A VICIOUS C

Amanda Craig's two previous novel. *Foreign Bodies* and *A Private Place*.

Praise for *A Vicious Circle*:

'A brilliant disquisition on the way we live now: as important a look at our capital city – and just as funny – as Martin Amis' *London Fields*. No wonder some people mention it in the same breath as *Vanity Fair*. Its treatment of ambition, of social rise and fall, warrant the comparison . . . a hugely entertaining book . . .'

Cressida Connolly, *The Oldie*

'An excellent novel' Fay Weldon, *Sunday Times*

'A novel of rare intelligence and ambition, which moves effortlessly from crime-ridden housing estate to the stately homes of the mega-rich and powerful . . . Funny, insightful, beautifully plotted, and steeped in the great tradition, this is a book that will catapult its author into the literary stratosphere.' Steve Grant, *Time Out*

'Amanda Craig has a sharp, aphoristic pen and she skewers her targets with enviable precision . . . The writing is crisp and the dialogue skilfully handled.'

David Robson, *Sunday Telegraph*

'Line after line of sparkling malice . . . a great tenderness . . . On motherhood in general, she is extraordinary. *A Vicious Circle* is a fierce and funny book.'

Allison Pearson, *Harpers & Queen*

A VICIOUS CIRCLE

Amanda Craig

FOURTH ESTATE • *London*

This paperback edition published in 1997

First published in Great Britain in 1996 by
Fourth Estate Limited
6 Salem Road
London W2 4BU

A catalogue record for this book is available from the British Library.

ISBN 1-85702-685-3

Typeset by RefineCatch Limited, Bungay, Suffolk
Printed in England by Clays Ltd, St Ives plc

For Sophia Bergqvist and Kate Saunders

CONTENTS

AUTHOR'S NOTE

A Vicious Circle is part of a sequence of novels which scrutinise different aspects of modern life. Many of the characters in this novel have already appeared in two previous works of fiction, *Foreign Bodies* and *A Private Place*.

Neither the characters nor the events described bear any relation to real people or events. When a small number of copies of an earlier version of this novel were first issued by the publishers in proof form, certain individuals believed themselves to be depicted in its pages. No such depiction from life was intended and the proof copies were issued in good faith. In consequence a number of changes to several of the book's characters have been made in order to dispel any question of there being similarities in this novel between living persons or real events. The author apologises to anyone who may have been caused any distress or embarrassment by the proof copies. Any resemblance of the satirical archetypes in *A Vicious Circle* to real-life people and events is therefore not only wholly unintended but entirely wrong.

London
October 1996

ACKNOWLEDGEMENTS

The advance in treatment of streptococcal meningitis described in Chapter 28 was discovered by Dr Crispin Best, a consultant anaesthetist at the Glasgow Royal Hospital for Sick Children, and reported in January 1996.

I would like to thank the following people:

Monica Appleby, Lizzie McGrah, Illona Dixon, Anthony Lane, Lola Bubbosh, Kate Saunders, Philip Weaver, Charlotte Mitchell, Peter Riddell and John de Falbe for information concerning various, non-medical, aspects of the plot.

Giles Gordon, John Rush, Andrew Franklin, Fanny Blake, David Hooper, Antonia Till, Hazel Orme, Robyn and Adam Sisman, Mark le Fanu, Paul Forty, Katie Owen, Joanna Prior and all at Fourth Estate for their guidance, patience and encouragement.

Lastly, my husband, family, friends and neighbours for their unfailing help, kindness and support.

SINE QUA NON

Thus interpretation is not (as some people assume) an absolute value, a gesture of mind situated in some timeless realm of capabilities. Interpretation must itself be evaluated ... Like the fumes of the automobile and of heavy industry which befoul the urban atmosphere, the effusion of interpretation of art today poisons our sensibilities. In a culture whose already classical dilemma is the hypertrophy of the intellect at the expense of energy and sensual capability, interpretation is the revenge of the intellect upon art.

SUSAN SONTAG, *Against Interpretation*

... self-reference has led into an infinite regression of storytellers and stories. This area of paradox is the meeting place between the paradoxes of self-reference and the paradoxes of infinity proper.

One might make the analogy of a mirror facing a mirror. Mirror reflects mirror, and so on to infinity. Furthermore, the archetype of the vicious circle, the ouroboros, the snake with his tail in his mouth, is sometimes known as the hieroglyph of eternity.

PATRICK HUGHES AND GEORGE BRECHT, *Vicious Circles and Infinity*

    ... O Love
You know what pains succeed; be vigilant; strive
To recognise the damned among your friends.
       'King Log', *Annunciations*, GEOFFREY HILL

A VICIOUS CIRCLE

Part One

A London Taxi

While the present century was in its last decade, and on one Thursday in midwinter, a boxy black taxi juddered and braked from Soho to Kensington at a rate of four miles per hour with two passengers bouncing uncomfortably on its back seat. It was a cold night, a clouded night, and for miles around the sky was stained a dull louring red, as if the city smouldered in heatless flames. All over London cars rumbled and jammed, spewing out invisible poisons in a general circulation of ill-temper as workers struggled to get home. Umbrellas locked spokes like cogs, circling in a slippery black stream of metal and flesh. People coughed and snuffled into paper handkerchiefs, not stopping to exchange apologies or insults. Every time the taxi stopped its doors clicked like the mandibles of a gigantic insect; but the passengers paid no attention.

Both were tense. They were going to a party, a big party, a party that would later be written up and cried down as a social event. One of the passengers had been invited; the other not. One of the passengers was considered, in certain circles, an important person; the other not. Yet it was this second person who was to change many lives, and most of all her own, because of her presence that night.

The first passenger was a man with short red hair called Ivo Sponge. He was thirty-two, unmarried, and combined corpulence, petulance and charm in unequal measures, according to how much he had drunk. Ivo's inebriation was so far confined to a bottle of wine at lunch – a comparatively abstemious consumption, occasioned by the fact that the party in question was being held to promote a travel book, *How Many Miles?*, by the daughter of his employer, Max de Monde. An acute observer might have recognized the minty scent of breath freshener masking an odour of sour grapes about his person.

Ivo had known Amelia de Monde since university. Flattery, flirtation and straightforward fibbing had resulted in something that passed for friendship. It was partly due to Amelia's patronage that he had progressed from lobby correspondent to reviewer, interviewer, and his present position as deputy literary editor of the *Chronicle*. But Amelia could not claim sole credit for Ivo's promotion. For it was one of the mysteries of Sponge's life that, though famously unsuccessful with women – and there was scarcely a woman in his circle who had not experienced the notorious 'Sponge Lunge' – he also owed his meteoric rise to them. Whether this was because he extended his devotions not just to Amelia and the prettier publishers' publicists but to the most raddled and acidulous of female hacks was a matter for some speculation. His friends compared him to Oscar Wilde, largely because of his dress, which was exotic, and his manner of speech, which was exceedingly rapid and flown with wit. His enemies called him the most dangerous man in London.

At present, he was sober enough to content himself with remarking to his companion, 'What the fuck do they put in these air fresheners? It's enough to make one puke.'

'What's Amelia like?'

'Perhaps I will puke. Why should we put up with this prole's bloody pong? It's even worse than his taste in music.'

'Mark says she's incredibly glamorous.'

'This is what those bloody anti-smoking fanatics have landed us with. Christ, London taxis! They're like the worst sort of woman – you hang around for ages until you're completely numb with boredom, and then when they finally come you almost wish you'd w-walked.'

Mary yawned. 'Not if you've been on your feet all day, you don't.'

'I wonder if Amelia realizes that I hardly ever go to book launches?'

'Of course, nobody ever does, but somehow you all know what happens at them.'

'Ghastly affairs,' said Ivo. 'The champagne always runs out after one glass, and then one has nothing to do but endure the unreadable in pursuit of the illiterate. Or is it the other way about? Still, Max does give very good parties.' Ivo, like all of de Monde's employees, always referred to the magnate as 'Max' behind his back. 'He's just taken over Belgravia, you know, which I expect is why Amelia has got into print at all. Someone told me he's spent twenty thousand on the flowers and catering tonight, but I suppose everyone who's anyone can't be treated like, well, anyone.'

'But I'm not everyone,' said Mary Quinn.

'My darling,' said Ivo, 'you aren't *anyone*. But there's going to be such a crowd, nobody will notice.'

'I don't really think I should be here,' said Mary Quinn. 'Only I'm – curious. Is she very beautiful?'

'She's rich and thin,' said Ivo.

'Oh,' said Mary.

'All a matter of taste. You're an unfashionable beauty and she's a fashionable one. Everyone can see that.'

'Everyone? Even anyone who's no one? The de Mondes are Society people, aren't they?'

'*We* are Society,' said Ivo. 'That's why anyone with any brains goes into the media now instead of the City or the law, and why a Lebanese counter-jumper like de Monde bought a newspaper.'

'People say he's a crook.'

'He probably is, but he owns the *Chronicle* so who cares? Mark will be there.'

'Indeed,' said Mary. 'But he doesn't really like my meeting his friends, I think. The last time I went to a party with him that outrageously stupid toff who's a Labour MP, you know – '

'Toby Jugg,' said Ivo.

'Yes, him – said, "Mary you're only a waitress, you've got to vote for us at the election." Then he said to Mark that nobody with a brain voted Tory, and Mark was rude to him. It was awful.'

'Oh, come now!' said Ivo, stroking his bow-tie as a cat might preen its whiskers. 'Mark is rude to everyone. You shouldn't be so thin-skinned.'

'Even Adam calls me a bogtrotter,' said Mary. 'He's like everyone in England, he thinks all the Irish live like tinkers, playing our harps and making bombs in the twilight while the waves crash against the shore.'

'Novelists,' said Ivo, 'are to the nineties what cooks were to the eighties, hairdressers to the seventies and pop-stars to the sixties.'

'Indeed. Which is what?'

Ivo was momentarily nonplussed.

'Merely, you know, an expression of the *Zeitgeist*. Nobody actually *reads* novels any more, but it's a fashionable thing to *be* – as long as you don't entertain people, of course. I sometimes think,' said Ivo, his eyes like industrial diamonds, 'that my sole virtue is, I'm the only person in London who has no intention whatsoever of writing any kind of novel, ever. Apart, of course, from Mark.'

'I sometimes think that every Oxbridge graduate has two degrees,' said Mary. 'one in their subject, and one in bitching.'

'You're not so bad at it yourself, my darling.'

'Well,' said Mary, 'I've taken night-classes.'

Ivo chortled, and thought with chagrin of how his best friend, Mark Crawley, had successfully seduced her five years ago after their encounter at the club where Mary worked.

The two men had an alliance based largely on envy and derision, the point being that they felt the same about everyone else, only more so. They had gone to the same Cambridge college and read the same subject; but whereas Mark had won a scholarship, Ivo had only just scraped through by bewitching his interviewers with a combination of Coles notes and charm. He was clever but not intelligent. This was tacitly agreed to be compensated for by the fact that his father was a doctor in Dorking, whereas Mark's was a dentist in Slough. Each had gone to a minor public school in the country, and each furiously resented the disparagement this information aroused among those who had gone to Eton, Harrow or Winchester.

It had been clear to both that at Cambridge, as in most societies, there was an élite destined, for reasons of family, energy, looks or talent, to succeed; and the other 95 per cent, who were simply not worth bothering with. Each had chosen a different route to this inner circle. Ivo, a born gossip and scandalmonger, had been intent on cultivating as many people as possible. He went to union debates, auditions, and college bars; joined clubs, attended parties, was sick over Japanese tourists and sat scoffing cream teas in the front window of Belinda's. In his last term, he had thrown a party for everyone of his chosen acquaintance, flattering them as 'Great Bores of Tomorrow'; as a consequence of this, and, it was rumoured, certain accommodations with influential homosexual dons, he had begun his career as a journalist.

Mark, on the other hand, had turned to an encyclopedic and esoteric knowledge of fashion, food and art. He believed in maps, guides, tips and timetables, read every style magazine he could buy and proclaimed himself without hesitation an intellectual. Where Ivo tended towards damask waistcoats and green carnations, Mark's wardrobe, purchased at Ralph Lauren or Hackett's sales, featured striped poplin shirts with button-down collars and thin silk ties. He was not handsome, for his features were sharp and his physique puny; but clothes, press-ups, and the weekly application of eyelash dye to his lashes and eyebrows overcame most of these disabilities. Furthermore the intellectual arrogance that fumed off him like the air round a glacier gave him a certain mystique. Abhorring any touch of undergraduate bohemianism he had furnished his rooms in college with monochrome minimalism. With the aid of a gyp-room fridge and a slo-cooker, he gave dinner parties, bought etchings and led a life of some sophistication.

These satisfactions initially outweighed the dwindling cash to support his tastes as a graduate, and for three years Mark, desultorily employed by the Cambridge University Press, had observed Ivo's undignified scramble through media London with amused disdain. 'I could write for any publication I wanted,' he would remark. 'I simply do not choose to prostitute my intelligence by becoming a hack. The attraction of driving a Porsche with a portable telephone is for the brain-dead.'

Gradually, however, both his ambitions and the pressing need to improve his finances had made Mark scrutinize his own prospects. While Ivo progressed from flat to flat, and finally to a small Victorian house in Clapham, it had become evident that, even with promotion to commissioning editor, he himself was never going to attain the affluence he coveted. There was no longer tenure or glory in academia, and his father, whose pride had initially been boundless, was fed up. Furthermore, after he failed to correct the index to an important textbook, Mark found himself ejected from his job. The number of pretty girls prepared to sleep with him then became distinctly thin on the ground, and one morning he awoke with an appalled recognition that, if he remained in Cambridge he could become a figure not of awe but of ridicule.

So Mark and Ivo met at the Slouch Club.

Ah, the Slouch Club! It is a rambling building in the heart of Soho which, having been a brothel, became a club for artists and writers in the 1950s; thirty years later, it had been saved from bankruptcy by opening its doors to the upper echelons of the media. Its Olympian array of personalities is screened from the public by a long black slatted blind, and by a revolving front door which deposits the unwary back onto the pavement outside.

Inside, the walls are covered with mirrors of every size, elaborately framed so that each moment of the present is made to seem like a moving picture – fragmentary, elusive and peopled with vaguely familiar faces. These decorations are invaluable for those who wish to gaze at themselves or spy on others; one or two gossip columnists claimed to have broken the most intimate of scandals by learning to lip-read. For fifteen years Slouch's distressed walls, eccentric chefs and pretty waitresses have passed into urban legend. Actors in West End hits, painters with East End misses, journalists short of a story, models long in the tooth, authors on the razzle, agents on the dazzle, politicians in a frazzle, they all congregate there. It is said that its name was inspired by 'The Second Coming'; and certainly, if you wish to participate in the millennial whirl of ambition, distraction, vilification and derision that constitutes a certain kind of London life, the Slouch Club can scarcely be bettered.

Mark Crawley had every intention of getting into this world. Ivo, who happened to be on the board, was proving recalcitrant about passing his membership. Obviously: he knew Mark to be more intelligent than himself, and did not want the competition. Yet not to get into Slouch's would be an inestimable handicap, for with the dissolution of Fleet Street it remained the quickest way to make contacts and get work.

Mark hated the place. Nobody was paying him any attention, and every other man in the brasserie seemed to be wearing a designer suit identical to his own. He felt miserably and angrily inferior.

'Miniature tomatoes, baby sweet-corn – it's vegetable paedophilia,' said Mark, loudly. Ivo smiled to himself: one of the first rules he had learnt was never to say anything that could be used as copy. Still, it was a reasonable joke, and he was able to throw back his head and, under cover of laughter, scan the rest of the room quickly for famous people.

'The best thing about this place is that they never fill in the total on your bill,' he explained.

'So?'

'It's essential, if you're a journalist, to find a good restaurant which gives you blank receipts. That way, you not only get back money you've spent – you make it. I get almost as much in expenses as I do through my salary. Not what I'd get as a political columnist, mind you.'

'You really are scum,' said Mark.

'Rules of the trade, dear boy. It's amazing how few restaurants cotton on to it,' said Ivo. 'The ones that do make a fortune.'

Their orders arrived.

> '"She was a primerole, a piggesnie,
> For any lord to leggen in his bedde
> Or yet for any yeoman good to wedde."'

'What?' said Sponge.
'Our waitress,' said Mark. 'The dark one.'

9

'Ah, Mary. Practically injection-moulded for sex,' said Ivo. 'Lovely girl.'

'She's not unattractive.'

'Iron knickers, all of them, unless you happen to be a superstar like Gore Tore.'

'What about starred firsts?'

'They'd think it was some sort of lager,' said Ivo.

'I wonder,' said Mark, watching as she flirted with an editor he particularly wanted to meet.

'Don't.'

'Girls are genetically programmed to find brains attractive, you know.'

'That's Cambridge,' said Ivo, nastily. 'In London, they only roll over if you've got money.'

'Oh, come on! Anyone who works here is bound to be a tart.'

'Don't know about that, old boy. She's Catholic,' Ivo said.

'In that case she probably does it with anyone.'

Mark knew this would annoy Ivo, who was lapsed but occasionally went to the Brompton Oratory for social reasons.

'She's an actor's squeeze,' said Ivo. Mark hated actors even more than he hated feminists, Americans and Old Etonians. On an impulse of pure mischief, Ivo added, 'But I think that's over. Want an introduction?'

As an undergraduate, Ivo had been known to heat up coins to near-melting point and leave them on King's Parade for unsuspecting passers-by.

'No.'

'Oh, that's "Felix" Viner over there,' said Ivo, brightening. 'You know, the cartoonist.'

'I know who Sam Viner is,' Mark said.

'He's been on a bender, you know, ever since La Bamber dumped him for Andrew Evenlode. Did you know Tom Viner? Oh, no, he was Oxford. The handsomest man of our generation, some say. Like an after-shave ad in the flesh.'

Mark was staring at Mary again. She looked round, saw him, and giggled.

'Worth having, if you could get her.'

'I could,' said Mark.

Ivo shrugged. 'Bet you a hundred pounds you couldn't,' he said.

'Is that serious?'

Ivo grinned. 'I need to pay my Turnbull and Asser account, old boy.'

'Then,' said Mark, 'I bet you I could.'

'Done!'

'By the way, you still owe me a magnum of champagne for the last election.'

'I've taken you out to lunch, haven't I?'

'But you'll only claim it on expenses, you've just told me. Listen: if I lose, I'll pay. But if you lose, you put me up for full membership here.'

'I would have done so anyway, dear boy.'

'You don't say.'

Like everyone who knew him, and many who did not, Mark regarded Ivo with unshaken mistrust. Ivo knew this, and was occasionally hurt by it: to himself, he was a benign figure – pragmatic, perhaps, diplomatic, certainly, and like most of his generation, operating with an eye to the main chance. But he did not accuse himself of anything more than venality, and that, after all, was a necessity for survival in London. Ivo knew what song the sirens sang, and was younger than the rock-stars with whom he sat. He had heard the voice of London that lives and breathes beneath the rumble of traffic, a voice like the continual high-pitched shriek you hear when you put your head beneath the waves of the sea. It is the sound of millions and millions of creatures living and struggling and dying and being born. It commands those who hear it to eat or be eaten; and Ivo had no intention of becoming anyone's prey.

2

The Queen's Estate

It is but a glimpse of the world of poverty we can afford this same winter's evening. It is not a large world, though, as it avoids census-takers, it is hard to tell its precise size. Its people are invisible, except when the more desperate or enterprising impinge on the purses of those such as Ivo or Amelia. Relative to this world of ours, it is a very little speck. There is much good in it, and some think it has its appointed place. But it is a world too much wrapped up in hopeless hopes, and cannot hear the rushing of the larger worlds, or see them as they circle round the sun.

On the Queen's Estate, some thirteen storeys up, a whole panel of polythene fell out of a block of flats where a group of young men had been buying and selling crack. The polythene had been taped to a window, broken for many months, when the dealers moved in. Before that, a young woman had jumped, holding her baby in her arms, smashing onto the concrete like a rotten fruit.

'Mum! Mum! Ghost!' said Billy, as Grace struggled to push the buggy over the rubbish on the path to their tower.

Grace glanced up, and cried out as a large transparent shape swirled overhead, jerked now towards, now away from their heads. Its surface caught the dim orange light, and it crackled as it flew.

''S'all right, stupid, it's just a piece of plastic,' said Grace, trembling. 'Don't worry, petal. Don't worry.'

Nevertheless, she quickened her step. She felt her stomach lurch, as though the concrete underfoot were moving. Perhaps it *was* moving. Grace had lived in awful places all her life, but the Queen's, well, it wasn't so much a sink estate as a toilet.

By day it looked a busy place. For months, council workmen dressed up like astronauts, with helmets on their heads, had been removing windows and bits of stuff wherever there was asbestos. There was asbestos everywhere, in the ceilings, in the heaters, in the walls, so the workmen were busy demolishing whole blocks of housing while terrified Bangladeshi families crouched in their front rooms, shivering in their thin clothes and trying to understand why their homes had suddenly become open to any passer-by.

Perhaps you have passed the place where Grace and her son lived, on your way from Hampstead or the West End. It is fronted by a row of small brick and stucco houses left over from an earlier era, which are now offices of a failing sort. There are signs to places suggestive of rural bliss, called Willowdale, Swallowbrook and Ashcoombe. Indeed, when the Queen's Estate was first built, during the early years of the present monarch's reign, it was a popular alternative to the squalid dwellings it replaced. Gleaming white towers of glass and concrete were flung up to give the poor views over London and its parks; wretched slums and workmen's cottages with outside lavatories were torn down; newly-wed couples were proud to live at such a modern address, with central heating and bathrooms, walkways and lifts.

But forty years on, the Queen's Estate had crumbled and decayed until the buildings were like a mouthful of rotten teeth. The concrete was grey and fanged with dirt, the glass radiating ruin. The only people who lived there were the powerless: the elderly, the insane, the immigrant and the unmarried. No one knew their neighbours except by hatred, inconvenience and distrust. The lifts were broken, and the stairs stank. Obscene graffiti and swastikas swam past Grace's eyes as she heaved Billy backwards up the stairs to her flat, racing to get to each landing before the timed light went out. The lights themselves were dim, coated by a thick mesh. Without this, someone would have stolen the bulbs.

Grace's flat was on the second floor, next to Mad Maggie from the Friern Barnet, who should really have been back there because she kept forgetting the pills that were supposed to keep her more or less sane. Mad Maggie believed she was Mrs. Thatcher; she was out and about at all hours, swinging her handbag, and denouncing her imaginary cabinet. She was quite harmless otherwise, and kept a number of cats, each almost as crazy as their owner. As Grace struggled with the buggy, she could hear Maggie singing,

> 'There was a crooked man
> Who walked a crooked mile
> And found a crooked . . .
> Pussy-cat, pussy-cat, where have you been?
> I've been to London to look at the Queen
> Shoo, shoo, shoo,
> How I wonder what you are . . .'

The songs would go on and on, yet somehow Mad Maggie remembered to feed her cats even if, to judge from the smells seeping from her door, she did not let them out enough. Billy, who loved animals, adored her.

Their stair was cleaner, and the smell less bad, for Grace would scoop up what was left from scrubbing the bath with diluted bleach in a bucket and throw it down the steps in a small, violent gesture every evening. 'Like a dog,' she said. 'My mark.'

If it wasn't for my Billy, I'd go stark staring bananas too, she thought; and then, if it wasn't for him, I wouldn't be here, neither. Those two thoughts buzzed round and round in her head like trapped bluebottles, until the main door to the block snicked open. Someone was coming up the stairs behind her, treading quietly and steadily in the dark. Everyone on the estate wore trainers, but the crunch of glass still made a sound.

Frightened, now, she gave the buggy another wrench. Billy was small for his age, and tired from his asthma, and she was always afraid he would pick up one of the things left on the stairs – used condoms, syringes, bubble-gum. At times like this it was like trying to move in a nightmare, the things that stuck or splintered or squelched underfoot. Well, she wouldn't give in, she wouldn't. Fear and anger made her wrench the buggy again, and suddenly it buckled and tipped to one side, Billy shrieking and just held by the belt while tins and cartons she had bought went bounce, bounce, bounce out of sight.

Grace grabbed Billy. 'My baby, oh, my baby, never mind,' she crooned, racing up the stairs with Billy and the buggy in both arms, fumbling with her keys. There were three locks, and she was shaking so much she could hardly turn them. He clung to her like a lover. The silence at her back was worse than any noise. Someone was listening, she knew.

Grace slammed the door, switched the light on and hugged her son until his sobbing subsided. The back wheel of his buggy had snapped off. She had bought it second-hand off another girl at the hostel – they'd all thought she was weird, didn't everyone get the best, brand-new, for their kid? It wasn't as if Grace didn't want the best, didn't crave for it with a dull, painful yearning, but she thought other things mattered more.

'Out, Mum-mum, out!'

'Not yet, sweetie.'

'Out *now*!'

'Wait, Billy. Don't climb about, it's dangerous.'

He understood that, of course: it was one of the first words she'd taught him. Don't pick up the phone, don't open the door, don't talk to strangers. She'd had to teach him about the bad in the world before the good. At nursery last week, when she'd been trying to do the thousand and one things she could only do alone, he'd had a tummy bug, and when one of the staff had come into the toilet he'd screamed, 'No! No! Nobody touch my bum except Mum!'

She unstrapped him. He could walk really well for a two-year-old, but they needed the buggy. The estate was so far away from everything – the shops, the post office, the Social, the library, the market – and her £73 benefit went even faster if she went to the Paki shop. As it was, she walked for miles, pushing him downhill and up to Sainsbury's, Kwiksave and Inverness Street market. Billy had been out of nappies since the summer, but he still burnt money; often she went without food herself so that he could have the chips and fish-fingers he loved. Once a week she bought a chicken from Inverness Street, and the giblets and bones got boiled so they could have soup.

But it was hard. Without the babysitting for Georgina Hunter, Grace didn't think she could stay straight. Half the girls on the estate were on the game. 'It's not as if we're talking the Virgin Mary, here,' Grace said, to herself. 'But I've never done it for money. Unless it means Billy starving, I never will.'

'Wead-a-book!' Billy chanted. 'Wead-a-book!'

Books were his toys, his comforters, his window onto another world. They showed children with all kinds of things he didn't have – children with gardens, pets, sofas; children like Georgina's, with brothers and sisters and fathers. Grace had to be and do everything for him.

'You've got to learn to read and write as soon as you can, Billy,' she said. 'You've got to make something of your life.'

She wanted so much for him to understand that she was doing the best she could for him. She had long, long conversations with him, even now, explaining.

'It's just you and me, petal.'

'And Nana.'

'Nana's sick, Billy. Like Maggie.'

'All the time?'

'Lots of the time.'

'Nana get better.'

'When she takes her medicine.'

Billy nodded wisely. 'Nana'll look after Mum an'Billy,' he said.

Grace became angry. 'Nana couldn't look after nobody, Billy. She's poorly. We look after her.'

At least once a fortnight, Joy rang at three in the morning, babbling with terror. 'I wish you were my mummy,' she said to Grace. 'I wish you were.'

Grace had seen Joy's date of birth when she was sectioned, and knew she had been adopted. What had gone wrong, she didn't know, but certainly there were no parents round now. Joy was forty-one, but looked twenty years older. Since Friern Barnet had closed, she had been living more or less on the streets, although there was a room for her in a sheltered house in West Hampstead, full of other nutters who forgot to take their medication, too. Grace had written letters to everyone she could think of, to try and get them to rehouse her so she could look after her mother, but it was no use.

Joy was fine as long as she took her pills, but mostly she didn't, and then she got crazier and crazier. It's terrible the things people would do to a madwoman. Grace knew her mother had been raped at least twice, and beaten up more times than she could count. Not even her filth and rags saved her.

Joy would walk for miles in all weather, dressed in no more than a sheet, barefoot on the freezing pavements of London, and people would laugh at her. She looked like a drunk, until you saw the expression of innocence on her red, raw face. People shrank away when she came near, from the stench, from the weirdness, though she was really quite gentle. She had done the best she could for Grace, although she had never told her who her dad was, and probably didn't know. She ought to be back in the bin, Grace thought, but it was all care in the community, and as far as the Government was concerned, she and Billy were the community. There was nobody else.

The buggy couldn't be mended: she could see the way the axle had snapped. From now on, they'd have to walk. If only Billy didn't wheeze so. Sometimes his lips and fingernails went quite blue, and he bent over double like a tiny old man. It was always worst in the cold, no matter how much she bundled him up, and it was always cold on the Queen's Estate because the water-pipes didn't have enough pressure to keep the heat going round. Even running a bath took an hour.

'But you live in a nice area of London,' Georgina had said to her, when she explained that the minicab would never drop her right outside the tower-block.

'Yeah,' Grace said. 'You cross over the road, and suddenly you're in Regent's Park, with rich people living in places that cost millions and millions, and shiny cars swooshing past, and flower-beds shaped like tarts. It's as if the life I live just doesn't exist. But it's there, all right.'

Grace and Billy were not starving, not homeless; there were many in London worse off than they. But it was a life devoid of anything but survival. If you looked round Grace's flat, there was not a single thing in it that delighted or relieved the eye. She'd cut out pictures from magazines, animals and suchlike, and Georgina had given Billy an alphabet frieze, but nothing could disguise the neglect, the draughty windows and splotches of mould.

She would have to wait until daylight to get her shopping. It was unlikely anyone would steal it, people were wary of food in case it was spiked with something to kill the dogs, although as most of it was tins she might not be so lucky. Grace made Billy a boiled egg, but he refused to eat it. So it was chips and ketchup again.

He raced around the room until he was exhausted, trying out all his toys before settling in front of a video from the library. It was their favourite *Beauty and the Beast*.

'"Once upon a time in a far-away land,"' said the deep, beautiful voice, '"a prince lived in a shining castle."' They watched, as one night an old beggar woman came to his gate, offering him a single rose in exchange for shelter from the bitter cold, then turned into an enchantress. Billy sighed with satisfaction.

How could Grace afford a video? By stealing from the insurance company. She and her friends had clubbed together to buy one and insure it. A month later, one friend claimed it had been stolen, and sold it on to someone else. With the money from this, plus a bit, they bought another video and put in another insurance claim, and so on, all round, until all the single parents got them. It worked out at about a third of the normal price. The only trouble was, nobody on the Queen's could get insurance now.

Grace wasn't a dishonest person. If someone dropped a fiver in the street, she'd give it back to them. But she needed a video like she needed a washing machine: without it, life would be almost impossible. Only when the video was turned on did she ever get a bit of peace, and most of the stuff on telly, apart from *Sesame Street*, was violent and horrible, Japanese cartoons that gave Billy nightmares.

It was such an effort to be cheerful, sometimes. Even plants died on her. She looked out of the window, washing up, and saw a whole gang of skins walking around with chains in their hands.

'Out, out, out!' they chanted. Grace moved towards the tele-

18

phone. At least her door was strong, with reinforced hinges and steel mesh. She'd stripped the floor right back to the concrete for a yard in case they poured petrol. Even so, she often couldn't sleep for fear at night.

'Nigger-lover, nigger-lover,' some of the kids on the estate chanted. She wondered how long it would be before Billy noticed that his skin was a different colour.

She rang the police station, and told them what she'd seen. A bored voice told her they'd 'look into it'. As they were well known for escorting the National Front through the Queen's Estate any time it felt like having a march, Grace refused to give her name.

Once, she'd been having a drink with a friend soon after Billy was born, and this man had bent over the buggy and said, 'My, my, a little golliwog,' and she'd chucked her beer right in his face.

'I'd never have done that,' said her friend, but Billy had made her brave. She didn't think of herself as brave, but she was.

3

A Five-year Plan

Mark Crawley won his bet, and Ivo never forgave him for it.

Perhaps you think this unlikely, but Mark – stiff, malicious, irritable Mark – could and did inspire extremes of love and loathing, frequently in the same women. Indeed, it was partly because of his very ill-nature that they so responded, for his shafts of malice made them laugh, and laughter is often the way the deadliest of cankers enters the feminine soul. Voltaire claimed that he could make any woman forget his appearance after fifteen minutes of conversation, and in any case Mark was not, as he might put it, unhandsome.

Mary was bored by any man who merely lusted after her; she encountered this every day in her job. When Mark remarked, 'Ivo fancies you, you know', she retorted, 'But he's the sort of person who thinks every apple tree needs a snake in it, for animation.' Mark had been surprised and charmed by this (as had Mary, for she did not yet know what she thought until she uttered it). Indeed, just as she yearned towards the regularity and precision of mind that she perceived in him, so it was her gift for the unexpected, together with her good-nature, which led Mark to become, he said to himself, fond of her.

Of course, she was very pretty. But then, so many girls were, in London. At Cambridge the standard of feminine appeal was still so low that an undergraduate who was no more than easy on the eye could acquire all the confidence and petulance of a born beauty; once outside, the increased competition came as a shock.

(It was this phenomenon, according to Ivo, which had caused Fiona Bamber, 'the Zuleika Dobson *de nos jours*', to take first 'Felix' Viner, then Andrew Evenlode, as lovers, even though she had been heard to remark, 'Whenever I try to remember what lies beneath Andrew's tweed suit, all I can see is another tweed suit.')

Mary was not in this league. You could not see her draped in chiffon for *Vogue* or sitting with a unicorn's head in her lap. Rather, she made you think of roses, and Renoir's models, with their pearly skin and teeth: the kind of girl, Mark thought, that makes any man feel vaguely randy and think in clichés. Ivo, it was clear to him from the start, was completely mesmerized by her – and this, too, added to her appeal. She was small, and walked with quick decisive steps, but she had the eyes of a seal waiting to be clubbed. At Slouch's he observed that she was, at least among the male members, something of a cult figure; and among his own peers she was known to be the particular friend of Adam Sands.

At first he assumed her mystique was of pure stupidity. She lacked that glistening, magpie sharpness which he associated with intelligence. Her expression was dreamy, as if she were not properly awake, though when making love she often laughed, revealing small white teeth and pink gums. Indeed, it was one of her charms that she slipped easily in and out of the animal self we call the sexual being, whereas for Mark it was always a violent dislocation of mind. She wore the uniform of any waitress at any Soho restaurant: Doc Martens, black Lycra leggings, white T-shirt, an apron wrapped around the hips, and a pencil, never used, behind the ear – except that Mary wore hers skewered through a toppling tower of hair, hair as soft and black as soot.

Her chief characteristic was a desire to please, coupled with a self-deprecation which was so baroque in its excess that her audience felt either a warm glow of self-satisfaction or a vague suspicion that they were being teased. Mary praised others extravagantly, and worried, openly and eloquently, about her waist, her legs, her skin and most of all her weight. 'The happiest day of my life,' she would say, 'was when I discovered potatoes were good for you. The worst was when I discovered I couldn't eat them without butter.'

At Slouch's she was tipped to become the next manageress, for she remembered every member by name, and knew all the latest gossip. In this respect, she was especially useful to Mark. Becoming her boyfriend instantly raised his profile at the flashier end of the media world. He had worked out that it would take him five years to get where he wanted to in journalism, and Mary, he thought, would be as good a guide as any.

Few of her friends liked Mark any better than his Cambridge contemporaries had, but all quickly recognized his intelligence. The other waitresses nicknamed him 'the Voice of the Mysterons', and thought Mary's choice a strange one.

'I don't see what's so special about him,' said Adam.

'He makes me feel I'm beautiful,' said Mary. 'And he teaches me such a lot. I never knew anything about books, or politics, or history of art, or even clothes until I met him.'

'He reminds me of the story about a peasant-woman who finds a poor little snake frozen in the field and takes it home,' said her friend.

'Does it turn into a prince?'

'No, it bites her as soon as it warms up.'

Her cousin, Deirdre, said bluntly, 'He's a shite.'

Love, even the happiest and most blessed of loves, is not a constant condition, but a state of self-censorship. All her life Mary had been waiting for someone who talked in the way Mark did. She perceived Mark's coldness, and pitied it, believing it to be the isolation of pure intellect, believing, too, that she could teach him how to enjoy ordinary life. He was always instructing her, moulding her by all the force of his personality into his own image and she was very eager to learn.

Now, you may have observed that anyone who tries to become popular themselves is bound to fail; but anyone who tries to make another person so will almost certainly succeed. Mary's character neutralized her lover's behaviour. She explained his ill-temper as shyness, and his opinions as the natural perspective of brilliance, so innocently persuasive in her support that some believed it. It had never occurred to her to ask any favours for herself, but where Mark was concerned she was fearless and shameless. She smuggled him in on Thursday night when Slouch's was crowded with the hack-pack, and forced him to circulate.

'Why should I associate with this scum?' he demanded. 'It should be obvious I'm in a different league.'

'It's not what you know, it's who you know,' Mary said, patiently. It was the kind of thing she overheard continually.

'Dunderheads!'

'Indeed they are' said Mary, 'but they have power and you don't. Yet.'

She even asked Ivo, although the request made her blush to the soles of her feet, if he could give Mark work. To her surprise, he did, adding, 'There are only three real ways into journalism, my darling. One is by gruesome toil, starting on a local rag and coming to London after years of covering dog-shows. One leaves that to very stupid people called reporters. The other is through patronage and nepotism, like myself. For this you need luck, and thanks to us, Mark is lucky.'

'What about the third?' said Mary, hoping there might yet be a way of not owing Ivo a favour.

'You could have such talent that – if you don't die from poverty, obscurity, disappointment, the usual obstacles – it will eventually drill through the hardest of skulls. But everyone will hate you, and suspect you got in by the second route anyway, so why bother?'

'Doesn't it . . .' Mary hesitated. 'I don't want to be rude, but doesn't that mean that a lot of people get work who shouldn't?'

'Of course. But to be a mediocrity among mediocrities is a perfectly pleasant thing,' said Ivo. 'Especially if one earns more than they do. Everyone goes on about our generation being Yuppies and Thatcher's Children and so forth. They forget, we came at the end of the baby boom and we've no choice. It's the survival of the fittest. Anyone who stands out from the pack gets left behind or torn to pieces.'

He grinned at Mary, running his tongue over his stained incisors. 'You should tell him that, my darling.'

Yet Mark needed no such homilies. He knew as if by instinct (but in fact after hours of reading back issues in public libraries) what each publication would like, and what he himself would do well.

He produced his copy exactly to length, on time, every time; he was never too pushy or off-hand in pitching an idea; and he learnt to explain it over the telephone in thirty seconds, which was the time between an editor's 'Hallo' and an editor's 'No'.

Furthermore, and this was a real part of his success, he deduced that the time he was most likely to get a piece commissioned was on Monday mornings, when editors came out of meetings desperate for new ideas, or on Friday afternoons, when, relieved to have survived another week on the job, they had all lunched long and well. The worst possible time – and this was particularly true of the features pages – was Wednesday or Thursday, when everyone on a newspaper is in a frenzy of deadlines, neurosis and panic. Yet it was the pieces he wrote that above all made him exceptional.

Few people learn to translate the charm of their conversation onto paper, and when they do they are said to have a 'voice'. Fewer still learn how to disguise their true personality. Mark's voice, ostensibly reasonable, civilised and humane, concealed the presence of quite the opposite characteristics from the reader.

His greatest gift, however, was sarcasm. It swelled and lifted him as helium does an empty ball of cloth, a monstrous glide of savage indignation, carrying him so high above the smog of mere journalism that it seemed as though he lived in purer airs. Only a few saw the little pilot dangling underneath.

Mary did not fully understand how her lover became successful so quickly, only that his intelligence was a kind of magic. Everything he said was taken by her to be a revealed truth, the further education on which she had missed out. Her admiration, her adoration, her gratitude were boundless, and he basked in it, and his creation.

'I see domesticity suits you,' said Ivo, encountering him at a Christmas lunch. He was annoyed to find him there, like an undertaker's model between the roaring red faces of the rest.

'She makes life very agreeable, you know,' said Mark. 'She must be one of the last women in Britain who will darn a sock, and besides, she's not unintelligent.'

'So, you're in love,' said Ivo. 'Congratulations.'

Mark shrugged.

'You'll have to watch it, old boy, or you'll find yourself frolicking down the aisle with someone who not only isn't Oxbridge but who didn't go to university at all.'

Ivo laid no emphasis on the last six words, but he scarcely needed to. Not to have gone to university was tantamount to being less than human. Mark sipped his wine. 'She has a lively mind.'

'A mind is either lively or it's dead,' said Ivo. 'That's not the point.'

'She reads.'

'Don't tell me.'

'Victorian novels.'

Ivo snorted. '"Reader, I loved him." Adolescent girls' stuff!'

'She has an ear.'

'All the Irish have an ear,' said Ivo. 'And an eye. The trouble is, there's nothing but a lump of green gristle in between. They get a handicap, you know, when they're up for any award. Twenty per cent off for the Blarney Stone.'

Mark uttered one of his machine-gun laughs. He actually said, 'Ha! Ha! Ha!' as if he had had to teach himself the approximate noise human beings make on hearing a joke, Ivo thought. 'I'm only shagging the girl, not marrying her.'

'Just remember Gissing,' said Ivo. 'The underclass are doomed, and they drag anyone who gets mixed up with them down too.'

Yet here he miscalculated. For though Mark feared and despised the poor, believing them to be stupid, violent and to be acknowledged only in so far as they were useful or deferential to himself, he had an uneasy respect for the Irish. That they were a drunken and superstitious bunch he had no doubt; but they had, after all, produced two out of the four modern writers for whose work he had any respect. As far as their struggles and sufferings were concerned he knew little and cared less, remarking that in a country which still remembered Cromwell with bitterness it was no wonder the incidence of madness was reportedly seven times greater than in the rest of Britain.

At the same time Mary's origins fascinated him. His own grandfather had been a pawnbroker in Manchester, and the middle-class status of the Crawleys recently and uneasily acquired; he was intensely conscious, as only an Englishman can be, of the exact social position of everyone he heard. Much of his stiltedness in conversation had originally been caused by dread of pronouncing certain words; he never forgot how he had had his accent derided by a hulking fool of an Old Etonian who had later scraped a third.

That Mary simply lilted over all the barriers that kept millions of Britons penned like sheep filled him with bitter wonder. She could talk to anyone and neither prince nor publican would be able to tell, well, what kind of school she had gone to.

'Your voice is like your face,' he told her. 'It makes you seem more intelligent than you really are.'

Mary accepted what he said. Mark was the man who would free her from bondage, uncertainty, the sensation that her life was passing in a stupor of anxiety and hard work. With him she felt that she, too, was five feet ten and dazzlingly intelligent.

What she feared most of all was boring him.

Mark cultivated this instinctive reaction, quite automatically. He had realized in his teens that he was unlikely to have any natural allies in life. Resentment fed his ambition at Cambridge. He knew infinitely more than these self-styled sophisticates, yet they rejected him from the start because he was shy and proud. Well, he thought, he would show them. Tutorials with Mark Crawley were something every undergraduate, and indeed many members of the History Faculty, learnt to dread. He despised them for coming from some place lusher and hillier than Slough; for not being able to parse a sentence; for being taller or shorter, beefier or weedier, richer or poorer, more or less Thatcherite. His intellect became a Procrustean bed, on which none could lie but one shaped and formed exactly like himself. Yet he could not despise learning that had been acquired largely as the result of intellectual curiosity: that was Mary's unexpected advantage.

'Why didn't you go to university?' he asked. 'Even a bunch of cretinous nuns must have realized you should have gone.'

'Oh, the nuns were marvellous, they had a grand idea for the uses of literacy.'

'Really?'

'Yes,' said Mary. 'They recommended that, in the event of sitting on a man's lap, we should place a book between his legs and ours. Seriously, the Mother Superior wanted me to go but I didn't.'

'You could have read English.'

Mary shrugged. 'Reading is something I do for pleasure. Besides, I wanted to leave Ireland as soon as I could. Everyone young does, especially if you're Catholic. There aren't any jobs.'

Mary had not been trained to be anything but a housewife. She knew how to roast the most delicious of chickens, by placing it upside down for two hours on a bed of salt and rosemary; and how to cook cabbage in milk and a pinch of soda. She knew how to turn sheets when they frayed, how to gut a fish, arrange flowers, preserve fruit, upholster a chair, hang wallpaper, grow tomatoes, charm both warts and neighbours, delight a child, strike a bargain and mend china. She learnt good French from another waiter – her first boyfriend – and knew a *cachepot* from gravadlax. But for all these she could not turn Mark into a marrying man.

In the beginning, this had not mattered too much. She was twenty-five, certain that Mark was as much in love with her as she with him. Poverty was nothing new to her, but with him it was an adventure. Everyone was making so much money all around them, but they would come out on top.

Mrs Quinn, who loathed Mark yet who rang up regularly to enquire on the progress of her daughter's status, always snorted and said that 'if he were a decent man he wouldn't care that they had nothing. Your dad and I didn't.'

'It's different now, Mam. Everybody lives together first.'

He rose, and her hopes went with him. He was talked of, first as a pundit, then as *the* pundit; and he became a well-known commentator on politics, featured as a young Turk of the New Right.

Mark bought a flat in Brixton for £50,000, where they lived. Mary paid the interest. They both called this 'rent', and until Mark got regular commissions it amounted to over two-thirds of her salary. Even then, there was somehow never quite enough. She waited, and pasted his cuttings in a big folder, thinking that one day she could show it to their children.

'If we were to marry and have a baby –' she began to say in the third year.

'I don't like babies,' Mark said.

'I would like to have one before I'm thirty,' she said in the fourth year.

'Do you really want to spend your youth pushing a purple-faced troll round Habitat every Saturday morning?'

'But do you think I'm pretty?' she said, in the fifth.

'I've lived with you longer than I've lived with anyone, and I'm as fond of you as I can be of anyone,' Mark said.

Mary gave him little presents and big ones. She would tell him every day how much she loved him. She wept, and said that if he didn't love her it was surely better to part as honest friends. She said that she would like to die in his arms. He sighed impatiently, in a way she had come to dread.

Daily, the cascade of padded envelopes stuffed with cuttings thundered through the door or were brought by messengers, helmeted and garbed in black with a crackling box strapped to their chests. To Mary, what happened next was infinitely mysterious, for in the small world of those who noticed such things, Mark's opinion became definitive. Yet it did not earn much money. The real power, the real plums on a paper came to a staff columnist. Here, Mark made no more progress than Ivo.

She earned £60 a week, together with another £400 in tips – £180, after the club and taxes had taken their cuts. Altogether, they lived on around £200 a week, which was fine when single but very tight indeed with Mark, who insisted on the best of everything.

In the 1980s everyone was bloated with confidence and loot – everyone, it seemed but Mark and Mary. It chafed Mark dreadfully. Mary tried to economize wherever possible. She brought home food, flowers and toilet paper from the club stores – a theft that horrified him. She walked for a mile on her journey to and from Soho in order to save 40p on the bus fare. After a night shift, when her stomach was empty and the cold came up through her soles, she sometimes felt herself to be on the verge of collapse. She worked overtime every other night and was often too tired to do anything but watch television.

'Your crowd are the worst,' she told Mark. 'They're the ones who wave twenty pounds in your face if you'll do it with them in the cloakroom.'

'Have you, ever?'

Mary was silent.

'Have you?' said Mark, with interest.

'I have not!'

'Don't you like being fancied?'

'Not when I've got some drunk trying to put his hand up my bottom,' said Mary. 'If you want to know, the ones I like best are the gays on Monday. They're the only members who treat me like a human being. And they leave tips in cash, on top of the service charge.'

'Was that how you met Adam Sands?'

'No,' said Mary. 'I met him because we both love reading novels.'

Mark sighed. It was axiomatic in journalistic circles that the novel was dead, though as with Cock Robin the precise cause of this demise was quarrelled over, and there were any number of self-appointed undertakers all jumping up and down on the corpse with tremendous glee. Some thought the novel had simply been run over and squashed flat by Hollywood, and that writers should now be producing scripts involving two car-chases and an upbeat resolution. Others maintained that fiction, wedded to its bourgeois roots, was failing to confront the urban reality of everyday life. Yet others taught that the novel was an inert text which the academic alone, like Dr Frankenstein, could bring electrically to life; or that it was a game reserved for members of a particular university; or that it should really be a short story, autobiography, or about football. Yet novels continued to be written and read, which had nothing whatever to do with this, and many of these were mysteriously successful – if only with the public.

Mary found it very puzzling. 'But what I want to know from a review is what a book is about, what the plot is.'

'Plot!' said Mark. 'Why, that went out with mangles and corsets!'

'Mangles and corsets are terribly useful, though. Mam still uses hers.'

'I'm sure your mother can peel a banana with her feet, too.'

Mary said, after a pause, 'I still like to know whether a novel is worth reading. Or buying.'

'Unlike the Irish, the English loathe reading, so anything we trash is a vast relief. What they want from a reviewer are reasons why they need *not* read.'

The balance of power in a couple's relationship can be judged by whose name comes first in their coupling. Over the years, 'Mary and Mark' had changed to 'Mark and Mary', and, most recently, 'Mark +1', or just 'Mark Crawley' on the top left-hand corner of invitations.

It was this, and more, that had caused Mary to accompany Ivo up the garden path to the house of Max de Monde.

4

At Max de Monde's

Max de Monde's house in Holland Park had many windows, and every one of them was blazing with light. A thin red carpet wriggled from the gateposts and up the tiled steps to the front door, apparently diving underground before coiling itself up the staircase inside. Beside the gate were clipped bay trees in tubs to which lemons had been wired, and beside these were two burly bouncers in black tie, standing so still they might have been made of wood.

Ivo said, 'Just wait until you see inside. Every stick of furniture is a brand-new antique.'

The roar of the party was audible even from Holland Park Avenue, and this, together with the presence of a couple of policemen, had attracted a small crowd, as well as a beggar slumped on the wet pavement.

'Pass along, please, pass along,' said one of the policemen, touching the figure with his boot. The beggar, an old woman dressed in a sheet, coughed and did not move. The policeman spoke into his walkie-talkie.

'Good God,' Mary muttered. 'Ivo, what have you let me in for?'

Ivo smirked. 'Mary, my darling, I'll sort out these flunkeys if you pay the driver,' he said, hopping down. 'They're probably expecting some dreary cabinet minister or something.'

Mary did so. The fare left her with less than three pounds with which to get home, and the taxi-driver sneered at her for not giving him a tip. She gave the beggar the change.

'You shouldn't encourage them, madam,' said the policeman.

'She's ill,' said Mary, 'She shouldn't be out here in the cold dressed like that.'

A hundred years ago, she thought, that beggar would have been one of her own countrymen, flying from famine and typhoid. Her indignation was more towards Ivo, however. He was such a stinge, Mark told her, he had even taken his curtains with him on a freebie to be dry-cleaned by a hotel abroad.

The wave of adrenaline she always got at the end of her shift was dying away. I must be mad to come, she thought. She knew that her dress was too small and her bust too large, that the gems on her ears were fake and her overdraft real, that she had no business being with all these thin, smart people who looked as though they had been dipped in varnish.

At least I'm young, she thought, for associating with people who were already in their thirties had this perennial benefit, and at least I'm prettier than most of Mark's friends, for Mary knew down to the last penny the advantage good looks give the poor.

Ivo was making impatient little noises in his throat.

'Are you *sure* it's all right?'

'Oh, quite, quite,' said Ivo, although he could feel his own heart beat faster as the unmistakable scent of the very rich, a scent consisting of beeswax, wine, fresh flowers and the skins of young animals wafted through the inner doors. 'Don't be a ninny. You'll be fine with me.'

The hall was tiled with marble. Much of one wall was occupied with a large, over-restored painting of a fleshy blonde reclining in a state of considerable undress and pleased surprise beneath a shower of gold coins. Opposite was an equally large mirror in a massive gilt frame, doubling the effect. Between the painted and the reflected canvas Ivo and Mary walked towards a little bandy-legged gilt table that stood like a submissive animal bearing an open leather-bound book. A Filipina in a dark dress smiled and pointed at it. 'Sign, pliss.'

They bent, and signed; Ivo giving his address in a dashing hand as the *Chronicle*, Mary, after some hesitation, leaving hers blank. Suitable for a nobody, she thought.

'Is that it?' Mary asked, after they had relinquished their coats and walked a little way out of earshot. 'I mean, we could be burglars – anybody.'

Ivo shrugged, and said, 'Max has a bodyguard, as well as those gorillas in front. He pretends to be his chauffeur, but you can see the gun under his jacket.'

He was beginning to feel annoyed with her, not because he regretted what he had done but because she was so obviously someone who worked for a living. Also, she wore far too much make-up, including a sort of brown cream on her skin that made it look at once lifeless and glittering. Really, Ivo thought crossly, if she had simply come along in her waitress's uniform she would at least have been sexy.

They passed through the door to the reception, and noise crashed around them suddenly like surf. Mary would have clung to Ivo, but Ivo knew that the only thing to do at parties is to circulate on a Gulf Stream of gossip. He surged forward. 'Ah, Lady Paddington!' he cried, to a woman who stood in his proprietor's presence. As with royalty, nobody spoke to Max de Monde before he addressed you, but the old man was evidently in a high good humour, and actually recognized Ivo.

'This is one of my staff,' he boomed. 'What do you think of my little girl's book?'

'Good evening, sir! Splendid, sir!' gabbled Ivo. '*How Many Meals?*, I mean *Miles*, is marvellous, quite marvellous. An absolutely brilliant débâcle, and such a fascinating country. It's our lead review this week, you know.'

De Monde, who had no idea of the quarrels that had preceded this decision, snorted. He was a handsome man, and had a large nose through which a snort sounded well.

'Think it'll sell?'

'Oh, absolutely,' said Ivo, biting back the remark that Amelia scarcely needed the money. 'Definitely. Amelia has so many friends and – people are frightfully keen on, ah – Thailand, that sort of thing.'

'Don't you mean North Africa?' said Lady Paddington, who had, many years ago, learnt geography.

'Then why,' said Ivo's boss in his giant's voice, 'have you not bought a copy at the door?'

Ivo goggled at him. Dead silence fell throughout the room.

'I – ah – I thought that if I bought it at Hatchard's it would go onto our bestseller figures,' he said.

Several listeners silently cursed themselves for not having thought of such a simple yet sublime way of saving themselves £14.99.

'My boy, come and have a glass of vintage champagne,' said the magnate. The party started up again. His manicured hand descended towards Ivo's shoulder, like a guillotine. Without a backward glance, Ivo followed.

Mary, standing on the threshold, looked for Mark. All the men were dressed in suits. They stood together in tight little knots, barely pausing for a canapé in their exchanges until, like a shoal of fish, they would suddenly break up and dart away. Mary overheard snatches:

'My agent says –'

'– a Japanese tour arranged by the British Council –'

'– only getting published because of her *father* –'

'– on location, and I couldn't understand why they kept shouting out, "banana!" but it's their code for "author on set" –'

'– d'you think I ever *want* to appear on *Snap, Crackle, Pop!*?'

They sweated with nervous animation, and smoked heavily. She saw one or two faces of members, and gave them timid smiles, but they did not recognize her outside the club. A Filipina approached with a tray of champagne. Mary tossed back a glass, and became instantly braver. If they would not speak to her, she would speak to them.

She approached two middle-aged women, both wearing black suits and enormous silver earrings like weapons. Their bodies opened slightly, twin valves of a mussel shell.

'Hallo,' she said.

'Oh, hallo,' they said, with the politely puzzled voices that the English use to say goodbye.

'You are?' asked one.

'Mary Quinn,' said Mary.

She could see their eyes flicker rapidly as computer terminals, trying to place her.

'Are you a journalist?'

'Oh, I'm not anyone you'd have heard of,' she explained, blushing. 'I just came along for – for the crack.'

'I hope you enjoy it, then,' said one.

The shell snapped shut, and the two black backs were turned to her. The pair began an animated conversation. Clutching her empty flute of champagne, Mary stared at them. She felt as though she had been hit in the face. This was not like Slouch's, nor like any party she had ever attended, either as guest or waitress. She looked around in desperation for Mark, but was confronted with a thicket of torsos. As the party grew more and more crowded, she was forced to duck and wriggle.

'Excuse me,' she kept saying loudly to people's stomachs or chests. 'Excuse me, please.' Why didn't all these rich people have their suits dry-cleaned more often? Why didn't they realize they were getting double chins, that their nostrils had hair up them, that their breath stank of booze? She became increasingly, silently, furious. Everywhere she looked between the chinks of bodies, and more bodies, she saw red and yellow, like flames roaring up around them, and people breathing smoke. Orchids gaped at her with green or red spotted throats, pots put out long tropical leaves, which scratched like barely sheathed claws.

She found a staircase. It went down, past a kitchen where more tiny Filipinas were scurrying, and down again to a subterranean swimming pool lying like a steamy blue grotto at the bottom of de Monde's fairy palace. All around a cold light went streaming through the broken marble columns, and at the far end a stone lion poured frothy water through its jaws. Here, two of the drunker guests were canoodling in such a frenzy that Mary turned round and fled. Upstairs, she thought; there were bound to be more rooms there.

I will go up, she thought, I will. I will. She saw a familiar face at last.

'Ivo, there you are,' she said.

It occurred to Tom Viner, sitting on the stairs, that there was not a single attractive woman of his generation present with whom he had not slept apart from Amelia. He wanted to get drunk and go home.

'I'm genetically preprogrammed to be unfaithful,' he had told his current girlfriend, Sarah. 'There's no point in you having a relationship with me. If I were to get married I'd behave just as my father did towards my mother. I may utterly despise it, but I don't think I'll be any better.'

'Can't you choose?' she asked.

'No. I don't believe in love. I don't want to lie to you. I like you, and I love sex, but you mustn't expect the two to combine.'

He had fallen into Amelia's world by accident, playing jazz at parties. He was without social ambition, and effortlessly popular; that his father was mildly famous made up for the lack of money in the Viner family – for in Amelia's circle, everyone was immensely interested in just how wealthy or well-connected other under-graduates were.

Tom offered what he himself craved, a kind of animal delight in being healthy and alive. He needed it. He worked twice as many hours as the hardest-pressed merchant banker, for a fifth of the money; moved around all over London during the course of his medical training, and off duty dressed in clothes that were almost rags. Of course, the Viner children had always been the shabbiest in North London because their parents had been too busy, vague or idealistic to notice things like unravelling jumpers. He never had time for a haircut, and had come to the party looking so ragged that de Monde's bodyguards had had to make a split-second deci-sion whether to let him in. He yawned, and closed his eyes. Six hours' sleep in three days and nights was not really enough to make anyone feel human.

'Loo busy?'

It was Fiona Bamber.

'Mmm.'

He suspected she had come up deliberately.

'Fag?'

'Thanks.'

She had not changed. Well, a little. Two fine lines grooved down the pointy mask of her cheeks where she drew them back to laugh.

Grub, Tom's youngest brother, called her Bambi but you could see the wolf coming through now that Fiona was in her thirties.

'It's so reassuring to see a doctor smoke.'

'The consultant I'm with at the moment stops in the middle of operations to have one. There everyone is, all scrubbed up, and he'll halt the whole show. Won't let any of us leave for a meal, mind you.'

It fell flat, like all his anecdotes.

'Isn't that dangerous?'

Tom shrugged. 'At least he's a real surgeon. Every now and again you get some nutter, usually a butcher, who wanders round in a white coat pretending . . .'

'Ugh.'

'There was one who performed an operation, and nobody realized. It was quite a neat job, actually.'

Fiona said, 'In journalism that's known as a minibar story – there's always a drink in there somewhere. With you I suppose it's a swab.'

Tom inhaled, shrugged again, then said, 'Congratulations, by the way.'

'Thanks.' She extended her long-fingered left hand, on which two large diamond hearts, surrounded by smaller diamonds, scattered light above a thin gold wedding ring.

'Must have cost a bob or two.'

'Oh, no,' said Fiona. 'An heirloom. It's got to stay in my deposit-box when I'm not wearing it.'

'I should think so.'

'Pity you couldn't make it for the wedding.'

'I didn't think it was really appropriate to rush back from the ends of the earth to see my dad's ex-mistress marry my former best friend.'

'Of course, your father was far more fun.'

Tom winced. 'If that's true, why marry Andrew?'

'Oh, Tom!' said Fiona, smiling at him from under her long blonde fringe. 'You're such a straight arrow, really.'

'Sex?'

Fiona said, archly, 'That's usually best kept to oneself, isn't it?

37

Money, professorship, small but perfectly formed . . . house in the Cotswolds. Even brains. That's what you marry for. At least the first time round.'

Tom looked at her, and she grinned. They had had an affair for a term in his first year at Oxford. Afterwards, she described him in *Cherwell* as 'worth paying for'. She had never understood why it had made him so angry.

She was like a little animal, he thought, instinctively amoral, always smelling of a musky scent as haunting as it was disagreeable. You could not stop thinking exactly what she would be like with her legs wrapped around you, how she would wriggle and giggle and yet be unmoved, unknowable. Some people, most notably his own father, claimed she was certifiably insane, others that she was quite innocent of the havoc she caused. Tom still remembered the first time he saw her, in Balliol. He had had an impression of an immense force, a sexual presence that made him turn round and stare.

'I'd no idea you were so old-fashioned,' said Tom. 'Surely you didn't need to marry anyone?'

'Marriage is the single most difficult thing for a woman to achieve nowadays. It's far, far easier to have a career. It's still the only way to get real money.'

'What a calculating way you have of seeing the world.'

'You're part of it or Amelia wouldn't have asked you.' She added, pensively, 'She probably thinks it's a form of medical insurance, in your case.'

'I hardly know her.'

'Few of Amelia's two hundred best friends are brave enough to say that,' said Fiona.

'Why are women such bitches about each other?'

'We see the truth.'

'I'm surprised you recognize it.'

'Oh, you always recognize what you don't like,' said Fiona. 'It's finding out what you do that's difficult.'

Ivo caught sight of Ben Gorgle, the portly Canadian editor of *Grunt*. Bearded, balding and bespectacled, Big Ben pursued young and fashionable writers with a view to getting them to submit long extracts from work in progress to which he could then add his own creative input. Ben had a vague enthusiasm for the printed word, possibly because he had never been known to read many. His especial love was for the school of 'dirty axle', a transatlantic formula that demanded little from the writer but the experience of having lived in a trailer park.

'Hi!' he said to Ivo, with the bonhomie that was his trademark.

'Well, hal*lo*', Ivo returned, and immediately regretted it, for beside the head of Percy Flage, poet, biographer, traveller, novelist, columnist and commissioning editor for Belgravia, he saw a writer whose second novel Ivo himself had trashed.

Percy swivelled his pale blue eyes onto him. 'Ivo! I was just saying, don't you feel a huge, orgasmic surge of *fin-de-siècle* creative energy washing over us?'

Big Ben blushed. 'Like, a tidal wave? It comes in, and it, it,' he waved vaguely, 'goes out.'

'Yes,' said Ivo. 'A hundred years ago, we were all part of the great sea, and now we're breaking up into little rock pools.'

'"The Rock Pool!"' said Big Ben. 'That could be a good title.'

'I'm afraid somebody else used it first,' said the novelist nastily.

Percy considered. 'There's a book in that idea, Ivo. Why don't we get together over lunch?'

Though Ivo knew that this was Percy's response to most people, his heart could not help beating a little faster for Belgravia advances were often six-figure, and the idea of cobbling together a few of his longer pieces and being paid twice for the same work was not unattractive. He was beginning to feel the need for a touch of gravitas. On the other hand, there was always the possibility that hard covers would be an irresistible invitation to everyone else to sharpen the axe for his own head.

Then Ivo saw Mary. It was time to put his other plan into action.

5

The Daughter of Midas

Where was Amelia, all this time? She was, after all, supposed to be the centre of the party given in her name, the very axis around which its glittering crowd spun and thrummed, and might be expected to be holding court in her father's drawing room, professing a modest but sincere enthusiasm for her own work, signing copies of *How Many Miles?* and in general behaving as every new author should. Indeed, Amelia had done all this for the first hour and a half. Confronted with the halitosis and neurosis of rival editors she had told them how clever they were, and how pleased she was they could come. Perpetually anxious that they might one day need a new job, the editors were charmed. To women she had confessed that she was terrified and covered in fake tanning lotion. (In fact, she had spent the previous week at a health-farm beneath a sunlamp.) To young men she was archly flirtatious; to old ones, girlishly appealing. She wore a tiny clinging dress of crushed gold silk, which had cost £9000 and which planted in the head of every gossip-columnist present the idea that here indeed was the daughter of Midas. Had there been half as much art in her book, it would have deserved the praise it reaped.

'It's marvellous, absolutely brilliant,' everyone assured her.

Amelia enjoyed it all immensely, and took it as no more than her due. She had grown up with the idea that her father was a powerful man, but she naturally failed to understand quite how much being Max de Monde's only child had made her passage through life an easy one. He had made his first million when she was a girl, owning a string of dull but profitable publishing concerns by the time she was at university. The *Chronicle*, which had turned him into a figure of national repute, had fallen to him after a round of fierce bidding and an attempted management buy-out in 1985. Amelia had been courted and fêted since puberty, and she had become a figure of startling glamour in Oxford. Yet this same glamour isolated her in ways that she did not wholly understand. She was at once innocent and sophisticated, the kind of woman idolized by homosexuals, older men and young girls who rarely inspires deep affection among her peers.

'I don't want to be told how talented and beautiful I am,' she would say. 'I want the truth.'

Amelia had never had to work at anything, except, perhaps, keeping her appetite under control. Her travels in the Middle East had been furnished with introductions to the pleasantest and most comfortable of private villas and her essays at writing guided by numerous mentors including her editor at Belgravia, Candida Twink. That her father now effectively owned Belgravia did not lessen her irritation at being asked for rewrites. She had no ambition to produce a good book, only to have published one that people in her circle would praise, but she believed herself to be exceptionally gifted, both as writer and journalist. Everyone was expected to have a successful career: leisure was for the unemployed.

She wrote an occasional column for the *Chronicle*, and pieces for other papers, but meeting deadlines was frightfully tiresome. Travel writing, by contrast, seemed ideal. One could get up late, shop, lunch, party, have love affairs, go all over the world and feel virtuous after only a couple of hours at the lap-top.

Of her father's early life in the Lebanon few now knew. Max de Monde claimed to be a Christian Maronite of French descent. Those of his family who had not died in the civil war fled to Paris and London; the women, with their exquisite chihuahua faces and enormous jewels, talked only of childbirth, clothes and spiritual matters, which bored him. The men were in business like himself, but less successful. Some of them could be seen now at Amelia's party, bunched together like the rings on their fingers. They did not speak to the English guests, and did not expect to be spoken to.

41

All sorts of rumours swirled around as to the sources of the de Monde fortune. It was said he was secretly an arms dealer or a drugs baron; some had it that he was funded by the KGB, others that he was the banker for the PLO. These rumours circulated solely among journalists, for de Monde had discovered that libel litigation in Britain was a lucrative sideline for the rich. His rivals had a tacit understanding that no newspaper proprietor would attack another for fear of what was hidden in his own closet. What was beyond doubt was the power of his personality. Even City lawyers felt uneasy when they saw him, for to the usual aura of a very rich man he added a distinct whiff of something altogether more sulphurous. He believed himself to be a genius, and would conduct his meetings, famously, like a chess grandmaster, moving from conference room to conference room, or from telephone to telephone in order to underline that his time was worth more than anyone else's. His energy, his insomnia, his womanizing, his fluency in six languages all added to his stature.

'Do you know why I chose to emigrate to this country?' he told interviewers. 'Because I am larger than life, and it is smaller.'

None of which made him popular with the Establishment. Yet here, too, he seemed invulnerable. He had married a minor member of the Kenward family then working at the embassy in Beirut during the 1950s. Though she was no particular catch this was sufficient to ensure a clan loyalty from other members of the Kenwards and their powerful cousins the Ansteys. Plain, shy and deeply romantic, the future Mrs de Monde had been easy to sweep off her feet, then under the carpet. Amelia's mother now spent most of her time in her own rooms, and those who saw her said she had not aged well.

Amelia had copied as many of her father's mannerisms as possible, especially that of being open in the enjoyment of her wealth. Educated at the French Lycée in London and a finishing school in Switzerland, she had acquired a gushing manner and a smattering of intellectual sophistication. It was common knowledge that de Monde had been obliged to fund a new Chair to get her into Oxford, and to do her credit, Amelia always cheerfully admitted this. 'Colleges never worried about taking people with money before, it was how most of them got built in the first place. Why should they have a nerd in an anorak when they could have *me*?' she would demand.

Amelia was generally said to be a beauty, and such was her aura of glamour, confidence and pure loot that many, including herself, believed it. She was tall, and had excellent legs which she displayed to advantage. Her hair was streaked, her fingers tapered, her skin tanned, her teeth capped; it was said that her nose had grown smaller with age. In motion, she flashed and winked and clanked with just the right amount of jewellery to be indiscreet.

She had a warm heart, or at least a hot temper, and liked to present herself as unpretentious and affectionate, never seeing the bad side of those she was fond of. But Amelia had a calculating shrewdness, and a shrewishness, which could take the unwary by surprise. Anyone suspected of slighting her or her family was spoken of with venom; disappointment was pursued with actual vindictiveness. But these displays of sourness were rare.

She was, indeed, very hard to resist, and only the lesser members of the upper classes – the most unaffected, rustic and suspicious of new money – did so. In any case, Amelia was not interested in these, but in an altogether racier and more cosmopolitan élite. Several of its members were claimed as her 'best and dearest friend', with Amelia extending invitations to share 'Daddy's box at the opera' or to swim in his heated pool in the basement.

Max de Monde doted on her, and she on him. Amelia was his darling, his poppet, his jewel; when he did not take his mistress on trips abroad, he would take his daughter. Throughout her twenties, he bought her one toy after another: a tiny silver Porsche, a diamond-studded Rolex, a collar of pearls once worn by the Empress Josephine. Only the Conservative Party received more, and from Amelia, de Monde did not expect a knighthood. What he waited for was an illustrious marriage.

Here Amelia ran into difficulties. Her father did not want her to leave home, and made it too comfortable for her to wish to do so. 'Why do you want to live alone in some miserable apartment when you have your own little mews house here, with a swimming-pool and the servants who have known you since childhood?' he asked.

'But everyone leaves home when they're grown-up,' Amelia protested. 'Why shouldn't I?'

'If you're restless, travel.'

So Amelia travelled, and when she was in England lived across the long lawn at the back of the Holland Park mansion in the mews house. It was the prettiest little place imaginable. There was a cobbled lane outside, dripping with windowboxed flowers and sporadically adorned with vintage cars. It had its own narrow front door, and a narrow staircase with ropes on either side, like a boat, leading up to the living rooms. Underneath was housed her Porsche.

At present, however, Amelia was not in her own house, but on the third floor of her father's.

Mark Crawley felt dizzy with champagne, exhilaration and fright.

'What is this place?'

'My old bedroom,' said Amelia.

'It's like something from *Come Dancing*.'

'Oh, I adore frou-frou,' said Amelia, with such confidence that even Mark began to wonder if this were not a mark of radical chic. In fact, he had seized upon the fondant pinks and gilts with a kind of relief. He could only cope with the evidence of so much money by despising the taste that had squandered it.

The sheer wealth of London still amazed him. Travelling from Brixton to Kensington made him feel like a diver with the bends. It wasn't like an American capital, where money sealed you off in a bubble; nor like a European one, where it hid itself away behind high walls and frowning concierges. In London, houses like these stood serenely behind a minimum of railings, displaying glimpses of the grace, the ease, the culture that enormous wealth could buy. Those who spoke of British reserve could only refer to their manners, not their urban architecture, for the privilege so casually displayed to any passer-by would have incited revolution in most other countries.

Mark knew himself to be more sophisticated than most, but the majority was not what concerned him. No matter how much he read and bought and looked and snooped, there was always an urbanity about, say, Ivo, which reminded Mark that he himself had grown up in the cul-de-sacs of Slough with a family who drank Blue Nun and read the *Daily Express*. The utter absence of intellectual activity in their lives still filled him with a dull, resentful misery. The happiness and ease of Amelia's nature astounded him even more than his possession of her.

Mark had never conducted simultaneous affairs for so long. He had met Amelia at a promotional lunch for travel writers; the kind of thing to which he did not normally go, but which Ivo had asked him to cover for a feature. Mark was so unresponsive that Amelia had exerted herself to charm him. Each had become mildly drunk, lightly flirtatious, then seriously so. When the lunch ended, they walked along Piccadilly together and into the Ritz for the afternoon. Amelia paid for their room in advance with her gold credit card, giving the man at the desk a huge, irresistible wink.

'I feel as if I'd just stepped into a trashy book,' Mark remarked, nervously.

'If this were Henry James I'd hardly have got through the door yet.'

Mark was astonished. 'You read him?'

'Naturally,' said Amelia, shrugging off her dress. 'He's the only writer who really understood about money.'

Nothing less than a viscount would satisfy Max de Monde when his daughter was in her twenties. Amelia, however, wanted love, and, increasingly, she wanted brains. It was a quest that had brought her to the age of thirty-two and the beginnings of panic. She looked as splendidly lithe and firm as she had at twenty, but she knew that things were not as they were. Mark was thrillingly keen on sex, and what he lacked in instinct he compensated for, surely, by a combination of intelligence and methodology.

'There's nobody else, is there?' she asked, as an afterthought.

Mark considered the implications of this. He did not want to be captured by anyone, even this nymph; but he was tempted. 'Would that matter to you?'

'Not particularly,' said Amelia. 'But one likes to know.'

'There is someone.'

'Long-term?' said Amelia.

'Yes, I suppose so. But not, you understand, permanent.'

'Good,' said Amelia. Then she giggled. 'I thought at first you might be gay, you know.'

'No,' said Mark.

The next day he sent her an enormous bunch of lilies. Amelia was touched by this for, like most modern women, she had received few of the conventional tokens of courtship. Used to the meanness of the very rich – the free sachet of cornflakes in the larder, the toiletries stolen from hotels, the bucket-shop flights to exotic locations – she was enchanted when these floral tributes continued, accompanied by a shower of witty, allusive postcards. He was her secret, and she was his – for the time being.

Only Ivo became suspicious. He knew Amelia well enough to sense when a serious love-affair was starting, and he saw them arrive together in Amelia's Porsche at a party in Fulham. Until then, he had not even known they were acquainted. He rang the Brixton flat one morning, ostensibly to speak to Mark.

'He's doing an interview in Edinburgh,' Mary said, sleepily.

'Is he?' said Ivo. 'Of whom?'

'Don't you know?'

'Oh, I expect so,' said Ivo. There was a long pause. 'Everything all right?'

'Yes,' said Mary, trying to clear her mind. She had got back from her shift very late. 'He's just working terribly hard. Shall I pass on a message?'

Mark no longer listened to her. Alone in Holland Park, while Amelia was out shopping, or having a massage, or attending one of the many social engagements with which rich young women fill their time, he prowled around her private things. He read her bank statements, discovered she used the mini-pill, flipped through her address book, her wardrobe and her teenage diaries. It was like being in a large airing cupboard, everything was white or cream. He approved of this monochromal taste. Her cashmeres, her jewels, her bottles, even the shell-shaped soap in her pristine basin delighted him.

Amelia was equally entranced by his approach to something as frivolous as her own handbags ('A metaphor for the vagina,' he observed, causing her to thank God she bought only Chanel). She had never been with someone who noticed so much, who knew so much, who could match her restless frivolity with sober taste. She was used to being with people who were stupid, or silly, bound together only by the money to pursue the same round of parties and holidays – whose social sophistication barely concealed the absence of almost any other quality. That he was still living with someone else was not a matter that especially concerned her. Yet it must be said that she had not planned what happened next.

'There's something I need you to know,' she said, smiling down in the pink and gold bedroom; and told him.

Mary climbed the stairs. Ivo followed. Red lasers winked from every cornice, the back windows were shuttered with folding iron grilles beneath their sumptuous drapery. Everything was rich and heavy and new; even the fittings in the bathrooms were gold-plated, the water falling soundlessly into hand-painted china. There were cartoons of de Monde in every conceivable guise – Max as the devil, as Rambo, as a burglar; Max gloating as he sacked print-workers in Scotland and editors in London; Max as the Demon King of newspaper proprietors. Mary was astonished that anyone could live with such portraits. It was as if de Monde revelled in his independence from the common need to feel popular, she thought.

'In here?'

Ivo shook his head. 'I've already looked. Don't worry, we'll find him.'

Mary lifted eyes full of anxiety to the next staircase, and for an instant encountered the gaze of a man above her. He was talking to a journalist she recognized from the club as Fiona Bamber. The man, too, seemed vaguely familiar – an actor, perhaps.

'Hi, Ivo,' said Fiona.

'Hallo,' said Ivo. 'What are you two doing up here?'

'Oh, just having a chat. Don't let him show you the etchings,' Fiona said archly to Mary.

'Who was that?' she asked on the next landing.

'Who?'

'That man, on the stairs, just now.'

'Not in your league, my darling.'

'As a matter of fact, I thought he looked rather conceited,' said Mary, hurt.

'Not conceited, exactly,' said Ivo. 'Let's just say there's not a dry seat in the house. That's Tom Viner.'

'Adam knows him. Where is Mark, anyway?'

They approached the third floor. Ivo pointed.

'In here, I think.'

Mary opened the door.

6

Adam Sands

Mary had begun to believe that she could direct her path towards the truth gaily and gracefully. For weeks now she had been dizzy, exhilarated, almost, by the vistas of misery filling her horizon. For an instant seeing him with Amelia actually came as a relief: she had not been mad, there was a real cause for Mark's behaviour. But then something seemed to drive her legs into her ribs and wrench every internal organ out of place. She was not crushed so much as impacted, dwarfed by a single blow. She watched Mark put the trousers she had bought over the boxer shorts she had bought, and was surprised to find herself breathing.

'I was going to tell you,' Mark said.

'You've always said it was better to show than to tell,' said Mary, and Mark felt a pang of surprise. They looked at each other.

Amelia said, 'What do you think you're doing, wandering round my father's house? How dare you come into my bedroom? Who are you, anyway? I know I didn't invite you.'

'Is it introductions you'll be wanting, now?' said Mary.

'This is Mary Quinn. My –' Mark made a gesture with one hand, as if flipping through a Rolodex.

'Oh. How embarrassing,' said Amelia, without a trace of this emotion. 'Well – what's done can't be undone.'

She spoke with complete ruthlessness, a ruthlessness so ancient and so female that Mary and Mark felt a kind of awe, as if she were laying claim to what was indisputably hers.

Mark made a decision. Had he not been discovered in this way, he would probably not have made it, but it seemed like the best way out of his predicament.

'Amelia and I are getting married.'

Amelia smiled her assent.

'Why?' said Mary.

'I'm pregnant.'

All those nights, Mary thought, all those weeks and months and years when she had forced herself to open and swallow that Advent calender of contraception, believing Mark would come to her of his own free will; all that time, yearning more and more for a baby, for Mark to marry her; and he gets caught by the oldest trick of biology.

She said, 'Congratulations. It is Mark's, I assume?'

'Of course,' said Amelia, frigidly.

Mary turned to Mark. 'You never intended to marry me, did you?'

'No.'

'Did you ever intend to marry anyone?'

She saw the answer in his eyes. Amelia had scored a double victory. Mary said, with violent humility, 'All the best, then. I'm sure you'll make a perfect couple.'

When she turned round, Ivo, who had been standing outside on the landing, and hopping up and down with glee, saw her face convulse. All at once he was filled with remorse.

'Thank you,' she said to him carefully, and ran down the stairs.

'Mary, wait!' said Ivo; but she did not. The crowds downstairs seemed to part before her effortlessly. She watched with a kind of surprise as the long red carpet carried her past the policemen.

'Enjoy yourself?' asked one, in a tone of half-envious sarcasm, and she gave a little wave, just as if she had.

Adam Sands was Mary's oldest friend in London, and it was to him that she went now, with tears streaming down her face. Her cousin Deirdre was closer, in Shepherd's Bush, but Mary could not bear the idea of her misfortune being chattered about by the people she had taken such care to leave behind. She stumbled down Campden Hill Road, then, at Notting Hill Gate tube station, remembered she had no money, and could not, in any case, go back to Brixton. Past the rasping buses, past the cinemas with their posters of giant loves and hates, round the public parks, past Marble Arch. It was a long walk, and by the time Mary reached Berkeley Square she had sunk into a deep freeze of the spirit.

Adam's flat was above an art gallery just off Bond Street. She rang the bell beside its narrow, scruffy front door, and he buzzed her up.

The stairs were steep and dirty and smelt of old socks. The first-floor flat was empty, its door covered by a metal sheet, having been repossessed by the pension company that owned it. They were trying to evict the other floors but without success, for below Adam lived Mabel, an elderly woman who was utterly tenacious concerning her rights as a sitting tenant. Adam was very tall, rather ugly, and spoke in a deep, lugubrious voice which was effective in repelling the various representatives of the pension company who tried to get him out. He had laughed when Mary told him that for a long time she had believed him a product 'at the very least of maids and marble halls'.

'Yes,' he said. 'It's lucky for me that in England a poor man working at appearing rich can look the same as a rich man playing at being poor.'

Mary knew how poor men dressed – the split, scuffed shoes of imitation leather that distorted the feet inside, the skimpy drip-dry shirts with huge collars – she had only to think of her own father, or the boys with whom she had grown up in Belfast. She did not think Adam poor, not when he had a bank account and a rent-controlled flat in Mayfair; but she supposed, with some accuracy, that part of her charm for him was that she made him feel his own privilege. He had an encyclopedic memory for social connection without himself attempting to participate in any kind of social scene – including the gay one, which he particularly scorned.

People believed him to be considerably richer and grander than he was, merely because he had grown up in Paris and had culti-vated a certain elegance of dress and manner. Adam wore what he called 'gardener's suits', old-fashioned tweeds bought from charity shops, which because of his odd shape fitted perfectly. This gen-trified persona was comparatively recent. At Cambridge, he had been flamboyantly camp: the kind of person, Mark observed, whom one really expected to see at Oxford. At his interview, he had pranced around in a long black cloak and a Borsalino hat; later, he affected cream linen suits with a miniature teddy bear in the breast pocket. He was a superb actor, wrote spiky little plays, one of which had won a prize at the Edinburgh Festival, was recognized by even the dullest Natural Scientist, and got a First in History. When he announced he was going to write novels, he was spoken of as someone bound to be a modern Proust.

Yet Adam had vanished. While his contemporaries, swarming to London, partied and networked and eyed each other uneasily to see who would be the first to become famous, he refused to circulate. Soon people began to sneer at his affectations and *bons mots*. There were stories involving leather and lavatories and bushes on Hampstead Heath; of Adam dancing in Heaven and modelling in pornographic magazines. Nobody knew whether these were true, and nobody cared.

When Adam reappeared, he was something of a disappointment. Quieter and more conventional, but still apparently writing while working in a second-hand bookshop on Charing Cross Road, he had become a recluse. The shop, Pocock's, was small, old-fashioned and mildly cultish, which made his choice of job almost respectable – but it was not what anyone had expected. He saw a few friends; never attempted to entertain, and only went to dinner parties if he knew the food would be good. During the past year his companions had been whittled down to four people: Tom Viner, Andrew Evenlode, Georgina Hunter and Mary Quinn.

Mary had never met these other friends, although she had heard about them. They were part of an Oxbridge clique who all seemed to have shared houses and beds with each other. Tom was a doctor, Andrew a don, Georgina a journalist who wrote romantic blockbusters. None of them sounded particularly nice, but she would have liked to meet these exotic beings, if only because the fact of her doing so might have impressed Mark.

Now she began to tell Adam what had happened in a voice that cracked with misery, while he made cocoa and Welsh rarebit on his rickety gas cooker. The windows had double glazing to cut out the rumble from the street, but otherwise the furnishings were all from the 1950s, down to the rounded fridge and the curling iron fire-escape out the back.

'I can't believe Mark would do this to me,' she said.

'Why not?'

'Why not? Because – because it's against everything I thought he was. Can you live with someone for five years and not know them?'

'Does it matter to you very much? Infidelity, I mean.'

'Yes, of course it does,' Mary said, almost shrieking. 'Of course – of course – it's the end of everything. He's going to *marry* her.'

'He might have just been drunk.'

'No, no, you don't understand. It's been going on for weeks, and that isn't the point. How can you be so obtuse? It means that everything he ever said to me was a lie. Oh, how can I bear it?'

'I've never liked him,' said Adam.

Mary stopped wringing her hands, and said furiously, 'No, I know, and he's never liked you, but I *love him*. I love him and I hate him, I think I'll go mad. I trusted him. I showed him – it's not just sex – the faults, the weaknesses, the little lies that – how he must despise me! I thought you could do that with someone you love. He must think that is who, what, I really am.'

'If you love someone you love even their faults.'

'But you don't love them for farting or having a silly laugh or being lazy.'

'I don't mean that. People are like planets, they circle you but only show you half. To love in the round is to know the dark.'

'Is that what it is? Isn't it more likely that you'll simply be a blur in space?' she said, tears pouring down her face. 'I believed if I gave him everything he'd love me. How utterly he must despise me. She must be perfect, for him to love her instead of me.'

'She's rich, and powerful in the world to which he aspires.'

'She talks as though she's gargling in double cream,' said Mary.

'Claws to the ceiling, darling, claws to the ceiling.'

'I can't believe money would count with him. He told me once that glamour meant "evil spell". He hates ambition.'

'People condemn their own faults most of all,' said Adam. 'They feel them, and loathe them, far more than any flaw which doesn't have its roots in their own nature.'

'You think Mark is ambitious?'

'Does a wasp like jam?'

'That awful party, I made myself go because he was always saying, why didn't I go out more? Nobody talked to me. Apart from Ivo, and that –'

She was yanking her hair, as if to drag the thoughts out by their roots.

'You know, I almost think he planned it, he told me where to find them, he tried to get off with me once himself –'

'The Sponge Lunge,' said Adam. 'I shouldn't take it personally, it's a kind of reflex, like a carnivorous plant.'

'No – no – of course not,' said Mary, who at that moment would have found some relief in the idea that even Ivo found her attractive. 'I don't know what to do. There must be some sort of protocol for these situations. Obviously, I must move out. Oh – do you really think he might just have been drunk? Or under an evil spell?'

'You've missed the last tube. Sleep here.'

For Adam to make such an offer touched Mary. She knew how he valued his privacy; he once said it was a lasting scar of boarding school that he was unable to bear the physical presence of others for more than two hours. She made up the bed on the divan.

'How quiet it is here at night,' she said. 'I'd never have thought it.'

'Mayfair's a morgue,' said Adam. 'All the buildings that used to be houses have been turned into offices. That's why I don't give a damn about being a sort of squatter.'

'You're so lucky,' said Mary. 'To have a flat to yourself for forty pounds a week, such freedom.'

For a single person, it was ideal. There was a front room, out of which a narrow kitchen had been carved, leaving a square for a table on one side and the divan on the other. An open fire smouldered in a white marble fireplace, incongruous as Cinderella's white foot beneath her rags. There was no central heating, so to save on fuel bills Adam would burn, quite illegally, any rubbish that looked combustible, with the result that his flat always smelt rather odd. The walls were grimed to the colour of melting snow. On one hung a small, unframed painting of a young man.

'Who did that?' Mary asked. 'It's new, isn't it?'

'A painter called Emma Kenward,' Adam said. 'Andrew Evenlode knows her. Some sort of cousin of Amelia's, actually.'

'It's rotten,' Mary said at once.

'No, it's not.'

The floors of both living room and bedroom were filthy. Every surface glistened with cake crumbs where it was not matted with dust, not just ordinary dust, but dust on top of dust, an infinity of dust continually being deposited by the city air. On the cooker, stalactites of grease met stalagmites of grease. The bathroom was encrusted in shaving foam that had set in leprous blobs and frills. Mary could never see it without longing for a bottle of bleach and a Scotchbrite.

Usually paper lay everywhere. Scrunched into balls, folded into wedges, shuffled into loose, towering piles that slowly leaned over and collapsed with a rustle into other piles; papers ringed by coffee and running with ink; papers stuck with yellow notes or black dog-clips; papers suspended from nails, from shelves, from walls. Open a cupboard door, and an avalanche of white would descend. Pull a drawer, and it reared like a lazy cobra. All was covered with Adam's slanting hand, which dashed forward across the page with a nervous speed and complete illegibility.

Now, though, she suddenly noticed that the living room was almost tidy, the paper stacked or greatly diminished. 'What's happened? Have you decided to spring clean?'

Adam beamed. She saw that he was static with excitement. 'I was going to tell you.'

'What?'

'I've got a publisher.'

'Oh, Adam! You mean, you've finished? I can't wait to read it.'

'It suddenly came right. I've been writing and rewriting for nine years, and then it suddenly wrote itself in three months. It's like tuning in to a radio, you know, nothing but snatches and static and then – clear! I typed it out and sent it to an agent, Francesca Styles, and she got an offer, all in a fortnight,' said Adam. 'I still can't believe it myself.'

'Who's the publisher?'

'Belgravia.'

'Oh,' said Mary. 'Like Amelia.'

'You're taking the de Monde shilling too, working at Slouch's. He's got fingers in every pie.'

'That horrible, horrible man!'

'You don't know that,' said Adam. 'You can't blame children for their parents or vice versa.'

Adam's father now lived with his second wife in Monte Carlo. 'The most ghastly woman,' Adam once said. 'She wears sunglasses with initials on them. All she's interested in is money, and making sure I don't get any. We haven't talked since I was twelve.'

Privately, Mary thought that if Adam's father and stepmother sounded bad, the first Mrs Sands was odious. According to Adam, she would cycle for miles over the Norfolk broads to find a garage selling petrol at a penny cheaper, and thought herself no end of a wit for continually 'sounding orf'. To Adam's own proclivities, she was blind, believing the convenient fiction that Mary was, as she put it, his 'little Irish popsy'. She also insisted on calling her 'Molly'. Mary endured such sneers for Adam's sake. He never criticized his mother apart from saying occasionally that she had been 'ratty', went home most weekends, and returned bearing a briefcase full of cake and cooked meat. Mary thought of the way that her own mother grudgingly thanked her for the money she sent, and received her visits with a sigh if it meant another mouth to feed; but she knew that Betty Quinn loved her more truly than Mrs Sands her only son.

Mary dreaded what would happen when her mother found out about Mark. Betty had never concealed her loathing of him, not after the disastrous holiday he had spent with them in County Cork, and Mary knew with complete certainty that she would be triumphant rather than sympathetic. Her conviction that Mary deserved better would have been flattering, had it not been entirely based on the utter conviction as to the moral supremacy of her own genes.

Mary put her head on her arms and sobbed again, though exhaustion was numbing her. She thought that she was regaining control over her feelings. Eventually, she blew her nose and said, 'Oh, it must be possible to avoid suffering, it must, it must.'

'Well,' said Adam, 'it's like the man on the double-decker with bananas.'

'What's that?'

'You know. There's a man riding on top of a bus who keeps throwing banana skins out of the window. Someone asks why he does it, and he says, "So that the elephants in London will slip on them."

'"But there are no elephants in London," says the other.

'"See?" says the man.'

Mary gave a little crockery laugh. Then she said, 'Haven't you been to the Zoo?'

7

Splitting Up

Mark's dislike of any display of emotion was extreme; so extreme that in the past Mary had wondered whether it was sensibility, rather than any manifestation of it, that he abhorred.

'Never say "I feel". Say "I think". Never say "moving", say "affecting",' he had instructed her, from the beginning.

They met at the Slouch Club, in a small room usually used for private functions. Mary had moved into the flat her cousin Deirdre shared with her boyfriend, Niall, in Shepherd's Bush. They meant well, and were kind, but she knew it was an inconvenience to them, for both were sociable, and thought nothing of always having other friends around. They both kept up with the Murphia, and between all their friends from the BBC, and those from Dublin and Belfast, Mary had no rest. In any case, she loathed their way of life.

There is perhaps no rack of torture in England as exquisite as that devised by social mobility. For twelve years, Mary had taught herself to enjoy the refinements of another class. She was used to listening to Radio Three and eating salads, to living with paintings on the wall, to having fresh flowers. Niall and Deirdre had aspirations, too, but they were of another, more modest kind. They shopped at Habitat, not Heal's, and drank beer instead of wine. By a thousand small ways they irritated each other.

'Let's face it, Mary, he was always out of your sphere,' said Deirdre. 'Prods are all the same, under the surface, so tight-arsed they shit charcoal briquettes.'

Oh, who will marry me, with such a family? thought Mary, weeping in the avocado-tiled bathroom.

Mark had moved into Amelia's house. The mews cottage accommodated two people with difficulty for its spare room was devoted to Amelia's wardrobe, but it was still agreeable, if rather too hot.

'It's almost tropical in here,' he complained to Amelia.

'Yes, Daddy and I find most English houses far too dark and cold,' she said, laughing. She had a lovely laugh: lush, gentle and practised a great many times in private. Hearing it on the telephone always made Mark want to tear her clothes off and bury his face in her scented flesh.

Their unofficial engagement was common knowledge within twenty-four hours of the party. At work he noticed the change, for a kind of wary deference crept into the eyes and voices of those around him, spilling out of Ivo's tiny fiefdom of Books in a ripple of gossip and speculation. Mark had been a name in freelance circles for some time, but to other editors, especially those in news and business, he had been relatively unknown. Now his telephone suddenly rang with invitations to lunch, with compliments, with requests to contribute a weekly political column.

Mark took this rise in his fortunes as no more than his due. He had been mystified before by the slowness of his success in comparison to, say, Ivo. He saw now that he had not fully appreciated quite how much Mary had counted against him. With Amelia, he was asked everywhere. Her glamour compensated for his silence, his intellect balanced her frivolity. Together, they were a golden couple, especially after the success of her book.

The reviews of *How Many Miles?* were so many, long and flattering that he became quite frightened he was going to lose her after all. She was interviewed by Merlin Swagg on *Snap, Crackle, Pop!*, profiled in the *Telegraph*, the *Standard* and the *Mail* and featured in *Harpers & Queen* as one of the rising generation of women travel writers. Everybody wanted to ask them to dinner, and to make a fuss of them. Nobody except her friends and relations bought her book, but it was still sold to America and Germany on the back of so much hype, and displayed on every coffee table of those in society.

Amelia's morning sickness prevented them from going out every night, but even so Mark had more exposure in one month to the glittering orbit in which she lived than he had enjoyed in three years. The people whose faces he had seen in glossy magazines now talked to him, to Mark Crawley from Slough.

Mark raged to himself when he thought of all the things he had missed out on by staying faithful to Mary in the past, blaming her for every slight and rejection. But for her, he might have been earning £50,000 within three, no two, years of leaving Cambridge, he thought.

Only Ivo said, 'I think you're making a mistake.'

'You were most emphatic about the underclass dragging one down.'

'Quite,' said Ivo, stroking his bow-tie. 'But I also said she was worth having.'

'So? I've had her.'

'I wonder whether you really understand what Mary could be.'

'I know what she is. Short of being hit over the head with a brick, people don't change their personalities.'

'Really? I think you may be wrong about that, old boy.'

'Well,' said Mark shrugging, and quoting Amelia, '"What's done can't be undone."' He felt masculine as steak.

'She's in a bad way. At least you should talk to her. And she needs her things from your flat.'

'Yes, I suppose so,' said Mark.

He did not like to think of going back to the Slouch Club. But there was something he dreaded more, and that was a formal request for Amelia's hand in marriage to Max de Monde. Mary had to be neutralized before she could make trouble.

'Daddy will be furious at first,' Amelia said. 'You'll have to talk him round. He won't do anything too terrible – as long as you marry me. We'd better hurry things up, though. My gynaecologist says I'm nine weeks now, and you start to show at fourteen.'

'Yes – yes, of course,' said Mark, in his gloomiest voice. 'I'd better have it out with Mary first.'

'I don't see why,' said Amelia. 'After all, there can't be any point of contact with our world and hers now you've stopped seeing her.'

'She has her things in my old flat. I'm still on the leash while they stay.'

'Oh, darling,' said Amelia, with her light, lush laugh, 'you're so funny when you're all Eeyorish.'

Walking through Soho to meet Mary, he clenched memory like a nettle. He disliked thinking of himself as in any way behaving badly, yet he would not, could not apologize to her. The girls at the front desk fluttered, smiled, directed him upwards. Climbing the narrow, twisted stairs his feet sank into pink and blue carpet patterned with a design of crushed peanuts. It was outdated for the 1990s, he thought; amazing to think that it had once mattered so much to him to be a member.

It was a shock for each to see the other, for to Mary Mark had become vast and shadowy, whereas to Mark Mary had shrunk to a wizened troll. The familiarity, the normality was surreal.

She's pretty, he thought.

He's ugly, she thought; and for a minute both were disarmed.

'That's a new dress. Where did you get it?' he asked.

'Fenwick's.'

'Ah,' he said, staring at her with his lightless eyes; and Mary wished she had lied and said it was from Harrods. He always asked people, especially women, about their clothes, and then somehow made them feel frumpy or ignorant. She had forgotten this trick.

A long pause.

'I would like to know some things,' she said.

'I don't think you should,' said Mark, gently. He was moved to sentiment, as people often are when they do not allow themselves to feel.

'Indeed? You surely have no right to tell me so.'

'What, then?'

'How long, for instance, have you been sleeping with her?'

'Ten weeks. And two days,' said Mark, deliberately.

'So there was quite a time when you were sleeping with us both?'

He shrugged. 'Yes.'

'Don't you think that was wrong?'

'As a matter of fact, it was quite . . . erotic.'

For a wild moment, Mary wondered whether she could bear it if she continued to share him, if she were sophisticated enough to survive a *ménage à trois*. She knew at once it was impossible.

'What if she's given me a disease? You can scarcely have been wearing a condom if you got her pregnant.'

Mark gave her a look of scorn. 'She has a gynaecologist,' he said, as if every woman who was not subhuman possessed this.

'Did you do it on our bed with her?'

'You don't want to know.'

'Oh, God. When?'

Mark said, with weary impatience, 'When you went home for Christmas. After a party at the paper.'

'Did she not know of my existence?'

'Oh, yes. But it didn't matter.'

'It didn't *matter*? Someone just destroys –'

'She's barely conscious of your existence.'

'And you're in love with her? Someone like that? An absolute idiot who knows nothing of the world?'

She found her voice rising.

'On the contrary, a part of her attraction is that she knows a great deal about it.'

'She knows nothing, *nothing*. What can you learn if you go everywhere in luxury or with your family, or with money wadding your every step?'

Mary's face flushed scarlet, and she began to pant. 'What does she know of what I know, of people, of suffering, of – of what it's like to have nothing but yourself? How can you love someone who goes through life as a bloody *tourist*?'

She saw Mark's composure waver. He hated tourists. 'Some of what you say is true.'

'Oh, my darling, my darling, what has she done to you? You're not yourself, how can you love such a painted bag of bones? How can you? Come back to me, I promise it won't matter to us. I promise. I can change – I can become anything you want me to.'

'You're thirty. Do you think you can change?'

'You did,' said Mary. 'Remember?'

For a moment she saw the face of the deep self, the face that miraculously becomes clear to lovers, welling up from the past. She held her breath. If only – if only – it was like trying to recapture his soul, she thought, to talk it back into him, when all the time, time was running out. If she were silent, she would lose him, and if she said too much, or the wrong thing, she would lose him also.

Downstairs, there was the noise of people passing and giggling. The clock on the mantel counted moments in its neat black voice.

She said, 'Mark?'

'But why should she know about poverty?' said the hateful, sneering mask. 'Do you think that makes someone better? Do you think I've enjoyed living the way we did?'

'I can't be blamed for not being rich or grand,' she said. 'I never blamed you for not being so.'

'But I deserve more. I am *worth* more. More has been invested in me by society. Can you blame me for wanting to take what's offered? If you had the choice between a first-class ticket and a third, would you take the third?'

'Yes, if it meant committing a sin for the first.'

'A sin! You never get rid of it, do you, that superstition that the universe is a moral creation?'

'Even if there is no God,' said Mary, her voice sinking, like a stream drying up, 'even if, you can still behave well. You still can. Even if there is nothing taking notice – don't you see it's braver? What you're doing to me, what you've done, is – you know what I say is true – and besides,' she said, fiercely, 'there's still other people. What do other people think of what you've done?'

'Why should they care? They have their own lives, people split up all the time.'

'Split,' said Mary. 'Yes, that's what it feels like.'

'I do dislike the way you are so self-consciously literary,' said Mark. 'It's like listening to bad blank verse.'

Mary was silenced. 'It's just the way I speak,' she said at last.

She was horrified by the hatred he clearly had for her.

'Even for someone so simplistic as to believe in moral absolutes,

63

you behave with striking naïvety. Your attacks on Amelia do you no credit,' he said. 'I am amazed by your self-importance at even attempting to do so. How can you dare judge someone you have barely met for five minutes?'

'*You* have often dared so,' said Mary.

He was getting bored with this conversation, by the way that she was attempting to put up a fight. He walked about the room, sighing impatiently, and flung himself down on the sofa. 'You must collect your things from my flat,' he said. 'Today.'

'I can't manage it today, I'm on shift until midnight,' she said. 'I've worked five shifts in a row.'

She sat down beside him, putting her knuckles to her eyes like a child and suddenly, unexpectedly, he was touched. 'There, there,' he said, patting her. She was just a small animal, he thought.

Mary thought, I must stop this, I must, but found herself with her head in his lap, her hot tears repulsed by his designer raincoat. For a moment it was as if they were companions who had reached a plateau after a long and horrible climb.

Mark said, 'It's a pity, there's so much of us still in each other, isn't there?'

'Oh, Mark, Mark,' said Mary, abandoning herself utterly. 'I love you so much. Don't do this to me.' With a movement of desperation she unzipped his trousers, and touched the cold, curled flesh inside.

'No. No!' He gripped her in fury, wrenching her hand away. 'You'll never understand how civilized people behave.'

Overcome with shame and misery, she sank down on the floor. 'I'm sorry, I'm sorry, I'm sorry.'

Triumphant, now, he stood up. 'You can collect your things at the end of your shift. I'll sort them out,' he said, and left.

Desolation dried her tears; she splashed water on her face, applied more make-up, changed into her waitressing clothes and went on with her work. Well, it's over, she kept telling herself. That's that. I never liked him anyway. We didn't even like the same books, not really. It's not as if he's handsome or nice or rich; it's not as if he's really worth breaking my heart over. If only I hadn't done that, just now. If only. I never liked him. Really, the whole thing is quite a relief.

'What did he say?' the other waitresses asked in whispers.

Mary tossed her head. 'He doesn't want a girlfriend, he wants a speak-your-weight machine,' she said, and they laughed.

All that long, long afternoon, she pretended to be cheerful. She had become used to looking at the sky, to stop the tears spilling out. It was a relief when it rained, for then, being small, she could cry under her umbrella instead of pretending she had a bad cold. The pain felt like a wire biting into her heart, wrapped round and round, making it harder and harder to breathe.

Yet she thought she was over the worst. Now she began to remember how he had said this thing or that – had told her that her face made her look more intelligent than she was, or that brunettes, being dark, were the first to go grey; how he had sponged off her and sneered at her for calling the sitting room a living room while accusing her of meanness and snobbery. It was a relief to see these things, but still she could not hate him.

Mary did not hate him even when she sat on the late-night bus from Tottenham Court Road to Brixton, and watched the familiar landmarks go by – the pub with its red sign flashing, Take Courage, Take Courage, the underground stations with their dim metal lights like the helmets of soldiers, the glittering ripple of the Thames. When she got off she felt only an immense tiredness, as though her legs were melting into the pavement. She walked from pool to pool of murky orange light, looking at the Georgian fan-lights shaped like umbrella spokes, like bat's wings. It was the time of year when it becomes impossible to believe in spring, when the cold seeps off the pavement in a dull mist, clamping down on everything: Valentine's Day.

Mary knew each tree and shrub she passed, for from many she had snipped leaves to bulk out the flowers she brought home. She loved flowers and plants, tenderly spraying and sponging down the leaves of her palm, her lemon (grown from a pip), her jasmine, her maidenhair ferns. All the thwarted maternal passion in her had gone into looking after her pots; yet she had forgotten them for three weeks.

Now she quickened her step. She had assumed Mark would care for them during her absence – but it struck her that, if he was spending most of his time at Amelia's, this was scarcely likely.

'Hold on, hold on, I'm coming,' she muttered, running up the steps. They seemed unusually full of rubbish bags, some of which had split open. She waded through the contents, felt for her keys, and found the Yale. It did not fit.

Mary tried again, jiggling it. Nothing happened. She took it out, and examined it. Yes, it was the right key.

On her third attempt, she suddenly noticed that one of the pieces of rubbish she was standing on was a bra. Moreover, it was one of her own bras. In fact, everything that was spilling out of the bin-liners was hers – her clothes, her books. Her plants, withered.

Her possessions had been dumped outside, rifled through, and the locks had been changed. Had Mark imagined she would squat there? Or would take any of the traditional revenges advertised by women's magazines, stuffing his curtain rails with prawns or running up vast telephone bills? Mary had too much respect for things to take revenge on what had been her home. She had bought the bed, and the chesterfield, which she had carefully re-upholstered; it had been her wages that had paid, piece by piece, for the Heal's cutlery, the Dualit toaster and Alessi kettle that Mark had demanded. Even if they had been included in the bags left for her, which she very much doubted, they must by now have been stolen, for it was clear that everything of any value had gone.

'You utter, utter bastard. You shit. You shit,' she said, rocking on her heels.

She would have liked to have left it there, the fragments of her ruin, but even underwear was expensive to replace. She took out her own bin-liners, and packed the clothes, the books, the plants, everything she could take in a taxi to Deirdre's. Then she took out a single hairpin from her bun, pushed it in the new Yale lock and snapped it off.

8

Tom Viner

Tom Viner, who loved his mother more than anyone, stood beneath five huge lamps which cast a shadowless ring of light. He was assisting at an abortion. Beside him was a monitor, registering blood pressure, oxygen and carbon-dioxide levels as ghostly waves of green, blue and red; before, the naked unconscious body of a woman with her legs in stirrups. He thought of how Confucius drew a series of circles around each individual, showing that one should love one's father most, then one's family, then others in lesser degree, as if love, like light, moves further and further from its source into the darkness of complete indifference.

The green overalls of the two other doctors and two scrub nurses were spattered with blood, as was the long sheet of hospital paper stretching from the woman's buttocks to the metal bucket directly beneath. A wide metal retractor kept the vagina open.

The obstetrician, who that morning had delivered one living baby from its mother's womb, was this afternoon rummaging with a pair of forceps and a wad of cotton, tearing a fifth limb from limb. He periodically inserted a suction tube. A noise, like a giant slurping at an ice-cube with a straw, filled the theatre, and more blood fell, splashing the white-tiled floor with a soft, scarlet smack. Tom looked at the kidney tray, and glimpsed a tiny, perfect hand, the size of his thumbnail, the nails the size of sand grains, float up before gently turning over and vanishing. He went back to his notes.

'That's it, bar the shouting,' said Mr Jackson, panting. 'Found a new place to live yet, Tom?'

'Not yet,' said Tom. 'I suppose I should buy, now that property prices are dropping, but it's such a pain dealing with estate agents.' Besides, he thought to himself, what can I buy on £21,600 a year? Nobody in their right mind wanted a long commute after an eighty-hour shift. But nobody in their right mind, he thought, would be a doctor now.

'We're trying to move ourselves,' said the obstetrician, gently sponging down the thighs before him with foamy detergent. Mr Jackson, who lived in St John's Wood and spent half his time on private practice, would doubtless be looking for something very different from the one-bedroom flat that was Tom's aspiration. 'But the slump is giving everyone problems. Mankind has a free market, but is everywhere in chains, eh?'

He hummed along to the Rolling Stones singing 'Bye, Bye Baby'. His taste in music was more than usually bad. Tom's favourite so far was Snell, who performed cardiac surgery to 'Every Beat of My Heart'. As Jackson's list drew to a close, everyone became almost light-headed with relief.

The woman's skin looked as though it was absorbing the light, swallowing it like a black star. She should have been draped, an impersonal mound, but in hospitals such delicacies often went by the board. It was easy to forget that each patient was a human being, once the look of terror had been replaced by an absence of animation deeper than any normal sleep. Of all of the doctors present, it was Tom who remembered: for during any operation it is the anaesthetist who bears the responsibility to ensure a patient survives. Anaesthetics is not a glamorous branch of medicine to outsiders, who worship surgeons, obstetricians, even general practitioners. Tom had actually been asked if he was a real doctor. Yet the moment when a patient relinquished consciousness was like that of an aeroplane taking off: once airborne, you were pretty safe, but getting there was when fatalities occurred. A knife could slip, a vein could haemorrhage but the single most dangerous moment for a patient was the time between consciousness and oblivion, when they could fight, choke, arrest, suffer an embolism. Going under was the closest a human being could come to death, and escape again.

It was Tom who reassured them as they lay on the trolley, vulnerable, naked, ill, that they would re-emerge alive, Tom whose hands threaded tubes down their throats and into their hearts and veins, Tom who relieved them from excruciating pain both during and after operations. Some even made a show of their detachment, sitting and reading the *Sun* or the *Evening Standard* in between taking notes. But it was Tom who remembered that this waxy doll, splodged with orange iodine or covered with green cloth, was a person with a heart and brain. An anaesthetist is the only kind of doctor who sees every kind of operation performed in a hospital, for every living patient will suffer that most terrible and frightening of human conditions called pain.

'If I still see you bending over me when I wake up, I'll know I've died and gone to heaven,' was what at least one woman a week said to him, as the anaesthetic took hold.

'No,' Tom would say tartly, 'you'll know you haven't.'

He sighed and stretched. Ideally, he would work in half-hourly shifts with his consultant, but half of them never bothered to turn up. He had now been in theatre for eight hours with only a cup of coffee to keep him going, and the blood in his feet was making his surgical clogs uncomfortably tight.

He checked to see that this patient was still under. Her stomach bulged, not from this pregnancy, which had been in its eighteenth week, but from previous childbearing. Tom wondered, briefly, what her history was, and whether those other children had lived and flourished; whether this foetus had been viable. That information would be on her records, under his hand, but there was no inclination to probe. One thing hospital work taught you, repeatedly, was that there were fates worse than death, and an unwanted child might find them all. Yet it was a dreadful thing, to end life. The suction tube made its harsh, greedy sound again. He often wondered whether the women who chose termination would still want it if they saw how perfectly formed a foetus was at eight weeks. Yet neither could a woman be forced to carry a child to term if she knew she could never want it.

This woman, for instance. Her hands and feet had the rough, misshapen look with which he was entirely familiar. She was twenty-seven and looked fifty. Few of Tom's friends ever saw such people, if they could help it.

'Even taxi-drivers now send their children to public school,' Georgina Hunter assured him. 'Everyone is middle class.'

'Balls,' said Tom. 'If anything, it's shrinking, at least as a cultural concept.'

It was not their fault. There was a constant, centrifugal force in London, separating the classes. Commerce pushed rich people out of the centre, pushing the middle classes into working-class areas, which had moved further and further out into the suburbs, or else become concentrated in the inner-city estates. These last corroded, sending out waves of dissolution from which people fled, if they could possibly afford it.

Not many now dared to say, as a contemporary of Tom's had, 'There is a class war, and we are class warriors', but many felt it. Fewer and fewer people had servants of any kind. During Tom's teens at Knotshead, the progressive public school, it had been fashionable to sound vaguely Cockney, with the result that many OKs had a curious Alf Garnett twang, copied from the taxi-drivers who shunted them to and from the school train – but during the 1980s even this had faded away. Most of the people Tom knew socially now lived in a world as hermetically sealed as those he treated professionally. He sometimes thought that without his mother's double alienation, as a Jewish American, he, too, would have been prone to believing there was something intrinsically superior to the professional middle classes.

It was not that his friends were particularly snobbish or unpleasant; indeed, the most frequent topic of conversation at their dinner parties was whether it was possible to be successful and remain a nice person. They donated money and blood, worried about the lack of good state schools long before they had children, and about the NHS even after they had private health care. They drove cars with unleaded petrol and used Ecover washing-up liquid; they recycled bottles, newspapers and ideas with conscientious efficiency. Though their politics crossed the spectrum from old-fashioned Toryism to Milettante socialism, they struck him as being, in many aspects, as homogeneous as apples in a supermarket.

It was the poor who were different, though they, too, had their similarities to each other with their chaotic lives, their inoperable cancers, the emphysemic lungs, their blind belief in medicine as something that could right the ills fostered by bad food, housing, cigarettes, drink, illiteracy and hopelessness. Their faces had a look, at once hard and worn, like coins withdrawn from circulation. Nothing in their lives was planned, and yet they followed a predictable path to ruin so often that it was hard to believe they possessed free will. They survived only by living from week to week and even from hour to hour; they were at once suspicious and credulous, resentful of authority and hopelessly enslaved by it. Who could not feel despair when seeing them?

At times, Tom, too, hated them, as any doctor can hate their patients. 'Just die,' he found himself thinking, when jerked out of sleep by his bleeper at three a.m. 'Just please, please be dead by the time I get to you, so I can go back to bed.'

Yet he still went, loping along the shabby mazes, like a greyhound chasing a mechanical rabbit. Every doctor he knew swore they would have 'No resus after 60' tattooed on his or her throat, but they'd still try to bring some old crone of eighty back from the grave. You learnt, you unlearnt, you joked and you fucked. Some saw patients in purely physiological terms, as problems to be solved. Yet Tom also saw that those who had wrestled with their work as with a demon, and made it in their own image rather than the other way about, made the best doctors. His own mentor, Professor Stern, was one such. Once, when Tom had spoken brusquely to an alcoholic about to have his leg amputated the Prof told him, 'There, but for the grace of God, go you and I,' and from him, this banal phrase had the force of revelation.

'Wonderful. Splendid,' said Mr Jackson enthusiastically. 'Off home, after this?'

'No. An "unsatisfactory birth experience,"' said Tom. 'They ask, "Doctor, what's the worst that could happen to me?", so I say, "You could die."'

'You know, I miss the old days,' said Mr Jackson. 'I had a patient

71

up in Leeds who kept complaining about pelvic pain, absolutely nothing wrong with her, so I gave her an anaesthetic, made an incision and didn't operate. Bingo, the pain was gone. Unethical, but it worked. It'd cause a riot now. That's it, well done, everyone.'

'One two three four swabs. One two blades,' said the scrub nurse. The runner ticked them off the chart, then wiped the whole board. Paper, blood, gobbets of dead foetus were piled into yellow bin-liners for incineration.

They wheeled the patient to the recovery room. The nurses smiled at Tom, and blushed. Sarah Meager divided nurses up into Old Boots and Flighty Tarts, possibly because, as a woman doctor and Tom's girlfriend, she was treated with unbending resentment.

By the time he was twenty-seven, Tom's ex-lovers, though very different in temperament, colouring, shape and background, agreed that it was a mystery he had remained single. Now he was thirty-two they had come to the conclusion that he would never get married. He worked too many hours, was addicted to bachelor slovenliness; he was selfish; he liked women too much and was impossible to imagine as monogamous. Materially, too, he would not be a good prospect for years, if ever. He drove the most beaten-up car imaginable, and had no flat of his own, lodging with friends or friends of friends as each job changed. Tom was wonderful for an affair, they told each other, but not, really, for life.

Tom had no idea he was discussed in this way. The grind from houseman to junior house officer to senior house officer to registrar to senior registrar to (you hoped) consultant was consuming. All he seemed to have done for six years now was work, study and sleep.

Even now, the demands hardly seemed to have lessened. He'd got two parts of his fellowship exam, but was still switching job every six months, being on rotation between four of the big teaching hospitals. Even consultants like Jackson worked a sixty-hour week while being paid for forty. Why the fuck shouldn't he earn £120,000 a year? People at the top of any other profession would expect double that, these days.

Driving from the hospital at the end of his shift, on his way to a dinner-party, Tom stopped off at the family house in Belsize Park for a bath and a change of clothes. He loved going home. During his nights on call in squalid cubicles with filthy sheets and no windows, he often thought that he could endure hospital life only because he had such a base to come back to.

Such comforts had made the Viner brothers lazy. For years they had never bothered to visit their friends; for years young men and women had fallen in love with the entire family without the Viners really noticing more than the number of coffee mugs in the dishwasher. When Sam had left Ruth for Fiona Bamber, half of North London had gone into shock; Ruth's psychotherapy patients would drape themselves over the cream-coloured Aga and weep sizzling tears of sympathy onto the hot-plates.

'Still flat-hunting?' she asked, kissing him.

'Yes. I've got to leave Highbury. James has been made redundant, and needs the spare room as an office.'

'Are you sure you don't want to move back?' Ruth asked him, as she piled his dirty clothes into the basket. Tom took it for granted that this foul swirl would be returned, within twenty-four hours, immaculate. Ruth watched him take off his jumper, seizing it by the scruff of its neck and hauling. It was a gesture that always made her smile.

'You've got Grub and Alice, isn't that enough?'

'You know me, never happy unless the washing machine is working night and day.'

'Oh, Mum! If I came back I'd feel as if I'd never grown up.'

'I know, I know,' said Ruth sadly. 'I wish you could be happier.'

'I'm fine. I'd just like certain certainties in my life. Like a consultancy.'

'There is only one thing certain, namely that we can have nothing certain, and therefore it is not certain that we can have nothing certain,' said Tom's mother.

'Yours?'

'Butler.'

Ruth loved aphorisms and jokes. She told Tom, once, that she had fallen in love with his father when she saw that he had drawn a little face round every nail-hole in his flat. When Tom had been three his most passionate wish was to marry her. She still laughed when she remembered the look of shock on his face on being told that someone else had got there first.

It was Ruth's work as a clinical psychotherapist that had inspired Sam Viner's first successful strip cartoon, *Felix the Black Dog*; and the souring of their relations which had produced *Dum and Mad*, syndicated to newspapers around the world. To see your parents' marriage publicly disintegrate by daily instalments was not, as the brothers agreed, the best introduction to adult life.

'There's always Phoebe's basement,' she said.

Phoebe Viner was Tom's great-aunt. She lived in Chelsea and had been an artist's model.

'It may yet come to that. Everyone I know is having children. The spare rooms are disappearing,' Tom said glumly.

'But not the spare women.'

'Nope.'

Tom was comfortable neither in America nor England. He felt himself to be a hybrid, neither one nor the other, at once insider and outsider. The Viner boys had all gone away to boarding school at thirteen, so had not even put down roots in the area where they lived.

The house was the heart of the family. Large, shabby to the point of decrepitude, it had a 100-foot garden and three libraries, each with its own piano. Even now, hardly a week went by without estate agents pushing letters through the flap, begging Ruth to name her price, and as she had no other assets, it was something of a temptation. However, the slightest mention of selling up was met with implacable opposition from all her children, who refused even to let her strip their yellowing childish paintings from the kitchen ceiling.

'Hurry up, then, and give me some grandchildren,' Ruth would retort, though she did not say this to Josh, who had recently married.

She hugged her eldest son, now, as he was going out of the door. He had been the most difficult: hyperactive, and so bright that he had been unintelligible until he was nine. Everyone else had thought him retarded until he learnt to control his stammer. She wondered how much this had damaged his confidence. He spoke perfectly, now, though always choosing his words with care.

'*Hazak!*' she said. 'Something will turn up.'

Even after five years Tom still checked any social gathering to make sure that neither Andrew nor Fiona was present. Arriving at the Hunters' house in Stockwell, he was relieved to see that the kitchen was without Evenlodes. Amelia's party had been unpleasant enough.

Andrew Evenlode had had rooms on the same staircase as Tom at Oxford. His family was large, rich, aristocratic and Catholic. Tom had expected to loathe him on sight. Instead, they had become friends – so much so that they shared a house in their third year – with Tom's passion for music matching the other's for art. Later, when Evenlode became, as everyone expected, a don and Tom was sunk in the grind of medicine, each continued to dilate the other's nature. It was because of Tom that Andrew had become less affected and less snobbish. It was because of Andrew that Tom had evaded the beefy insensibility and cultural illiteracy into which many medical students sink. Andrew was the only person in whom Tom confided his distress when his father started his mid-life crisis affair with Fiona Bamber. When Fiona left Tom's father for Andrew, the embarrassment was almost equal; although, of the two, Tom felt the loss most.

He could have gone out every night, but he was lonely. More and more of his friends were married, while he continued to live much as he had at university. Once upon a time, parties were occasions to which you brought wine and ate fish pie and chocolate cake. Now you brought boxes of Belgian chocolates, and drank vintage Bordeaux with *bœuf en daube*. Once, he could have gone to an evening like this knowing that at the end of it he would probably be in bed with a new and deliciously pretty girl. Now there was Aids and Sarah, who wanted to marry him.

He liked her, of course. She was clever, attractive and in the same profession. Marriages between anaesthetists and GPs were almost a medical cliché, supposedly because the former were sociopaths and the latter empaths. If only she didn't remind him so much of a horse! If only she wasn't so inalienably English! He could tell exactly what their life together would be like: house in Hammersmith, Colefax and Fowler downstairs, cartoons in the loo, a Volvo and two children.

But who else was there? All but one of the women here at the Hunters' had children. The indestructible bloom of propriety was everywhere: their prettiness was that of a rose in a public park, he thought, too general for poetry. The men discussed politics; the women were laughing over Georgina's story about how a jammed video machine had been taken apart by a succession of male relatives over Christmas, none of whom spotted that little Cosmo had pushed a raw Brussels sprout into it. Tom prepared himself for an evening of mild tedium, rendered palatable by gossip. He knew everyone slightly, and recognized Professor Stern's daughter, Celine, as the only unmarried female present.

'My nanny can't understand why English people are so unfriendly,' said Georgina. 'I keep trying to explain, it's nothing personal, it's just that we all live half an inch away from each other, physically and socially.'

'There should be a "Who Hates Whom" or a "Who Owes Whom",' said Dick, her husband.

Georgina concealed her irritation admirably, for although, like so many women, she had married her intellectual inferior, she was sufficiently pragmatic not to remind him too often of this. There was a certain usefulness in having a husband whom most people could barely tolerate: it deflected envy, for one thing. Georgina was fantastically prolific as both journalist and writer of romantic blockbusters. She was quite intelligent enough to write literary fiction, and had indeed produced one example which had been widely praised and had sold two hundred copies; after which she had decided to write for money. Unfortunately, what she earned did not go far. Dick was an architect, and had not had a real commission for years; but it was Georgina who got up in the night when her children were ill, and Georgina who did most of the household chores. As a result everyone felt extremely sorry for her.

'Have you heard about Amelia de Monde? She's engaged to someone on the *Chronicle*!'

'Who?'

'Mark something. Ivo Sponge's best friend, apparently.'

'Didn't know he had one.'

'Ugh, Ivo! I shared a taxi with him once, and the next thing I knew his tongue was half-way down my throat.'

'I wouldn't like to have him as a father-in-law – de Monde, I mean. He's a crook, isn't he?'

'Nobody knows. Still, it's time she got hitched. One can't be glamorous for ever.'

'And children are *the* fashion accessory for the 1990s.'

'Only because we're all so broke.'

'God, it's hard work. I'd no idea. My parents must have been saints.'

'They didn't work the hours we do. Middle-class life used to be civilized. Now it's the most stressful thing imaginable, both partners working, everyone scrabbling round just to pay the mortgage on some place miles from the centre with a minute garden. It's amazing there aren't more divorces.'

'Oh, there will be. We're just a little too young yet.'

'I find it interesting,' said Tom, 'how everyone whose parents aren't divorced seems to stick together and make their own happy families. Children from broken homes increasingly don't have children. It's almost as if a process of natural selection is at work: if your parents' marriage survived, however rockily, you'll reproduce yourself. If not, you're at a biological dead end.'

'I don't think it's biology, it's fate,' said Dick. 'When I met Georgie, I just knew she was going to marry me.'

Everyone laughed. His wife was known to be a very determined woman.

'Tom doesn't believe in love at first sight,' said Georgina.

'Actually, it's about the only thing that would make me marry. The trouble with us is that we do it when the steam has run out of everything, if you see what I mean.'

'What I want to know,' said Celine, 'is how you have two children and such an orderly house full of pretty toys.'

'Oh, Georgie has two sets of toys,' said her husband. 'One lot are plastic, for the children to play with, and the other are wood, for display.'

'Really?'

'No, of course not,' said Georgina, blushing.

'*Ooooh*,' said everyone. Georgina had been head girl at Cheltenham Ladies', and it was always fun to catch her out.

'Have you heard, the Evenlodes are completely desperate to have a baby?' said Celine.

'No, *he* is and *she* isn't,' said Alex.

'Didn't they discuss it first?'

'Apparently not.'

'I've heard that when blokes die they get a huge stonker, and then the nurses hitch up their skirts and go for a ride,' said Dick.

'Don't be disgusting!' cried the women.

'Isn't it true, though, that seeing people die makes doctors incredibly randy?' Alex asked.

'Well,' said Tom, 'it's a bit like that joke. There's a husband says to his wife, "The doctor told me I won't live 'til tomorrow. Let's drink champagne and make love one last time." His wife says, "That's all very well for you – you don't have to get up in the morning."'

He noticed Celine smiling at him. She was dark and neat, and would have breasts like damsons. She was Stern's daughter, he thought to himself, alarmed. The image of Sarah faded in and out of consciousness.

'I used to think the national average of twice a week fantastically low until we had children,' Alex was saying. 'Now I think they must be sexual athletes.'

There had been a time when all that these people would discuss was estate agents and holidays; now it was nannies and schools. Hardly anyone drank, because you could not risk a hangover if woken at six every morning. Nobody except Tom and Celine dared take coffee or brandy. They smiled at each other, again, the spark of attraction jumping from eye to eye, in collusion against those neutered by parenthood. Georgina, who did not like Sarah, saw it and was pleased. She was less pleased when they stayed on, past midnight. She wondered how to get rid of them until Dick, having eaten all the remaining Bendicks, said, 'Scarcely any point going to bed now, is there? Flora'll be up in two hours.'

'I must get a minicab,' said Celine, taking the hint.

Georgina yawned and said, prodding, 'Tom, are you still in Highbury?'

'Yes. I drove here.'

'Could you give me a lift home?' Celine asked; and Tom, after a brief struggle with the inevitable, said, 'Yes.'

9

In Camden Town

On the Queen's Estate it rained and rained. The bad weather there was so bad that it seemed like a different climate from other parts of London. Drip, drip, drip, day and night, the rain fell, puddles joining puddles, blotting and blurring into each other so that the people in the tower-blocks were doubly marooned, for each was surrounded by a kind of lake, several inches deep. Drip, drip, drip, until every window was a weeping eye. The water could not drain away, except through a few holes in the glass tiles over the boiler room by Grace's flats, and soon the trickle into the basement meant there was no hot water and no heating.

Grace and Billy found it harder and harder to get up every morning. They snuggled together in her bed, under the little pockets of heat trapped by the mound of old blankets, each with a large hole that had to be concealed by another blanket, itself torn and worn in a different spot.

'Billy float 'way, Mum float 'way. In der Ark,' said Billy. He wanted to help Grace around the flat, although mostly his efforts doubled her work. She could hear the wheeze, as though each breath set little fans whirring in his chest. He never complained, but sometimes, if he climbed the stairs too quickly, his lips went blue.

There was mildew on the walls; originally cream, they were speckled with dark blotches that sent out long, spidery tentacles almost overnight, as if searching for something. Grace had rung the council every week for months, but nobody seemed to be in charge, and so nothing got done, even if she got through. Outside the sky was so drear she would have believed it was evening, if it were not for the clock of the church where they went every Sunday. The church had a subsidized nursery for under-fives, otherwise Grace would never have gone.

Drip, drip, drip. The gaunt chestnut tree in the middle of the estate looked like a giant pouring tears from its very bones; Father Time could scarcely be greyer or more scarred. The tree was so large that it must have been planted long before the estate was built, perhaps dreaming in a green field with sheep and cows rubbing against it, or as part of a rich man's private garden. Its scabby trunk was carved with initials and swastikas, although crossing to where it grew was a feat of which even the dogs on the estate were wary. Bottles, syringes, nappies, polystyrene boxes, shit, wire had made a shameful conquest of this fortress built by Nature for herself, this little world, this precious green set in a concrete sea.

'C'mon, petal, breakfast,' Grace said. 'Your nappy's wet, pooh!'

'Need my potty.'

'Magic word?'

'PLEASE! Mummy-hug, Mummy-hug,' Billy chattered. 'Park, park, park.'

'All right, after breakfast,' she said, but the thought of having to carry him for much of the way made her tired already. 'We'll stop off at the library on the way, OK?'

'Yeth!' said Billy. 'Wead-a-book. Wead-a-book. *Please!*'

He demanded at least one book with every meal. The offer of being read to soothed any pain or woe. Grace seemed to spend half her life reading to him, feeling his warm, light limbs burrowing into hers, his curling hair tucked under her chin. She thought how strange it was that health visitors nagged new mothers to breastfeed, and not to read. Words poured out of her like milk, thin and sweet. She told him about birth and death and wickedness and bravery. She was desperate to equip this child for life, as she herself had not been equipped. Poor Joy, she thought, at least she kept me out of a foster home.

'Mummy's *good*', Billy said, with satisfaction. 'And Billy's *good.*'

'But some people are *bad*,' said Grace. 'What do you do if you see someone is bad?'

'Run 'way.'

'Good boy!'

'Garnian angel'll help.'

'Yes,' said Grace firmly. 'Remember: you can't always see your guardian angel, but it's there. Like God. Looking after you.'

'Playin' hide 'n' seek.'

Billy was very interested in the invisibility of God and he was now a determined God-spotter. On the way to the library, he told his mother he could see a bit of God's hand sticking out. Grace couldn't see it; she was too anxious that it might rain again. Without the buggy and its hood, Billy would get wet, a thing she was terrified of because it might make his asthma worse. She carried a small collapsible umbrella in her bag, but it wasn't enough to cover both of them.

The library was where some semblance of a local playgroup took place on Mondays. There were others, but they were too far away from the estate for those who needed them most; and the nicest, the ones with proper heating and clean floors and lots of books, were in rich places like Hampstead. All the libraries in Camden shut every Wednesday, and very often on Monday and Friday as well, because the council had run out of money – or spent it on refurbishing councillors' homes, depending on whom you believed. There were fewer and fewer books each year as the stock was sold off. The toys were mostly broken and filthy, although there were crates of brand new ones kept locked away, and racks of CDs although the players were beyond most people's means. All the same, the playgroup made some attempt at welcome – at Christmas, a librarian dressed up as Santa Claus, and handed out presents of Smarties. This was very popular, especially among the fatherless, to whom all men were either alien or positively dangerous.

Currently, spring was on the walls, lumps of pink and white cotton wool representing blossom or lambs. Some older children were painting egg boxes and toilet-roll tubes, to turn them into rabbits and chicks.

Billy had never seen a lamb, or a cow, or a rabbit or a chick although he had, of course, seen plenty of dogs and ducks and pigeons and crows – even a few cats when Mad Maggie's escaped. There was a city farm, in Kentish Town, which Grace had promised to take him to when he was older, because there were real horses there, and Billy was mad about horses. This was useful, for it meant that he begged to be put into reins, unlike some kids. Sometimes Grace asked him, 'What do you want to be when you grow up?'

And he would always say, 'A horse!'

His other favourite animals were the elephants at the Zoo. Grace and Billy had never been inside the Zoo, it was far too expensive, but they could see quite a lot over the fence in Regent's Park, especially if Billy sat on his mother's shoulders.

He wanted to go past the Zoo now. Playing with other children didn't interest him. None of them had his ability to concentrate (the ability, though Grace did not know this, of a sick child), and every nose except his was joined to the mouth by a thick slick of green slime, which periodically got smeared over the rest of the face. Grace was disgusted by this. Every five minutes she swooped on her son and gave his nose a swift double wipe. She gave him malt and multivitamins, and this, too, helped him, she was sure. Most of the women she saw, mothers or minders, weren't fit to keep a dog let alone a child, she thought. They treated the library as a place to dump their kids and moan to each other; only at the end of the session, when a determined librarian made everybody sit down in a circle and sing did they make any attempt to control the little ones.

It was a long walk to the Zoo, so Grace persuaded the librarian to give her the key to the toilet. There were four other librarians doing nothing except gossiping and occasionally wheeling round a trolley of returned books, but the toilet was filthy, and stank because the window was never opened and the last person to use it hadn't flushed it. Grace put down paper between Billy's bottom and the seat.

She couldn't remember much about her own childhood with Joy, except that one day she had understood that she had to look after her mother, not the other way about. At seven, she could fry chips for them both and was washing all their clothes and sweeping the floor. At twelve she had the maturity of someone twice her age. She made her mother take her pills, and cooked. They could not afford meat, so she bought vegetables at the end of the day, when things were cheap, and learnt how to make soup and a kind of omelette – kids' food, really, but it had come in useful later on. When she realized that her mother was ashamed to go out because of the big gaps between her front teeth, she had started babysitting every night to pay for cosmetic dentistry. Joy had been a lot better after that.

She would tell wonderful stories, on good days, about swimming in the sea with dolphins and mermaids, and of having lived in a white palace with blue flowers on the walls that changed colour in the afternoon. 'I was a princess in a far country, until I was stolen away,' she said.

'So where's your treasure?' Grace asked.

'You're my treasure,' said Joy, 'the only one I have. But one day I'll make sure you get what's yours. I know where she lives, you see, only they won't let me in.'

Grace lifted Billy up so he could see the animals over the double row of railings. A lion roared, a melancholy cough as though it, too, was choking in the dank dark air. All the creatures inside looked bored and miserable. They turned their backs on visitors and trudged round the same patch of concrete like convicts. Grace could see the elephants, all females, shuffle from leg to leg while their pens were cleaned.

'Lion says hallo,' Billy chirped happily. His wheeze was getting worse in the cold.

'He's having his dinner,' said Grace.

'Chips an' egg.'

'Meat,' said Grace, longing.

'Mummy lion an' baby lion go home now,' said Billy.

'Let's go to Sainsbury's first,' said Grace. 'You can ride round on the trolley.'

'And *eat* things.'

'Yes, but very quickly, without people seeing.'

This was how they managed to get real grub, as well as some of the sweets Billy craved. They would go in at a busy time, when nobody was too sharp on the uptake, and wheeling the trolley slowly between the aisles, stuff themselves. Pork pies, sausage rolls, chocolate, bananas, all sorts of treats would find their way into their mouths, while the wrappers went back into the shelves. Lots of mums on the Queen's Estate did this; she had been shown how by her mate Angie. 'They won't arrest you, or nothing,' said Angie. 'Not when you've got a kid.'

It wasn't shop-lifting, exactly, Grace reasoned, but she was always nervous doing it. If only you could lift a whole packet of sausages, or a joint of beef! If only she could take cartons of apple juice and bags of oranges! But they were too bulky, and she was scared of getting nicked by the security guards. So they would ride round for an hour or more, and if any of the other shoppers noticed them, Grace would sigh and roll her eyes as though it were all Billy's fault, and they would sigh, too, in the great freemasonry of parenthood.

Across the pelican crossing and through the automatic doors, into the lovely warm air, past the pot plants and the exotic fruit and vegetables. Who were they, these people who could pay £1.20 for a tiny polythene bag of ready-mixed salad? It astonished her. She bought a bag of potatoes and some Bold with the money Georgina had paid her, and they left, thawed and renewed by the sugar and stodge in their stomachs. Heaven must be a bit like Sainsbury's, Grace thought to herself dreamily, except you wouldn't have to walk, just float about on your wings, nibbling.

Back through Camden Lock, the water frozen into icicles round the edge of the gates, and the smell of patchouli on the air. The market was always good for a laugh, all gaudy mobiles and smiling suns, clinking and clanking from the stalls, the blokes and girls with fingerless gloves and funny hats. Grace couldn't say she blamed them for wanting to pretend – after all, who wanted to be a grown-up if you could avoid it? Grace held her son's hand tightly as they walked along the canal. It always frightened her, doing this, the water so flat and murky, the bridges echoing tunnels dripping large sad drops of water and grease from the railway overhead. Anyone could come up behind you and push you in.

'Ducks!' said Billy.

'Are they mummy ducks or daddy ducks?'

'Mummy ducks!'

'No,' said Grace. 'There's just one mummy duck, the brown one. All the rest, the ones with white collars like Father Pat, they're daddy ducks.'

Billy gazed interestedly. 'Dwagon!' he said.

'No, petal, they're ducks.'

'Dwagon, dere.' He pointed and, to Grace's delight and astonishment, there was a dragon, sculpted out of tin cans and wire, with a piece of corrugated steel for wings, almost invisible against the old brick wall. She would never have noticed it without him.

'You're right, clever boy.'

'It's a *good* dwagon,' said Billy, and they walked on, Grace blessing the unknown person who had made such a thing, and put it there.

They walked to the Chinese restaurant boat, then up to the playground in the park. It was deserted in the misty drizzle. Billy climbed on the blue sea-horse, his favourite, and said, 'Rock-Lippe-horsey! Rock-rock-rock! Past wolves, past Beast, past wood, rock-rock-rock-*rock*!'

He was being Belle in *Beauty and the Beast* which had puzzled him because the hero was clearly Belle's horse, Philippe. Grace could see why. The Beast was selfish, domineering and not all that nice. The horse was consistently more sensible, helpful and affectionate, not to mention better-looking. So Billy had decided to change the story. Belle and Philippe galloped on together endlessly, in blissful union.

'Careful, petal,' she called.

'We're living happily everafter!' he said. 'Happy everafter!' and Grace saw that spring was coming, and smiled.

10

A Literary Editor

The office of the literary editor, Marian Kenward, and her deputy was the smallest in the *Chronicle*. It contained some seven hundred books, of which the most frequently read were *Who's Who* and the *Oxford Companion to English Literature*, two desks, two telephones, an answering machine, two computer terminals, and a young girl whose main job, apart from skimming through the books as they arrived, and wearing a very short skirt, was telling anyone who called that Ivo and Marian were 'in a meeting'. Lulu Anstey was a distant relation of Marian's, recently graduated from Bristol. Apart from this, she was unusual only in that she took her job very seriously. 'We in the World of Books,' she would say, or, 'The whole of Literary London thinks –'

Ivo found this exasperating, not only because he badly wanted to get out of Literary London and back into politics..

' "Literary London!" What *do* you mean?' he said. 'There isn't one world of books, there are twenty – twenty-one if you count Oxford.'

'But they all join up,' said Lulu. 'You know – they're all neighbours, or intermarried or having affairs –'

'Every profession is an island whose inhabitants earn a precarious living by taking in each other's washing,' said Ivo. 'If you and I were to go to bed together – I'm talking purely metaphorically – would that mean we thought as one? No, we'd probably be at each other's throats even as we scratched each other's backs.'

'Oh, Ivo!' said Lulu, giggling nervously. She had received the

Sponge Lunge at the Christmas party, and often entertained her friends in private with it. Like every assistant, she had ambitions that she discussed rather more openly than was wise. She was allowed to write and commission the *Chronicle*'s page of paper-back reviews, blissfully unaware of her impotence, for by the time a book reached the general public at £5.99 it was dead in the water to everyone who counted. Lulu prattled on as if fifty words in shrunken type could outweigh five hundred in bold.

'Hallo?' said Lulu into the telephone. She rolled her eyes. 'You've sent your copy off by taxi? Well, I'll ask, but I can't see it here.' She mouthed the words, K. P. Gritts, and Ivo groaned. Gritts was one of the few first-rate reviewers they had but he was always late with his copy, and rather than admit to this he would tell elaborate lies along the lines of 'the dog ate my homework'.

'Couldn't you just fax it to us here? It's broken? Bad luck.' Lulu rolled her eyes again. 'I'll send a bike round, then. We must have it by two o'clock. Bye. Sometimes I wonder whether we're really dealing with grown-ups,' she said.

'Better check with deliveries, just in case. Every now and again, he does tell the truth,' said Ivo.

The life of a deputy literary editor is not an especially enviable one. The job had been handed him as a sop. Angus had promised to make him a political columnist, but the present incumbent was hard to shift. Few people seemed to realize that in any practical sense it was Ivo who wielded the real power. It was Ivo who – unless Marian put her foot down – decided who got what to review, Ivo who manipulated the wheel of fortune, or put a spoke in it, Ivo who rigged the table and laid out the page. Yet it was his boss to whom those soliciting work or coverage usually demanded to speak and, really, almost everyone wanted to review these days. Anyone with something to sell, or something to hide, anyone long in the tooth or fresh out of college, rang Marian.

Marian, however, spoke only to those she considered her social equals – which, as she was considered upper class by the middle classes and middle class by the upper, caused considerable offence all round.

Ivo, meanwhile, had worked out his own system. Not for him

the dreary banquets, prize committees and air of moral probity. No: Ivo was there as the entertainer, the hired gun, the Jeff to Marian's Mutt. He was there to be rude, to pour scorn, to make publisher's publicists slam down the telephone screeching with rage. Ivo could be relied upon to savage anyone, from Right Hons to right-ons, for the *Chronicle*'s stance of being at once anti-élitist and pro-lifestyle meant that nobody could predict which way he would jump. On a more modest level, Ivo was there to uphold the impression that the *Chronicle*'s books page was not merely a small room staffed by two incompetent females and a boulevardier with a second-class degree, but an Olympian fortress of considered opinion, from which even a thunderbolt of extreme prejudice was better than none.

That fortress was currently under siege from a most alarming quarter. Ivo was waiting – actually waiting! – for Mark to appear so that they could both go out to lunch and discuss Mark's meeting that morning with Max de Monde.

Ivo did not know whether Mark suspected that he had had a hand in his discovery by Mary, but he was taking no chances. The announcement of his friend's engagement to Amelia had come as a bombshell. There was still hope, of course, that the shotgun nature of it all would cause de Monde deep offence, but it was a slim one. Amelia had to get married some time, and she had decided Mark was her man. What was infinitely more alarming was the possibility that Mark would now get a job, perhaps *the* job on the leader pages for which Ivo himself had been quietly angling since his arrival. To think that he himself had promoted Mark because of his chagrin at being surrounded by women. Angus McNabb longed to get rid of Marian also, but she had resisted all attempts to make her resign and was too well connected to be sacked. She would be there forever, and if Mark was made a columnist someone else would be axed. Where, oh where, would that leave Ivo? Even deputy editor was better than, say, Lulu's job, or, horrors, no staff position at all beyond the vague title of 'correspondent'. Someone had to go. Clearly, it could not be Lulu, because that would leave a vacancy into which he would then fall. So, it had to be Marian.

'Come on, Mark,' muttered Ivo, racking his hair.

'I can't understand what Amelia sees in him,' said Lulu.

'Brains,' said Marian, hoarsely. 'He's got one of the best minds I've come across.'

She was in the office for once, chain-smoking like a beagle. The jungle sense which all journalists must possess in order to survive after thirty had told her that change was in the air, which meant appearing more than two days a week instead of writing novels at home. Marian was the author of two previous works of fiction. It was as axiomatic that these were received with rapture as it was that they were bad: Ivo was thrilled whenever a literary editor published a novel because he or she could usually be relied on to quit their jobs and swank off into the sunset. In the case of his boss, however, the reading public sniffed such a large rat that less than seven hundred copies, the norm for literary novels, had been sold. Marian's response to this had been to enter a kind of permanent sulk. She blamed her publishers, she blamed bookshops, she blamed public libraries, she blamed her agent. She blamed the picture on the dust-jacket. She even blamed the hand-picked critics who had reviewed her. At the same time, she knew perfectly well that she had received an advance ten times what anyone else could expect simply because of her position.

'We in the World of Books understand brains very well,' said Lulu, offended.

Marian had finished the most inspired piece of writing any journalist produces each week, her expense sheet, and now rattled her keyboard, sending letters into frenzies of duplication across the screen.

'Christ, this bloody technology! Give me a typewriter any day,' she said. 'You knew where you were with a typewriter. Oh, the lost purity of print and paper! The smell of correction fluid, the delicate resistance of each letter, the friendly ping at the end of each line . . . Now we have to be subs, technicians, layout supremos as well as the fucking thing we're supposed to be any fucking good at.'

Ivo beamed at her, as he took a blue biro from his desk. He had just had a brilliant idea. 'Heigh-ho, my darling!' he said, in his most sympathetic tone. 'We're all handy-dandy these days, with hacks turning authors, authors turning agents, agents turning publishers and publishers turning hacks. Like that ass Percy Flage. He's failed at absolutely every job in the business, but is he on the skids? No, he's on at least fifty thousand a year.'

'Turned down your book, did he?' said Marian.

'Did I sing? Did I dance? I almost paid the bill at the Ivy myself. He kept saying, "Yes", and looking round to see who else was there. In the end I lost all pretence of subtlety and said, "Well, what do you think?" and he said, "I think you need to unpack your ideas a bit." Yes! Hallo,' said Ivo, into the phone. 'It's on my shelf. No, I haven't had a moment to look at it yet. Goodbye. Don't you think it's time we ran a feature on the uselessness of people like Percy? I mean, I was – Hallo? Hallo. Yes, I've skimmed it. Oh, well, my darling, just for you. No, I haven't forgotten. Let's see. Cover a piece of piss, blurb a piece of piss, first page a piece of piss, author photograph. Hmm. Not bad. Is all that hair her own? Ye-es. Well, it's possible, but it looks like it needs unpacking a bit. I can't promise anything, but I'll see what Marian thinks. God, publicists,' he said, putting the phone down. 'They get more and more like pimps every day.'

'Obviously,' muttered Marian. 'They know who they're dealing with. Get me a ham bap with apple juice and a yoghurt, will you?'

'I'm going out for lunch, Marian darling,' said Ivo. 'Sorry.'

'I'll get it,' said Lulu, staggering under a pile of books which she was attempting to shelve. 'If you can just hold on a sec. Oops, sorry!'

A pristine pile of hardbacks, still with yellow Post-it stickers on the covers, crashed onto the floor.

'I thought I told you to sell those,' said the literary editor.

Once a month, the office would, for a couple of pounds each, sell any leftover books to colleagues on the *Chronicle*. The profits from this went into a china pig called 'Lunch', and so eager were Marian and Ivo to feed it that many authors went unreviewed unless the publisher had the prescience to send more than one copy.

'Sorry, Marian, sorry. They just keep on coming and coming. I keep telling them not to send proof copies, but they're frightfully thick. D'you know,' said Lulu, rubbing her knee, 'there are times I almost think I *hate* books.'

She said the last in a shriek because Max de Monde's helicopter was landing. Twice a day everyone from the editor to the canteen staff had to communicate with each other by a kind of frenzied sign-language, so deafening were the propellers of their proprietor's ego.

'At last,' said Marian, rolling her heavily kohled eyes. 'The penny drops. The cock crows.' The noise diminished, and Marian was left bellowing, 'A single cell in your useless brain has stirred into life.'

Lulu began to sniff and ran out.

'Girls,' said Marian, her voice ringing through the open-plan offices. 'Why must they take everything so personally?'

She stomped off to the canteen. Just as he had hoped, she left her expense sheet in her Out tray. Bending over casually, Ivo drew a zero in blue ink on a restaurant receipt and her claim, both of which were in black. It was exactly the kind of thing even the stupidest of de Monde's accountants would spot as a sackable offence.

'The pen is mightier than the word,' he murmured, and breezed down to accounting. Marian was so chaotic she would never remember whether or not she had handed it in herself.

When he returned, Mark was waiting for him. They walked through the empty maze of desks, each with its lutescent computer terminal, to the lift. Ivo found himself uncharacteristically nervous.

'Do you remember how idealistic we all were about capitalism at Cambridge?' he said at last, feeling that a note of shared nostalgia would be best. 'All those discussions about Macaulay and the mystique of monarchy? Whoever would have thought we'd descend to this?'

'I don't remember you being idealistic about anything,' said Mark. 'Except, perhaps, your overdraft.'

'But we still believed in an academic élite. You know, the other day I bumped into that chap Nick Posely, you remember, the punk who shaved his hair off and lived on speed and Night Nurse? He went into making pop videos, and now he's a bloody millionaire, has a house on Clapham Common as big as a palace. I nearly had a fit. I mean, maybe we should have been listening to the Clash or whatever, not slaving in the UL. Orso's all right for you? How did it go?'

'Well,' said his friend. 'All right, I think.'

Mark had walked three times round Holland Park, becoming more nervous with each circuit, before approaching the de Monde house. The screeching peacocks trailing their bedraggled winter plumage through the muddy lawns filled him with foreboding, and when he came across a little girl, accompanied by her uniformed nanny, kneeling down to change the nappy of a life-sized doll, he felt as if he could not go through with it at all. He had written to Amelia's father, a short and businesslike letter devoid of irony, saying that in view of Amelia's situation he would appreciate a meeting. Amelia had gone over to the big house to tell her parents about her pregnancy.

'How did he react?'

'You never really know what Daddy's thinking,' she said. 'We'll just have to wait and see.'

'And your mother?'

'Oh, she just sighed and said something about heredity. I don't really care what she thinks, it's Daddy who counts.'

Then de Monde's secretary had telephoned, to say that Mark could have an appointment at 11.55 on Tuesday the following week, when Mr de Monde had a 'window' in his diary. Mark had wondered whether this diary was a book as cheerless as the building where the *Chronicle* was produced. There were no windows there, either, apart from skylights – inserted, it was believed, so that MDM employees could watch their proprietor arrive by helicopter.

There was no bouncer or red carpet at de Monde's mansion this time, only the chirr of a security camera as it tracked his progress to the front door. The Filipina housekeeper answered. She was almost identical to the maid who cleaned Amelia's mews house, and seemed to know all about him.

'Yith? Ah-ha. Misthtah Murk. Come in, pliss.'

Under her mocking simian gaze, Mark removed his coat. The

house was furnished in even worse taste than he recollected, the sofas over-stuffed, the chandeliers modern, the curtains swagged. The light switches and fingerplates were brass. All gilt and no shame, he thought, his lip curling. Then he was guided not as he expected into the drawing-room or study, but down to the basement where his employer was swimming in the eternal blue of his subterranean pool.

Waves rippled and slapped in a trough all around, faltering into filters with a sound at once lascivious and sad. The air curled with steam, which dripped slowly off palms and orchids and ferns, all so unnaturally green they might have been plastic but for the bulbous blue lamps supplanting the sun. The walls were painted with *trompe l'oeil* columns and cypress trees. There were newspapers from around the world, and a number of glossy magazines on the mahogany table beside the steamer chairs, a large fridge, malachite cigarette-boxes, and a chest of drawers marked 'Swimming costumes'. A number of inflated water toys were piled in one corner.

Mark had ample time to consider these features, for de Monde swam up and down, ignoring him. He wore nothing, not even a pair of goggles. At first Mark was amused by this. To witness such a powerful man in a condition his own newspapers would have bought for a large sum of money seemed to promise a kind of intimacy. It was hard to believe he had produced Amelia's slender form. De Monde was not just overweight but pelted on shoulders and back with thick, coarse, greying hair of the kind that anyone else would have had cosmetically removed. But as the magnate continued to swim up and down, up and down, Mark's best gabardine suit grew limp. He sat down on one of the mahogany steamer chairs, grinding his heels into the white towelling upholstery, and began to read.

De Monde had shown not the slightest awareness of Mark's presence, but such insouciance produced rapid results. In less than no time he was standing in front of him, dressed.

'Max de Monde.'

Mark rose to his feet. 'How do you do,' he said. 'I'm Mark Crawley. I want to marry your daughter.'

'Well, naturally,' said de Monde. 'Cigar?'

It was extraordinary, Mark thought, the way very rich people, especially men, always spoke in just the way you expected them to. It meant that either they were all the same, or that they had modelled themselves on what they had read in airports.

'I don't smoke.'

'Come,' said de Monde.

He did not say another word, but ushered Mark out of the house and into the waiting Rolls-Royce. Half of Mark's mind concentrated on the disharmony between the yellow rose in its silver holder on the door and the pink Wilton carpet, the other with wondering it he would be executed, gangster-style, by the chauffeur. It was the first time Mark had ever been in a Rolls, and he was profoundly unimpressed. The grey leather seats, for instance, were so sticky and pristine they might as well have been plastic. De Monde, on the other hand, was petrifying.

Mark was not unfamiliar with the phenomenon of men who exist in a force-field so powerful that it alters the perceptions of those around them. Anyone who got too close to, say, 'Felix' Viner started to believe that the world was a bad joke perpetrated by a female deity, and that vast quantities of booze were the only possible response. Yet Max de Monde was something else. He seemed not so much to exude power but to have absorbed it like a sponge so that what came out was superfluous. His sheer physical bulk, the bulk of a man both tall and fat, woke childhood fears of ogres in the most unimaginative. Even his comic elements, such as his occasional attempts to present himself as a 'man of the people' complete with reversed baseball cap, served to underline a monstrous playfulness which could, at any moment, explode into something terrible. Sitting beside him, Mark was conscious that he had at last encountered someone whose selfishness was so complete, so absolute as to constitute invulnerability.

The magnate ignored him, and talked loudly into his portable phone. Only one of these conversations was in English, and about the cost of newsprint.

'Then we need to print more pages than our competitors, not

less,' he was growling at Angus McNabb. 'The market is all about appearances. I don't care if you haven't got enough news to fill it. People don't want news any more, they want features, they want lifestyle. That's what the advertisers want, too.'

The legendary smoothness and quietness of the car, together with cigar smoke, made Mark feel increasingly sick. The Rolls slid across Battersea Bridge and along the Thames to a steel gate and the concrete wharf of a helicopter landing-pad. Three were poised for use, like enormous dragonflies.

Mark took a deep breath. He had never flown in a helicopter before, and he knew already that he would hate it.

'Enjoy flying?'

'Yes.'

'I pilot myself this morning. Glyde will take the Rolls to the office.'

Amelia had made him promise that, whatever else he did, he would not show that he was intimidated by her father.

'He despises anyone he can bully,' she had said. 'I mean, he'll put a detective onto you, darling, I should think he's done that already to check you aren't a fortune-hunter or a bigamist, but he won't tolerate cowards.'

Mark thought of his own father, and winced.

'Tell me, truly, is it because of my money that you want to marry me?'

'Well, of course I'm glad you're rich. I would be a fool if I wasn't. But you know yourself, what has always interested me are the finer things in life.'

Amelia sighed, contentedly. It was so good to be appreciated at last by someone of real calibre. 'This will be his first grand-child, and that's your trump card. He can't stop us. Only he can make our lives a great deal more comfortable. I haven't been getting much from my trust fund, because of the recession,' she said.

Mark climbed into the helicopter, and fastened his seat belt as the blades overhead started to roar. He thought to himself it was one of the bravest things he had ever done, for they were sitting in a kind of perspex bubble which would make his vertigo worse on take-off. Rain flew off the propellers into puddles that now reflected blue sky. De Monde flipped more switches, and the dashboard suddenly glittered with coloured lights. Noise swirled, exploded, and Amelia's father gestured towards a pair of earphones. Mark put them on. The foam pressed into his ears uncomfortably, but muffled the blurry ring of wrung wind overhead. Through the side window, he saw the Rolls disappearing again.

The ground suddenly collapsed, and he was looking down at the Thames, and London. It seemed to spill quickly in all directions, a vast organism of brick and concrete, each street a vein along which cars flowed in viscid clots. There was Battersea power station, shrunk to an overturned footstool, and the gaudy bridges of London spanning the river. Vast and still vaster, London opened its packed organs beneath the cockpit. Now and again, a pane of glass or metal gave a swift, collusive wink in the bright sunlight, but for the most part the city heaved and fell with ugly indifference. Only in the parks did the eye experience any relief from the inorganic, their green lawns and great trees breathing peace.

Around the heart of the capital the streets formed patterns, squares and semi-circles opening and closing, but further away it all became a seemingly random mutation, ranks stretching on and on, barely contained by the belt of the giant ring-road. The helicopter juddered, following the Thames, faster than any of the coloured corpuscles below. The only thing that kept pace with them was a dark patch roughly the shape of a fly. As Mark watched, it swelled suddenly, breaking in two on the walls of an office block before shrinking away, whole.

It was their shadow.

'Tell me what you see,' said de Monde, suddenly.

Mark wondered if this was a trick question.

'The City,' he answered, for it rose ahead of them.

'It is indeed the City,' said de Monde. 'If you love it, it will make you. Otherwise it will break you.'

A kind of shudder went through Mark, independently of the continual vibration in the cockpit.

'Would you like to try and fly?' de Monde asked, his mocking voice shrunk to that of an insect.

'I've no experience.'

'It's quite simple. You just hold the joystick steady. Here.'

Before he could protest, de Monde had given the controls to him, and suddenly, the helicopter was plummeting, no longer a bubble but a boulder, a ball of metal and flesh. You fool, you'll kill us both, he wanted to shriek, but was too terrified to utter a word, his tongue, like his stomach, left flapping some hundreds of feet above him. Buildings swelled and spread, streets turned into canyons, rooftops pitched and steepled – and then, just as suddenly, they rose again. De Monde was chuckling. 'All those fools going about their dull lives, and suddenly – bang!'

Mark said nothing. He was afraid that if he opened his mouth he would vomit.

'So, you want to marry my daughter.'

'Yes.'

'Why should I let you?'

Mark was not the kind of man to make sentimental declarations, nor De Monde one to credit them. 'She's pregnant.'

'So? These days, the absence of a father hardly matters. What have you to offer? You have no money, no family worth speaking of, you are currently earning an income which would not keep Amelia in shoes. You are said to be clever, but so are a thousand others. Why should I let my daughter, my only child, marry such a one as you?'

Mark swallowed his hatred and humiliation. A hundred answers chased each other through his brain. 'Because she wants it.'

'Ah,' said de Monde. 'Yes, perhaps that is the only answer that counts. When I wanted to marry Amelia's mother, that was the answer I gave, and in those days a Lebanese salesman was even more despised than a Cambridge graduate with nothing but his degree. Now, of course, her relations all come to me with their share offers and useless children to employ.'

De Monde fell silent. 'Are you interested in her money?'

'I am not uninterested in it,' said Mark, with what he felt was convincing honesty.

'Then it is as well for you to understand that she has very little of her own until her trust fund matures, and that I am the sole trustee. I am a generous man, but I do not believe in children being given too much independence before a certain age, and in my daughter's case that is thirty-five. Then she inherits what I have set aside for her. It will not, however, be much. She may look like a rich young woman, but her real income is little more than thirty thousand a year. I have paid for the rest, but once she marries that will fall to her husband.'

Mark shrugged. This news was surprising, but she still had the mews house, he thought. De Monde seemed to read his mind.

'The house she lives in belongs to me. You will understand that I will only allow her trust to pay for half of whatever house you choose to buy, up to two hundred thousand pounds. You will also be required to sign a pre-nuptial contract stating that in the event of a divorce, you will receive nothing from her trust fund.'

'Quite,' said Mark. He happened to know that such contracts were not enforceable.

'It is not appropriate for my daughter's husband to be a journalist,' said de Monde. 'You wish to stay a freelance? Its opportunities for promotion are very limited.'

'A political column would be more . . . appropriate perhaps,' said Mark. He remembered the conversations he had just overheard. 'I can think of several aspects of the leader pages that could improve if I joined the staff. It needs more features, more lifestyle, to attract increased advertising. It's a great paper, and should be more profitable.'

'Yes,' said de Monde, and afterwards, as the helicopter dropped light as a feather onto the roof of the *Chronicle* building, Mark thought that this was the moment he really married Amelia.

11

Going Down

Now all days and nights became alike to Mary. She could not sleep until dawn. When she slept, she would always have the same nightmare.

She would be plodding up an escalator on the Underground. On either side, stretching into infinity, were more escalators, some going up towards a circle of light and some descending to a circle of dark, constantly moving. Everyone was silent and sad, their faces drawn, as if at the end of a long day's work.

Then, just in front on a parallel route, she would see Mark. He would turn and look at her, sorrowfully; she would stretch and strain towards him; and at the instant her fingers touched his, he would push her away so violently that her escalator reversed itself, descending with sickening rapidity while people fell backwards on top of and beneath her, while a huge mechanical voice boomed: 'THE WAY UPPP IS THE SAME AS THE WAY DOWNNN!'

On the whole, Mary preferred the nights she could not sleep.

Everything that reminded her of Mark caused agony, as though she had been flayed, and everything did remind her. She did not know how to fill all the hours that they had spent together, going round museums, art galleries, out to films and plays and restaurants – in paradise, it now seemed. She could not bear to walk down some streets, they reminded her of him so strongly: this was where he had taken her out on their first date, and this the patisserie where they would meet when she was between shifts, he had said this about that painting and held her hand there. There was a Soho hairdresser called 'Mark's' that she would now make a long detour to avoid. She tried very hard not to read the newspapers in which his byline appeared, but she could not screen out everything, especially once his engagement to Amelia hit the gossip columns.

The shock of seeing his name never seemed to grow any less; every time, she thought she was going to throw up, even when she knew that he was bound to have a piece in on a certain day. She did not know whether it was worse when rage or despair were uppermost, only that she was trapped between their twin poles, an alternating current raging between dreams of murder and dreams of her own death.

At work, she became increasingly silent and absent-minded, forgetting orders or getting them muddled up. Very happy or unhappy people disappear, and often even the other waitresses forgot she was there. Her arms ached from carrying plates, and when she recited the menu she sounded so gloomy about it that people found themselves choosing one course instead of three. She had a cold all the time, and the most exquisite relief of her existence was blowing her nose until it bled. She could not sit on the front desk, being in perpetual terror that Mark might walk in. Anyone who looked remotely like him made her feel as though she had stepped into a manhole. Yet she also longed to see him more than anything in the world, and would run after anyone who looked a little bit like him in the street, even if it was just a passing resemblance, high cheekbones, perhaps, or a particular cut of hair.

A hundred years ago, people had perfectly understood that you could die of a broken heart, now they thought you were making a fuss about nothing. When she told Ivo about how he had changed the locks on their flat and left all her belongings outside to be rifled, he laughed, and passed the story round as a joke. She often thought that if one person, just one, had understood then it would not have been so bad.

Yet, in learning what it was to lose, she also learnt for the first time what it must be like to win. She had never thought of winning before – of what it would be like to possess fame or money or even the thing for which she had modestly hoped, a husband. Certain kinds of suffering are like radiation: they cause furious growth and mutation of the inner self. Mary had always been conscious of the difference between herself and the rest of her family, but this, though it had equipped her with a degree of intellectual curiosity, had also leached her self-confidence. Now this difference was growing into a monstrous language that reached and curled, so that she was at once liberated and sunless, like Jack when he wakes up to find the beanstalk stretching all the way up to the land where the giants live.

'I have thought and thought on him and Amelia so deeply that it is as if everything he has ever done or will do has become clear to me,' she said to Ivo. 'He thinks she will make him live, but he will freeze her too, for it is not me he hates but all women. He has tried to kill me, and there are things that will never come back, but the rest – the rest – will do such things – I feel as if Mark is punishing me for a crime I have never committed – unless loving him was such a crime, and if that is so, what does *she* deserve?'

Amelia, to whom Ivo had mentioned this, said, 'Well, a sadist is a person who is kind to a masochist,' and went on leafing through *Interiors* with fastidious incuriosity. Mark admired her indifference. She was so poised, so glowing with the kind of artifice he found most attractive in a woman – no mess, tears, hair, blood. She had her father's strength of character, yet her mother's docility. What a life they would have together, he thought. The only trouble was, as usual, money.

They had begun to look for a house, but it was depressingly evident that they would either have to live in a flat, or a considerably seedier area of London than Holland Park. At least it would mean a fresh start. All the complaints he was receiving about Mary were tiresome. He wondered if she was having a nervous breakdown. The idea rather flattered him.

'Would you like to ask her round for a drink or something?' Amelia asked. 'One would prefer to be civilized, after all.'

'God, no.'

'Well,' said Amelia, laughing, 'Whenever I see a small woman I want to rest my glass on her head.'

Mary wrote letter after letter. She posted none, being too afraid of exposing herself to further scorn. It was out of the question to telephone, for she knew that she would be instantly struck dumb; and besides, Mark despised the telephone as 'instant communication for imbeciles'. His silence was so impenetrable, and she found herself scribbling, 'If you don't get this letter, it must have miscarried. Please write and let me know.'

She would lie on the narrow sofa of her cousin's flat in Shepherd's Bush, watching headlights flicking the ceiling like white dusters until the urge to write became intolerable. Every letter, scribbled between shifts or at three a.m., would begin with violent humility, followed by the realization that for Mark there was no impulse of remorse. This understanding came to her slowly, and at first she could not believe it. Yet she could not stop writing. It was like being on a treadmill: fury, despair, hatred, desolation, fury, despair, hatred, desolation. Every letter-box was a temptation, another return to the wheel of fortune. Tomorrow he could get this, she would think, tomorrow or the next day, and then he might write back; and for three days she would live in suspended animation, waiting for a reply to a letter she had not sent.

'I always said he was a shit,' said Deirdre. 'Forget him.'

Mary knew her predicament was putting strain on her cousin's own life, but she felt too exhausted to look for another flatshare, and knew that her misery would make her as unwelcome as a blocked drain.

He wrote: once to tell her the date of the wedding, to which she was not invited; once to send a postcard for her thirtieth birthday; and, lastly, to say that they were skiing in Switzerland and were happy. This, from a man who had condemned skiing as 'Torremolinos on ice', made Mary wonder whether Amelia had drugged or hypnotized him.

Most of her energy was taken up with trying to postpone crying until she was unobserved. There was no privacy, except when she found herself alone in one of the club rooms. This happened more often than usual, because of what was now happening in the world outside.

*

For over a year, the money that had been keeping London in motion had stopped descending and ascending like the handle of a spinning-top. Some said this handle had become too hot, so that it could no longer move smoothly or efficiently; some that it was suffering from metal fatigue; some that the wrong hands at the Exchequer were pumping it, at the wrong time. Heads rolled, faces changed, knuckles were rapped and reputations plummeted – it made little difference. The great teetotum that had spun serenely on its axis for over a decade began to wobble in wider and wider orbits, crashing into lives that had never before known poverty or unease. The recession had come to London.

In Soho it took longer to hit. Everyone was still in fancy dress; the fronts of restaurants sprouted vast torsos, chiming clocks, flaming brands and ever-changing names. Secretaries pretended to be ballerinas, ballerinas to be tourists, tourists to be Londoners and Londoners to be film extras. Men in skirts grew their hair, women in trousers had a short back and sides, East met West and swapped places. Taxis and dispatch riders still fought pitched battles in the narrow streets for inches of space, but from one week to the next, something faltered and died. More and more beggars filled the doorways of offices, solitary figures of indeterminate sex and age, bedding down on cardboard. Everyone felt poorer, even those whose mortages had not suddenly doubled.

At Slouch's, the two restaurants were only half filled and the party rooms were empty more nights than not.

'They disgust me,' Mary said to Adam, one evening. 'They disgust me so utterly, you cannot imagine.'

'You want people to behave as though they still believed in God,' he told her.

'So do you, or you wouldn't love Henry James,' said Mary. 'Selfishness is ugly. You can't separate morality and aesthetics.'

'Can't you? I rather think you can. I don't give a shit if someone believes in eating babies if they can really write. In fact, just about the worst thing an artist can do is to try and be a nice person.'

'Niceness is not the same as goodness,' said Mary, and Adam, for once, was discomfited.

'Mary, most people no longer believe in moral absolutes.'

'More fool they.'

'No. More fool you if you expect them to believe in an exploded system. You wouldn't expect someone to fly an aeroplane believing that the sun goes round the earth, would you?'

'I wouldn't give a shit if they could really fly,' said Mary, with a faint smile.

Adam shrugged. Her depression grated on his elation. His novel was being advertised as the lead summer title at Belgravia, and his agent had told him in some excitement that their publicity office was 'doing a number' on it. After a decade of introversion, Adam was, in his own way, coming out. He had spent nine years in London without lovers, holidays, new clothes or restaurant meals and he wanted to enjoy.

'Everyone else has been mortgaged to a house, I've been mortgaged to a book,' he told Mary. 'Now it's paytime.'

His employer at Pocock's was irritatingly unenthusiastic. 'I hope you aren't thinking of throwing in your job,' he said.

'I was thinking about it,' said Adam, a little embarrassed.

'You aren't the type to become a tart,' said Malcolm. 'So don't get your hopes too high, dear boy.'

'Surely talent has something to do with it too?'

'Talent is just another word for promise,' said Malcolm.

What turned Adam's head most of all was the photograph of himself for the dust-jacket. He was used to being ugly, cutting his mouse-coloured hair himself so that it stood out all over his head in lumps. But with his nose slimmed down, his jaw tidied up, his pupils darkened and his face carefully lit, he looked almost handsome. He began to believe that this was what he really looked like, just as he began to believe that he was a writer of exceptional gifts. Everything about being published struck him as delightful, a massive dose of ego-massaging earned by talent.

'Oh, God, I want sun. I want sex, I want food, I want wine, I want boys with bums like apricots,' he said. He was going on holiday, to Sicily. 'It's like an English summer there, now. Jacaranda trees and wisteria and nightingales, Malcolm says. Do you know what a jacaranda is? Neither do I, but it sounds wonderful. Listen, I've an idea –'

For one moment, Mary thought he was going to ask her to go away with him. To be abroad on the day of Mark's wedding was what would make it bearable, she realized.

'Why don't you stay in my flat? I'll be gone for three weeks, it's mad to let it stand empty, what with the pension company trying to evict and you needing a place.'

'Thank you', said Mary, after a pause. 'I'm sure I can find a flat of my own by then. I'll pay you rent, of course.'

Adam made no protest as she scribbled a cheque for a month's rent to the pension company, though had he known what bitterness was in her heart as she wrote out the sum of £120 he would have been wiser to refuse it. He had a vague apprehension that she was almost as poor as himself; but Adam, though he was quick to condemn stinginess in others, had his own blot where money was concerned.

'Thanks,' he said, carelessly.

Mary moved into the flat the next week. She had never lived alone before; solitude and the propinquity of Bond Street gauzed her thoughts. She had long hot baths, cried, drank half a bottle of Jameson's each evening, cleaned Adam's flat, and slept heavily. After a while, she began to drink in the mornings as well. The blood hummed in her veins, and the spirit in her stomach. She could not imagine why she had not thought of drink before. Every time things became unbearable, she would have another little sip, and then she would feel if not exactly happy then numbed, able to continue from hour to hour. Once Mark was actually married, she felt she could really start to put the rest of her life in order. Only five more, three more, two more days, and then she would be free.

On the morning of Mark's wedding, she went to the Soho hairdresser's which she had avoided, and asked him to cut off her hair.

'Are you sure? It's lovely stuff. Not often I get to do anything this long.'

'Yes,' said Mary. 'I want all of it off. Make it short, like a boy's.'

'You don't just want a long bob? That's ever so stylish.'

'No. I need a change of image. Cut it short.'

All around her, women sat with their heads in large plastic eggs, emerging with the blanched fluff of baby birds as born-again blondes. The scissors crunched round her ears, and the radio broadcast an old Dusty Springfield song. Mark had played it repeatedly in the flat around Christmas. It was called 'You Don't Have to Say You Love Me', about how you could make the one you loved proud of you if they returned your love. She had believed, uneasily, that he meant to reproach her for not showing how pleased she was about his success. Now she understood it had been an entirely private mantra, concerning his intentions towards Amelia.

The hair fell from her head in dull black loops: so many years gone, chopped off. Mary felt light and cold when the hairdresser had finished. Her face was grey. I look like Mam, she thought. I've never seen it before, but I do.

'Like it?'

'Oh, yes, yes.'

'Cheer up,' said the hairdresser. 'It'll all grow back in a couple of years.'

'A couple of years!' said Mary, trying to smile. 'I could be dead by then.'

She was late again when she got back to the club. On the reception desk, there was a front-page picture of Amelia and Mark coming out of the church together in the *Evening Star*, and the headline GOLDEN GIRL WEDS GOLDEN BOY. Mary went into the lavatory, vomited, had another swig of Jameson's and rushed into her shift. Half-way through the afternoon Gavin, the manager, called her to his office.

Mary climbed the stairs to the second floor. Her legs were shaking, and when she reached the half landing she had to stop and sit down. Everything was reversing itself, like a negative, the grey skies outside turning black, the carpet white. She sat quietly, like a sick animal, until her head cleared, then knocked on the door.

Gavin sat behind his desk. 'You've taken your time,' he said.

Mary made a frightened movement.

'I'm sorry to say, there have been complaints about you, Mary,' he said.

'Is it my hair?' she said, stupidly.

'What? No.' There was a long pause. He put his feet up on his desk and swivelled his chair so that he could look out of his window. 'It's your general manner. People seem to feel that you aren't, well, putting what you should be into your job, acting the shrinking violet and so forth. This is a very special place, you know – very particular – and you've been here a long time, but even so –'

Mary was being sacked.

'But –' she said. 'But – why – I –' Her voice died in her throat. She remembered that this man had, more than once, tried to feel her breasts, in the accidentally-on-purpose way of all creeps.

'I think it's best if you don't go back to your shift,' said the manager. 'I've got the rest of your week's wages here.'

He handed her twenty-five pounds. Mary stared at it. She thought about her £1800 overdraft which, living at her cousin's, she had just begun to pay off.

'What about my tips? I've earned four hundred pounds in tips this week, I'm entitled to half.'

'I have only your word for that.'

'Ask any of the other waitresses. No, no, there's the tips book. You can look there if you want proof,' said Mary, trembling. 'I've never had a day off sick, I've earned thousands and thousands for this place in tips – and – and good publicity. The least I'm entitled to is fairness.'

'I'm not going to make a fuss about this,' said Gavin, whose face had changed a little at the mention of 'publicity'. He smiled, and swivelled his chair again, as though grinding an insect. 'Let's split the difference and say you get an additional hundred. It's at my discretion that you get anything, you know.'

He took five twenty-pound notes from his desk, and held them out, with her P45.

'It's nothing personal. Pity about the hair, though,' he said. 'It doesn't really suit you.'

It was nothing personal. All over London, the recession was closing restaurants or causing them to lay off staff. In any case, she knew that she was getting too old for it, for waitressing, like all unskilled labour, devours the young. She was thirty years old, and had mutilated her one real beauty. Mark did not love her. Her mother had not addressed a single kind word to her in years, and the people she had believed to be her friends had all withered away. She had nothing. When Adam came back, she would once again be homeless, and now, having no job, she had no hope of finding another flat-share. Without a flat, she could not get a job; she could not even claim the dole.

What was she to do? What *was* she to do? It was so cold on the streets of London it was a wonder people did not freeze like statues between one step and the next. They looked less alive than the dummies in shop windows, all decked out for a spring that never seemed to come. Her head was enormous. She had to have a drink. She needed it so badly. The windows of Bond Street were full of beautiful things, but none of them useful. She remembered what William Morris had said: 'Have nothing in your house which you do not know to be useful or feel to be beautiful.'

'I am neither beautiful nor useful,' she said, sadly.

Mary bought a bottle of whiskey and a bottle of paracetamol. Then she lay down on the bed in Adam's flat, and swallowed them.

Natural History

A vast, shadowy hall stretched up and tied itself into gilded knots. Arches filled with spring flowers loaded the air with scent. Thick white tapers sidled up the wide marble staircase at the far end of the hall to join behind the main table for the de Monde and Crawley families. In the middle, the gigantic skeleton of a dinosaur, fifty feet long, perfectly articulated from its mean little head to its broad, curving tail, stood frozen. Circular tables, laden with cutlery, crockery and small cards, surrounded it. Overhead, the glass ceiling, turned mirrory by the thunderous afternoon, reflected hats and heads, all wheeling and turning, with the creamy dress of Amelia blossoming in their midst.

'The English wedding represents the failure of hope over experience,' said Ivo. 'They marry in summer, knowing that it will pour with rain. They marry in winter, believing they will get snow, and it pours again. They drag guests to the countryside, or even out of England altogether, advertising this sacrifice of an entire weekend as an adventure instead of the tiresome and expensive ordeal it always proves to be. They expect you to fork out a hundred pounds for a morning suit, a hundred for a wedding present from the General Trading Company, and at least fifty on transport. They attempt to mix friends and family, ignoring the intolerance of the one and the dullness of the other. They provide too much chardonnay and too little champagne, too many canapés and too little food. Yes, for any cynic a wedding is not to be missed, especially your own.'

'I know a man with six daughters who says he'll provide them with a ladder and a suite of luggage from Aspreys if they'll elope,' said Andrew Evenlode. 'So far, none of them have taken him up, though.'

'Catholic, of course,' said Fiona.

'I do dislike the phrase, "of course",' said Evenlode. 'It's the hallmark of a lazy mind.'

'What a pity my lazy mind should be paid so much more than your active one,' said his wife. 'I'd never have invested in Lloyd's.'

'Oh dear, are you in one of those syndicates?' asked Sarah Meager.

'I'm afraid so.'

'We're probably going to lose everything,' said Fiona. 'Including Lode.'

'We don't know that, yet. I think you should wait and see, before broadcasting our misfortunes.'

'Here we are, in our least comfortable clothes, freezing, ravenous, preparing to be bored,' said Ivo. 'Already, I have had to negotiate the sneering exchanges of several department stores in the attempt to buy a present from the wedding list – thank God Mark and Amelia are conventional enough to have such a thing – only to find there was not a single thing under a hundred pounds.'

'Ivo, you're drunk,' said Georgina.

'Of course I am. I could swear, for instance, that there's a megalosaurus in the room.' Everyone laughed.

'Awfully original place to have a wedding,' said Sarah, her tone, like her lipstick, a little too bright. 'I didn't know you could hire the Natural History Museum for this sort of thing.'

'Appropriate, don't you think?' said Tom Viner, looking up at the great ribs curving over their heads.

'Glorious flowers,' said Sarah. 'I wonder what they cost?'

'Thirty thousand pounds,' said a Lebanese relation of their host. Silence fell across the table.

'It's so hard, finding presents for people who already have everything. What did you get, Ivo?'

'A cafetière.'

'Did you? Us too.'

'It's the modern equivalent of a fish slice,' said Georgina. 'It was that or pillowcases, and that always seems faintly indecent.'

'Not in this case,' said Ivo. 'She's got a bun in her oven.'

'Ivo!'

'It's true, my darling. You can't not know. That's why Max had to give in. He's given them an absolute pittance, too, considering.'

'Oh?' said everyone.

'Yes, only a hundred thousand. I mean, what can you buy for that, these days?'

'How shocking,' said Georgina. 'I was expecting they'd get some nice place in Ladbroke Grove at the very least.'

'That's the trouble with new money,' said Andrew. 'Awfully tight.'

'We're all hard up, suddenly,' said Ivo. 'Even those of us who haven't been Members of Lloyd's.'

Ivo's plan to get Marian sacked had worked beautifully, in so far as she had been escorted off the premises and was now unlikely ever to get a job as a literary editor again. But her position had not been filled. Ivo was only Acting Editor, on the same salary as before, ignored at conference while Mark was grovelled to. This did not lessen Ivo's intense disappointment, or his desire for revenge.

'Hasn't Mark got a flat or something?' asked Fiona.

'Yes, but it's miles away across the Thames, and nobody's buying.'

'Oh dear, no comfy hole to bolt to,' said Georgina. 'How wretched for Amelia. Still, I'm sure Max will forgive her once she has her dear little babby.'

'Awfully common, these shotgun weddings nowadays,' said Andrew Evenlode. 'I wonder why?'

'They happen when one half has money and the other doesn't,' said Sarah. 'It's a popular misconception.'

Andrew laughed through his nose, like a horse.

'You have children?' asked the Lebanese relative.

'No,' said Fiona.

'Ah, you should, you should! They bring so much joy. But no doubt you have some important career, like so many young women these days.'

'Quite,' said Fiona, and the look she darted him from beneath her long blonde fringe was that of a basilisk.

Tom thought, Coming to this wedding was a stupid mistake. Why do I keep on seeing these people, most of whom irritate and depress me even more than my patients? Is this the best my life will hold, socially and emotionally? He looked at Celine, chatting to someone across the room. She kept darting glances at his table. She wanted to go to bed with him again, it was clear from the number of times she had left messages on his answerphone, but though it had been nice he really didn't want more complications. He felt guilty enough as it was.

'It's fun, isn't it?' said Sarah. It didn't matter to her that she didn't fit in, he realized suddenly: just being around people with lots of money was enough.

Tom said, 'I was thinking, can I really bear, ever, to go through this procedure myself?'

So, this is what it's like, then, Amelia thought, while she smiled and smiled until her jaws ached. This is what happens when they all live happily ever after. Nothing about the dress being let out at the seams three times because the bride's bosom had grown from 32B to 38D. Nothing about the dressmaker making a false waist to conceal the fact that her own was vanishing by the day. Nothing about having to wear shoes a size larger than normal, with no heel, gigantic underpants, and a brassière at night.

Worst of all was the sickness, a bit like a really bad hangover and flu combined, the rings of nausea tightening, then relaxing into shivering lassitude, over and over. The smell of meat, frying fat, exhaust fumes, cigarettes, coffee, the altered smell of her own urine – almost anything triggered it. For the first time, Amelia realized what it meant to be female.

Amelia was not especially stupid; few pretty and privileged young women really understand the essential injustice of biology. She had controlled her fertility, concealed menstruation, toned her muscles and owned her own cheque book since the age of thirteen. For most of her life as a woman, the rules had been perfectly clear cut: other women were the enemy, and all love was war. She had rejected feminism, quite openly, as a crutch for the envious and ugly, and regarded married women as holding the upper hand if, unlike her own mother, they had any strength of character. The weaknesses and dependencies imposed by fecundity had never entered into her calculations.

'It's obvious,' she said bitterly to Mark, 'God is a man. A woman would never have designed such a silly means of reproduction. Why can't I lay a nice little egg, and take it in turns with you to sit on it?'

'What makes you think I'd sit?' he said.

Sex was impossible. Her head spun even while lying completely still in bed. She felt, in some mysterious way, blocked, sealed off, and furiously resentful at any attempt to breach this. Whenever Mark tried to touch her, she either winced or said no. Quite often, he ignored this. Amelia's set were quite used to discussing sex, but about this, and childbirth, they were, like books, enragingly reticent. Nobody explained that during pregnancy you *dried up*, thought Amelia angrily. Nobody said that your breasts would become, first, as hard as a Barbie doll's and then painful, floppy bags that the stretching hurt. Oh, no, it was all supposed to be blissful ripening and mellow fruitfulness. The thought of their honeymoon filled her with dread.

'We've had it before we got married,' she said.

She kept reassuring him that her libido would come back in the second trimester, when pregnant women were supposed to bloom and look gloriously fecund instead of miserably bloated – although Georgina Hunter told her not to put too much faith in the idea.

'You don't feel better than you would if you weren't pregnant, just not so sick. It's a bit like when you stop banging your head against a brick wall.'

Mark found her resistance exciting. He had begun a new habit of rubbing himself against Amelia's thighs. She was too ashamed of her loss of desire to protest. Just as her palate had returned to its pre-pubertal taste, yearning for sweet things and revolted by coffee, so lust had become at once grotesque and incomprehensible.

'If only I could hire someone to have a baby for me,' she said to

Mark, not entirely joking. 'They could go through all the morning sickness and delivery, and I could have the nice bits. Breast-feeding is supposed to be orgasmic.'

'I'm sure I'll be jealous,' he said, politely, but she could tell he found the idea repulsive.

The actual wedding service had not been so bad. It was all very familiar, of course, the hymns sung lustily by the middle-aged, and in a sort of meandering bleat by the rest, the flowers, the clothes, the vows, the crying of small children. Every year, Amelia had sat though almost identical services, interspersed with readings of Sonnet 116 and Kahlil Gibran, attended by almost identical congregations in identical locations. There was the wedding list at Peter Jones and the General Trading Company, the cream – never white – silk dress, the ushers looking as though they were back at school, the King James Bible and the vicar addressing God rather as one member of a club might address another. There was the entrance to Mendelssohn's 'Wedding March' and the exit to Widor's 'Toccata'. But it was all so different when it was your own! There was no etiquette for trying not to be sick at the altar. She had just made it to the vestry in time, where her mother had whipped out a bucket for her to retch into.

She kept glancing at Mark, to see how he was taking it, but he had retreated into himself. His face was that of a stranger. She knew his opinions about Degas, Bagehot, Marx, caviar and the efficacy of Lancôme face-cream, but she did not, she thought, know whether he loved her. Perhaps he was simply above such banal expressions.

If only she could stop feeling ill. At least the pouring rain prevented an excessively long session in front of the photographers, both hired and from the national press.

'So glad you could come,' she repeated endlessly, charmingly. 'How nice to see you. How lovely. *So* glad you could come.'

Beside her, Mark was seething. His parents were behaving themselves about as well as could be expected but, even so, their social status was painfully clear. They had met their son's future in-laws once, at a restaurant. De Monde had been courteous to them, rather in the manner of Lucifer confronted with a pair of

Martians, Mrs de Monde vaguely vivacious, and Amelia at her most effulgent.

'She's very glamorous,' his mother whispered to him afterwards. 'I do hope she realizes we're not used to society people.'

Mr Crawley, on the other hand, could scarcely have been more talkative. 'You're not so much losing a daughter as gaining a lifetime of free dentistry,' he remarked jovially. 'Ow! Who's kicked me under the table?'

Mark's cousins were both drinking champagne as though determined to prove true every observation about suburbia. Who had told them to wear blue eye-liner and flesh-coloured tights? Where had they got their screechingly provincial suits in two-tone black and white? Could they possibly be – *mail order*? Their sharp cheekbones and fair hair, which looked faintly Slavic on himself, were simply those of peasants when translated onto feminine features.

There is perhaps no place as cheerless as the table of a bride and groom at a wedding. All polite conversation has long ago been exhausted by the strain, and any comment on the success or otherwise of the occasion is deeply resented. Max de Monde sat in thunderous silence, looking down at his serfs. When Amelia attempted to charm him, he stared her down; she had failed to give him the obedience he demanded. For Mark, she thought, he had utter contempt, now that he had bought him, or rather sold her, for such a pittance. She knew how he could turn on all the heat and charm of his personality like the sun, assuring anyone who found the courage to defy him that they were 'one of the family'. He would shower such rebels with money and flattery, and afterwards roar with laughter at the ease with which he could manipulate and corrupt them, but she had not expected him to employ the same tactics towards herself and her husband. Mark was one of his creatures, now, that was clear.

'Your father's a genius,' he told her, after their meeting; and she had not been surprised to learn of his promotion.

All this magnificence was pure show, she thought sadly. Her father no longer loved her. He looked splendid in his pearl-grey morning coat, with sapphires down his shirt-front and at his wrists. Even in his sixties, he was what used to be called a fine figure of a man, a little portly beneath the tailoring, a little large of nose and small of eye, but tall and imposing, his head adorned with crisp waves of silvery hair, his brows bristling, his teeth white. Despite the presence of two viscounts, an earl, the Archbishop, four baronets, and half the Cabinet, he looked the most aristocratic Englishman in the room: Max de Monde, who had risen in the decade when appearances counted for everything. Who could not admire the way his energy and ingenuity had built him a fortune in this tolerant, idle country? Who did not admire the ruthlessness with which he had cowed unions and undercut competitors; had dragged the *Chronicle*'s printing presses into the twentieth century; had survived the prejudice and antagonism of both the City and Fleet Street to become that mighty thing, a press baron? When he stood to make a short, graceful speech to the assembled guests there were few who did not think he would not look well in ermine.

'Jumped-up foreigner,' said Andrew Evenlode's uncle, Lord Windrush, as the toasts were drunk and the cake finally cut. 'Who is he, anyway? Where does his money come from?'

But these questions, quite properly, were thought to be as superannuated as the creature whose remains they all sat round, eating and drinking until the long, shiny black cars came to take them away.

13

The Wheel Turns

Adam Sands believed himself set apart from the rest of humanity, a spectator, an unacknowledged legislator and all the usual nonsense that writers wish to be true of writing.

'For me to like someone is the greatest compliment to their good qualities,' he had once said to Mary. 'It means that something exceptional has outweighed the bad.'

'Do you always see the bad, then?' she had asked.

'I see the bad, and the badness of that bad, down to the last drop. Most people talk and behave as though nobody is watching, as if nobody is taking down what they say as evidence to use against them. It's quite incredible how little attempt they make to change.'

'But, Adam,' said Mary, 'what about your own faults?'

'There are some things you just have to learn to live with,' said Adam.

He had a nervous, brooding self-belief that perennially threatened to curdle into vanity, particularly now. For there is no time in a writer's life as happy as that when their first novel is accepted. It is a little like getting a job which you have long wanted, or being in love with someone who, you suddenly discover, returns your affection. Adam believed, when signing the contract for *A World Elsewhere*, that his troubles were over. It was for this that he had hungered and thirsted, for this he had laboured in poverty. He was almost delirious with optimism. For six months he felt like a genie let out of a bottle.

He had taught himself to read, to write, and to rewrite; he had analysed other people's novels; he had learnt to make language move, twist, fold back on itself. Often he would lie sleepless all night, thinking about this detail or that, worrying and gnawing at his novel, round and round, until his sheets were drenched.

'Candida really understands Hugo,' his agent assured him. She was an elegant middle-aged woman who spoke in a mournful coo, which Adam found at once soothing and annoying. 'A lot of editors didn't.'

'Really?'

'They hated him,' said Francesca. 'Do you think this heather needs a squirt of Baby Bio?'

'He's meant to be hateful,' said Adam, surprised. 'That's the point.'

'Yes, well. That kind of thing is fine if you're writing about a yob or a paedophile, but someone like Hugo, well, they thought you must be some sort of fascist. Oh dear, this dust, it's making your poor leaves dull, but yes, oh, yes, I can see a bud! Adam, can you see it?'

'No.'

'Just poking its head out in the middle, there. Oh, my darling. Yes, well, Pat liked it, but thinks it needs a lot of editing. I think you'd like her, she's very motherly, especially to young men, but she's only offered five thousand. I think we need grit.'

'Gritts? Surely not.'

'Grit, maybe some ground shell. This earth is getting water-logged. Candida, though, just adores it. She thought Hugo fright-fully sexy, and she's bid two and a half thousand more.'

'He's not meant to be sexy,' said Adam. 'He's meant to be ludicrous.'

'Of course, Belgravia doesn't have quite the high profile of say, Slather and Rudge, but apart from the money they'd make a fuss of you,' said Francesca. 'To be honest, you may need repotting next year. If we weren't in a recession I'd have got double, but it's vital to get into the right environment for your first novel.'

'I don't think most book-buyers even notice who someone is published by,' Adam said, his mind's eye filling with all the things he could get for £7500: a word-processor, for instance, and a printer. 'If you think I should go for the higher bid, that's fine by me.'

He liked Candida – after all, she had bought his book. She took him out to lunch at the Slouch Club, apologizing for the banality, and Adam found himself enjoying it. Everything from the heavy, scratched silver cutlery to the hand-crafted sugar-lumps spoke to him of a kind of low-key extravagance that had been absent from his existence since university. He liked the gossip that splashed across the tables, the sensation of being at the centre of a particular kind of life; and he was tempted to stay on board this floating world, as thinly colourful as a slick of oil on water.

'You write like Evelyn Waugh crossed with Nancy Mitford,' said Candida, flattering.

'Well – thank you,' said Adam. 'More Fournier crossed with Huxley was my intention.'

'So many young men only write for men,' said Candida, for whom lunch was not a noun but a verb. 'I really think we could market you as an upmarket women's writer.'

'But I don't write for women,' said Adam. 'I mean, I don't for men, either.'

'That doesn't matter,' said Candida, briskly. 'Women buy more than seventy-five per cent of fiction; if they like you, then you're a commercial proposition. You're young, single, good-looking, you write about sex and class – they'll be falling over you. You want to sell, don't you? Well, then.'

Slowly, it began to dawn on Adam that he was being marketed as a real-life version of Hugo, his protagonist. At first he was amused. He knew perfectly well the two people who had given him the germ of Hugo, and neither was himself. Yet everything he mentioned about his own life emphasized this misconception. In a way, he found it fascinating to observe how old-fashioned publishers were. If you had lived abroad, gone to public school and spoke with a certain accent you had to be upper-class. In fact, his parents, who were barely middle class, had lived abroad as thousands of other professional people did, because work demanded it. His school fees had been paid by the company; there had been no option of sending him to a local school. His father was a tax exile because he was mean. His mother lived in Norfolk because she was broke. He wore tweed suits because he could buy them cheaply from the Sue Ryder shop. His Mayfair flat was rent-controlled, and had been acquired by pure luck. Yet these superficial details of his life were interpreted as the stuff of grandeur. The photograph they had chosen, of Adam in a silk dressing-gown (borrowed from Mabel downstairs), emphasized this.

'It doesn't look anything like you,' Tom Viner remarked, when Adam showed him the results of the photographer's wizardry with airbrush and lens.

'I know. Nice if it did, though.'

'You should tell them you're gay,' Mary said.

'Look, my mother doesn't know that. Why should strangers?' said Adam, waspishly. 'Besides, if I come out now, I'll sink into the ghetto. It's like declaring yourself a feminist, or a Catholic or whatever because it means that everything you write becomes specific to that one aspect. There's so much crap about coming out, and what they really do is shove you into an even smaller closet, full of blokes with loo-brushes on their upper lips. What I am is private. I don't have a lover. Why should anyone be interested in the writer rather than what is written?'

'Maybe because it takes less effort.'

'Less effort!' said Adam. 'Do people really imagine that they can understand a single other human being if they can't even manage fictional ones? Do you think that, even if you had everything I'd ever written, you would even come close to what, in myself, I *am*?'

Belgravia seemed particularly excited about his contacts. They had compiled a list of all the journalists he knew, to whom copies of his book might be sent for favourable coverage or review.

'It's such a welief when we have an author who's part of the Oxbwidge mafia,' said Caroline, Belgravia's publicist. 'It saves so much time.'

'If a mafia exists – which I personally doubt – then it spends its time assassinating its members, like the other kind,' said Adam. He suddenly felt a wicked urge to talk like Hugo. 'You didn't go there yourself, I take it?'

Caroline's smile froze. 'Well, no.'

'I thought not. This idea that Oxbridge graduates spend their time helping each other is a complete myth. You don't get in if you're not fantastically competitive, and the people you compete against are your peers. It's non-Oxbridge people who form the real mafia. They're the ones who need it. Unless, of course, they happen to be dazzlingly pretty blondes.' (This was Hugo, too; Caroline was not at all his type.)

Caroline blushed. She had wondered – there had been rumours – but now she was quite, quite sure they were wrong.

'I still think we'll send out pwoofs to everyone on your contact list.'

Next there was the puff. Any reputable author who could conceivably owe the publisher or the novelist a favour was sent a copy in the hope of receiving a letter in return, which could be quoted on the dust-jacket and press release.

'It's standard pwactice,' said Caroline.

'But it's dishonest.'

Both Candida and Caroline were firm, however.

'Look,' said Caroline. 'You've done your job, and we'll do ours. The best thing you could do is some timely journalism.'

So Adam tried; and this was the second mistake he made. He had no idea how literary fashion is manufactured, and made a nuisance of himself by suggesting half-baked ideas for features to editors with whom he had been slightly acquainted at Cambridge. None of them was published, for he had no idea how to write journalism and the two commissions he managed to extract were spiked – but his actions made him achieve a vague notoriety.

'People are weally excited about your novel,' said Caroline, ringing him. 'All the litewawy editors I've spoken to say it's off their shelves.'

With this, Adam went on holiday.

He was happy. Yet one night in Sicily, a fortnight after he had arrived in Taormina and was lying in bed listening to the nightingale outside his *pensione*, he was suddenly overwhelmed with an apprehension of disaster so intense that he staggered to the basin and was violently sick. They can't think that, he thought. Hugo isn't me, nobody could be so monumentally stupid. Yet the nightmare persisted. He could not stop shivering and sweating. The sight of his own vomit, rimming the plug-hole with lumpy slime, filled him with dread.

The boy who had been curled up beside him asked, '*Sei malato?*'

'No,' said Adam. 'Bad fish.'

Gradually, he stopped sweating and retching. The worst that could happen was that his book would not be reviewed anywhere, and Caroline had assured him there was a lot of interest. All the same, he thought, he had better fly back to London.

Mary gagged. Her throat, her tongue, had something pressing against it, hard and unyielding. She struggled and fought. Needles of remorseless light made her eyes stream. She went on gagging for what seemed like a very long time, then sank into thick black glue.

The second time she woke, she felt as though she had been punched all over especially on her throat and stomach. She was surrounded by a rippling, clinking fog. There was a vile taste in her mouth. A needle in her hand, under a sticking plaster. It hurt, in an itchy way. After a while she noticed that a tube led up from it to a transparent bag, half full of liquid, on a pole. Her mouth was covered with a mask, and she was breathing in a kind of gas. It was very quiet, apart from a strange, persistent hissing. They had made her swallow a snake, she thought.

Voices drifted in and out of her head.

'– cheers, guv.'

'– beds. We're mostly full all the time.'

'Not enough ITU nurses. They're buggering off because –'

'– suggestion your brain's a bit swollen.'

'Mary, are you awake?'

'Pre-eclampsia clotting disorder. Basically, you had a fit, but I don't think there's any stroke. How's your vision?'

'Fine.'

'He's a beautiful little boy.'

'Looks just like the urologist.'

'Mary?'

Her throat felt as if it had been crushed in a mangle. She had fought and fought, but there had been too many. Footsteps. A loud, precise voice.

Sighing. Breathing. Footsteps. A dreadful thirst. She was shrivelling up, every cell of her, and there was a juice dispenser full of beautiful round oranges just out of reach. It was part of their cruelty. They had forced her to swallow a long white snake, miles and miles of it, no matter how she fought and begged to be left alone.

' – don't know. Paracetamol at the levels we found in her blood has a high risk of mortality. Basically, it makes your liver rot, but we won't know how bad it is yet. Patients can seem fine, then collapse. I think you found her in time. We've given the antidote. Also, she doesn't appear to have aspirated her stomach contents, which is lucky.'

'She'd been sick on my bed.'

'The point is, she didn't breathe vomit in, otherwise we'd be looking at lung injury as well. She's off the ventilator, now, as you see.'

'There was no note. It might not have been deliberate.'

It was Adam, speaking.

'I hope not. She was bloody l-lucky to get a bed. All the intensive care units are full. We've been turning people away over the weekend.'

'She's been very unhappy. I should have realized.'

'She should try being riddled with cancer and crapping through a colostomy bag. Look, I'm sorry for anyone who gets depressed enough to try and off themselves, but she's young and healthy. An operation has had to be cancelled because of this.'

'What a place. Half the patients look dead already.'

'She is. She's been like that for years, but her father refuses to accept it. He comes to read to her every day. Every expert in the country has told him she's a corpse, but he won't listen. If it were up to me I'd switch off life support. We need the bed.'

'What a bloody awful job you have.'

'Oh, I love it.'

'Any sleep?'

'Not since Friday. The cleaner woke me at seven thirty this morning just as I was getting off. A nurse will be round again soon for some more blood samples. The intensivist you've met. I'll send the psychiatrist round.'

'That was awful, seeing you shove that big tube down her throat, and all the water. I never thought pumping a stomach was just pouring jug after jug down, then that black stuff –'

'Charcoal.'

Adam moved, and Mary saw the face of the doctor. She recognized him at once. It was the man she had seen at Amelia's party, whom Ivo had known. Tom Viner. She had a vague memory of him shouting, hurting her.

'Don't tell Mam,' she tried to say.

'She's awake. Mary?'

'War.'

Adam handed her a glass of water, and removed the mask.

'What happened?'

'More,' said Mary, croaking. She felt completely empty, like a balloon, in this clear, clean white place.

'You took an overdose.'

'Yes –'

'I'm sorry. I never thought it was so bad.'

Tom moved away, discreetly, to the monitors.

'You can't let it take you over, Mary,' said Adam. 'Men have died, and worms have eaten them, but not for love, remember?'

'That's men. Women are different. When you give someone your whole heart, and he doesn't want it, you can't take it back. It's gone for ever.'

'Nothing is for ever except death.'

'You've no idea,' Mary said.

'Everyone does,' said Tom, sternly. This was the enemy, the thing he hated. 'Everyone has the death-wish. It's always there, always waiting until you're weakened by something, illness or disappointment or even bad weather. It's the counterpoint.'

'I can't see that there'll ever be any point,' said Mary.

Adam said, 'Nothing is constant, neither happiness nor sadness. You shouldn't expect it from people, either.'

'I tried. Clothes, work, drink –'

'No. If you drink you'll drown,' said Adam.

'Alcohol is a depressant,' said Tom Viner.

'How the hell do you know?' she said, resentfully.

He looked down at her, and she thought, Oh, right, spin me some line about chemicals.

Then he said, 'My father's an a-alcoholic.'

Mary spoke without thinking. 'Mine too.'

For a moment, she almost liked him. She said urgently, 'My family mustn't know. Please, please, don't tell them. They can't cope –'

'You have a right to privacy,' said Tom Viner. 'But you must see the psychiatrist.'

The two friends walked out of earshot.

'Has she ever done this before?'

'Not as far as I know.'

'Well, the shrink will go into all that. If there's anything you can think of to help, tell him.'

'I should think losing your lover and your home would make most people pretty suicidal. She's not normally neurotic or depressive, I'd say.'

'*Cherchez l'homme.* It's always that with women, isn't it?'

'Well, you should know,' said Adam.

Tom shook his head. 'I've never made someone unhappy like that. Perhaps I've never inspired l–devotion like that. Has she somewhere to stay when we discharge her?'

'Only with me, and that's difficult. I've only one bedroom, as you know.'

'I see,' said Tom. His bleep whined.

'No, you don't,' said Adam, suddenly impassioned. 'She's not like us – she's struggled out from under this great *boulder* of poverty and disaster, and now it's about to roll on top of her again. I want to help, but I don't know how.'

Tom thought of the time when his father had left his mother, and he himself had moved out of Andrew Evenlode's house to fail his exams. He thought of all the hopeless people he saw every day in hospital, and of the need to remain detached. 'My great-aunt Phoebe has a flat,' said Tom. 'But she's barking.'

'Where?'

'The basement of her house in Chelsea. Grotty, I should think, but better than nothing. I'll ring and find out if it's still available. Don't say anything to – what's her name?'

'Mary Quinn,' said Adam. 'Only you would have such a thing as a great-aunt in Chelsea.'

'So that's Mary. Pretty hair,' said Tom.

A nurse, overhearing this, said, 'I've always wondered what it was about short girls.'

'They bounce up and down on you,' said Tom.

'So do big ones, if you ask nicely.'

To Mary's surprise, the person who came to see her next was not the psychiatrist but Ivo Sponge. Another fool, she thought, but a certain vivacity returned to her, although he brought only a bunch of wizened narcissi. 'How did you know where I was?'

'My spies are everywhere.' There was an awkward silence.

'Does *he* know?'

'Mark?' Something flickered in Ivo's black eyes.

'But someone's told him. And he's sent nothing, not even a card. God, I always knew he was a cad, but I'd no idea he was this much of one.'

'What *have* you done to your hair?'

'It's a disaster, isn't it?'

'You do look – different. Sharper, somehow. Well, if you botch your own suicide, the time has come.'

'It wasn't –'

'To sort you out.'

'Why?'

Ivo reddened. 'Oh, well, you know – I'm fond of you. Also, just between ourselves, we share a common enemy.'

'Amelia?'

'Don't be stupid.'

'I thought he was your friend.'

'Not any longer.'

Mary looked at the map of her pain, and understood. 'Mark got your job?'

'Three hundred a week expenses, real power and Westminster. I'm just acting literary editor. He used both of us.'

'More fool us,' said Mary, with a faint smile. The ventilator on the next bed hissed rhythmically.

'No, more fool you,' said Ivo. 'The trouble with you, Mary, is that you've never understood how London really works.'

'Ivo, I just can't take any more lectures from people.'

'Listen to me. *Listen*. You are at a turning point in your life. Either you accept what other people have forced on you, or you rebel. Don't you want to revenge yourself? I see, you're listening now. I'm glad there's still some Celt in you kicking the pricks. There is a market, you see. At the bottom end of it, where most people are, you trade something ordinary – time, say, or muscle. That's pretty much what you were doing, waitressing. But at the top end, there are only two commodities: fear and favour.'

'I don't understand,' said Mary.

'Yes, you do if you think about it. Mark trades in fear. I trade in favour. People do what Mark wants because they're frightened of him. The worse he behaves, the more people will rush to lick his arse. Not only is he one of the most savage hacks around, he's part of the in-crowd. If you cross him you could be made into a running joke and, believe me, nobody, no matter how good their sense of humour, wants to be a joke in his column. And now, of course he's got Max behind him.'

'And the favours?'

'That, my darling, is an equally good commodity except that you need a very good sense of market value, and whether somebody is likely to understand tit for tat.'

'Oh, backscratching.'

'No, it's much more complex than that. It's a different kind of power. The point is, I operate the favours market. It is less immediately effective, but better for the long term.'

'Ivo, I don't think you can do much for an unemployed waitress.'

'I thought,' said Ivo, 'that you might become a reviewer.'

Mary gaped at him. 'Me?'

'Why not?'

'I've never done any journalism.'

'So? You've read more than almost anyone I know. Even Mark thought you might be able to write. You could learn. I'll teach you.'

'Indeed,' said Mary drily. She thought about his proposition. 'What about Mark?'

'He's away on his honeymoon.' Mary swallowed. 'By the time he gets back, if you work hard, you could have three reviews out. If they're good enough, other people will commission you. Mark won't want to look any meaner by getting you spiked.'

'Mark never worried about looking mean before.'

'You forget,' said Ivo. 'The thing that makes him powerful now makes him a target also. He's Max de Monde's son-in-law – and I, it so happens, write for the *Eye*.'

Part Two

14

Amelia Slums It

Spring comes earlier to some parts of London than others. In the quiet squares of Kensington and Chelsea camellias and magnolias, warmed by abundant central heating, had been in bloom since Christmas. Elsewhere, the city remained in the grip of winter. Everything seemed frozen beneath grimy clouds. For weeks people trudged through dirty puddles and dirty rain, disappearing underground and coming up miles away with scarcely the consciousness of having missed daylight. As the pale sun set, every large doorway in the centre of town was filled with animated heaps of rags; and as the sun rose, more and more doorways displayed rags only.

Yet one day there were crocuses flaring on every roundabout, and daffodils pointing their long lenses at landmarks throughout the city. Patches of blue blinked across the sky. Pneumatic drills shook the air, tar charred it, and the yellow-white flesh of the city was exposed in the annual quest for – what? How wretched and denatured this London earth looked, starved of light and air! Yet still tall trees struggled and stretched into the sky, their roots scorched by salt and strangled by wires; still they grew; and as they swelled, so did Amelia.

She was not enjoying pregnancy.

'My dear, I can completely understand why so many women have abortions,' she said, to those of her girlfriends who remained childless. 'When I think I've got a whole summer of this, I could *just die.*'

She spent most of her time on the sofa, a rather pretty chester-field Mark had brought from his flat, reading or sleeping in the one habitable room of their new house. Food was repellent, yet the only thing that made her nausea recede. As soon as she did eat, it was as though something inside her opened a giant maw, like the plant in *The Little Shop of Horrors* and growled, *'Feed me!'* If she did not then immediately shovel food into this inner mouth the sick-ness became intolerable. It seemed particularly keen on Cadbury's Fruit and Nut and Dover sole. She imagined the foetus to be like a lamprey, all mouth. Amelia's role in the process was simple: she had to stuff herself until the maw closed. Then it ordered her to sleep. That was all it wanted from her – no beautiful thoughts, entertainment, exercise or even good humour, just another organ-ism as primitive as itself. I could be paralysed, or mentally defect-ive, or practically dead and it wouldn't matter, she thought, resentfully.

Mark was now on a salary of £60,000 a year, which together with her allowance from her trust fund brought their income to around £90,000. There was her 20 per cent share in her father's company, but no significant income accrued from that at present. The *Chron-icle* was known to have lost £10 million over the past twelve months, and everything was being hit by the recession. Amelia was vague about the exact sums at their disposal, but she felt terribly, terribly poor. Mark was still paying the mortgage on his flat in Brixton, which remained unsold, despite the asking price having been twice dropped by £7000. The estate agents kept complaining about not being able to get in to view the property with the keys he had given them, but this must be incompetence. The interest on what he had borrowed to buy their undistinguished Victorian house in Kentish Town swallowed up £1400 a month. They had calculated on spending £20,000 to install a new kitchen and two bathrooms, strip the walls of the usual woodchip wallpaper, and the floors of beige carpet and layers of old varnish. To their horror it soon became apparent that not only would their plans cost double that but the back wall of the entire house needed under-pinning. Their survey, which on Mark's insistence had been the cheapest possible, had not revealed that the entire street was subsiding down the hill. As soon as the hideous Formica kitchen and wallpaper has been removed, a crack wide enough to insert a paperback appeared. Out of their joint income, a mere £1000 a month was now left with which to pay for food, clothes and anything that could not be wangled as a freebie.

'At least you can't possibly commit adultery,' Amelia said. 'It would be too much of a cliché, in our postal district.'

'That's NW3,' Mark said sourly. 'In NW5 people have babies.'

Bang, bang, crash, crash, down came the walls and up rose the dust. All day troops of goblins and trolls marched through the ground floor with spades and shovels and mallets and picks, drills and wires and hammers and planks. The same top ten pop songs reverberated around the back gardens, almost drowning the incomprehensibly guttural shouts of the builders. Their foreman seemed to have equal difficulty interpreting Amelia's crystalline requests for all wires to be buried in plaster, or for the radio to be turned off. They hung up sheets of plastic between the ground floor, where most of the work was going on, and the rooms where Amelia and Mark lived, but the cold air still gusted through, coating everything with grime. She had to have her hair done whenever she went out to lunch simply to look presentable. Not that it was enjoyable to go to places like San Lorenzo any longer when one had to spend at least an hour crawling across London in a traffic jam; and anyway, most of her acquaintance was skiing.

If only they could have gone on living in the mews house while it was all happening. Max, however, had made it clear that this was not on the cards, and it was put up for sale. Amelia was more upset at having to sell her Porsche. They would need something dull like a Volvo once the baby was born. In any case, it was the only way they could afford all the extra building work, and a new bathroom was better than a number-plate any day.

Mark bottled up his rage like a new wine. This was not at all what he had envisaged when marrying Amelia. De Monde's meanness, or shrewdness, humiliated them both. To be demoted from Holland Park to North London would have been tolerable had they been in something suitably graceful, a Georgian square in Islington, perhaps, but this – it was scarcely even the muesli belt. They could not afford to entertain, even without the rubble everywhere, and the neighbours! Always complaining about the noise their builder made, as if they themselves were not suffering ten times more inconvenience, and always trying to chat over the back-garden wall.

'They're just stupid,' he told Amelia.

'They're not really our sort of person,' she agreed. 'They all vote Labour.'

There were plenty of media people around, but they happened to be left-wing politicians, and this, too, was fraught with potential embarrassment. It was one thing to trash someone from the safe remove of the *Chronicle* and quite another to find yourself standing in the same Sainsbury's check-out as your victim. Mark lacked Ivo's imposingly bad manners. He preferred his victims to be at one remove. He was as murderously funny about politicians as Ivo was about authors, but his temperament was still that of a scholar. Stories abounded of him listening at doors in Westminster, of scandal lifted off other pundits' screens, of vendettas. He was dropped from a lunching syndicate after running a story early, and a piece on a Shadow Minister had the latter in tears for a week. He did not care, reminding himself that persistent prophecy assured the event, and that it was the historian's duty to tear away the mask of chance, as it was to prevent any repetition of the past. Mark remembered the intellectual thrill of the early 1980s, when each new issue of *The Spectator* seemed a rallying-call to those like himself, the Young Turks of the New Right. Class was risible: merit, all.

His coarseness of speech in private astonished his wife. 'It's only verbal,' he said, surprised, when she told him how much she disliked it.

'Don't you think there's a connection between what you say and what you think?'

To Amelia, middle-class poverty was a novelty, quaint and rather exciting until she learnt that she would have to have her baby on the National Health.

'But I've belonged to BUPA for years!' she exclaimed to Dr Wright, her new GP. 'Surely there's some mistake?'

The doctor smiled frostily.

'Not unless you have a Caesarean.'

'Well – couldn't I?'

'It's not advisable. Perhaps I should explain,' she said, with barely concealed satisfaction, 'that private hospitals of the kind you are thinking of are not equipped to deal with medical emergencies. Should something go wrong during your labour, you would be transferred to an NHS hospital, which in itself is a dangerous procedure. No responsible doctor would recommend that you have your first baby outside the NHS, though many teaching hospitals now have private wings which may answer your requirements.'

Amelia rang round, and discovered that to have her baby privately would cost a minimum of £900, with every extra night another £450. A consultant would be £2000. A year ago, these sums would have been a mere pinprick but, now that Daddy was no longer footing the bills, they suddenly seemed immense. She had no idea what ordinary hospitals were like, but they did not sound like nice places. Imagine having to share a room with other people! Imagine having to use the same bathroom!

'Oh, my dear, now that we're living in North London, it's not at all the thing to go private,' she lied. In her circle, anywhere north of Harley Street was a mystery, rife with socialism. 'Besides, I expect the whole business will be so frightful that not having a television won't matter a bit.'

The weight of her enlarged womb pressed down on the small of her back, and she was breathless after climbing the stairs. Dr Wright told her that she was putting on too much weight. Still Amelia could not stop eating. On her way out to lunch she had to stop and gobble down sandwiches. You were not expected to eat more than a mouthful of any meal, no matter how tiny, but she felt quite faint these days if she did not have two puddings.

Soon she could not fit into any of her largest dresses. She took a taxi to South Molton Street, the nearest point of civilization, to buy some maternity clothes.

'My God,' said the proprietor, watching Amelia struggle into one dress after another, 'you must be 'aving an *enormous* baby.'

After this Amelia did not dare go back. She sent off for clothes in mail-order catalogues, and resigned herself to Lycra leggings and extra large silk shirts.

Amelia told Mark about her suffering in great detail, together with daily bulletins on the development of their child. She did not see why she had to endure this tedious process without sympathy. 'It's got everything now, eyes, heart, lungs, fingers. I never realized that by the time you know you're pregnant it's already there. Don't you want to read about it?'

'I will – later,' said Mark, sheafing through the folder of builder's estimates.

'It's so awful, this. I bleed every time I go properly. Apparently I've got something called a rectal fissure.'

He looked up, interested. 'Have you? So did Auden. His was from buggery, though.'

He would not even come with her to the hospital for her first scan. His new position on the *Chronicle* seemed to demand an inordinate amount of lunching, and whenever she rang him he was either in a meeting or at Westminster. On Wednesday and Thursday he came home close to midnight, and even during recess, when most political staff on the *Chronicle* were relaxing, he was off in his study, researching his next column. Any noise roused him to a searingly bad temper, so much so that they had to ask the builders not to come, which delayed work still further.

'Darling,' said Amelia one day. 'We really do need more money.'

'I can't ask for a rise yet. You could do more work yourself.'

Amelia sighed. 'I might in a month or two, if I feel up to it, but not yet. I thought I could take some time off, after my book.'

'Other women manage,' said Mark. 'And they have to commute by tube.'

'What I was thinking is, we might have a lodger. The top floor has its own bathroom, and there are two rooms just standing empty. We could be getting five hundred a month for them.'

'We couldn't possibly have a total stranger living in our house. Are you mad? The next thing we'd know they'd be selling the story of our life to the *News of the World*,' said Mark.

'It wouldn't be a stranger,' said Amelia. 'Tom Viner needs

somewhere to live. He's a doctor, he was at our wedding. We'd practically never see him, he works so hard, but he's terribly nice.'

Mark said, 'The himbo? You'd fall in love with him.'

'Oh, darling,' said Amelia. 'Of course not. I've known him for donkey's years, he's not my type. And it would be awfully useful to have a doctor around with the baby and everything. It would mean we could have a live-out nanny. The one would pay for the other.'

So Tom moved in, and although it meant the extra expense of plumbing in a kitchen sink and buying a second-hand cooker and fridge to furnish it, the arrangement was a success. He could sleep through any amount of builders crashing about, and the dust seemed not to rise to the third floor. Somewhat to her disappointment the double bed she put up there seemed to be unused: whatever philandering Tom did was discreet.

'I was rather hoping to enjoy a vicarious sex-life,' she said on the phone to Fiona Evenlode. 'Living in a haze of hormones, as one does, it would be nice to be reminded of something other than maternity bras.'

Fiona laughed. 'Oh, Tom never brings girlfriends back. He always wants to have a getaway. You must have heard the story about the time he slept with Arabella, and put her alarm-clock forward a couple of hours just so he could leave without a big scene? The poor girl turned up at work at five o'clock.'

There was no danger, Amelia thought, of falling in love with her lodger. She saw rather than felt Tom's attractions, and congratulated herself that this was the case. After all, he was extraordinarily nice to look at, and sympathetic to talk to. He told her to get a syrup called Lactulose when she confided her miseries, and this worked a kind of miracle on her digestion, although she still felt sick much of the time. She had given up any pretence of working, though Candida Twink encouraged her to write a novel: 'You're a name, and you've got a track record, now. Just knock it off in your spare time.'

But Amelia could not think about any subject for more than a minute without the realization of her condition blotting out all else. Pregnancy obsessed her. She felt as though she were fighting a pitched battle with her foetus, not just for nourishment but for control of her personality. As her bones softened, so did her heart. A world of suffering, over which she had floated with serene indifference, suddenly touched the luminous bubble in which she existed. She was resentful of this. Why should she feel guilty for being born to privilege and beauty? Yet a dozen times a day, she winced and felt her eyes fill with tears, at pictures in the news, at ordinary everyday cruelty – a toddler in the street, crying and trailing behind its irritable parent, a baby with a black eye, a quarrelling couple.

Then one day she woke up and found her face and breasts covered in powdery dead skin, as though she were literally sloughing off her anxiety. A deep peace suffused her, as though her body and her baby's had laid down their weapons and decided to look after each other. Now she began to feel excited, as well as tired. At least five times a day she would pull up her shirt to scrutinize her stomach. It was definitely rounder. She looked at her reflection in shop windows. When would she stop looking fat and start looking pregnant?

Amelia, unfamiliar with the less affluent parts of London, had never seen a high street to equal Kentish Town's for dreariness. At the top end was a pretty glass and iron shelter, originally designed so that the intelligentsia of Kentish Town could lift their eyes to Hampstead while sitting on the two wooden benches. These benches were permanently occupied by drunks, sleeping off their latest binge, and saturated with urine and beer. At the bottom stood the last in a series of depressed pubs and estate agents. There were no trees, only a dismal clutter of concrete tubs planted with withering shrubs. Intermittent steel railings bent by the passing traffic sheltered an astonishing procession of grotesques. There were days in which every other person she saw was either crippled, or mentally defective, or drunk, or enormously fat. Yet nearly all of them wheeled buggies in which their boil-in-a-bag progeny lolled beneath plastic hoods.

Amelia was especially fascinated by the children. At the surgery she now attended she could tell within weeks of birth whether a baby was middle class or not, according to the frilliness of its clothes, the jewellery it wore and the way its face rose from or sank into stupefaction. In all the time she visited, she hardly ever saw a child being read to, or sung to, or talked to. If a baby screeched it was either ignored or had something shoved in its mouth; when the dummy or bottle were dropped on the surgery floor, the mothers would swoop down, suck the teat themselves, then pop it back.

Yet now, walking along the high street, it seemed the most beautiful and human of places. The blackened concrete tubs bobbed with daffodils, the fish shop gleamed with rainbows of iridescence, the florist spilled colour and scent. She still distrusted it, however.

'As far as I can make out, Camden is nothing but a breeding ground for thugs and criminals,' she remarked to Tom. 'The other night, I looked out of the window, and there was a boy with a sledgehammer going down smashing in all the car windows. He'd have done in every car, except I leant out and told him to stop.' She expected him to applaud her doing so.

'Mmmm,' said Tom.

'And the litter they throw into the front garden! Beer cans and crisp packets keep landing on my bulbs.'

'I expect they won't, once passers-by see flowers growing,' said Tom.

'I have visions of all my roses being picked the moment they come out.'

'No,' said Tom. 'They aren't wantonly destructive like that. Poor people crave flowers. Haven't you ever looked at the balconies of housing estates? You wait, you'll find a front garden is better than a dog at keeping burglars away – as long as you don't put out anything too nobby like bay trees in pots. It's just that nobody teaches the young ones about not throwing litter.'

'Or not eating fast-food in the streets.'

'A lot can't cook.'

'Well, they jolly well ought to learn,' said Amelia, crossly. 'I mean, no wonder they're gross and broke if all they eat are Big Macs.'

'Yes, cooking lessons at school would help, but where's the

money for that? State schools can't even afford textbooks, let alone raw food.'

'Why can't their mothers teach them? Why should it be schools?'

'Most of them don't know how. You've no idea how much working-class culture has been destroyed in the past forty years. Everything conspires to produce a state of ignorance and inertia at the bottom end of society. The food they eat is crap, because increasingly it's only people like us who can afford the fresh vegetables and fruit, and the meat that hasn't been pumped full of shit. We're becoming more and more like America, where you can tell how low someone's income is by the size of clothes they wear.'

'You sound as if you think it's deliberate.'

'I do. Nobody gives a damn about them. They're not even called the poor – that might stir people's consciences a bit too much when they read articles in the Sunday papers. They're not good for cheap labour any more; their only role is to terrify people in under-paid jobs that if they dare join a union they can be sacked. Oh, and they keep the social services in business, of course.'

Amelia laughed.

'No, I mean it. There's nobody a medic hates more than a social worker, except perhaps a politician. What was the single biggest advance in health in this country? What do you think?'

'Penicillin?'

'No.'

'Disinfectant?'

'No. It was when the Victorians put down public sewers. Just think – all the drugs and operations and advances of medical science couldn't equal basic urban planning. They're crumbling to bits, of course, now. Everything is done to make things look good, while the infrastructure rots away underneath.'

Tom was always entertaining, if a bit of a lefty, Amelia thought. She was sceptical about his claims, and Mark dismissed them out-right as typical Hampstead nonsense.

'It's middle-class socialists like him who destroyed the grammar schools while educating their own children privately,' he said. 'If your father had sent you to your local comprehensive, you bet it would have had to pull its socks up.'

'Oh, but, my dear, Holland Park was much too expensive,' said Amelia. 'The drugs you had to buy to keep up there cost the earth.'

15

Tom in Casualty

Tom was now the registrar on call in an East End hospital. It was one of the worst jobs in one of the worst hospitals in London, but the nearest District and General he could get. He counted himself lucky, for the consultant who organized rotations for all registrars hadn't got a clue about who was supposed to do what, and he could have found himself high and dry.

If only he could get a consultancy! Nothing had gone right since he had failed his part three fellowship exams a couple of years ago, fluffing the viva with a stupid answer about the parts of the heart, his stammer suddenly erupting and the wrong answer coming out. Nearly everyone failed at least one exam in medicine, but that didn't make it any easier.

It had taken Tom two months of writing and telephoning to remind the co-ordinator that he still had to spend six months in a D and G; he had been hoping for the comparative civilization of the Whittington, but had got this instead.

'I hear you're seeing something of my daughter, Celine,' Gabriel Stern had said, when his protégé rang to keep in touch.

'Yes,' said Tom, startled. He did not think that one night of inebriated sex exactly constituted a relationship, though he had been surprised by the frequency with which she had suggested subsequent meetings.

The Professor cleared his throat. 'I'm very close to my daughter, you know.'

'She's a lovely girl,' said Tom politely, although he felt acutely embarrassed.

'Would you care to spend Pesach with us?'

No, he did not want to have Passover dinner with the Sterns, but Tom could not see a way to avoid it without giving offence. On the other hand, he was increasingly worried, both by Celine's persistent attempts to see him again, and by his own failure to get a better posting. Could the Professor, his referee, be saying the wrong things? Was he bent on revenge for Tom's supposed seduction, or trying to arrange a marriage? Anything was possible, in the Byzantine way that hospital medicine worked.

Driving out, the end of 'Oranges and Lemons' ran through his head:

> '. . . Here comes a chopper to chop off your head
> Chop, chop, chop, chop.'

This was the dead zone of London. No busy politician or royalty bothered to press the flesh out here. For mile after mile there was nothing but tarmac, concrete and broken glass. Half the shops were boarded up or wired over, although the pubs had scalloped metal awnings over them and grey satellite dishes. Only bookies, off-licences and massage-parlours remained in business, interspersed with a few Asian shops. Trains crawled across the cindery plains like metal slugs. Unlike the smart robots transferring journalists to shiny new offices in the Docklands, these old engines slipped along overgrown sidings as though ashamed, the cadence of their wheels exhausted. Some carried commuters to and from the dark of the Underground system; others, it was said, bore toxic waste. You could hear their slow progress for miles, a ghostly whispering along the rails long before and after the wheels had passed.

Centuries ago this had been a fashionable village outside London, considered healthy and agreeable. There had been pleasure gardens, farms, small businesses, streets of exquisite Georgian houses. Bombs and successive waves of development had demolished almost all of it. The original East Enders had mostly moved out to Essex to neat bungalows with chiming doorbells and the highest murder-rate in England. Nobody came here now unless they were forced to. Tom put on a tape of Glenn Gould playing

Bach's fugues that Grub had given him for his birthday. Amelia had been shocked by Kentish Town, but North London was green and pleasant compared with this. East of the City was the real desolation, where the Thames, passing beneath Tower Bridge to the sea, writhed like an intra-uterine loop.

His car stereo would be stolen in seconds if he parked here. The estates were simmering cauldrons of boredom and delinquency, in which virtually the only source of income was crime. When you saw people gathered, it usually meant trouble: twelve-year-olds in stolen trainers lighting a fire, joyriding or worse. Most of the obstetrics cases here were either fourteen-year-olds or the tired-out hags who were their mothers. The places they lived in could have been designed to oppress. Every window was proportioned and positioned to induce claustrophobia inside and disgust outside; every open space a lot to park cars and rubbish; every Saturday night a time for bedlam as the inhabitants of this area tried to stupefy themselves or each other.

Lately, a new and terrible illness had begun to fill the wards. Tuberculosis, which had been almost eradicated for fifty years, was increasing by the month, especially among the homeless. Cold, badly fed, filthy tramps – most of them men – coughed their lungs out, spewing blood over the gowns and sheets. Often they were mistaken for drunks until too late, for nobody wanted to get too close to the sour reek of old beer and vomit.

Medics hated working in D and Gs which, with a couple of exceptions, were the pits. The media, for all its exaggerations and intrusions, kept London's teaching hospitals on their toes, and other places, like Bristol, Oxford and Edinburgh, were in rich enough areas to support first-rate staff. Otherwise, well, it wasn't just north of Watford that your chances of mortality went up, thought Tom. If anyone from Kensington had to be treated here they'd think themselves in the Third World. It was the Third World, effectively. All the monitors were over twenty years old, the doors were just sheets of plastic, the walls were visibly falling apart and the lino so cracked that it looked like they'd had a minor earthquake. Only last month, a dead patient had been found mummifying in the vast heating ducts beneath the hospital, and nobody had any idea who he was. One nearby hospital had had its A and E department closed, following the Tomlinson report, with the result that the sick in its area could not now be treated.

By eight o'clock that night, Casualty was swarming with people vomiting, moaning, spouting blood, coughing in the thick fug of cigarette smoke or just lying like marble effigies on trolleys, waiting for a bed. One lethargic cleaner pushed his mop carefully between the pools of effluent, spreading it more thinly over the floors. The lifts were even worse, and none of the cleaners would touch the loos.

Patients slumped in chairs, row on row of them. A boy had a wodge of cotton wool taped over his eye. An old man had been stabbed for telling a kid not to throw litter. A woman had stomach pains, possible appendicitis, and was taken to X-ray. Another, a heroin addict, had an abscess in her groin. The stench of rotting flesh and pus was added to the rest.

'Put a drip in her. She'll have to be operated on,' said the duty officer, after seeing the addict.

'When?'

'I'll try and get a slot in surgery for Monday, but we're cancelling appointments as it is.'

'Seventeen years old,' said the nurse, despairing. 'Why do they do it?'

'Fuck off, you silly cunt!' shrieked the addict, as Tom tried to find a vein for the drip. Most were ruined, imploded in a mass of scar tissue. Her legs were criss-crossed with scars where she had laid heroin on neat. Her feet, fingers, hands looked as though they had been burnt. Tom had even seen those who had tried to inject their eyelids, such was their desperation. She was pale brown with dirt, and each time he tried to insert a needle he had to wash her skin. Everyone wore rubber gloves, and his hands sweated horribly inside them.

'You fucking cunts,' the girl shrieked. 'What the fuck d'you think you're doing, you fucking fuckers? Lemme go!'

Two of the porters held her down, and Tom, after washing her more or less all over, eventually managed to find a vein for the drip.

'No food, no fags, no drugs for six hours,' he said grimly. Addicts were generally loathed; they were not only filthy and unpleasant but manipulative and almost impossible to form any kind of relationship with as patients.

He left the trolley and hurried on to the next, and the next, and the next. Each case demanded twenty minutes of paperwork; people could literally die in a fog of bureaucracy because every hospital was now so frightened of being sued if anything went wrong. All sixteen of the trolley bays filled up, and soon patients were being held in the corridors. The doctors seemed to do everything, from clerking patients in to rushing them off to theatre.

'Why don't they get more bloody porters?' someone asked.

'Because junior doctors are cheaper,' said a houseman.

One man had an axe in his head, and two policemen were trying to take a statement from him.

'Dunno nuffink,' he said to every question. 'My brains is scrambled, isn't they?'

When he saw Tom, he gave him a wink. 'How's the motor?'

'Fine, thanks,' said Tom.

'Any time you want a new one, you give us a shout.'

This patient was known as Bruv, of Bruv & Bruv. He was a used-car dealer of sorts, and gave medics a special deal, arranging for their old cars to be stolen so they could claim on the insurance. Bruv was involved in some sort of gang warfare, and turned up in Casualty at least once every six weeks with more and more exotic wounds. Tom was quite fond of him, although he had prudently declined his offer of a Peugeot 'not hot enough to warm your hands by'.

A Bangladeshi woman, clearly in agony but unable to speak English, was trying to tell a houseman what was wrong with her, while her two terrified little girls clutched their father.

'Does it hurt here? Or here?'

The woman nodded politely and smiled each time.

'I should have been a vet,' the houseman muttered.

The casualty officer, a woman whose hair stood out of her head as if electrocuted, was shrieking at a houseman.

'He needs a chest X-ray and his blood done. This patient has been here twenty minutes, that's unacceptable! Do it!'

'I've done it.'

The woman had worked herself up into such a froth of rage, she seemed not to hear. 'You must work faster, that's what Casualty's about. There are people who've been here for over four hours! To think I'd just phoned your next post to tell them how good you were!'

Bitch, thought Tom.

'Don't worry,' he said to the houseman. She was on the verge of tears. 'She can't do a thing. It's not her job.'

She was Asian, probably of Indian origin, and her name was Laili. Almost half the housemen were Asian: only the children of new immigrants wanted to be doctors. Medicine had once been dominated by Jews, thought Tom, but now the only ones who entered it rather than the City were those like himself, who had inherited the rabbinical ambivalence about money. Asians, thank God, still saw it as a way of both rising in and repaying the society that had taken them in, although the racism they endured from their hosts sickened him. More than once Tom had had to take over because a patient refused to be touched by 'black hands'. The rings beneath Laili's eyes were like bruises.

'I think I've got flu.'

'Don't be silly,' said Tom. 'You're a doctor, not a nurse.'

'I've got a fever.'

'If you're ill, some other houseman has to cover for you. You see anyone who's prepared to do that? You think they're going to get a locum out of thin air? Take paracetamol.'

Faces, faces, faces. A woman dressed only in a sheet arrived, entirely naked, flesh hanging from her skeleton like raw dough.

'Picked up in London Fields,' said the policeman who had brought her in. 'We think she may have concussion.'

'Any name?'

'No.'

The woman coughed, and a spurt of brilliant red blood gushed out of her mouth.

'Oh dear,' said the nurse. 'Here's another.'

'There's a Yiddish proverb: "If the rich could hire other people to die for them, the poor could make a wonderful living,"' said Tom. 'Test for TB.'

He ran backwards and forwards to Intensive Care as his crash bleep went off. By two a.m., the trolleys were jamming the corridors, and a second shift of nurses came on. Half of them were agency nurses, costing the hospital a small fortune, because the nurses had a proper union that demanded they worked no more than an eight-hour shift. It was one of the hardest things to bear, that medics had so much more training and responsibility and no proper union. On call, over week ends and bank holidays, Tom thought angrily, we're paid less than the cleaners. Any overtime was paid at half the normal rate. From time to time, someone dredged up the energy for a protest; but nobody really expected junior doctors' hours to drop. Those who had suffered in the same system underwent a miraculous conversion as soon as they became consultants.

'What are you complaining about?' one, in his late thirties, had said. 'You only do a one in three. We did a one in two. You've got it soft.'

Tom's consultant had decamped at six on Friday to go to Covent Garden, leaving the registrars in charge. Consultants were always doing that, they thought they'd earned it, and the bugger of it was, you had to stay on their good side because at least one had to be your referee for your next job. What do I do if Stern expects me to get serious about Celine? Tom thought, cursing the impulse of shyness and randiness that had got him into trouble again. You couldn't afford to piss anyone off, least of all your precious patron.

Casualty was like being in the trenches: the only thing you could do was hope to make it through with a couple of mates. Tom was relieved that his partner was Klaus. Klaus was a good bloke, Tom thought. He'd never known a German before – being instinctively prickly about even visiting the country where so many of his mother's family had died in concentration camps – but Klaus was a different generation, even taller than himself and polite to a fault. His accent got him spat in the face at least once a week by older patients, but he had never been known to lose his temper. Like a lot of young German medics, he could only get the necessary hours to qualify outside his own country, but he couldn't believe how drab and run-down British hospitals were.

'Before I came here, I worked with Simonaides at King's. A world expert in obstetric radiology, and you have him in an office the size of a – is it dog-house?'

'Enjoy the film last night?'

'Yes. Your girlfriend, she's very beautiful, very *gemütlich*.'

'D'you think so?' said Tom, surprised.

'Yes,' said Klaus.

'I'm very fond of her,' said Tom. 'But she wants to get married.'

Without the Germans and the Asians, British hospitals would simply cease to function, Tom thought. Every doctor he knew now told their friends' children, 'Do anything, anything at all except medicine.' It didn't seem to stop them, of course. It was a vocation; and hospital medicine in particular. What he did, the practical fascination of seeing a drug work immediately, of getting someone to trust him with their life, was a kind of seduction.

His mother had got out, as soon as she qualified, unable to take the strain of being on call on top of having two young boys. Tom still had dim memories of her going off to work, not daring even to hug them goodbye in case she broke down, of creeping into his parents' bedroom to smell her scent because he missed her so much.

'I don't ever want to have a wife with a career that takes her out of the house once we have children,' he had said fiercely to Josh.

'What you want is impossible,' said his brother. 'You'll never be happy with someone who isn't as bright as you, and she'll never be happy without a career.'

'I know,' said Tom. 'And neither can I afford to marry anyone who doesn't work, unless she has a private income.'

He thought of Sarah's large, white, slightly protruding teeth, her thin brown face, at once sexy and predatory. She was adamant that she would go into private practice as soon as possible, and make some 'real money'. He sometimes wondered whether what she really liked about him was the people he knew; her curiosity and social ambition to be introduced to people like Andrew Evenlode and Amelia were almost as embarrassing as their complete lack of interest in her. Generations of hard-living, hard-working middle-class ancestors showed under her like bedrock. She would not be the kind to take an overdose if he chucked her. He wondered, briefly, how Adam's friend was, little Mary Quinn. She had rung him up to ask him to dinner in a fortnight. Out of curiosity, he had accepted. Another mistake, probably.

His trauma bleep went off, and voices crackled over a message about a car-crash – eight on the coma scale. His heartbeat accelerated. There was a rush for the stretcher as a young man was brought in, screaming, smelling like a burnt potato. Even the registrars began to gag. Blood was one thing, everyone was used to that smell, but burns upset even those who had seen thousands die. Everyone moved with incredible rapidity. Three nurses began cutting off the remains of the boy's clothes while Tom pierced the crackled skin with diamorphine. The screaming stopped. The drip above the trolley was emptying so fast the nurse could hardly get the next up quickly enough.

'Is there a bed in intensive care?'

'I don't think so.'

'Jesus Christ. Start phoning.'

'He won't make it if we move him again.'

'He probably won't anyway, but ring, ring! There's got to be somewhere. Anyone know his name?'

The rapidity with which they moved stirred the other patients in Casualty out of their own apathy. One pounced on Tom as he sat down to write up his notes.

'Hey – you – I'm talking to you, sunshine! What about my mother? You doctors are all the same, sitting on your arses like bloody layabouts.'

Tom looked at her with bleary eyes. He had been working now for thirty eight hours, and was having difficulty in focusing. 'I'm sorry. You can see, Saturday night's not the night to have something wrong with you.'

Through a glass door he could see Klaus desperately trying to find a bed. A consultant could pull one, but all the consultants were, of course, at home asleep. His accent would count against him. Tom knew he should try to help, but exhaustion made him selfish. Let him sort it out, he thought.

'None of your bloody lip! We've got a Patients' Charter now, and some of us have been waiting for well over four hours. I could have you in court.'

'The reason why you are waiting,' said Tom, 'is because there aren't enough doctors as it is to see to everyone at once. If you want to tie up even more of us in useless litigation the queues will get even longer. On the other hand, if you would care to write to your MP about the state of this hospital, and about the others all over London being merged and closed down you might just possibly get better service. Though I very much doubt it.'

Laili rushed up. 'Have you seen that IV woman?'

'No. Isn't she in the ward?'

'We can't find her anywhere. It looks like she's got out with the cannula in her.'

Tom sighed. 'She'll be shooting up somewhere through it, then. Old addicts' trick. Don't worry, the vein'll block off in a couple of days – if the abscess doesn't get her first.'

At five a.m. on Sunday there was a lull. Everyone who was going to die had snuffed it, and the rest had decided to hang on, at least until Sunday lunch was over. He walked along the endless corridors to the cafeteria, watching the dawn.

'Sorry, dear, the caff's closed.'

'Can't you just give me a sandwich?' Tom begged. 'Or a piece of fruit?'

'Sorry. You doctors should learn to bring your own.'

The man who used to run the café was now a hospital manager, earning three times what Tom did, with offices overlooking the grounds, and his brand new car. Clearly, his replacement had ambitions in the same direction.

Back along the corridors to the doctors' room. It was furnished with sagging, filthy old chairs and overflowing with cigarette stubs. Laili was snuffling in one corner, in rhythm with the Kenco coffee-maker which, after seven applications to various committees, had been bought by the doctors clubbing together. The milk was all powdered.

'Perhaps one of the nurses will have a biscuit,' said Tom.

'Here.' She held out a packet of digestives.

'Thanks. Thanks very much. How d'you feel?'

'Like death.'

'That's medicine,' said Tom. 'Cure the patient, kill the doctor.'

'I fought so hard to become a doctor,' she said. 'My family didn't even want me to take A levels. And then I –'

'You mustn't let it get to you,' said Tom.

'All I want to do is help people, and they won't even let me touch them because I'm black.'

Utter weariness made him silent. Either you survived or you went under: three times the average rate of suicide, three times the rate of alcoholism, seven times the rate of divorce.

'So, grow a thicker skin. You know what Yeager said to me when I joined? "We always try to get a few Jews and Asians on board around Christmas because they can cover for everyone else then."'

There was a pause, then a watery smile.

Klaus came in, yawning.

'What happened to that burns patient?'

'Airlifted to Manchester. You missed the helicopter.'

'That'll cost a pretty penny.'

Tom's bleep went off.

It was the woman who had been brought in earlier. The tuberculosis was too far advanced to be stopped by the drugs being pumped into her. Another hopeless case. Her skin was almost as white as the sheets on which she lay, so white it made her hair look yellow again, but in her cheeks the bright red spot gave the illusion of health. Probably not more than fifty – forty-five, even, thought Tom. Her voice was not at all what he had expected, in so far as he expected anything these days, being soft, almost educated.

'Am I dying?'

'Yes,' said Tom.

The nurse who had called him said urgently, 'What's your name? Do you have any relations? Family?'

'Grace,' the woman said. 'Tell Grace – Queen's Estate – Camden –'

A violent spasm of coughing.

'Your surname? What's your surname?'

The woman opened her eyes, and said, before the light went out of them, 'Kenward.'

16

Mary in Chelsea

To be a single woman in London is not pleasant after the age of twenty-seven. There were those who claimed to be free of any wish for a partner, busying themselves with the cultural life of the city as spinsters in the past once devoted themselves to charity. They proclaimed the joys of childlessness, worked long hours, wore clothes so fashionable they looked demented, and were rumoured to be lesbian.

Then there were those others, only a couple of years older than Mary, who stacked up like aeroplanes waiting for a landing slot: every year you could see them reappear until one day, having either run out of fuel or found a mate, they vanished from the horizon. They, too, could be seen at every book launch and private view, laughing a little too often. It was a mystery why these women remained single, thought Mary, for they were pretty, intelligent, pleasant, entertaining, affectionate, and above all successful. Were they too choosy? Did they frighten men off? Or was it simply that, once over thirty, they were too old?

This last thought worried, but did not preoccupy her as it had formerly. She wanted revenge, not a husband; she did not think any man after Mark would be capable of holding her interest, and she did not think she could possibly attract anyone else. She would never get married, have children, a home – but she might, she thought, get her own back, somehow.

Hatred bears all things, believes all things, hopes all things, endures all things. Something in her hardened. All sexual feeling had died since the day of her attempted suicide: she felt as if it had been amputated from her body, occasionally itchy like a phantom limb but otherwise gone. She had believed herself radically changed by Mark, but now she understood that she had remained as naïve as if she had just stepped off the ferry. She saw that she would have to construct a network of new friends – for everything, as Ivo had told her, depended on networking – and that to do so she would have to have dinner parties. Parties were no good. You could meet the same person a dozen times a year, and have the same inconsequential conversation; but dinner parties provided more intimacy and incurred, therefore, a greater debt. It would be difficult to entertain people, living in a bedsit on a disposable income of about ten pounds a week, but not impossible. Nothing was impossible to one who hated as Mary did.

She had three advantages. One was that she could cook, and people were so exhausted by work they would do anything, including driving through London traffic jams at eight thirty, in order not to face the dreariness of thinking about food and washing up. The second was that, if she invited Ivo, other people would want to come to meet him. The third was that in London, address is destiny. Even in the property slump, Londoners were as snobbish about your address as they once were about your ancestry: better a bedsit in Chelsea than a mansion in Muswell Hill.

Phoebe Viner, her landlady, was an odd creature. When Mary first met her she thought she was some sort of Indian workman, for she was wearing a purple turban and mending the front doorstep. Then she saw that Phoebe's thin brown hand was adorned with an enormous gold and amethyst ring.

'I've been icing a cake all morning and I keep getting this bloody stuff mixed up with the marzipan,' Phoebe said, in a deep hoarse voice. 'Whisky? Gin? Cha?'

'Tea would be grand,' said Mary, unsure if that was on offer.

'So,' said Tom's great-aunt, 'I hear you need somewhere to live, in exchange for housework. Have you done cleaning before?'

'I've practically got Harpic in my veins,' said Mary.

'And you're a friend of my wicked great-nevvew.'

'A friend of a friend,' said Mary, cautiously. Phoebe looked at her shrewdly, eyes blue as gentians in the shale of her face.

'Well, it's an utter tip, but quite habitable, I suppose. Now, I need six hours a week, hoovering and all that, not being so steady on my pins and pretty bored with the whole caboodle. That OK? Such a bore, moving dust from one place to another. Gardening's my thing. You smoke?'

'No.'

'Ah. Pity,' said Phoebe, putting a cigarette in a long lacquer holder and lighting it. 'No point in stopping just to hang on for another twenty years as a dribbling old crone. What are your vices?'

'I'm not sure,' said Mary, startled. She felt dull and rustic. 'I tried drink for a bit, but that didn't really work.'

Phoebe laughed, her face wrinkling up under the purple turban. 'Not men?'

Mary shook her head.

'Women?'

'No.'

'Can't see the point of women, really,' said Phoebe.

Mary could see that Phoebe suspected she had had an affair with Tom, and flushed. 'I was living with someone for years, and then he decided to marry someone else.'

Phoebe gave a Delphic sniff. 'Well shot of him, then.'

They drank their tea, and went downstairs to the hall. It was an exquisitely pretty house, with wisteria twining up to a balcony in front, but a mess inside. Phoebe jabbed at the walls with her cigarette, scattering ash. 'I was a Muse, you see. Most of the pictures here are of me. That's Bonnard. That's Kitaj. And that's Augustus John.'

'Most gratifying,' said Mary, politely.

'They'll all go to Tom, you know, when I croak. He's the only one with an eye for paint. All my nieces and nevvews chose something to be theirs, and they went for dull things like grandfather clocks and rugs. He chose my Whistler.'

'You've got a Whistler?'

'He'll get a surprise one day when it's valued. It's the only thing worth having, art, you know. Not all these dull stocks and shares people tell you about.'

The basement was dingy, and full of junk.

'Would you mind very much if I did a bit of painting?'

'Good heavens, child, of course not,' said Phoebe. 'As long as you don't block the drains or play loud music you can do what you like. Provided I get my six hours. No cleaning, no flat. That's the deal.'

'You will. Thank you,' said Mary. 'Thank you very much.'

She rang her mother in Belfast, who sounded as relieved as she felt.

Adam, who was largely responsible for her stroke of good luck, said, 'Just keep your legs crossed if Tom comes round to call.'

'You sound like the nuns.'

'I've already had to scoop up one emotional meltdown. Don't have another.'

There was a multiplicity of pipes and little direct sunlight. The bathroom, tucked under the stairs, had a cast-iron bath, with ball-and-claw feet. The bedsit had a Victorian fireplace, a sagging brown sofa and brown velvet curtains that absorbed much of the light seeping through the small square window. Her view from this was of two boarded-up coal holes extending under the street, railings, and passing feet; from the kitchen she could look up to Phoebe's garden, where cats wandered over the trellised walls and marble urns. Later, during the summer, she could hear the chatter and clink of drinks parties, all of which seemed to be attended by people with the loudest, most self-satisfied voices in the world:

'There's Jonty Paddington, now he's a silk –'

'Spot of trouble at the Dragon, Summerhill's a better bet –'

'The *most* divine little man –'

'Just a drop.'

Mary bought two large mirrors from a junk shop across the river. The most speckled she fixed outside, on the whitewashed wall below the railings, framed by three pieces of trellis. Two large pots planted with clematis and jasmine were trained up it, and she planned to plant a trough with flowers in front. The other mirror she fixed opposite the window, doubling the light.

'What d'you think?' she asked Adam proudly.

'It looks like every other basement in Chelsea,' he said.

Everything Mary did next was a private act of defiance against the memory of Mark's regime of tasteful beige. The walls of her bedsit she painted yellow, flecked with gold. She stitched long pieces of calico to the short brown curtains, extending them to the floor, and looped them back with gold-painted rope and a large tassel. The sofa and her narrow single bed she covered with more calico, printed with gold stars. The haircord carpet was irremediable, but acceptable when scrubbed. She made new calico lampshades for Phoebe's lamps, fixed six candelabra, twisted out of wire and painted gold, on the walls, blacked the fireplace and stuck cut-out cherubs and angels from wrapping paper onto the ceiling. She did not have the money for pictures.

The kitchen was papered with old sheet music, varnished, and given a new light. The stove dated from the 1930s, but cooked beautifully, and the small fridge worked after she had turned it upside down and jiggled it. She threw out two cupboards and kept only a card-table, on which to work, eat, prepare food, and, joined to its twin next door, entertain. The bathroom, already gloomy, she painted deep blue, and the bath deep pink. Another mirror, its frame stuck with shells, hung over the basin, and a plastic lobster held the toilet roll in its claws. By the end of a fortnight she was caked in paint, her head swimming from the fumes. Yet she had achieved very nearly the effect she wanted. It was clean, and stylish, and not the kind of place in which you would expect to find Betty Quinn's daughter living. It was to be the place of her re-creation.

Adam visited her at least once a week, partly to make sure that she was not about to let the muscle of resolution go slack, and partly, she could see, out of pure terror as the day of his publication approached. She had thought him as self-contained as an egg, but now he was cracking and running all over the place, unnaturally polite to anyone in journalism while making it clear he despised them. He reacted to her sudden transformation into a critic with irritating censoriousness. 'Those who can, do; those who can't, review.'

'I have no ambition to be a writer,' said Mary, annoyed.

'No, but you are a reader. A reader is to a critic what a – a rose is to a begonia. Come on, Mary. There must be something better. Proper journalism, if you must.'

'What? – "The house had once had balconies. Closing my ears to the cries of women mourning their dead, I inched along Snipers Alley." I've already spent most of my life hanging round a bar, thanks.'

'You sound different.'

'I *am* different,' said Mary. 'I intend to become a monster.'

Adam smiled.

'No, I mean it. You can either accept the awfulness life hands you, or you can rebel, as Ivo said. What good has it done me to be obedient to the idea that any moral order rules my existence? Mark was right. I've been trying to live as if God were taking notice, and the fact is, there's nobody, and as long as I refuse to play the game, I'll be nobody, too.'

'It isn't a game. What goes around, comes around.'

'But it doesn't, it doesn't!' said Mary, fiercely, running her hands through her hair until it stood up in shining spikes. 'That's the whole point. People like Mark and Amelia get rewarded for their sins. People think I'm mad even to think of sin. Nobody gives a damn; if anything, they admire them for it. It's like Darwinism – only the fittest wins.'

'You misunderstand Darwinism, if that's what you believe,' said Adam. 'A species survives as much by co-operation as by competition. The world is not overrun with predators. Furthermore, human predators are not generally admired, even by others of their kind.'

'You think so?' said Mary. 'Well, we'll see.'

She asked Adam to dinner with Ivo, Tom and two other single girls she had vaguely kept in touch with despite Mark's disapproval. She told herself she was doing Adam a favour, that it would help him, for the rumours concerning his novel were not good.

It was not Mary's fault that the evening did not go well. She had cooked watercress soup and *coq au vin*, but not even the chocolate bread and butter pudding seemed to lessen the tension. Part of it was Tom's fault, she thought, for the other girls could do nothing but giggle and gawp at him; and part was the antagonism between the three men. She had not realized that Ivo disliked Tom so much, or that it was mutual. The worst thing, though, was the way Adam behaved.

She had never seen Adam in company before. He hardly ever went out, and clearly believed that he had to perform in some way. The result was painful, for all his usual wit was translated into a caricature of his true nature.

'How long did your novel take to write?' asked Ivo.

'Oh, two months,' said Adam, smirking. 'And a lifetime.'

'Really? What sort of thing is it? A novel of ideas?'

'Well, yes, but it also has a plot. It's about a young man who spends his gap year in Provence and discovers a lot of things, especially about his own nature.'

'Oh, rite-of-passage,' said Ivo, dismissively. 'I do wish aspiring writers would stop picking their spots. You should do some reviewing if you want to distinguish yourself.'

'No,' said Adam. 'My opinion is much like Flaubert's: a man becomes a critic when he cannot be an artist, in the same way that he becomes an informer when he cannot be a soldier.'

'This will not do,' said Ivo, reading Mary's copy after everyone had left.

'I'm sorry,' she said, wringing the dishcloth. 'What an appalling evening. He's not usually like that.'

Mary had read *Other Feet* by Flora Payne three times: first in hospital, where she thought her inability to understand why it had been published must be due to ailment, second to try to find some redeeming features about it, and last to check her quotes. She now felt she knew every sentence of its two hundred pages by heart.

Ivo ignored her apology. He had already decided how to deal with Adam. 'Did you think this a good book?'

'I've never loathed a novel so much in my life.'

'Well, why didn't you say so?'

'I thought my hatred might be irrational.'

'That's the first thing that happens with any piece of journalism,' said Ivo, genially. 'Profiles are the worst. You interview someone, you get on, and then when you sit down to write, the whole thing is such a pain in the arse that you'd prefer to shoot them. Any more Armagnac?'

'I did tell you I'd be useless. I haven't been to university, I'll never be any good.'

Ivo sipped. He had already drunk half the bottle. 'Oh, you will be. You know what you're talking about, you just don't know how to make it readable. "This novel is about a housewife living in North Oxford –" Your reader will be asleep by the second sentence. Look, what's the first thing a review has got to do?'

'Tell you about the book?'

'No.'

'Tell you about the author?'

'No.'

'What, then?'

'It's got to make you want to read it. Look, forget anything Mark may have told you.' Mary blinked. 'A review is a piece of journalism, just like any other. If you get someone to read what you write, you've done half your job. Every single article in a newspaper isn't just so much information. It's a pitched battle with the reader's indifference, laziness, telephone or wish for another cup of coffee. You have to grab them by the balls and hang on.' Ivo looked at her and smiled. It was not a nice smile.

'That sounds –'

'Like a tabloid? Well, all journalists who are any good learn from tabloids, not from posh broadsheets. Of course,' Ivo added, sighing, 'once you become famous, people will read you simply to know what you think. That's why most of our reviewers are crap. We have to have big names, but most of them have forgotten how to write, assuming they ever knew. And the absolute dregs of them write for the Books Pages. Why? Because it's the lowest form of journalism there is. And the lowest form of that is reviewing fiction. You don't have to go out and discover things for yourself. You don't have to sit at the end of a telephone line. You don't even have to know anything about the subject. All you have to do is read a couple of hundred pages of someone wanking their imagination, and write five hundred moderately clever words about it'

Despite her tension, Mary laughed. Ivo slid down onto the floor beside her. 'Christ, I'm pissed. Where's that bottle?'

'You make it sound so easy.'

'It is, even if you bother to read what you review.'

'Do you mean – people don't?'

'Good heavens, no. Skim, my darling, skim.' He began to stroke her knee, in an absent-minded manner. 'You read the first chapter, last chapter and the blurb. It's immensely important to learn how to skin. I mean skim. Someone like myself skims a dozen books a day. That's why real pros put all their best effort into the beginnings and ends of books. You can't possibly be expected to read every word; reviewers are paid far too little for it to be worth their while.' Mary seized her courage, and his hand, in both of hers. 'Ivo, don't. Please. I'm not – I just can't.'

'I'm feeling sentimental.'

Inside herself, Mary laughed indignantly. If this was his technique with women, no wonder it met with so little success. She patted him awkwardly, and said with determined briskness, 'I read the book you gave me three times, just to make sure I was accurate.'

'Well, even if you've got something completely wrong, there's nothing the author or the publisher can do about it,' said Ivo. 'Anyone who writes a letter of complaint about a review practically commits suicide.'

'But if I made an actual mistake, wouldn't the newspaper owe the author an apology?'

'Good heavens no. Nobody except the author ever cares about inaccuracy. Who gives a toss if you say their hero is a one-legged Spaniard called Mary when in fact he's a blind Mexican called Jesus? After all, what is any kind of review but free advertising? Why do you think newspapers get free books? Because any publicity, even the most unfavourable, is better than none.'

'Yes,' said Mary, sadly. She pondered what he had told her. 'What if a reader catches you out?'

Ivo erupted. 'Reviewers don't write for *readers*,' he said. 'They write for each other. On the whole, it's safer to damn than to praise. It always makes you look better.'

'Isn't it awfully unfair? I mean, most books aren't wholly good, or even wholly bad. They're a sort of mixture.'

'Yes, but what *we* want is an opinion,' said Ivo. 'Any newspaper thrives on opinion. Who are the highest-paid hacks in the land? Not some clod in Hush Puppies who writes the news. It's the movers and shakers. We're diseased with information, so that people are less and less able to make up their own minds about anything. Your job is to make it up for them. Look, this isn't a charity. You have to ask yourself, "What has this book done to *deserve* to be published?"'

'I see,' said Mary slowly. 'Put like that . . . But what if you miss out something good by mistake? It's often a matter of taste, and –'

'Short of major crime, once you're on the circuit you practically never get off – unless the editors who commission you get sacked. Most are like Angus – they know fuck-all about literature and just see it as an incidental way of adding to their circulation and advertising revenue. But every now and again they mumble something about "spicing up the Books Pages", and then you have to drag in a semi-literate actress to do "Sex Tips for Cats" or whatever. No, the real bane is that lit. eds resign once they write a book, like Marian. Of course they get raves everywhere, because nobody in their right mind wants to antagonize a source of commissions by saying, "Actually, this is a pile of old tripe." So then the editor thinks he or she can really write and chucks it all in for Art. And you lose your patron.'

'There's no chance Mark might write a book, I suppose?' said Mary.

'Not a hope. Don't fret, my darling, Uncle Ivo has other plans for Mark. Now, go away and strike out your first paragraph. Always strike out the first paragraph, it's what you write before you've started to think. Try and start with a joke. The English hate culture, so you've always got to sugar the pill. Make sure your first paragraph and your last link up, like an O level essay. If possible, make a joke at the author's expense. On the other hand, if you're going to praise, use two adjectives instead of one; then you'll get quoted on the paperback.'

'As in, "absolutely fabulous"?'

'That's right. Personally, I think that to be quoted on a paperback is a sign of failure, authors are never grateful enough. Oh, and if you want to operate in the favours market remember that there's a whole code for it. If you want to say someone is a snobbish, humourless poof you should write their book is "civilized, dry and graceful". Anything that's "lyrical" is rubbish, "off-beat" is unreadable, and "original" means the author is practically certifiable. You'll soon get the hang of it.'

'You make reviewers sound like estate agents,' said Mary.

'Estate agents,' said Ivo, stroking his bow-tie with a happy smile, 'have just had a code of practice forced on them.'

17

Grace and Favour

Grace and Billy picked their way along the street that led to the Outer Circle of Regent's Park. The scarred plane tree was in leaf now, but all the saplings planted on the pavement had been snapped off by bored teenagers. Ghetto-blasters echoed round the dull air as though in a canyon. A Wall's ice-cream van did a slow circuit, suffocating the competition with its jingling yell.

> Girls and boys come out to play
> The moon is shining as bright as day!
> Girls and boys come out to play
> The moon is shining as bright as day!

The tune stuttered, and repeated itself, again and again. But it was the sun that shone, blanched by the haze overhead to a dull coin. There had been no rain for weeks, and the air was yellow and foul. Everyone had stinging eyes and a dry throat. Nobody wanted to travel by Underground; just going past the stations you could see the filth rolling slowly out, like smoke. The traffic jams lasted until late at night.

All over the estate mothers, wound up into a pitch of hatred, lashed out at their children, whining for ice-cream. It was not ice-cream at all, but a dollop of emulsified pig fat and sugar, aerated, and as expensive as the genuine article sold down in Chalk Farm. Yet the children were mad for it.

'No, Billy,' said Grace. 'It's full of naughty-bad germs.'

Billy trotted alongside her, holding her hand and wheezing.

Warnings had been broadcast about keeping asthmatics and children indoors, but how could you stay cooped up in a boiling one-bedroom flat with the park just round the corner?

'Gorgeous cars,' he said. 'Wed car. White car. Yellow car. Bus.'

'What colour is the bus?'

'Wed.'

'What letter and number can you see on it?'

'C2', said Billy, after a pause, for this is what the bus that passed the Queen's Estate had been designated.

'Clever boy!'

'We're going to Sainsbury's.'

'Later.'

Across the pelican crossing, through a passageway, and there ahead was the park, a sweep of green ringed by great houses gleaming behind the private gardens that set them back from the road. Some had white statues on their roofs, in classical drapery, others imposing fluted columns.

'Hallo, stone people, hallo,' Billy said, waving to them. He talked happily to statues, especially the two of babies in the Rose Garden. They commented admiringly on his new trainers from Woolworths, with velcro straps, and he asked them why they were wearing nappies. Grace laughed, and laughed again when he pointed to the statue of a merman in the middle of a fountain, surrounded by nymphs, saying, 'There's Daddy.'

'That's just like him, petal.'

'My daddy's big an' strong. My daddy's vewwy vewwy handsome.'

Billy had never seen his father. Grace, who had seen him once since the birth, had crossed the street to avoid saying hallo.

There was a time when all men were 'Daddy', but now he knew there could be only one. Anyone he liked the look of, black or white, he'd go up to.

It was terrible, trying to live on the dole, but she would never go back to her husband. I must have been mad, she thought; but it was madness that she had wanted to escape. Billy was growing like a weed, and he really needed new shoes every three months. He was going to nursery school in the morning now, and that was

£100 a term. Even the extra £20 a week babysitting money from Georgina only went so far in lifting them out of the debt-collector's clutches. She owed money on everything – that was the trouble with having to buy from catalogues; they let you have credit and pay it off every week, but it meant that a washing machine cost you double in the end. Yet you had to have a washing machine, because of all the mess a kid made, and launderettes were too much.

She was registered with a cleaning agency, but so far they had only come up with terrible jobs – women in St John's Wood who followed her round and tried to knock a couple of pounds off the hourly rate, although they were dripping with money, a single bloke who had scared her so much she had taken the spray of Flash with her, just in case, an old lady who had rung up complaining Grace had broken her Hoover though it was fifty years old and on its last gasp. In desperation, Grace had trudged round all the libraries, putting up a handwritten card saying, 'HONEST RELIABLE CLEANER, CAMDEN', with her phone number.

Grace had faith in public libraries. They were the only places that sheltered those damaged by London, or by life – the homeless, the elderly, the lonely, the single parents like herself. There was always a smell, especially round the newspaper tables where the tramps and winos sat, and the floors were all filthy, the toys and books torn and bashed. But they existed, despite all the cuts. She had no more hope of escape than someone on a desert island sending a message in a bottle, but the libraries were that bottle.

They sat on the short, prickly blond grass, resting. Billy loved to run and play, but his asthma would catch up with him and force him to stop. If only we could get out of our flat, Grace thought, but the only other flats for single mothers were hundreds of miles away, in the north of England, and she didn't know anyone there. At least here she had some mates, and Georgina to babysit for. Couples were lying on top of each other, or eating sandwiches. A group of self-conscious young Japanese played frisbee while one plucked at a guitar and sang a Beatles tune.

'Mummy's sad,' said Billy, after a while, putting his arms around her.

'Mummy's sad,' Grace agreed.

'Nana's dead.'

'Nana's gone to heaven, to live with God,' said Grace.

'And Mary,' said Billy. He liked Mary, and always went up to the statue of her after Mass. Last Sunday he had given Grace no end of a turn by asking, 'Where's Baby Jesus?'

'Somewhere else,' said Grace, not wanting to explain yet that he was the man hanging from the cross over the altar.

Grace said, 'Nana was my mummy, and I'll miss her.'

'Will you die?'

'One day, but not for a long, long time. Not until you're grownup and have a home of your own.'

'I don't want to grow up,' said Billy, passionately. 'I want to stay with you, for ever.'

A hospital in the East End had traced them. She and Billy had to have tests to see if they had picked up TB as well. Grace was not looking forward to holding her son still while they took blood from him.

They walked slowly through the park to the benefits office, where Grace had to sign on. The queue stretched round the block, people standing docilely, shuffling forward every five minutes. Once inside, it was worse. There were rows of moulded plastic chairs to sit on, all facing a bank of desks behind steel mesh and glass. Most people chain-smoked, and Billy's wheeze became louder. They could not go out, in case they lost their place. This was what the dole did to you: it leached your initiative and your self-respect until you were afraid even to make a fuss for your child. Grace tried reading to him in a soft voice, which made the others stare at them, but nothing could distract Billy. At last, she screwed up her courage and walked over to yank on a metal chain to try to get some air in. The windows were painted shut. There was silence, apart from a low murmur of acrimony at the desks in front, and the wail of children. People read tattered copies of the *Sun*, or stared, stupefied, into their inner darkness. It took three hours to get to the desks to sign on. Nobody protested, for the only thing they had to spend was time.

'I'm sorry, petal,' she said. 'It just couldn't wait.'

Once a month she had to go through this horrible, grinding humiliation, being asked whether she was earning anything. She kept quiet about the babysitting, of course, though that extra £20 a week was what really kept them both afloat, and Georgina didn't seem to mind about bringing Billy too.

'He's such a good little boy, isn't he?' she said, marvelling at the way he just fell asleep as soon as Grace put him down on the sofa. Cosmo and Flora always took an hour or more of coaxing, crashing about and demanding games. Georgina was a nice one, though, so grateful, and always paid for a minicab back.

At last, released from the office, they made their way to the tube. Grace tried to quell her worries about her son by thinking that if he got any worse they were going to a hospital anyway. She held Billy against her thin side, trying to comfort him, but the heat was so intense that he squirmed away.

'Not long, now, petal,' she said, soothingly.

They could not read on the train, the swerving made them both sick. She tried to amuse him by pointing out advertisements. On and on the train went, miles out to the East End, so far that it actually came up out of the ground, and everyone looked around, blinking frowzily in the sunlight, the smell of cinders replaced by hot rubber, and pink London Pride blowing in the wind made by their passing.

It was better out here, and the hospital itself was set in trees and green lawns, like a grand house.

'Used to be a loony bin,' said the bus driver; and Grace grimaced.

The body was Joy's, of course. There was no doubt about that.

'It just took us longer to trace you because she gave a different surname,' said the clerk.

'What?'

'Kenward,' he said, looking at Joy's notes.

Grace shook her head. 'That's never been her name. Our name's Bailey. But that's my mum, poor soul. What'll you do now?'

'You can make arrangements to have her buried, now she's been identified.'

'Me? I can't afford a funeral. I'm on the dole.'

'Well, someone from the social services will have to talk to you about that,' said the clerk, uninterested.

'But she's Catholic,' said Grace, distressed. 'They won't do it properly.'

'She can't stay here.'

They were directed to have blood samples taken, queuing for another hour in Outpatients. Billy was not crying, like most of the kids; he didn't have the energy. He just sat there, slumped against her, his tawny head lolling, and the fans in his straining chest grew louder and louder.

'Excuse me,' said Grace, worried.

'Number, please.'

'I haven't got a number for this.'

'Then I can't help you. What's your name?'

The woman at the desk began to tap into her computer.

'Grace Bailey. And Billy Bailey.'

'Date of birth?'

Grace told her.

'Address?'

'Look. It's not about the blood test.'

'I can't help unless I've got you down on my computer.'

'It's my boy. His asthma's really bad. Please,' said Grace, 'stop looking at that machine, and look at him.'

The nurse looked at Billy then. 'Dear, dear,' she said, and became another kind, tired mother like Grace herself. 'Let's just get a doctor to come and look at you, hmm?'

Grace never forgot the next hour. A young doctor came and looked at her son in Casualty, tapping gently on his chest and listening, asking if he ever took Ventolin. 'Poor little fellow,' he said. 'We'll get you onto a nebulizer right away.'

'Oh, thank you, thank you, Doctor – Viner,' said Grace, screwing up her eyes to read the name on his lapel. Tom smiled and walked away, forgetting her, as she forgot him; but his smile stayed with Grace as she sat up all night in the children's ward, staring at the balloons and coloured clouds painted on the walls, and it made her a little, a very little, less frightened.

'You'll need to go home and get his stuff,' said the matron, the next day. 'He's breathing much easier, but we need to be sure because of the exposure to TB.'

Grace dragged herself across London, glad that at least her pass meant she didn't have to pay the full fares. By the time she got back to the Queen's Estate she was convinced her son was going to die. She packed his little clothes, crying into them, and had nothing to blow her nose on.

The phone was ringing and ringing. She was so tired, but it might be something about Billy.

'Is he dead?' she asked, but no sound came out.

'Hallo?' The voice on the other end was so posh she had difficulty understanding it.

'Yes?'

'Hallo, I saw your card in the library and was wondering whether you're still looking for a job as a cleaner?'

'Yes,' said Grace.

'Do you smoke?'

'No,' said Grace.

'I live in Kentish Town,' said Amelia, 'and my name is Mrs Crawley. Why don't you come over?'

18

Amelia's Accouchement

For weeks Amelia had been getting bigger. Her stomach was tense, jagged with livid stretchmarks like a dinosaur's egg cracking in slow motion. She could actually see her skin tear from the pressure inside when the baby kicked.

Its tickling flicker had become a rolling heave between heart and bladder that made it difficult to breathe. Her stomach tented, peaked, bulged with force. At times the outline of a whole limb showed clear, rippling as though under thick water; but never the face, for which she longed.

The tranquillity that had come over her continued. It was as if all her anxieties had been transferred to Mark who was in a state of frenzy at the slightest hitch. He shouted at the builders; he shouted at the lobby correspondents and his secretary on the *Chronicle*; and although he did not shout at Amelia, he greeted almost everything she said with chilling indifference.

'I hope you don't expect me to be in at the birth,' he said.

'Well, yes, I do, rather,' said Amelia.

'I suppose you know that most women shit on the delivery table,' he said. 'I happen to be a coprophobe. If you force me to watch –'

'No, no – I'm sure it's best you don't, then,' said Amelia, miserably. Her body had already let her down in so many ways. She could not believe she would ever be slim and healthy again; and neither could Mark. All through their twenties each had enjoyed the illusion of stasis, of perpetual youth. Other people had become fatter, balder, sadder, wrinklier: not they. Diet, exercise, the daily application of sun-block, avoiding the moving finger was merely a matter of will-power and common sense. Now Mark remained static while she sank, overwhelmed by tides of flesh.

At times, she would think about resuming her career. It seemed futile now, except as a means of earning a little more money. She had almost forgotten all the fuss made over her book, but Mary's appearance in the *Chronicle* books section had given her a shock.

'Isn't it odd how many Mary Quinns there are?' she asked Mark.

'There's only one.'

'I thought she was a waitress.'

'Ivo has decided she can write.'

'Has he? She's quite witty, I suppose,' said Amelia. 'So you've seen her?'

'I don't want to see that mad Irish slag again.'

'Oh. Why have her write for you, then?'

'It's Ivo's section,' said Mark, arousing more suspicion. 'I suppose he's done it to annoy. Or because he wants to screw her.'

'Really,' said Amelia, disapprovingly.

Mark shrugged. He hated Mary, with all the venom of a bad conscience, and would have spiked her pieces had he been able to. But he did not wish to make an enemy of Ivo, whom he still thought of as an ally. Mark knew himself to be deeply unpopular at the *Chronicle*, where his artificial manner and intellectual arrogance, combined with nepotism, made him a figure of almost universal loathing.

At editorial meetings he even made Angus McNabb uneasy. Sympathy for Mary now ran high, and she began to get commissions from editors on other newspapers as word of Mark's behaviour and her entry into freelancing spread. Lulu, in particular, was overflowing with friendliness towards Mary, when she rang up.

'He's in a really terrible mood today – Hang on, it's K. P. Gritts – Oh, hallo. Yes, your copy's arrived, I'm looking at it right now – Ha! That'll teach him not to lie – even the dispatch riders have been shaking like jelly.'

'Oh dear,' said Mary, maliciously. She had a sudden inspiration. 'The girls at Slouch's called him the Voice of the Mysterons.'

Lulu squawked with laughter, and e-mailed the nickname around the building. Mark's secretary, meanwhile, responded to his malice with all the weapons at her disposal. Faxed cuttings failed to arrive, pieces were misattributed, photographs and cartoons switched. Ministers seethed at finding their quotes more than usually badly edited. In order to maintain even the appearance of being in control, Mark often had to work until midnight. Everything for which he had worked and schemed over the past five years had come to fruition, yet his mouth was permanently twisted – not, as many believed, from contempt so much as from an acrid taste, which others might have called disappointment.

Amelia knew nothing of this. She had not thought of Mary since Mark had transferred his belongings to her flat: had dismissed her from her mind. Her natural self-absorption had been augmented by pregnancy. The rich are not different but indifferent. Amelia had seen more of her Filipina maid than either parent, even when doted on by Max. She saw nothing unusual in this. The nuisance was entirely financial. Max had paid for everything, and now that she had to cover her own bills she realized how little her trust fund actually yielded.

'At least I'll get the capital next year,' she said to Mark. 'Daddy only set it up when I was fifteen, you see.'

'How big is it?'

'Oh, not that big, only a million. Daddy doesn't believe in giving away too much,' she said.

The heat of the city was perpetual torture. Her extra weight and blood pressure made her temperature soar at the slightest exertion. She had not shared a bed with Mark since June. London rumbled and sighed through her open windows, exhaling dust. Voices rose up from the streets around, merging with her dreams.

'YER FOCKIN' USELESS CONT.'

'Get out, *get out*!'

'All the lonely people –'

'NONONONO.'

'EEEEEEEEEEEEEEEEEEEEEEEEEEEEEEEEEEEEEEEEEE.'

'Bricks and mortar will not stay, Will not stay, will not stay . . .'

Five times a night she lumbered out of bed; often what came out was no more than a tiny, agonizing trickle for although she was careful to drink no more than a mouthful during the night, it seemed to go straight through her.

'It's nature's way of breaking you in for all the nights to come,' Georgina Hunter said. This did not cheer her. Everyone seemed insistent that she was unlikely to love her child at first.

'The general consensus is that newborns either look like a bright blue bulldog or a mass-murderer that's shrunk in the wash,' she said brightly.

'If only one could still farm them out until they could read,' Mark said. 'It really is a great nuisance, this post-Romantic idealization of infancy.'

Wearily, Amelia was scanned, gave urine samples once a fortnight, then once a week. Wearily she had her blood pressure taken and her weight increase measured. She had put on five stone. 'I'd give half my inheritance if I could just stop eating,' she said to Tom, with tears in her eyes. 'It's like being walled up alive by flesh.'

'Don't worry, it's just hormones,' he said, in his slow, gentle voice.

'Just hormones! The worst thing about this whole business is discovering my hormones are *me*!' said Amelia. 'I used to enjoy clothes and sex and fast cars, and now I feel like the Virgin Mary.'

All she could do on hot days was lie in the bath and try to get her belly under the water. She dreamt of her father's swimming-pool, but travelling across London, with its pot-holes and fumes, was impossible. In any case, he had not telephoned once to ask how she was. The person who had, to her great surprise, was her mother.

Amelia had not really talked to her mother for years, not since Mrs de Monde had attempted to tell her teenaged daughter that wearing no bra was unladylike. Amelia had laughed in her face and dull, quiet Anne de Monde had retreated still further. Her mother was not stupid. She had been a secretary at the British Embassy in Beirut when she had met Amelia's father, and every now and again she surprised everyone by coming out with a dry remark. Amelia had vague memories of some tempestuous rows between her parents when she was a child, of jewellery being hurled across the room on her father's return from a business trip. Presumably, Max's infidelities no longer mattered, for at Amelia's book launch, where her mother had made a rare appearance, she had chatted quite cordially to his mistress. Mrs de Monde had her own friends, the kind of people with whom she had been at school; she had quiet lunches in quiet restaurants off Sloane Street, she went to the Chelsea Flower Show and the London Library and her relations in the country. Amelia occasionally wondered why on earth she had married Max de Monde, instead of making the kind of marriage expected of a Kenward, all cut-glass and Hanover Square; but then her father was so very handsome, so magnetic, so glamorous a figure that it was not altogether surprising.

The telephone calls began cautiously.

'I just wondered how you were,' said her mother.

'Broke,' said Amelia, bluntly. 'And filthy. We don't even have a cleaner.'

'Ah. It's difficult finding help in this country now, isn't it?'

'What I really need,' said Amelia, 'is a maternity nurse for after the birth. They cost a bomb, but for three hundred a week they'll put up with anything.'

'Perhaps I can get you one, as a present,' said Mrs de Monde. 'I was wondering what you really needed.'

'Thank you.' There was a pause. One of the things she found particularly hard was that it was quite impossible to charm her mother, Amelia thought suddenly. 'Is Daddy very angry with me?'

'I don't know.'

'He was so sweet about the wedding and everything, and then it's as if I've dropped off the face of the earth.'

'You're his little girl,' said her mother. 'It's difficult for fathers when their daughters become mothers.'

'Was it for yours?'

Her mother made no reply. Amelia had not known either of her grandparents, but she knew they had disapproved of her mother's marriage and cut off all communication for many years. She suspected that this was one of the reasons why her mother was sympathetic now. There was so much she wanted to find out about, suddenly, but when Amelia asked her mother about her own experiences during pregnancy, she replied, in her vague way, 'It's all so long ago, now. I really can't remember.'

How could you not remember exactly what having another human being inside you felt like? Yet clearly she did not. Amelia had been born at St George's, before it got turned into a hotel, yet once, when she had been complaining about the heat, her mother said, 'Yes, when I was in labour I was dying for water and the nun refused to give me a sip until she'd finished her rosary.'

Nuns at St George's? Perhaps, thought Amelia, her mother really was a bit strange in the head. She wasn't Catholic, why was a nun in her room? Yet after this, they spoke once a week.

'Why don't we make a list of what you'll need, and I can get it for you?' Mrs de Monde suggested.

'I don't think we can afford anything new,' said Amelia.

'It can be my present.'

Amelia longed to decorate her child's room – Mark mocked her for calling it the nursery – with pretty wallpaper of the kind she had seen at Georgina's, but this was forbidden. Her husband vetoed colour or pattern, insisting that their walls be painted white or cream and already resented every penny she spent preparing for their child. She bought Babygros from Woolworths in secret, as though they were pornography.

They went out, occasionally, as a couple – squeezing into cinemas that depressed her because, unlike Kensington or Chelsea, she never saw anyone in the audience whom she knew, and to dinner parties in thin, fashionable houses in Islington. They were chillingly unlike the parties she had been to before. Everyone sat on Shaker chairs, eating trout off thick plates, and discussing the Labour Party.

'We're going to end up like the Americans, living in ghettos patrolled by private guards,' said one host. 'It would be much more cost-effective to raise taxes and do something with the unemployed instead of letting them rot into crime. If I were a young black man I'd be out mugging people like us, too.'

Eight weeks before her due date, it seemed as if Amelia's

abdomen could stretch no more, that the baby would punch right through it. She lay on the sofa sipping Waitrose lemonade and watching *Star Trek*. All the television she watched now seemed to be science fiction, about human beings being taken over by aliens. There was no position in which she was comfortable. Her fingers swelled to the size and complexion of Italian sausages; she had had to go to the local jeweller and get her wedding ring sawn off.

'You could wear it through your nose, like a pig,' Mark suggested.

A part of her was appalled at what she had become, so appalled that she could no longer bear to look at her reflection. Another part found it profoundly soothing. She had been imprisoned in her narrow, fashionable body just as she had in her narrow, sophisticated mind, and the fact that change was very nearly to cost her her life did not make it any less wonderful.

'I'm so sorry about all the mess,' she said, swaying up the stairs to see Tom. 'I can't seem to find a decent cleaner. If I could just get the house clean, I wouldn't mind so much.'

'Have you looked in the library?'

'No. Is that a good place?'

Bang bang, crash, crash.

'*Capital Radio-o-o!*'

'Oh, those *bloody* builders.'

'It's OK, really. I can sleep through anything, and I hardly notice the rest, as long as it doesn't get into my computer,' said Tom, politely.

'What are you writing?'

'An article for the *BMJ*. Pain relief for children.'

'Have you invented something?'

'No.' Tom smiled. 'That sort of thing is more inspiration than perspiration. You know, like Crick dreaming of the double helix.'

Amelia looked blank. Amazing how people knew so little about the stuff they were made of, he thought.

Pain was a subject that haunted her. Women who had had children spoke to her with the sly sympathy of initiates, as though she were about to lose a second virginity. It occurred to Amelia, with increasing force and frequency, that this baby had started life as something the size of a full stop, and was only going to come out in a way that caused agony in all the tenderest parts of her body. All the pregnancy books she read and reread kept emphasizing that it was a perfectly natural thing – but so was death, Amelia thought. So was death.

'Is labour very bad?'

'Just make sure you have an epidural as soon as possible,' Tom said. 'There's nothing worse than being woken at three in the morning by someone who's screaming her head off when it's too late.'

'What do you mean, too late?'

'If you're ready to give birth. It takes about ten minutes to get an epidural in, and after a certain point the risks are too big.'

'I'm not sure I wouldn't rather have the pain than a socking great needle in my spine,' said Amelia.

'Oh, for God's sake,' said Tom. 'It's something the size of a thread. I can show you.'

'Really?'

'Yeah. I spend half my time doing them.'

'Is it safe, though?'

'Nothing is entirely without risk. Common aspirin wouldn't be passed now by any drugs committee, because in a tiny minority of people it causes massive bleeding in the stomach.'

'What about not being able to feel your legs?'

'Look,' he said. 'You may be one of the very lucky ones who has a quick and easy birth but most first labours are pretty bad. Do you really want to go through so much pain that you'll hate the baby because of it? I've seen that happen. The second time is much quicker and easier, and that's why all those bloody NCT women who had a forceps delivery the first time and a natural birth the second become so fanatical. They think the first time could have been that easy too, and it's us wicked patriarchal doctors who've prevented it.'

'If you were going to have a baby, how would you do it?' she asked.

'Me? Elective Caesarean. It takes longer to heal, but you and the baby are guaranteed to survive. That's why it's more and more common in America. Also, you don't get all the problems of incontinence later on.'

Amelia grimaced. 'I don't think I'll risk it,' she said, faintly. The only thing that comforted her was the thought that he might be her anaesthetist when she went into labour. He was back in the teaching hospital where she was booked, and she made him promise to visit her if he was on call.

The day she was supposed to go into labour came and went. Then the week. The midwives recommended raspberry leaf tea, curries, driving over sleeping policemen.

People stopped phoning up to ask how it had been. The French cheeses she had lined up on top of the fridge to eat as soon as the baby came out became putrid.

'Perhaps it's a phantom pregnancy,' said Mark.

'If you'd come to see the scans you'd know it wasn't,' said Amelia, but nevertheless she began to feel uncertain.

She went to see the consultant, descending into what looked like the lower intestine of her NHS hospital to meet a man in a Jermyn Street suit, whose office was tucked away beneath a large yellow duct pipe. They quacked at each other about the heat, each establishing to the other that they were only in this appalling place by default.

'Yes, yes,' said the obstetrician, his eyes barely flickering over her jewellery. 'My dear young lady! Of course you can't go on.'

Two days later, she went into a dingy little room on the second floor with her bag. At dawn, a midwife with the face of a Greuze angel put prostaglandin gel inside her. There was a burning sensation, but nothing happened. Time passed. More prostaglandin. Amelia wept with frustration, then reapplied her mascara. She did not wish to lose all semblance of femininity in this place, and had already been appalled by the way the other women waddled around the corridor of the labour ward in old T-shirts and fluffy slippers.

The monitor showed contractions, but she could feel nothing. Then, quite suddenly, it began, the pain mounting like a whale coming up for air while her mind tilted. Down, down, down, a clenching sickness, and then – nothing. For a whole ten minutes, she was completely normal, wondering if she had just imagined it.

Then up, up, up, the whale bigger and blacker than before, pushing her down, down, down into churning sickness.

'Oh, oh, *oh*, this isn't nice,' said Amelia, in shocked surprise.

'Try to breathe, dear. One, two, three . . .'

Violent heat and cold coursed through her. Up, up, up, down, down, down. A blank, in which to function, drink, breathe. Up, up, up, she could hear herself moaning and retching, down, down, oh, this was dreadful, worse than anything, worse than the worst helter-skelter, worse than a falling plane, worse than food poisoning! The blanks in which to be human became shorter and shorter, so that she barely had time to get over one contraction before the next was convulsing her.

'You're not in labour yet,' was the reply, when she begged for the epidural.

'What do you call this?' she gasped.

'False labour.'

'It feels bloody real to me.'

'You're not dilating yet.'

The midwife injected her with pethidine. It did not take away the pain but the hands of the wall-clock began to move very fast, leaping from minutes to hours like water on a hot-plate.

'Epidural!' she screamed. 'I want an epidural *now*!'

'You're not dilated enough yet,' said a stranger. Gloved fingers thrust inside her, measuring, probing. The blue waves of the monitor throbbed.

'We're going to try syntocinon to speed it up.'

'Please, please.'

The walls swelled and bulged with agony. Up, up, down, down, endlessly tossed. Her mouth was parched. I promise, she said childishly, that if this stops I'll be a better person.

'Not long now.'

The Greuze angel was back. 'Dear, dear, I didn't expect to find you still here. Hang on, love. Yep, five centimetres.'

'EPIDURAL.'

'Can you get into the wheelchair? Good girl. Upsadaisy!'

She was pushed with interminable slowness down a corridor.

'Don't worry, dear. The anaesthetist's here.'

Amelia was helped onto the delivery table. Next door, another woman was bellowing, 'FUUUCK! Oh, FUUCK! You BASTARD, FUUCK!'

All along the corridor, there were terrible, inhuman jungle noises, women growling like lions, grunting like seals or just shrieking.

The anaesthetist was not Tom, but another tired young man with red hair. 'Lie on your side, Mrs Crawley.'

'Please, please hurry.'

'Try not to move,' said the doctor, spraying her spine with something cold. 'Little prick now, and then you'll feel your legs get warm.'

Two more terrible contractions, and then – and then – she was sane again.

'Oh, thank you. Thank you. Thank you.'

'Can you wriggle your toes?'

Amelia was so happy that she scarcely noticed when the drip was put into her hand, and a catheter into her bladder. She watched the long plastic coils of it turn yellow as the day went on, and chatted to the succession of midwives who watched her monitor. They were all so nice, especially the young ones. Amelia was full of love for them, with gratitude and amazement that such kindness existed. 'You won't let them hurt me, will you? I don't want to be cut.'

'We'll try not,' they said.

In the afternoon, Tom came by. Amelia was lying there like a queen, with a succession of wet white flannels draped across her forehead.

'Oh, Tom, Tom, isn't this marvellous?' she gabbled. 'What you do. To give birth without pain, it must have been a dream for centuries, it was so terrible before. Will you be with me when it's born? Will you? Please?'

'Yes,' said Tom. She was as high as a kite. Not surprising, with two shots of pethidine. 'Isn't Mark here?'

'No,' said Amelia brightly. 'He's a shit, isn't he? I wish – you know, I wish I'd married you. Oh, I shouldn't have said that, should I?'

'Don't worry,' said Tom.

'Promise me, promise me you'll stay when it's born.'

'I'll be here.'

And, when at last Amelia had to be cut all the way back so that her daughter could be dragged out with forceps, spattering seven doctors with her blood, he was.

19

Mary Ascendant

In no profession but journalism is it possible to ascend with the rapidity Mary now achieved. With Ivo's patronage and a lively turn of phrase her success was almost guaranteed, but what made her notorious was her reviews.

Every critic has his or her own private agenda, which ripples through the surface of their writing while remaining invisible to the ordinary newspaper reader. For some it is the simple wish to make their byline better-known. For others, it is the proselytizing for a particular aesthetic, religious or moral perspective. Others still wish to alert publishers that they have an uncommissioned book on the same subject in them, or to pay back scores of an entirely professional nature. A few churn out reviews as they would almost any other piece of journalism, but these do not really concern us, and they do not, as it happens, last long.

Mary's novelty was not that she was prepared to be rude, or witty at the author's expense, for both of these were commonplace enough. Nor was it even that she was so well-read. She had suddenly discovered that she had a voice. It was not the voice she used when talking to people, any more than the voice Mark used as a columnist reflected his conversation. It roared and railed and spat and hissed all the things she had kept silent about; and when a writer discovers such a voice it is usually heard even if what it is saying is mistaken.

'I, too, am someone who can make a difference to somebody's career,' she said to herself; but it was not this that impelled her.

Once, Mark had told her that to read fiction to find out what life was like in other places, or to identify with the protagonist, was the hallmark of stupidity; that to prefer a story with plot and dialogue was middlebrow; that to be interested in the given order of things rather than pure language was utterly common-place.

'Yes, yes,' she had said humbly. But what had his precepts actually upheld? Politics in which every cruelty and callousness were displayed as admirable or avant-garde, in which character, charity and compassion were non-existent, in which the party's manifesto devoured itself like a snake attempting to swallow its own tail. It was consistent with his behaviour. He had chosen Amelia, had chosen style over content: that was what his philosophy had led to, and that was what boiled and suppurated beneath Mary's reviews. Of course, language was half of it, the delirium of words ran in her blood like fever, but language was also a system of deceit, a confidence trick. She hurled sentences at Mark like javelins over a wall, not caring who else got hurt, not caring if she made a fool of herself.

Occasionally, Ivo even found himself toning her down. 'This is a bit harsh, isn't it?' he said, of one piece she sent in.

'Is it?'

'Well, yes. He writes for us,' said Ivo.

Mary snorted.

'And – well, the thing is, his wife has cancer.'

'Ivo, you surprise me. What has that to do with his writing?' said Mary.

'Remember what I said about the fear and favour markets.'

'I'm not in this for the long view,' said Mary.

In the past, she had wondered how Ivo had spotted which books to review; now, trawling through newspapers and magazines in the local public library, she saw that it was largely to do with completely extraneous factors. It went without saying that there was a first division of big names, but these Ivo always gave to men, or reserved for himself. Women were generally regarded as inferior, both as writers and as critics – too kind, too thoughtful, not, well, *ballsy* enough. The one thing female reviewers could be guaranteed to get was books on feminism, and on the *Chronicle* Ivo had even broken with this.

It was in the second division that competition raged, because to pick out an obscure author who went on to win a major prize shed glory on the reviewer. You could, Mary found, judge a book by its jacket. The first division were presented as austerely cerebral, the favourite design being of horizontal lines or a minutely costive single image. The second division had dust jackets with a detail from a classical painting, or an old photograph, modishly rent, to denote approachability and post-modernism. Anything pastelly, which had the author's name or the title in gilt letters, could usually be safely trashed or ignored. Also significant was the author's potted biography. The chic limited themselves to two sentences, such as: 'Ed Cropper was born in 1975. This is his first novel.'

The stupidest included everything. 'Barbara Higgs-Barker is the author of thirteen previous novels, including *Lilies and Roses*, winner of a Betty Trask Award, *People in Palaces*, serialized on *Book at Bedtime*, *Some Other Lover*, runner-up in the Romantic Silver Pen Prize, and the best-selling *Sandwiches at Sandringham*, a book of Royal picnic recipes. She lives in a Georgian manor house in Wiltshire with her husband Hugh, a solicitor, two children, three dogs, five cats and a hamster.'

The only important information an author's biography could yield was whether he or she was also a reviewer, for nobody except the insanely honest or the determinedly malign wished to antagonize someone in the same small world. Novels by media celebrities, producers of arts programmes or mere journalists were fair game, though, because however strong their fiefdom within their own particular field they were unlikely to have real influence in the world of books.

(Ivo explained this. 'If you attack the latest novel by Merlin Swagg, you look brave and outspoken because he's such a big cheese in broadcasting. But the fact is, he's not a mover and shaker: he only has established authors on *Snap, Crackle, Pop!*, and he's much too soft to give them a hard time. He can't affect prizes. Prizes are the gift of a caucus of critics.')

Then there was the blurb, which mattered rather less than whether or not the advance copies were sent out with a personalized letter from the author's editor, or, better still, publisher. Publicists' letters, which always ended with the plaintive announcement that the author was available for interview, went straight into the wastebin. They usually repeated the information on the dustjacket, but with more misprints.

What really tipped the scale, Mary realized, was the publisher. Slather and Rudge marketed itself rather than its authors, who tended to be hip young men. Virtually every book on its list would be given prominent notice, largely because so many editors and critics were also hip young men. Harpy adopted a similar policy, but their books rarely received critical attention because nobody, especially not the handful of female reviewers, wished to bury their talents in a feminist ghetto. Others, who tended towards the academic or the eccentric, might get a look-in on a dull week. Others still were thought to be mass-market: they published too many blockbusters for their literary fiction even to be glanced at in the catalogues – though bestsellers were always good for a drubbing. Adam's publisher, Belgravia, fell into the middle market.

'But why is it important to be reviewed at all?' Mary asked. 'I mean, I can hardly remember who said what about whom, so why should anyone else?'

'Oh, quite, quite. If it were only the opinion of five or six hacks, nobody would give a toss. The point is, *booksellers* take note. The bigger chains position a hardback entirely according to how many inches you've had in the quality Sundays, and that in turn dictates how well you sell, and *that* dictates the size of an author's next advance. So a hardback really is important. What sells a hardback is reviews. Real pros simply count the number of inches they've got, rather than read the actual words.'

'But don't people write for something other than money?'

'That's how they start out, poor lambs, skipping about among the daffodils. By the time they've been turned into chops, all they care about is the size of their advance,' said Ivo. 'Haven't you heard them at Slouch's? Well? Were they ever discussing the finer points of the objective correlative?'

'No,' said Mary. 'But – do they need to?'

In the beginning she could not believe that she was making a profit out of what she did for pleasure. She began to go to launch parties, for even if Ivo was too grand to descend on such affairs more than once a fortnight, she knew she had to make allies in journalism if she were truly to infiltrate Amelia's world.

There were parties every night for those who cared to go to them: parties in clubs, parties in pubs, parties in houses, in flats, in boats, in gardens, in bookshops; parties in museums and parties at the Zoo. How did publishers continue to afford such things? Why did they bother? Mary did not know or care. There was the escalator going up, and she took it. It was quite easy, as long as she had a little Jameson's. Not that she was going to overdo it again, just keep a little bottle in her bag. The same people spun round with their glass of white wine and line of patter, and soon they became familiar, less frightening, more frightened of her, almost friendly, as long as you didn't look too closely at the eyes. The women all wore skimpy black dresses, even in the middle of winter, and they were seemingly prepared to have sex in public if it would advance their career. You could always blame it on the drink, and literary life was so incestuous everyone had probably seen it all already.

There were neighbours who heaped praise on each other's work before modestly declining to review it 'as a friend', publishers who proclaimed every one of their authors as brilliant, agents touching down from auctions, gossip columnists truffling for a snippet, freelances exchanging telephone numbers, hacks in search of a free meal. All this industry, generated on the back of a book that would, if anything, make a loss. The main thing was to get her name and face known, while not giving away anything that could be useful. You had to circulate all the time, exchanging snappy opinions on fashionable authors. Most of these were negative, but it did not do to trash everyone. There had to be enthusiasm for one or two promising young iconoclasts, judicious applause for an elderly survivor, ardent advocacy for a possible winner of the Booker Prize. It was like working on the Stock Exchange, but whereas the trading in dead authors took decades to rise or fall, buying Donne here, selling Kipling there, living writers barely had time to acquire a reputation before it declined.

Of course she was still poor, for a review only brought her between a hundred and two hundred pounds, and the *Chronicle* took nearly three months to pay her. This was a shock, although she remembered that it had been the same for Mark before he got his staff job.

'Sorry,' said Ivo. 'It's nothing to do with me. The *Chronicle* is always a late payer.'

'That's outrageous! It means I'm paying for Max de Monde's overdraft.'

'That's right. To those that hath shall be given and to those who have not shall be taken away. Look, if you're stuck, I'll see what I can do. Profiles are much more lucrative, you can make up a few expenses.'

'But I haven't got any,' said Mary. 'I can't afford to go out to restaurants.'

'It's amazing what a few phantom taxis can notch up,' said Ivo.

She took out an even bigger overdraft to cover her debts. New jewellery, new flat, new life: two thousand pounds. She realized that she could get away with wearing the same black dress over and over again because in a crush nobody looked below your bosoms, but a change of earrings was essential. Butler & Wilson became the most frequent name on her credit-card bills. Yet her poverty was of a different kind from that experienced as a waitress. She was somebody: she existed. Had she met those women who had snubbed her at Amelia's party now, she thought with satisfaction, they would have paid attention instead of turning their backs. The first few times she saw the words Mary Quinn at the top of a review, she was mesmerized. It seemed she had never seen her name before. She fell in love with it, with the beautiful symmetry of the M and the curly tail of the Q. Every word she had written concerning *Other Feet*, was far, far better than anything else in Ivo's section. That joke about athlete's foot – it was inspired. The whole thing was a masterpiece of compressed intelligence, far too good for what it described, in fact. She wondered what Mark would think. Even now, choosing a new dress, she would find herself checking to see if it was the kind of thing of which he would approve, sometimes buying things out of sheer, stupid defiance. His pale face was always in her mind, bitter as lemons.

Ivo was pleased. The week after her first review came out brought a furious letter from Flora Payne. Ivo was in ecstasies of laughter reading it. Mary was relieved to see this.

'Can she do anything? I mean, legally?'

'Not a thing. A review is a statement of opinion. Of course, she'll hate you for ever, but frankly, my darling, you're not in this game to make friends, are you?'

'But neither, apparently, is anyone in it for money,' said Mary, drily. 'So what's the attraction?'

'Power,' said Ivo.

Adam's party was in one of the rooms at the Slouch Club. Had his book been a success he would have gone downstairs to have dinner with his agent, editor and a few friends. What precluded any real possibility of this was a review in a paper a fortnight before publication when there was still, supposedly, an embargo.

'FRENCH LEAVE FOR SNOBS,' said the caption.

Adam had been reading the *Chronicle*, when his own face, or rather the smirking and airbrushed version of it, suddenly jumped out of its pages. It was so unexpected that he began to read the copy beside it quite automatically, gratified to be given so much space. This gratification rapidly changed to astonishment. 'But that's just not right,' he kept saying to himself, as one sentence after another bowdlerized events, names, locations, characters and intent.

A paragraph later, bewilderment was replaced by incredulity. 'But Hugo is *meant* to be awful.'

And then, as the awfulness of Hugo was elided into the awfulness of his book, and by implication, his own nature, as everything he had intended to satirize was reflected back, monstrously distorted, upon his own personality, Adam went into shock. Hugo was 'transparently autobiographical', and his novel 'a tissue of clichés and sexual fantasy typical of the overgrown public schoolboy'. Adam, whose chief anxiety had been that he might not have been able to depict an upper-class heterosexual convincingly, felt as if he had slipped into a bad dream. That he had grown up abroad ('apparently educated in France'), gone to Eton and now worked at Pocock's was turned into something of which to be ashamed. 'Sands, a second-hand bookseller, has all too obviously been infected by his shop-worn wares. We should not stop reading Victorian novels, but we should now stop writing them,' was the conclusion.

It had been written by Ivo Sponge.

Adam had not gone up to Norfolk to stay with his mother that week. Mrs Sands had worked herself up into a frenzy of maternal pride over his book. To Adam's mortification, she had gone round all the major stores in London, announcing herself as his mother and bullying managers to order *A World Elsewhere*. 'A lot of people will want this novel, it'll simply walk orf your shelves,' she said, and the managers, taken aback by this, had allowed themselves in one or two instances to be swayed.

Adam, who was already dreading her presence and the possible conjunction with his father and stepmother at the launch party, had decided to stay in London. Perhaps it would have been less bad in company, or perhaps the thing that had been waiting in him for years would have emerged then anyway. All he knew was that he felt terribly weak and frightened. He was afraid even to go too close to the windows of his flat. He sat in bed, rocking backwards and forwards with his head on his knees, saying, 'Nine years! Nine years completely wasted!'

Then rage filled him, and he thought of killing Ivo, of stabbing him, or beating him to a bloody pulp. But what was worse was that he suddenly saw his novel from a different perspective, saw how bad it could be, after all, how unoriginal, how grossly malformed, how unfunny. The revelation made him want to faint.

He tried to gain control over his feelings, but instead became more and more distraught. A dozen times an hour he jumped up and reread his own words, his fingers sweating so much that smudges of newsprint blurred the text. He could no longer tell if what he had written was good or bad. How could someone he had met only once hate him so much? What had he said at Mary's dinner party to cause such antagonism? Of course, he had quoted Flaubert on critics, but was Ivo so pusillanimous that any attack on his profession should be so monstrously revenged?

By noon he had written a letter, rather a good letter he said to himself, acknowledging Ivo's right to free speech but wittily pointing out the factual and literary errors of the review. This helped to calm him for a while. He posted it although a dozen fresh points occurred to him even as it left his hand.

Exultation filled him. He wanted to rush round to the newspaper, and shake Ivo by the throat, saying, 'Don't you understand? It hasn't worked!'

But the mood did not last. He wondered how many people he knew had read the *Chronicle* that day, how many of his friends and enemies, how many former lovers, tutors, schoolmasters, relations. He thought of all the regulars who came to the bookshop, of having to face Malcolm the next day, of all the utter strangers who at some point would learn of his fate; and he knew the thing that gave him so much pain would cause them all a small stab of joy.

Towards evening, his telephone began to ring. It was Candida Twink.

'Marvellous space the *Chronicle* gave you.'

'*Marvellous?*'

'I hope you haven't done anything silly, like write a reply,' she said.

'Well, yes,' said Adam. 'I can't let them get away with such a travesty. To condemn a novel as bad because the protagonist is unpleasant – I mean, that sort of *bêtise* was exploded by Henry James.'

'Don't post it.'

'Too late,' said Adam. 'Besides, why shouldn't there be a right of reply?'

His editor sighed. 'There just isn't. It's unsporting.'

'I wasn't aware,' said Adam, through gritted teeth, 'that writing fiction in any way constituted a sport. And if it is, it should be run by professionals not amateurs.'

'Oh, well,' said Candida. 'You can always do a spot of reviewing yourself, and get your own back.'

'Never!' roared Adam.

Next was his agent. 'I've just got back from the country. Just remember, aphids and sap suckers always cluster most thickly on new shoots,' Francesca said, in her mournful boom.

'I have been thinking along the lines of insecticide,' said Adam.

Francesca sighed. 'It's not ecological.'

Next was Andrew Evenlode. 'Bad luck.'

'It's full of mistakes,' said Adam.

'Is it? I'm afraid I haven't had time to read the copy you sent yet.'

So it went on. Some pretended not to have read the *Chronicle*, but Adam knew perfectly well that they had. None, he thought, had so much as opened his novel.

'I lent it to my mother, and she really enjoyed it.'

'I'm taking it on holiday.'

'I've asked my local library to order it.'

'My local bookshop hasn't stocked it yet.'

It was like trying to grapple with fog. There was a universal consensus that *A World Elsewhere* was snobbish, obscene and in every way unmemorable – and yet nobody had read it. A joke went round, quickly incorporated into the *Guardian* review, that he gave a new meaning to the phrase 'to run like Sands'.

Ivo's review, and Ivo's gossip, unleashed a downpour. The roiling soul of the city that twisted and turned on itself, writhing with poisons visible and invisible, seemed to gather and empty over his head.

The *Evening Standard* had K. P. Gritts write on the extraordinary foolishness of responding to criticism, taking the publication of Adam's letter as his excuse.

'Do we wish to become as absurd as the Americans, whose vain, self-pitying authors fill more than four thick pages of bleating correspondence in the *New York Review of Books*?' Gritts demanded. 'It is the hacks, the egoists, the amateurs and the publicity-maniacs on the borders of vanity publishing who wish to "clarify misunderstandings". If a bad review has made an author look like a twit, a letter of fury makes him a fool. Sands has invited publicity, and he must take the publicity that comes along.'

It was with difficulty that Adam restrained himself from pointing out that it was not he but his publishers who had invited publicity.

The *Independent* ran a feature on author photographs, taking as its main theme the fact that Adam's nose was larger in life than on his dust-jacket. The diaries of the *Telegraph* and *Sunday Times* poked fun at public schoolboys and Provence. By the end of the first week, Adam was cowering as if beneath a succession of thunderclaps.

None of this seemed to distress Belgravia, who were delighted by all the coverage. They sent him cuttings of everything, until he wondered whether the whole exercise was designed to provoke a nervous breakdown.

Then his mother rang. 'How could you do this to me?' she demanded, in a voice quivering with fury.

'Do what?' said Adam.

'Haven't you seen your reviews?'

'Yes.'

'Well, aren't you ashamed of yourself?'

'No,' said Adam, surprising himself. 'It isn't anything to do with me, Mummy.'

'What about all your friends? Why haven't they done anything to help? What about little Molly, eh? I see she's writing for the *Chronicle* these days.'

'I thought it would be dishonourable to ask.'

Mrs Sands sniffed.

'Have you read my book?'

'No, I have not. It sounds perfectly appalling. I've got a pretty good idea from all the papers, and it really doesn't sound like my cup of tea. If you had to go in for this sort of thing, you might have done it under a different name. I bought three copies in Norwich, but I can't even give them to people as presents if what I hear is true.'

'Mummy, there was *one page* of sex, which my agent told me to put in, and which was meant to be funny.'

Adam was used to concealing mortification: it was like being back at prep-school, alternately buggered and bullied, with no hope of escape. In the past, he had always been consoled by the secret knowledge of himself as a writer, a knowledge that came long before he had ever attempted to write anything. Now even this was stripped from him, made, like his anguish, ridiculous.

Malcolm was the only person he saw who was genuinely kind during that time. Adam felt so shaky that he could do little besides check off books bought at auction, and had to keep dashing to the lavatory. Malcolm dealt with anyone trying to offload review copies, while Adam unpacked boxes in the basement and cried. Trade was slack, even in midsummer when Americans wandered in and out of the dusty second-hand bookshops along Charing Cross Road and bought out of sheer nostalgia. Half the shops in central London were closing, because of the recession, and they were lucky at Pocock's to make as much as fifty pounds a day. Malcolm brewed pots of Lapsang Souchong – a tea Adam detested, but had never had the heart to tell him so – and patted his hand. 'Don't take it to heart, dear boy,' he said. 'First novels are just the cream off the top of a writer's imagination, it's what comes later, when you're forty or so, that shows what you're really made of. The few people who write something good before that age are always one-offs, like Thackeray and Fitzgerald. You should just get on with your next.'

'I'm not sure I'll be able write another.'

'Then you aren't a real writer, and you should be glad to have it pointed out to you. If you are, you'll get better with practice, just as you would with anything else. Look at *Titus Andronicus*, one of the worst plays ever written. Look at *Endymion*. Look at Jane Austen. Look at the mess of *The Pickwick Papers*, or *Roderick Random* or *Barry Lyndon*. Every major figure in literature starts off as worse than the norm, not better.'

'But everyone will remember.'

'Less than you think. Besides, readers might have a very different reaction. I enjoyed it.'

'You did?'

'Yes,' said Malcolm. 'It's completely over the top, but it was meant to be, wasn't it?'

'Yes,' said Adam, dully. What did it matter to him if ordinary people like Malcolm understood? It was the world of the Slouch Club he had wanted.

On the day of his party, Tom Viner rang. 'Can I drop in on you? My shift has just ended, and I wondered if I could stop off at your flat rather than wander about Soho in the heat before your party.'

'Are you going to it?'

'Yes, of course. Aren't you?'

Adam gave a shaky laugh. His head and neck ached. 'I had been thinking of not.'

'Your book very nearly made me give someone an embolism,' Tom said. 'I was at the bit where Hugo was chasing the peacock across the castle. Brilliant! It's Andrew, isn't it?'

'Um,' said Adam, thinking to himself that his protagonist had also had a fair bit of Tom in him, too. 'Mostly.'

He rushed into the shower, and was bumbling around nervously with shirts all over the bed, when Tom came up the stairs.

'You've lost weight.'

'I can't eat in this heat,' said Adam. 'Which should I wear?'

'You know I'm no good about clothes.'

'You don't need to be,' said Adam.

Tom looked away, then back as his friend sighed, and put on another. 'Have you seen anyone about losing so much weight?'

'No,' said Adam. 'Don't worry. "'Tis strange the mind, that very fiery particle, Should let itself be snuffed out by an article".'

'Sorry?'

'That's what Byron said, about Keats, I think. Don't worry, I'm not going to shrivel up and die just because of a bad review. Sod them all. Let's go.'

20

Adam's Fall

'How could you do that to Adam?' Mary asked Ivo.

He shrugged. 'Rite-of-passage novels are two a penny. People used to be entitled to one, like free travel for under-fives. I've decided they shouldn't.'

'And you can do that?'

'Yes,' said Ivo, and Mary was conscious that he had said it as much to show her his power as to show Adam. 'It's a wank, to be frank. *A Year In Provence* by a public-school git.'

'Is that what it comes down to?' said Mary. 'The fact he went to Eton?'

'If he'd written about life on a council estate in Manchester it might have been a bit more original.'

'But Adam doesn't know about council estates in Manchester. He wrote about what he knew.'

'The trouble is,' said Ivo, 'too many of us knew it already.'

'And do you think we want to learn about the rest? For God's sake, Ivo, I grew up in one of the worst slums in Britain. Do you think I want to read about it? Do you ever hear me talk about the things I've seen? The people who've come from misery want to escape it, and the people who've never known it don't want to know – apart from a few trendy Trots who thinks it gives them street cred.'

Mary would have said more, but self-interest made her fear that she had already overstepped the mark. Besides, her own conscience was uneasy. She had enjoyed Adam's trashing, if she was honest; his lack of sympathy for her over Mark, his meanness in taking money off her his flat, his frequent observations *de haut en bas* had rankled more than she admitted to herself. Ivo's hatchet-job, which she knew to be full of fallacy and half-truths, had caused her precisely that stab of malicious pleasure Adam had feared.

But when she saw him looking so ill and nervous, she remembered only how fond she was of him, how he had been the one person to stand by her, and the small cindery thing that was left of her heart glowed with indignation.

Adam's party was no worse than many other launches. Belgravia had expected three times as many guests, and Caroline had informed Adam that several celebrities had been invited. 'There's Merlin Swagg, Sally Dunkin from *Night Calls*, various literary editors, and of course Jules Martian.'

Needless to say, none of these people appeared, and nobody had expected them to. Of Adam's acquaintance, some never answered, some never turned up and some turned round in the doorway to return to the restaurant downstairs, afraid that failure might be contagious. The Belgravia staff and their partners made up at least a quarter of the guests, and another quarter were either gate-crashers or alcoholic hacks from magazines in search of free booze. (It was noticeable that Caroline, who manned the table with the wine and copies of Adam's book, guarded the former ferociously, while allowing anyone to take the latter for free.) Mrs Sands, draped in beads and flowing garments, talked loudly to anyone who would listen about her son; the young man whom she buttonholed turned out to be a gossip columnist from the *Evening Standard*, and he repeated her most offensive remarks the next day with possibly the greatest accuracy of anyone who wrote about Adam that month. There was, of course, no lack of conversation:

'A real come-down.'

'D'you think Sands's hair is meant to look like that?'

'Perhaps he's been tearing it out in chunks.'

'Frightful. Ivo must really have enjoyed himself.'

'I think I've had enough. Where are the chips?'

'The lonely vigilance over language is all that matters.'

'Adam, darling, what can I say? Just don't give up the day job.'

'I hear it's pure pornography.'

'Any more canapés?'

'Well, I heard it was choir boys. He used to hang around outside King's, ogling.'

'I'm working part-time in a theatre while I finish it.'

'Well, it sounds more like a comedy of manners to me.'

'No, I can tell you with absolute certainty that he's not posh at all.'

'*Ciao*, everyone.'

'It's about a young man, an Oxbridge graduate, living in Notting Hill and, well, working part-time in a theatre. But, really, it's about the gap between appearance and reality.'

'Oh, it's useless sending women reviewers books by men. Men review men and women review women.'

'Never mind, Adam. I'm sure Ivo'll be feeling guilty enough to be nice about your next one.'

'Not after the letter I wrote.'

'Ah. Mistake. Never complain, never explain, that's the rule.'

'The first person who said that was Disraeli. I wonder whether the Jews who went to the camps thought it such a good thing?'

'I hear you're getting sued by Gore Tore about that piece you wrote about him and his son.'

'Not me. The *Mail*. I don't think a superannuated rock-star with a history of drugs and sex-scandals is going to cut much ice in court.'

'Fiona looks well.'

'I bet she's having an affair.'

'Filofaxes were so bulky.'

'You *must* try my crystal therapist.'

'You should do it for its own sake. Not for money, or success.'

'Have you started your second?'

'Only the synopsis.'

'I hope we'll get first offer on it.'

'Yes, if you want.'

'Fiona's such a vamp.'

'More of a *femme banale*, in my opinion.'

'I've thrown away my Chanel earrings. I can't believe I ever wore such things.'

'You're selling well, you know. Two thousand gone already. Most first novels are lucky to sell eight hundred hardbacks, especially in a recession. The bottom line is sales, not reviews. That's all that matters, in publishing.'

'Is it?'

'Look: if you'd written a novel about how frightfully clever and literate you are, which I'm sure you're perfectly capable of, all the people who dumped on you would be fawning – and nobody would buy it. To invent a story with characters and a setting is much harder, but of course it's working in a convention so it's easy to pull to bits.'

'So who do you think she's bonking?'

'With Fiona, it could be anyone.'

'If I were earning millions, it might not matter,' Adam said. 'But the sums are so minuscule –'

'Don't you want to make money?' asked Candida Twink. 'Because you could, you know. There are only about thirty novelists in the country who make a real living from writing, and the rest would do better as typists.'

'She used to go out with Mark Crawley before he married Amelia.'

'No!'

'Oh, yes, and it gets better. She used to be a waitress here.'

'There's more inspiration in a good plot than in style, any day.'

'Can't you do both?'

In the months that followed Adam thought about the advice he had been given but he could not take it to heart. How could you do something for its own sake if all pleasure in it had been demolished?

'I can't stop looking over my shoulder all the time,' he told Mary. 'And then, like Lot's wife, I turn to salt.'

He spent five days a week trying to write, for Malcolm had asked him, very apologetically, if he would mind working part-time. 'I'm so sorry, dear boy. There just aren't enough customers in this recession. Maybe when things improve,' said Malcolm, blinking.

Adam knew his employer was right; knew, too, that he was terrified of losing his boyfriend, a pretty Brazilian window-dresser with a taste for designer clothes and exotic holidays. When Adam thought of what Malcolm suffered over Carlos he was glad he had nobody. It was bad enough being gay, without being in love with a tart as well. All that stuff about coming out and being proud of homosexuality – that was for the sort of people who called spastics 'differently abled' or 'educationally challenged'. They were as blind as those who insisted that all heterosexuals were closet gays. Something he had read long ago had stuck in his mind, about how a writer must have the power of facing unpleasant facts. It was no good telling himself that he would be less lonely if he sought the companionship of others.

Nothing consoled him. Belgravia sold his paperback rights, but the money went to balance his advance, and in any case he could not have cared less. He wondered whether he should have given up his job at Pocock's, should have realized the snobbish opprobrium of being in trade; but what would he have lived on? Had he been on the dole, or independently wealthy, he would have been more respectable, apparently.

Adam had believed himself brave, or at least tenacious, during the long struggle to write his first novel but that was nothing compared with what was demanded by the second. He looked back on that time now as a period of happy innocence. Then, his only real worry had been whether or not he was publishable. Now it was as though he had entered the gates of hell, and every new book would take him further down into it.

He woke every day in tears, and went to sleep crying. He went back to Heaven, watched the throbbing, pulsating crowd gyrate. I could get laid, he thought. Even though I'm over thirty and ugly. I have a black leather jacket and can call myself a writer: some dipshit is bound to be impressed by that. There were some beautiful boys there, who had at least a hundred men watching them greedily, boys greased front and back for action, but all had the same predatory look in their eyes. Eat or be eaten. The bodies writhed beneath the stroboscopes like maggots on dead meat. In the beginning he had imagined a finer sort of love, not this oily gristle heaving and lurching in the heat. He stayed, gripped by the beat that went on and on, swirling and churning men into a mass, dissolving the boundaries between dancing and sex until, one after another, they were spent. There was pleasure in this, the pleasure of repeated temporary oblivion, of being reduced to so much anonymous flesh, but it was not for him.

He felt ill with misery, a misery that went on month after month, and impotent fury. He wrote out something he found in Dr Johnson's *Life of Pope*: 'An author places himself uncalled before the tribunal of criticism, and solicits fame at the hazard of disgrace.'

'I don't know how to get past it,' he said to Mary. 'You see, I know that there'll be faults in the next book, and the next, and I don't know how to survive if there's nothing but hammering each time. I mean, eventually I might do something faultless but not in those conditions.'

'Oh, come on, Adam,' said Mary, irritably. 'It wasn't all bad.'

'Yes, it was.'

'Well, then it won't be next time.'

'There's no guarantee of that. People like Ivo'll just think I've got the hide of a rhinoceros and am coming back for more.'

'Ivo thinks you're too thin-skinned.'

'Thin-skinned! Isn't that a prerequisite for being a writer? Oh – those who can, do: those who can't, review.'

'I've never wanted to "do", as you put it. Besides, it seems to me to be a perfectly valid way of earning a living.'

'It isn't a living, it's your life. What kind of a creature wants to spend his or her life in such a parasitical activity?'

Mary had never seen Adam like this. She had admired him in the past for a kind of sardonic dignity, for being at one remove from everything around him; it had given him a mystique not unlike Mark's. This tormented, egotistical bore, whose every conversation returned obsessively to his own maltreatment, was not someone she even pitied.

'I don't know what to say to him,' she said to Tom Viner. 'I do feel sorry he's so hurt, but it's embarrassing, especially when he keeps on about Ivo.'

'Perhaps he doesn't want you to say much,' said Tom. 'When you were unhappy, didn't you just want him to listen?'

'No,' said Mary, with a flash of her small white teeth. 'I wanted him to go out and punch Mark on the nose.'

Tom felt the strangest sensation, as though he might faint. It was her voice, he thought. It reminded him of a clarinet, or an oboe, the way it swooped and rose, at once haunting and full of laughter. 'What did you think of his book?'

'Well,' said Mary, 'so unlike the home life of our own dear queen, don't you think? But strangers could scarcely be expected to know that.'

This was their third lunch together. Tom was now working just north of Soho, and Mary had joined the London Library, which, despite its horrifying paucity of contemporary fiction, saved her a small fortune in newspapers and periodicals. They would meet at the Patisserie Valerie for a sandwich; it always amused her to see how intensely every woman in that small, steamy, vanilla-scented room was aware of him as though, no matter how silent he was, his body spoke. He talked easily and pleasantly, but gave away very little about himself. She knew he had a girlfriend called Sarah, also a doctor, and that he lived with, of all people, Mark and Amelia.

'I never return dinner-parties,' he said, to her mingled disappointment and relief. 'I'm too lazy to cook.'

She wondered whether it was because she was indebted to him for her flat at Phoebe's, or whether his interest was professional, a follow-up on her mental state. It could scarcely be gratitude for a pleasant evening. Perhaps, she thought, he just wanted uncomplicated companionship, or perhaps it was something altogether more sinister. Mark had always been so prying about her life. It was not inconceivable that he had put Tom up to this. She was careful to make no demands on him, to expect nothing, to be as different as possible from the creature she had been in hospital. He didn't fancy her, there were hundreds of other girls prettier and richer and in every way more desirable than she was, and that was fine.

'Is Ivo a great friend of yours?'

'Not really. I find him quite repulsive, physically. But he does grow on one, you know. Like fungus.'

She would say or suggest things to test him out. One day she said, 'Have you ever been into a sex-shop?'

'No.'

'There's one opposite. Don't you think, as a doctor, you should know what it's like?'

'I think I've a pretty good idea.'

'Where's your curiosity? It might be a good crack.'

'All right,' he said, amused. 'Let's go in.'

The impulse of cruelty that had made her suggest it lasted long enough to take them across Old Compton Street inside the smoked-glass door. The shop was dimly lit, like an aquarium, with its merchandise displayed in bright glass cases. Most of it consisted of gigantic plastic penises.

'Dildos, I suppose,' said Mary, scornfully. She looked at some steel rings of varying circumference with what she felt was scholarly interest. 'What on earth are those?'

'They're for putting on an erection,' said Tom. 'Supposed to make it last longer.'

'Jesus, Mary and Joseph. How do you know?'

'Seen them in Casualty, occasionally. Some poor sod gets them stuck and gangrene sets in.'

'What d'you do then?'

'Cut their plonkers off,' said Tom. It took Mary a moment to realize he was joking.

A woman's breathy voice said, 'Uh, uh, uh,' over the sound system. Behind the cash register a bored man turned the pages of the *Sun*. Mary looked at the underwear on display, spidery pieces of red and black nylon. 'So unaesthetic,' she murmured, thinking miserably of Mark.

There was a dummy with handcuffs on, and chains through its nipples. Further on in the dimness was a demonstration model of an inflatable woman wearing a black G-string with a hole in the crotch. A TV showed a video of frankfurters.

'What a horrible place.'

'You wanted to see it.'

'Does it turn you on?' she asked. She had wanted to embarrass him, and yet it was she who was blushing and uncomfortable.

'No.'

'I suppose, as a doctor, you've seen everything, haven't you?'

Tom knew that his having seen thousands of people without clothes on was found erotic by an extraordinary number of women; they never seemed to understand that for him they were clothed in their humanity. 'No,' he said. 'It's nothing like the reality, is it?'

'I've forgotten,' she said, and all her bitterness against Mark welled up so tightly in her throat that she could hardly breathe.

He glanced down at her, angry, embarrassed, and, despite what he had said, lustful. 'Let's go, shall we?'

They came out, blinking, into the daylight.

'You're not spying on me, are you?' she asked, suddenly.

'Spying?'

'For Mark and Amelia? I know you live in their house.'

'No,' said Tom; and this time she saw she had hurt him. 'I'd never do that.'

She knew he was telling the truth; knew too that she had damaged something by asking. He would always somehow expect you to be better than you were. It was very tiring.

'Has Amelia had her baby?'

'Yes. Last month. A girl.'

'Are they – happy together?'

Tom said, 'As far as I know.'

He knew she would think him over-diplomatic, but his parents' divorce had taught him the value of silence. I don't really know what I think about anyone, he realized; and Mary knows too much.

'Oh?'

He looked at her. 'I don't discuss people, Mary. Not like that.'

'Why not? Gossip makes the world go round, so they say.' She had tears in her eyes, and glanced away. It upset her to discover how much it still hurt.

'Not my kind of world.'

'You mean there's any other?'

'Yes. What you live in now is just a tiny fraction of all the possible ones there are, even in London. There are people who don't exist on a currency of malice.'

'Indeed? Why do I never seem to come across them?'

'You move in the wrong circles,' said Tom.

Amelia in Love

Amelia was ill for a long time after the birth of her daughter, Rose. It was not just that she haemorrhaged on delivery, and that the hospital neglected to give her a blood transfusion for five days. She had a urinary tract infection from the catheter, infected stitches in her episiotomy, and, as she discovered a month later, a verruca courtesy of the hospital bathroom. Peeing made her stitches burn like red-hot staples; she could stand it only if she trained a jet of cold water from the hand shower onto her, which meant, disgustingly, doing it in the bath or bidet. Anything bigger made her nearly faint.

'I can't, I just can't,' she whimpered, straining, soaked in sweat from pain, fear and effort. 'It'll rip me apart all over again.'

'Don't be silly,' said the nurse, who helped her into the bathroom the first time. 'The stitches are stronger than you think. Just push.'

Amelia tried and fainted.

All the calm and kindness of the delivery room had vanished. Two overworked nurses trying to look after twenty women, all stunned by pain and shock, told her briskly that she was making a fuss about nothing; after five days her bowel began to leak. Then there was another infection, complete with delirious dreams of floating on an iceberg, and then an enema. At around the same time, she got mastitis, and more fever.

'You look like Paddington station down there,' said the midwife, checking her stitches. 'Never mind, you'll soon be as good as new.'

She had never been in so much pain. As the epidural wore off, it caught up with her like thunder after lightning, rumbling endlessly through the haze of drugs. Everything hurt, her bottom, her breasts, the hand where her drip went in. Her veins had contracted from lack of blood, and the transfusion she eventually received felt like a bar of steel going into her flesh. Breast-feeding was so far from the ecstasy described in books that she could endure it only by writing imaginary letters of unparalleled ferocity to Sheila Kitzinger. Every time Rose clamped her jaws on, it felt like an electric shock; but if she did not allow her daughter to suck, her breasts seethed and stung, as if bitten by writhing worms just under the skin. She was unable to stop herself flinching, and then the baby would scream with her.

When Amelia looked at herself in the bathroom mirror she saw a middle-aged woman. Her skin was pale grey. Her hair clumped together like wet straw. Her stomach hung in streaky folds of wrinkled flesh like an emptied balloon. Nine months ago I wore a size ten gold dress by Karl Lagerfeld, she thought. Now I understand about corsets and Monsoon.

But something astonishing had happened to her on the delivery table as soon as she heard Rose's hoarse, imperious cry. She said, stupidly, 'So there really was something in there after all!' and, in that instant, her old life was consumed.

'Is it all right?' Amelia kept asking. 'Is it all right? Please, Tom, is it all right?'

'She's fine,' he said, and that was when Amelia knew she had a daughter.

She had lost any sense of modesty, spatchcocked on the birthing chair with six doctors cutting or sewing or, for all she knew, basting her for the oven. She suddenly realized she had been gripping Tom's hand. He gave her some water, and grinned. 'Don't worry. She's beautiful.'

'Can I see her?'

'Just checking,' said the paediatrician; and for ten minutes, Amelia forgot to breathe until at last she had her in her arms, her perfect daughter, blotched and bruised, smelling of iron and sex, still turning with each breath from stone to flesh, but with such eyes! They were blue, the blue of deep space melting into air, as though she had hurtled into being like a meteor instead of pushing her way out through an earthquake of torn muscle. They seemed to know everything already, to understand and forgive everything Amelia had been before this moment.

'Oh, darling, my darling,' she said, and was sick into a kidney dish.

She refused, absolutely, to let the nurses take her. When one of them tried, Amelia snarled like a wolverine. She was too weak to stand up, but she knew, and the nurse knew, that she would kill anyone who tried to take this exquisite weight from her; so they left them together. All night long, and for many nights after, she lay staring into her daughter's eyes, with her own red-rimmed ones, examining the miniature fingers and toes, the scrawny limbs, the bracelets of fat, the rayed lashes, the flattened, primitive, angelic face. She was mad with pain and love. This was not the delight in a sympathetic heart or the pulsing rut of adult lust, not the meeting of minds, nor the adoration of beauty, but something so fierce and instinctive it appalled her. You could no more enjoy it than you could enjoy a shower in the Niagara Falls.

She knew her baby was frightened by everything except her, just as she was frightened by everything except it. It nuzzled into her, a tiny animal, and she nuzzled it back, a large one. She almost forgot how to talk, existing in a world of smell and touch and heat and milk and pain. When the pressure on her bladder became too much she pushed the hospital bassinet to the lavatory with one arm while gripping her drip with the other because she was so frightened of somebody stealing her. When she dozed, she kept Rose wedged in between her arm and her side.

A blushing junior doctor came to lecture her on contraception.

'Do I *look* as if I'll be remotely interested?'

'Well, ah, you might be sooner than you think,' he said. 'You'd be surprised the number of women we get back within a year.'

'Brutes,' said Amelia. 'They're all married to brutes!'

It was not infants who were sexual, but sex which was infantile, she thought, hazily. She had never really read Freud but he had got it completely wrong, just like a man. What idiots they all were.

Next came a physiotherapist to instruct them on post-natal exercises. She was a bouncy young woman, glowing with health. 'In order not to suffer from incontinence in later life, you have to imagine you're holding a pencil in your vagina and squeezing it.'

Amelia glared.

'Squeeze and – squeeze and – squeeze.'

Amelia asked, icily, 'Won't you give me a demonstration?'

'Now, to get your tummy back, you need to do fifty sit-ups a day, starting *now*.'

Amelia managed three before collapsing.

'Come on, come on,' said the physio. 'You can do better than that.'

Amelia asked, 'Have *you* ever had a baby?'

The girl gave her wide, bright smile. 'Nope.'

Amelia lay back and closed her eyes. 'Then sod off.'

The other women in the ward uttered a faint cheer.

There were lessons on how to bath her baby and put a nappy on. She handled Rose with her fingertips, afraid she would break if she picked her up too roughly, and consequently nearly dropped her. Alone of all the babies in the ward, Rose remained in the hospital smock, which seemed far more sensible in a heatwave than Babygros. The radiators were on, notwithstanding. 'The one person who knew how to turn this ancient central heating system off got made redundant last spring,' Tom told her. 'Keeping it on costs sixty thousand a year. Sorry. Eventually this will all be knocked down and merged with another hospital in a whizzy new building, and then it'll be wonderful. Except that you won't be able to get a bed.'

The ward emptied and refilled. The woman whom Amelia had heard yelling appeared the next day as a smiling Australian who left with her husband the same afternoon. A fourteen-year-old girl who had given birth to a boy was visited by her admiring schoolfriends.

'Oooh, isn't he cute?' they all said, one after the other.

'Yeah,' said the girl, indifferently. 'He's a doll.'

She left after zipping herself into a pair of size ten jeans, with her mother, who looked little more than twenty-five herself.

A Muslim girl of about sixteen was berated by her husband and relations for producing a female. She left her baby to whimper, and walked grimly up and down the corridor while the family sat on her bed and filled the ward with smells of curry.

'Her daughter'll be dead in weeks, poor little mite,' the nurses prophesied. They spoke to anyone foreign with quite a different tone of voice, cold and hectoring – even though, with the exception of two Irish girls, they were nearly all either Chinese or West Indian.

'She won't breastfeed,' said the Irish nurse to Amelia. 'Those Muslims never do, if it's a girl. She'll be back within a year, too.'

'Does it upset you? The things you see?'

'I'll tell you something, darlin',' said one. 'I think it's a crying shame that you have to have a licence to have a car and not a baby.'

Amelia wondered whether she would have qualified. She felt divided between a surging tide of goodwill to all women and disdain for the common herd.

Mark did not visit until the Friday, although she knew Tom had told him of their daughter's birth. He arrived with a magnificent bunch of white lilies – he had always been good about flowers, she thought – and a bottle of champagne, most of which he drank himself. 'A daughter,' he said. 'Well, well.'

'She's called Rose. Isn't she just the most beautiful thing you ever saw?'

'She's all right, I suppose,' said Mark. 'Is her skin supposed to be that funny colour?'

Amelia looked anxiously at her baby. 'Oh, she's a bit jaundiced.'

'Hair's a bit lank, too,' said Mark, beginning to enjoy himself. 'I thought they were supposed to be bald.'

Amelia looked at him calmly. She felt beyond his power to affect her in any way, contemptuous, even, of his attempts to do so. 'It's just newborn stuff. She's a red-head, though. See?'

'How is that possible?'

'It's a recessive gene. Look how alert she is. This is your daddy, Rose.'

'She can't see anything,' said Mark. 'Newborns are blind.'

'Yes, she can. If you'd read my pregnancy books you'd know. She can see up to ten inches, which is the distance between my breast and face.'

'Looks more like twenty to me.'

Rose began to grizzle, and Amelia, not without defiance, undid her nightdress and nursing bra. One enormous, green-veined breast flopped out like a peeled Stilton. The baby splayed her hands across it and began to suck ravenously. Mark watched in undisguised horror. This grey ogress bore only the faintest resemblance to the woman he had met less than a year ago. Their withered infant hung from her livid dug like a leech, twitching obscenely. He could never love it, he thought, and relief made him almost kind. 'Is there anything I can bring you?'

'Food,' said Amelia. 'There's nothing edible here except corn-flakes. And some more batteries for the portable phone. They've only got an awful old thing on wheels here, can you imagine?'

'When do they let you go? The maternity nurse has arrived. A New Zealander, looks like a sheep in a shellsuit.'

'Oh, good,' said Amelia absently. 'Have you rung our parents?'

'Yes. Your father sent a crate of vintage champagne. This is part of it.'

'Is he coming?'

'I don't know,' said Mark. 'The last I heard, he's in America, trying to buy a paper there.'

'He hasn't forgiven me, then,' said Amelia.

There were visits from her mother and parents-in-law. The latter were arch and embarrassed, terrified that she might breast-feed in front of them, and brought a musical mobile with fluffy teddies. The former was the only person Amelia trusted to hold Rose while she had a shower and washed her hair. Mrs de Monde had tears in her eyes, seeing her daughter's naked body for the first time in twenty years.

'It's so ghastly, isn't it, darling?' she said. 'Nobody who hasn't been through it can imagine. But your baby is lovely.'

'Oh, Mummy,' said Amelia, overcome with sentiment and guilt. 'I'm so sorry if I made you suffer when I was born.'

'It wasn't your fault,' said Mrs de Monde.

Amelia went home. She was still bleeding so copiously that she used up the entire stock of maternity pads in the Camden Boots. Shirley, the maternity nurse, had to help her in and out of the bath. 'You leave your dignity at the hospital door and don't pick it up until six weeks later,' she said.

Ten days after the birth, the stitches began to fall out in clots of black and blood. Amelia spent all day in bed, feeding and sleeping and gazing at Rose. Even television was too much effort. The washing machine shuddered continually; the bathroom steamed up with all the ironing. Shirley prepared what she called 'slickers', strips of incontinence pads smeared with frozen arnica ointment, which placed inside underpants gave Amelia's burning perineum three whole minutes without pain, and bought calendula ointment for her cracked nipples.

'I can't do this, it's too sore,' she said, getting mastitis for the second time. 'I'll have to stop.'

Shirley folded her arms. She had told Amelia that breast-fed babies grew up happier, healthier and more intelligent than their bottle-fed counterparts.

'Don't you want to breast-feed?'

No, no, Amelia screamed silently, but meeting Shirley's righteous indignation said, 'If it helps Rose.'

'Righty-tighty.' Shirley bent down and forced one throbbing globule into the baby's mouth.

'*Aaaaah!*' shrieked Amelia, but Shirley would not let go. Rose sucked furiously. Five minutes later, the worst of the pain had vanished, although she had to have another course of antibiotics to kill the infection.

'Thanks,' said Amelia, when she could speak again. 'I suppose that was the right thing to do.'

'Yis, it was. Now, you eat up everything, especially those dried apricots and the red wine. Your figure'll come back soon enough. Rose'll suck off all the fat, won't you, chucklechops?'

Shirley made her laugh, although she had a reverence for the Royal Family and a hatred of black people that continually amazed Amelia. She also thoroughly disliked men. 'Blokes are good for plying hide the salami, otherwise yer better off with a dog,' she would say. 'Just you make sure you don't give your husband yer money.'

'Oh, my money's quite safe. Daddy took care of that.'

There was now a shortage of beds. Mark slept with his wife, but as far away from her burning, milky flesh as possible. He was appalled that Rose needed seven changes of nappy a day.

'You mean, it's begun already?' he said, gagging as his wife cleaned their daughter's yellow bottom for the first time in front of him. 'I thought we'd have a few days before the torrents started.'

'It's not too bad,' said Amelia, adoring.

Every day, florist's vans drew up with baskets and bouquets, most of them silky pink carnations, scentless roses and sypsophilia from employees of her father and colleagues at the *Chronicle*. From those she had counted as friends she received baby clothes, mostly smocked and smothered in lace, utterly impractical for the first year of life.

'I'm the one who's suffered,' she said, tearfully. 'Rose couldn't care less if she wears a towelling vest. I'm the one who needs the presents.'

She hated everyone for being more concerned with Rose than herself; she even hated Rose for making her love her so much. She couldn't sleep for fear that Rose would stop breathing. When she did manage some sleep, she would be woken by milk spurting from her nipples.

Little by little, she became more active. Georgina sent her a long spidery thing called a Wilkinet sling, which freed her hands and kept Rose wonderfully close and happy, tucked in between Amelia's gigantic breasts and dreaming, presumably of the womb from which she had been forced.

Half the time Amelia was in ecstasy, and the other half she wanted to throw herself under a bus. Every day, she thought she could not possibly get any tireder, but every day there was another level to sink. Her hair fell out in clumps, and she had no time to have it streaked, so its gold dimmed and faded. She could not wear contact lenses, and reverted back to some ancient glasses like goggles. Wodges of fat rolled around her torso and legs.

'You look like the Michelin Man,' said Mark. She was surprised that he still wanted to have sex with her, but it did occasionally happen. She was still completely dead inside, not just dry or numb but gone as if there had never been anything in the first place. She could not believe that those wonderful rings of muscle would ever come back, however many pelvic-floor exercises she did.

It was worse once Shirley left. Mark moved back into the spare bedroom, but that was the only relief. They still had no cleaner, and no nanny. The sound of Rose's screams seemed to go through her head from ear to ear, reverberating. It was, she thought, like having the most passionate affair of your life with someone who tortured you every night. Every day, Rose was so charming, so exquisite, so utterly adorable that Amelia forgave everything, and every night she turned into a demon who drove her to the very edge of self-control.

'Just go to sleep, darling, go to sleep,' she said, over and over in a demented chant.

'I'd like to have my wife back, now,' said Mark, giving her his black look; but Amelia, who was to see every single dawn for the next three years, lived perpetually in three o'clock in the morning. It held no terrors for her, only a weary familiarity.

'I can't get my figure back until I get some sleep.'

'So, get it,' he said.

She tried rocking, hoovering, tapes of the womb. She tried long walks, more breast-feeding, less breast-feeding, driving for miles around London. She tried silence, she tried stimulus, she tried reading aloud and singing. Every night she would lie down with her baby in a darkened room, counting up to a hundred, then to another hundred, then another hundred, in an agony of tenderness. Still Rose would not sleep. She tried patting her daughter's bottom. She tried dummies. She tried bottles.

Occasionally, something would seem to work, and then after twenty-four hours, Amelia would find her spirits soaring.

Aha, she said to herself, so *that*'s what I was doing wrong. How simple. But after a couple of nights, the magic wore off, and she was back to where she had started, only tireder. The exhaustion was so great that she was barely conscious of it, pressing down on her like a vice, flattening everything into two dimensions. She lived in a world devoid of logic, radiant with feeling, in which she was so tired she thought that at any moment she could fall asleep on her feet, and yet so strong that the slightest threat to Rose filled her with a surging maniacal strength.

It did not occur to her that there could be a danger from any other direction.

22

A Literary Banquet

Over the *Chronicle* rumour pressed. People worked in murky air, foul-tempered, sore-headed, unaware of this until they went on holiday – which few now dared to do. News is misery, uncovered or concocted, but were you to look beneath the cream-coloured Burberrys of these busy cynics you would see that they were almost as wretched as their victims.

Everyone had been disgruntled by the move from Fleet Street to paperless offices, but the shadow that crept now upon even the youngest and most enthusiastic of journalists was deepening. The user-friendly dwarf conifers on the steps, the £500 tubs of pansies outside and weeping figs inside could not distract de Monde's employees from the high fences of razor wire, security patrols and sniffer dogs. They were producing a newspaper in a prison, and the fact that they could leave prison every evening did not lessen their depression.

There was a further cause for despondency. Max de Monde and his empire were in deep debt; quite how deep nobody knew except that the banks, who were his creditors, were refusing to roll over his loans any longer. People said his debt amounted to that of a whole country in Africa, or South America, but then people always exaggerated. The recession had damaged everyone, but for news-papers and magazines it was catastrophic. Who, really, needed newspapers when everyone had radio and television? People had once defined themselves as *Times* or *Guardian* or *Chronicle* readers, but now that all the broadsheets were competing for the middle market such readers were fickle. The *Chronicle* in particular was losing circulation to other papers by the thousand every week. All the dailies had been weakened by the growth of Sunday supplements and, no matter what scandals Angus McNabb's team unearthed, nothing could stop the slide. Week after week new victims were exposed, yet the public did not seem to care for it. Both Max de Monde and Angus McNabb believed the punters, as they called their readers, to be stupid, gross, venal and incapable of making up their own minds, but no matter how low they sank, the level appeared not to be low enough. Should they go tabloid? Merge with a Sunday? Relaunch the magazine?

There are few things worse for a journalist than to work on a sinking newspaper. It was, as Ivo said, like being trapped on the *Titanic* with the brass band. Everyone wanted to move, and no one, except for a couple of star columnists, was able to breathe a word of their discontent in case the dagger should suddenly stick out from between their own shoulders. When friends lamented to each other they went into the lavatories and whispered under cover of the hot-air machines. Those who could take redundancy did, but most, faced with soaring mortgages and a shrivelling of staff jobs on all newspapers, were miserably resigned to hanging on.

'It has to pass,' they said to each other. 'Property prices have to go up, and then the recession will be over.'

Each month, however, saw another rise in interest rates, another fall in the value of their flats and houses, another pinching of the national pocket. It affected everyone, from de Monde, who had boasted that the *Chronicle* had been grossly undervalued by the Paddington family because its former site alone was worth the price, to Mark, who could not even rent out his flat. The thought that had he behaved less ruthlessly towards Mary he might have at least gained some income from her made him even angrier, especially once he discovered he had to spend £120 on new locks. Angus insisted that all freelances in Ivo's section be paid half the amount for which Marian had previously budgeted, and that nobody take any more contributors out to lunch, a move that made him spectacularly unpopular. Such was the desperation among freelances, however, that many thought even £85 a review was better than nothing.

Yet de Monde continued to expand, buying a tabloid in New York and a TV station in Hong Kong from which he planned to broadcast to the Pacific rim. He was listed by a rival paper as the twelfth richest man in Britain, an accreditation that astonished those who worked for him. His hirings and firings were reported in the *Eye*, the only publication his libel writs could not gag. He seemed unable to turn down anything that came on the market, especially if it was being pursued by other, bigger, media barons.

What drove Max de Monde to such excesses? Some believed it was greed for money, or for more power; others that he was bent on revenging himself on the society which had initially ostracized him as a foreigner. There were stories of how he, alone among proprietors, had never been asked to Chequers or to the Queen's garden party, how he had been snubbed by his wife's family so that he had a rooted aversion for the entire Establishment. The simple-minded believed him an incarnation of evil, and it is true that, were the devil to exist, he could find no better way of fomenting trouble than by owning a newspaper.

The *Chronicle* literary banquet was, like Christmas, a nadir of ill-will advertised for months in advance. Only the fact that it generated a small profit stopped the management from axing it, but it was a nightmare to arrange. In the past, Marian had persuaded Angus to let her lead with something serious by saying, 'Look, Angus, this book is *the* most stylish accessory around. Everyone will be wearing it on their front page, and we'll look like idiots if we ignore it.'

Angus, who aspired to join the chattering classes even if he attacked them every other week, would fall for it. With Ivo, how-ever, the situation was difficult. He was smarting at remaining in Books, at the same lowly salary, and insisted on a high literary tone. Angus had started to rebel, and demand that the middlebrow take precedence; no argument could suppress the evidence of their own bestseller lists. Ivo was equally determined not to compromise his position in the favours market. He liked patronizing academics from his Cambridge years by commissioning articles from them, publishing young poets – as long as they were male – and elder statesmen. It consoled him for the political future now lost for ever. For it was one of the strange aspects of Ivo's nature that, steeped in mischief and prejudice as he was, he retained a kind of reverence for those he considered to be, within the narrowest of bounds, gifted. Angus could no more understand this than he could learn to knit.

'Why can't ye kick off with something our readers will really enjoy, like the new George MacDonald Fraser?' he would demand. 'This Steiner fella is a total turn-off.'

The literary banquet became a new battlefield.

MEET YOUR FAVOURITE AUTHORS, said the advertisement, with photographs of what resembled, and sometimes were, raddled ex-convicts with a bad hangover. For only £75 a head, readers were informed, they could meet these giants at the Savoy Hotel. Over a hundred star-studded authors, agents and publishers would be present at what the *Chronicle* claimed was the Oscars of the literary world.

'There is one thing as a judge I would like to make absolutely clear,' Mark said to Angus. 'We are not having any women writers as guests or speakers.' He had been brought in as a non-literary figure.

'Why not?'

'They're all crap.'

'I say, old boy, don't you think that's taking things a bit far? After all, one or two have actually won major prizes, you know,' said Ivo.

'Only by default,' said Mark coldly. 'Or because they were shagging the judges on the side.'

'We cannot ignore one half of the human race,' said Angus, his liberal credentials jabbing him sharply like an under-used credit card. 'The prizes are up to you and the other judges, but my decision is final.'

Mark hated the idea of a literary banquet even more than Ivo did. The idea of meeting any of the politician-novelists he had disembowelled was embarrassing to the point of discomfort – it was bad enough to receive angry letters, public or private, complaining about their treatment in the leader pages. 'Why can't they behave?' he said to Ivo, in genuine bewilderment.

'That's the trouble with living people, dear boy,' said Ivo. 'They just won't take it on the chin. They aren't gentlemen.'

'Neither are we, of course,' said Mark, with his usual dour honesty.

'Speak for yourself,' said Ivo.

Angus always had a private party in a little room off the ballroom for the guests of honour. This banquet was no exception. Five hundred *Chronicle* readers, dressed in black tie and their best evening gowns, were cordoned off from those they had paid to meet, and had to content themselves with drinking Buck's Fizz and the odd glimpse of fame.

'Ooh, is that Fay Weldon?' said one, craning her neck.

'No, it's Lady Antonia Fraser,' said another. 'Isn't she beautiful?'

'Do you think Salman Rushdie will be here?'

'Christ, I hope not. We could all be blown sky-high.'

'God, look at them,' said Percy Flage, turning his back on the other side of the rope. 'What do they think we are, animals at the Zoo?'

'They have to buy their own wine, poor things.'

'It's probably better than this rats' piss.'

'Who's getting the awards?'

The awards, a hollow silver book for the Author of the Year, and a cheque for £2000 for the publisher, were supposed to be kept secret in order to heighten the tension.

'No idea. Flora Payne, someone said.'

'Not after Mary Quinn hatcheted her.'

'Darling! Mmmwaah!'

'Darling! Isn't this frightful?'

'Worse than Cheltenham.'

'Marian's got a hundred and twenty, just for the UK rights. It was a stroke of luck, getting sacked, she says.'

'The publishers are all furious. Six hundred a table, and they don't dare refuse.'

'They can afford it. When did you last see a poor publisher?'

'Just remind me what your name is? Of course, I know the byline.'

'There is no longer any distinction between high and low culture.'

'Yes, but the trouble with post-modernism is that it's unable to deal with relationships between people. It can only relate screens, images, texts.'

'The nineties aren't shaping up too well, are they? Not a trace of naughtiness, just a lot of long faces.'

'God this food is vile. Sun-dried tomatoes gently wrapped in millefeuille pastry.'

'Yeah: sun-dried dog turd gently wrapped in old newspaper.'

'They've just paid Marian an advance of a hundred and fifty grand.'

'Bitch! I can't bear it!'

'Have you heard, Georgina Hunter's left her husband?'

'Good God, I'd no idea she was in her forties.'

'She isn't. The new generation are precocious.'

'Well, in my day people used to wait until the children were at boarding school.'

'In my day, it used to be when they went to university.'

'That husband was a crashing bore. Georgina, darling! Mwaaah! How's the new novel?'

'How did she lose all that weight?'

'Oh, my dear, she's found a Harley Street doctor who prescribes amphetamines. I was on *Snap, Crackle, Pop!* with her last month and said how I wasn't used to getting up at seven thirty, and she said, "Why not have a quarter of my pills? They make you talk rather fast but —"'

'You mean, speed?'

'Well, how do you think she manages a blockbuster a year?'

'Of course, she's an admirer of Mrs Thatcher, what can you expect?'

'I thought it was really rather good.'

'Absolute crap. School of Laura Ashley.'

'AND they've just paid her a hundred and sixty for the paperback rights!'

'The coming thing is popular science books.'

'All that stuff about incest, one's so tired of it. Book after book at Frankfurt, half of them in languages one had never heard of.'

'Yes, but nobody dares *say* it's crap. Sorry, is he a friend of yours?'

'His wife found out they were having an affair, and came round and threw a brick through the window. So then he had to pretend it was vandalism, and ever since he's been banging on in his column about the failure of the police to combat street crime.'

'We can't give this award to Red Herring Press, they're a left-wing publisher.'

'I'm sorry, but it is their turn, Angus.'

'Was this your decision, Mark?'

'They're not unworthy of it.'

'Why isn't Belgravia on the shortlist? They're part of the Group.'

'It's so hideous. Why can't they give a cheque?'

'I've promised it to my son if I get it. He thinks it's like a football trophy.'

'Oh, bad luck. I suppose it would go to Percy Flage, wouldn't it?'

'I wonder if you could melt down the silver?'

'It's bound to be dipped.'

'Boo!'

'Boo!'

'Piss off, McNabb!'

'Outrageous, to make jokes about redundancies in publishing.'

'Boo! Down with fascists!'

'Excuse me, madam, may I see your invitation?'

'What? Let go of me! Fuck off, pig!'

'Out you come, please. Now then, don't make any trouble or someone will get hurt.'

'Ow!'

'Who was she?'

'Some old tramp who bluffed her way in.'

'I thought her dress was Westwood.'

'More like Westway.'

'Oh dear, poor old thing, at least she got a decent meal.'

'She did smell rather peculiar.'

'Darling, it's been marvellous to see you. Mmwaah!'

'Mmwaah! Will you be at the Paddingtons'?'

'Of course.'

'*À bientôt*, then, darling. At last. What a bore that woman is.'

Ivo, green with anxiety, slipped round the room like butter on a hot pan. Angus could do nothing to Mark because of his position as de Monde's son-in-law, so the blame for the catcalls during his speech would fall on Ivo. Will I still have a job by the end of this evening? he thought. Why had he ever helped his nemesis escape from Cambridge in the first place? Out of the corners of his eyes he watched Fiona Bamber talking to him from under her long blonde fringe with her peculiar mix of archness and animality. It was well known that Angus would offer any money to woo her from the *Mail*. Mark bent his head towards her, in the manner of Dracula.

Ivo went over to where Mary was standing. 'Look,' he said.

'I've seen.'

'Do you think –?'

'Oh, yes,' she said. 'But what are we going to do?'

Afterwards, Mary walked to the Underground. Its hot metallic reek thickened the further down she went, swirling exhaustedly as trains entered and left far below the surface of the earth. It clung to clothes, parched throats, furred nostrils. It tasted of blood.

I am desolate, desolate, she thought, horrified to find herself crying again. Even if she now hated Mark more than she had ever loved him, the pain was no less. It had shocked her profoundly to see him at the Savoy, to see him look at her and look through her, as though she, who had lived with him for most of her adult life, were so much thin air. If he would only say sorry, she thought, if he would release me from feeling so much hatred. That's all I want. She wished with all her heart that she had never written those letters, she saw that they had been as hopelessly ineffectual as those sent to her by wounded authors.

She had marked the anniversary of Amelia's launch with a party of her own, noting with grim pleasure that many of the faces she had seen there came to her party also, and no longer snubbed her.

Every time she found herself in a street down which she had walked with Mark, or in a cinema, or restaurant, she experienced a small sense of triumph, as another piece of the past was overlaid by the present. Even if she now had debts of £4000, even if she spent the hour before going out to yet another party crying and drinking in terror of encountering him again, it was all progress. What she dreaded was stasis. In London, you had to keep moving or you would die. Yet the one thing that would cure her, if anything would, remained impossible.

She could not take another lover. She could not sleep with someone without falling in love, and that was what she most dreaded. I cannot, ever, be so vulnerable to someone again, she thought. That is the scar Mark has left on me for ever. If only she could just do it, as heartlessly and joyously as, say, Tom Viner. She was almost tempted to say to him, 'Look, I have this problem, would you mind doing it, lay the ghost?' But the idea was too comical and too embarrassing.

She knew what Ivo wanted, and really, if she were at all sensible, she would let him. He was always dropping round at the Chelsea flat, supposedly on his way home to Clapham or bringing her a book to review. He had actually ended up on his knees in front of her, once. So far she had managed to keep him at bay by talking about how miserable Mark had made her, but in the end, she was either going to have to give in or make it clear that she found him repellent.

A movement caught her eye as she waited for the tube home. It was a rat, scurrying like speeded-up clockwork, moving between the rails in a blur of fur and naked tail. There were supposed to be more rats than people in London, now. That was how you survived, she thought, living off scraps, in between the lines.

23

The Zen Art of Motherhood

"'Allo, do you spik Turkish?'

'Hallo, I'm a Kiwi, I saw your ad in the *Lady*, I –'

'This is Carla I am ringing about the *Lady* magazine –'

'Hallo, I am ringing to enquire whether you really need someone with a driving licence for the nanny position –'

'Hallo, I saw your ad in the *Lady* and wondered if you've given any thought to paying nanny tax –'

'This is Sondra, I am Serbian I need help pliss –'

'Don't you dare hang up on me, you rude bitch –'

'I was just ringing to ask, is that two hundred a week before or after tax?'

'Hallo? Hallo? Hallo?'

Amelia was exhausted. She had got a nanny through an agency that charged her £480, on top of the £200 a week she paid to the nanny herself. By Christmas, the girl had gone back to Italy, unable to endure either English weather or, she had said, with an angry, flashing look, English men. Amelia, who was still being woken five times a night, promptly went down with flu. As soon as she got better, Rose caught it, and they lay in bed together, the baby crying and wheezing, running a temperature. Nothing stayed inside; she writhed in agonies like a caterpillar, contorting so violently that she half suffocated herself if not watched. Amelia's back and shoulders hurt as though a blunt knife had been inserted between each muscle. Rose became too heavy for the sling, yet could only be calmed if held close, face down, while her mother walked up and down in a convict's shuffle, terrified of waking Mark, whose temper, when he had enjoyed less than eight uninterrupted hours of slumber, was unspeakable.

Sleeping and waking merged into viscid waves. Amelia tried to get another nanny, but each one she employed turned out to be mad, slatternly or so lazy that they would not even scrub out the teats of Rose's bottles, let alone clear up the glop left on the floor and high chair by her mashed fruit and vegetables. Each stayed just long enough to be instructed on the correct way to stack a dishwasher, then left. Amelia found that, apart from the days her new cleaner came, she was doing all the housework while her nanny played with Rose. Thank God for Grace, who came in unfailingly twice a week, and who was like the fresh air she let in, cold but bracing.

'You shouldn't let him boss you around,' she said, when Amelia told her Mark wanted this or forbade that.

'I know.'

Amelia had never, ever, felt so ill. She would lie on her side, the baby clamped to her breast, dreaming that she was a corpse whose flesh was being sucked out with tiny fishlike nibbles. 'How did you survive?' she asked other mothers with older children, but all they could tell her was that they had forgotten, that it was like entering a black tunnel of tiredness from which one day, perhaps five or ten years older, she would emerge. Rose cried and cried. It made her get up even when she was so tired she could hardly see, when she had a fever, when her legs and arms shook.

I have to be strong, I have to survive, I have to be strong, I have to survive, Amelia said to herself. All that she had luxuriated in, all the money, the servants, the order, the parties, the *time* . . . I could have done so much more, if only I'd known, she thought, and this was her greatest regret. Every now and again, there was a window of perhaps two days in which she had a half-decent nanny, and Rose was well enough to sleep for six hours, in which real life almost reasserted itself, and during that time she had to do everything – mountains of laundry, see the dentist, the hairdresser, shop, send things off to her accountant, write, go to the lavatory. Then

Rose would become ill again, and these brief moments of normality would vanish even from memory.

She learnt to live from hour to hour, always with the consciousness of incipient disaster. At any moment Rose could start shrivelling, the fat melting off her bones as if burnt. Then a time out of mind would begin, rocking her baby as she cried herself hoarse until Amelia thought she would take on any agony for her child in order not to see her suffer. When ill, Rose would not take anything except breast-milk; the sweet, scalding smell of it was sicked up, curdled, to cool on every garment they both possessed and turn to rancid cheese. Every half-hour Amelia would force the digital thermometer under the baby's armpit, and watch it blink from 38 to 39, from 39 to 40, almost longing for it to rise higher so that she could take her to Casualty and relieve herself of responsibility. Nobody suggested anything useful. 'If I meet one more bloody woman who tells me the solution is to visit her acupuncturist or Chinese herbalist or homeopath, I think I'll hit her,' she said to Mark. They were sitting in a Hampstead restaurant, on one of their rare evenings out together, the usual affair of distressed apricot walls, tortured hazel twigs and, on every table, a single pink tulip in a blue glass vase wilting under halogen spotlights.

Mark dissected his smoked salmon blinis and asked, 'What do you expect?'

'I'd like someone to tell me I'm doing a hellish job well.'

'The trouble with you is you've never done a job of any kind before,' said Mark, disagreeably.

'I'm a journalist just like you, and unlike you I've written a book.'

'You wrote rubbish.'

'Well, it might not be your sort of highbrow stuff, but a lot of people liked it,' said Amelia. She knew by now that she was not a genius, but she still thought of herself as a professional.

Mark, however, would not give her credit for anything. 'You've never done a day's honest labour,' he said.

Whenever they went out together, they quarrelled. It was as though they saved up all the bile they dared not express at home for public. Amelia was increasingly demoralized about going out in any case, because she could barely squeeze into the largest of her old clothes.

Without Tom, she thought, she would have gone mad. He arrived back from the hospital greenish-white, with livid bruises of exhaustion under his eyes, yet after crashing out for a few hours would always come down to help. Sometimes it was just taking Rose out of her arms and making them both a cup of tea. Sometimes it was getting her a pint of milk and some chocolate from a corner shop, or chatting about trivia. Amelia learnt to recognize the sound of his tread outside the front door, as though he and not Mark were her husband. Sometimes she would slip into fantasies in which this was the case. Why had she not seen how good a husband he would make? Because she had not been brought up to think of men that way, with the sort of rational romanticism of Jane Austen. She had married instead out of – what? Neither love nor lust, it now seemed, but a sort of intellectual awe. What was so great about Mark's brain, anyway? He couldn't do what Tom did in a million years. He didn't make her laugh, as Tom did, or think about other people; he wasn't up against the very stuff of human existence, just sniping at politicians.

She said to Tom, 'I don't know how you do it. I've only had a few months of broken sleep, you've had years.'

'Practice.'

'It's not just that.'

'No . . . There's something you need in medicine called *caritas*. Do you know what it means?'

Amelia blushed, overcome with a shame that went over her like scalding water. '"Charity suffers long and is kind" . . . Yes. I know what it means.'

'It's that, you see,' he said, reddening.

'How can you bear it, though? Looking after – them – ordinary people – when they're so ugly and smelly and boring.'

'There are days when I think I can't. But I'm not asked to like them.' He put a spoonful of sugar in his coffee. 'Nor even to feel sorry for them, or remember them the next day.'

'But do you?'

'Yes. Some. They're all human.'

'Did you always want to become a doctor?' asked Amelia. 'So you could help people?'

Tom smiled at the naïve respect in her eyes.

Grace came in with the Hoover. 'Mind if I do your rooms, Tom?'

'No, go ahead. I was interested in science, but that was too nerdy.'

To have a doctor in the house was even better than a live-in nanny, Amelia thought, especially if he belonged to what she had begun to think of as North London aristocracy. Sometimes she had a vision in which the awfulness of Mark was ranged against the niceness of Tom. Sometimes, too, the only way she could stand having Mark in her bed was to shut her eyes and think of floating upwards into Tom.

'Couldn't you let me have a lie-in just one morning at the weekend?' Amelia asked her husband.

'No.'

'Just "no"?'

'I'm working, you've got a nanny and a cleaner. I can't think what it is you do all day.'

'I haven't had more than six consecutive hours of sleep for seven months,' said Amelia.

Mark looked at their daughter. As usual, her face was splotched in red spots, through which she was drooling and chattering like an idiot. He blamed Amelia's genes for the eczema. 'Can't you drug the brat? Tom must have something.'

Mark did not talk to their lodger more than was strictly necessary. When the two men met, they edged round each other with the wary politeness of two large dogs who knew that they might fight.

'No. They don't let you drug a baby, and it doesn't solve the problem.'

'Well, just let her scream, then,' said Mark impatiently. 'That's what our parents did, and it hasn't done us any harm.'

'Hasn't it?' asked Amelia, with the new, tired little smile of martyrdom he found intensely irritating.

If only she could get a proper nanny! The dirt and dust subsided under Grace, but Rose was driving her mad. She felt like a grain of wheat being mashed between two granite wheels. Each nanny stayed no more than a couple of months, and then there would be another fifty pounds to the *Lady*, another two weeks of interviewing and answering the telephone while Rose screamed in the background, another two weeks of showing them how everything worked, and then perhaps a month before they'd call in sick every other day or split up with their boyfriend or walk out in a huff at being asked to hang up the washing.

Amelia tried everything, more money, more friendliness, more help. She tried foreigners, English roses, ex-nurses, NNEBs, people with qualifications and people without. They simply didn't understand how to look after the most precious thing she had, because they weren't mothers.

Mobility only added to the mess. Walls, curtains and sofas became covered with tiny hand-prints. Glass, china and books tumbled like thunder. If Rose was silent for any length of time it meant that she had discovered a new and yet more ingenious method in which to commit suicide: choking on a tampon, say, or garotting herself with a steel tape-measure. Amelia learnt that the only way to preserve her sanity was to stay calm until the last possible moment at which disaster could be averted, then spring forward at supersonic speed to snatch Rose out of danger. She called this the Zen Art of Motherhood.

There were other, more brutal methods of maintaining life. Two weeks after she had written a piece for the *Observer* on why she would never ever hit her child, Amelia discovered that this was the only way to prevent Rose from biting through live electric wires. Otherwise, she was too beaten to care. She used the baby's dirty muslins to mop up the worst – dust, mud, shit, juice, milk, fruit – flailing wildly around whenever she heard a knock at the door.

'How are you finding it?' friends would ask, and Amelia would say, 'Oh, fine, fine,' because it was too awful to begin to describe.

Her heroic efforts were neither appreciated nor noticed. 'This mess is intolerable,' said Mark. 'Every step I take I'm either skidding on baby-sick or stumbling on another soft toy. It's not necessary to have all this junk. She'd be just as happy with a wooden spoon.'

'She gets wooden spoons as well.'

'Why can't you make things?' Mark said. 'You don't even have any hobbies.'

'I do have a hobby,' said Amelia. 'Sleep.'

'I find all this very stressful,' said Mark.

> 'This little piggy went to market
> This little piggy stayed at home
> This little piggy had roast beef
> This little piggy had none
> And this little piggy went wee-wee-wee
> I can't find my way home.'

Rose burst into giggles, and Amelia felt the rucksacks under her own eyes bulge with sudden fury.

'Oh, and I don't, I suppose? You've been in a nice clean office all day, with intelligent people talking to you and making you cups of coffee. Why don't you do some clearing up? Or hold her for a while. I'm so tired of holding her, so tired, I think my arms will come out of their sockets.'

Mark had once, early on, attempted to change a nappy. It was unfortunate that on this occasion, Rose grunted and covered his favourite Hackett's suit with noxious orange.

'It's not radioactive, you know,' Amelia said, laughing at the frozen horror on his face – but from then on he flatly refused to touch their daughter.

'Da-da!' Rose would cry, when she saw Tom.

'You should have children of your own,' she told him, probing.

'I've got six godchildren,' he said.

'Don't you want a family?'

'I don't know,' said Tom slowly. 'Everyone has the draw-bridge up, these days. But I don't want to marry just for company.'

Every day Amelia was determined to be the perfect wife and mother, serene and clean, with supper on the cooker. At six o'clock, she would change into a fresh T-shirt, put on mascara, empty the nappy bucket, squirt on some scent, sweep the floor and just about manage to fry some onions. Then it would all collapse. Within five minutes of her husband walking through the door, she was screaming at him. 'Why can't you *do* something?'

'What?'

'Something, anything. Put on some laundry. Take her for a walk round the block. Even if you changed one nappy in the morning it would help.'

'I'm not cut out to play the role of a father.'

'You're not playing a role. You *are* a father,' said Amelia.

'I never asked to be one.'

'*I* didn't ask to be a mother, but HERE WE ARE. This is our life. It's hell, I know, but you can't pretend she doesn't exist.'

'Really,' said Mark, in his measured way, and she felt the immense silence between them, and was frightened. He so seldom smiled. When he stared at Amelia with his small dark eyes she felt her will, already weakened by repeated wakening, as the foundations of a building are by the passing of heavy lorries, tremble on the point of collapse.

'How do you manage alone?' she asked Grace, when she came in to clean. Amelia regarded her with a kind of awe, as though she had Superwoman as a servant.

'I'm younger than you,' said Grace, simply. 'That's why, when I fell for my Billy I thought, it's now or never.'

This simple explanation for the number of young single mothers had not occurred to her employer. 'How old are you?'

'I'm twenty,' said Grace.

Amelia sighed, thinking of all the things she had done at that age. How pretty Grace was, with her clear skin and cheerful face. 'Wouldn't it have been better to wait until you found someone, a husband, I mean?'

'Oh, I was married, but it didn't work out. All the blokes I know are useless,' said Grace. 'No job, no sense of responsibility, no nothing. I wouldn't mind another kid, in a year or so, though.'

'Another!' said Amelia in horror. 'I'd shoot myself.'

Her cleaner sniffed, and muttered something.

Amelia suspected that Grace did not like them. Tom, of course, could do no wrong: Grace made his bed and she ironed his shirts while Mark's somehow remained wrinkled. Yet it was Grace who told her to take iron tablets and stop breast-feeding to get her strength back, Grace who told her never to let Rose go without socks, even in summer, Grace who told her to make up formula milk with boiled water that had cooled, instead of pouring it directly onto the powder, which made it taste vile. Amelia thought her presumptuous, and a bit eccentric, but all her advice seemed to work. She was scathing about the nannies Amelia employed. 'Most of them wouldn't be fit to look after a dog,' she said. 'When you ask them what they'd do with Rose, all they can think of saying is, take her to the park.'

'What would you do?'

'Well, by her age, my Billy was having books read to him,' said Grace. 'And doing fingerpainting.'

She was horrified to find Amelia slept with Rose.

'You've got to get a baby out of your bed now, or you'll have her there for the next six years.'

'I can't, she'll scream.'

'It's not as bad as it sounds. She won't die of it. We all took turns at the hostel, holding on to each other while our kiddies screamed, bit like Alcoholics Anonymous, and that's why they all sleep.'

'I can't, I just can't.'

'Then she'll never let you have any peace.'

'I know, I know,' said Amelia, resentfully. 'But I haven't the strength to say no.'

'That's what being a mother is,' said Grace. 'You want to say yes all the time, because you love them, but when you really love you learn to say no.'

There were no weekends for mothers, no breaks or treats or time out. It was like being chained to a lunatic. Sometimes Amelia would imagine that Rose was dead, swept under the wheels of a passing car, or drowned in the bath during an instant's inattention. She would see this in minute detail, the way Rose would fly up in the air, or sink down in a cloud of silvery bubbles, hallucinating so completely that for a moment she would actually believe it to have happened. What horrified her was that in these moments she would feel not only the most intense grief but an equally terrible relief that life could now go back to normal again.

But life could never go back to normal. The stretchmarks faded, her breasts shrank, her shanks slimmed but there were permanent signs of what had happened. Her nipples would remain brown and stumpy, stamens in overblown flowers: only red-heads, said her pregnancy book, stayed pink. She had a flap of flesh under her jaw that dropped down like the gill of a fish when she laughed. Each new tooth in Rose's gums cut another line on her forehead. Oh, that arrogance of her youth, when she had condemned every woman who failed to look her best! She was gross, lumpen, frumpy – ruined.

Month after month she walked round the bedroom, round the house, round the block. It was a vicious circle. She could only get Rose to sleep by rocking, which is made it less likely that the baby would ever to go to sleep alone. Amelia kept going on biscuits and chocolate.

'Amelia, my darling, I'd never have thought you'd turn into an earth mother,' said Ivo.

'That's just another name for any woman who's size sixteen,' said Amelia.

'Oh, look at that cheesecake pose!' said Ivo. Rose beamed at him, and Amelia felt a gush of adoration for her. 'What a little flirt you are!'

'For God's sake, Ivo, you can't lech at someone that age.'

'Why not?'

'Ivo! Don't tell me you're getting broody.'

'What, me? Never! You got nabbed by Mark.'

'Tease!'

'You're a respectable married woman, my darling. One can but admire from afar.'

All the same, there was a look in his eyes when he played with Rose that she would have given much to see in her husband's.

Time slowed to a crawl, buckled, looped back on itself, sped past. Adult business had to be crammed into the brief periods when Rose slept. She had started writing an article a month, mostly for women's magazines. Mark, of course, despised this kind of journalism so much that she kept quiet about where the extra £400 or so came from. Nothing felt like the work she put into Rose. 'Look, look,' she said, showing her a snowdrop, a catkin, a butterfly, a cat: and for a moment, it was as if she herself were seeing these things for the first time also, the radiant archetypes of infancy. She remembered that she had once loved her mother, and this compensated for some of the hurt she felt about her father. 'I know he's frantically busy, but why won't he talk to me any longer? Doesn't he love me, now I'm married?'

'Just be patient, darling. He's having a bad time. The banks keep finding excuses not to lend him more money,' said Mrs de Monde.

Somehow, everyone knew her father had cut her off. Nobody rang her any more, except other mothers. All her rich, smart friends had no time for her now that she could not run with the crowd.

Of course, she was still immensely privileged. Whenever she went to the doctor's or, later on, to playgroups, she would see babies the same age as her own, and want to weep. Week by week their faces were closing up, their eyes shrinking back into their heads like frightened snails. It almost broke her heart. Suddenly, she had something in common with someone like Grace, and yet such a gulf was opening between Rose and the babies of the poor. They reached out for things, and were shouted at; they were hauled about like so much laundry. You could look at each one of our babies naked, she thought, and tell which was being talked to, sung to, polished with attention. Their trouble was that they had no connections. What would Grace have become with my education and advantages? she wondered. She just doesn't know anyone.

Yet here Amelia was wrong, for one day, when the answerphone played back a message from Georgina Hunter, her cleaner said, 'I know her.'

'Who?'

'Georgie.'

Had Grace grown a pair of wings, Amelia could scarcely have been more astonished. 'Really?'

'Yeah. I babysit for her once a week. I had my Billy when she had her Flora. We were in the same ward.'

'Good heavens,' said Amelia, intrigued by the way the remains of a socialist state could connect its citizens. Suddenly she had a brilliant idea. 'I don't suppose I could pay you to *look after Rose*?'

'Sure,' said Grace. 'Not all day, just when Billy's at nursery school, nine to three.'

'Even that would save my life,' said Amelia.

Rose smiled, stretched, grasped, laughed, rolled, crawled, tottered to her feet and walked. Her snuffles and squeaks escalated from the cooing of a dove, the crowing of a rooster and the riot of a complete jungle to syllables: Mama, Teddy, Cat, Book, No, Want. Grace was brilliant with her, full of simple ideas about keeping her happy. She took her swimming at Archway, and made crumbles; introduced her to other children and put her in trousers to give her more confidence about running. Her only drawback was that she couldn't drive. 'I don't like cars.'

'Daddy made sure I could drive at seventeen,' said Amelia.

She was hurt and angry at her father's complete neglect of his granddaughter. Yet it was also a kind of relief. For so long Max had loomed over her like a vast planet which drew all lesser objects into its orbit. Now he had moved on.

It was a relief, too, when Mark was away. Not only was he hairy, sweaty, too large and the wrong *smell*, he had nothing of a baby's instinctive sensuality. She was consumed with guilt for feeling this, yet defiant.

'Does it ever come back?' she asked other mothers; and they all said in a year, two years, it would. They told each other rude jokes about the awfulness of their lives, rather like Russians during the Cold War. Grace egged her on to underground resistance.

'Why d'you put up with him, if he's giving you a hard time?' She asked. 'You don't need a man about the house. You can stand on your own two feet and earn a living, can't you?'

'I'd no idea you were a feminist,' said Amelia, drily.

'What's that?'

One day, when Grace was off work, she was pushing the buggy round the Highgate Ponds, leaning on its handle as if on a zimmer frame. It was very hot. Her large, shapeless bag ('A metaphor for the vagina,' she reminded herself, bitterly) was crammed with baby wipes, tissues, emergency juice bottles, emergency juice, raisins, teething gel, Calpol, sun-block, rattles and pop-up books. The usual assortment of mid-week North Londoners were jogging, walking dogs, going to and from the Lido, or looking after small children with a public display of affection that Amelia knew was the only thing that prevented them from infanticide.

Rose had stopped grizzling and, with luck, would calm down enough for her to be able to sit on the sloping lawn above the water and read a newspaper. There was a smell of drying grass and chopped dog turd everywhere. She had told Angus McNabb that she would like to start writing her column again. He had been surprisingly unenthusiastic. 'Well, I've more or less told Georgie she can keep going in your slot until the end of the year,' he said. 'She's worked up quite a following.'

'I've been on maternity leave for over a year. That's long enough.'

'Yes, but you're freelance. Georgie's staff.'

'Angus, darling, I do *rather* need the money,' said Amelia, wondering whether she was making a mistake in telling him this.

'Hmmm. Well, now, I'll see what I can do,' he said.

Amelia was most dissatisfied with this conversation. This was no way to talk to a shareholder, and his boss's daughter. She thought of ringing her father to complain, then sighed. It was not the same any more. She could not delude herself that she was in the same league as Georgina, who had been in the public eye ever since an actor had started libel proceedings against her following a novel she wrote. Nothing for the de Mondes seemed to be going well these days, she thought. Everyone liked to gang up on him because he was foreign. 'The Levanter', he had been nicknamed, by smooth Etonians in pin-striped shirts who had never known what it was like to be poor.

Rose crawled off a little way down the slope to examine some daisies. Amelia's skin prickled. Then she realized that what she felt was not only sun.

Mary Quinn was standing just below her, glaring at them.

24

A Second Chance

Adam wrote. He did not know where it came from, only that there was occasionally a kind of clear space in which he could function again. During that time he went to the computer and typed. It was not good. So much mental energy went into bolting the door between himself and disappointment that there was little left over for the actual work, and this, too, made him despair.

It's just work, he told himself. Writing is just a job, nine to five, low pay, lower expectations. There was no hope, no wealth, no fame, only effort and endurance. He was used to examining everything put before him and judging it; why had it taken so long to realize that he, too, would be judged?

'I think you're taking it too much to heart,' said Andrew Evenlode.

'How else am I to take it?'

'As you should take success: get on with the next.'

This was, indeed, the only thing which was possible to do, apart from giving up. Adam wondered whether it was always this bad. Malcolm told him of those who, having had nothing but approbation throughout their careers, were roasted for one book and found themselves unable to continue.

'The only question is whether you're an amateur or a professional. If you're the latter you don't give up, you accept that criticism follows publication as night follows day, that they're doing their job and you must do yours.'

Gradually, the blanks in which Adam wrote became longer and

more frequent. It was like trying to spin a lifeline at the same time as falling into an abyss: impossible, yet the only thing that could save him. There was no energy for anything other than satire of the crudest kind. If people wanted comedy spelt out for them they would get it. If they wanted depths sounded, rather than suggested, so be it. He would tell rather than show; the bad would be clearly labelled, the good unambiguous. As a technical exercise it quite amused him. There were still words to combine and re-combine, there was the arc of plot, the booby-traps and flies. He could not forget the things he had learnt. And what was also strange was that once he was inside his book, really inside it, something very like happiness came. There was no way forward if he thought about money, or praise, or anything except failing as well as possible.

For of course this book, too, would fail. In a curious way this realization gave him courage. It was as if a novel existed in some ideal Platonic state, and he had to transcribe what had already been written.

His second advance had gone within four months, half of it spent on a lap-top computer to replace his battered Olivetti. The part-time job at the bookshop barely covered his rent, and in any case he felt guilty at being too weak to help Malcolm with the labour of lifting boxes of books. His employer made no comment for several months, but Adam knew he was concerned, and this touched him. Malcolm, he realized, had been a kind of benefactor to him for so long, giving him a job in the bookshop, getting him the flat, dispensing gentle advice. He was one of the few homosexuals Adam knew who never proselytized.

'I was camp as a row of tents for thirty years before I told people,' he said, 'and that was after my mother died.'

Malcolm had even attended a Gay Pride march. It made Adam smile to think of his owlish, reserved employer holding a banner among all the drag queens and leather clones, but he respected him for it, too.

'Dear boy, have you seen a doctor?' he asked, eventually.

'It's just flu,' said Adam.

There were days when he would hurl himself at the glowing

orange screen and bounce back, as if from a hard wall. Before, he had simply been concerned with conveying a kind of liveliness. Now every sentence had to be idiot-proof: not only balanced, charged, faceted, polished, but made clear to the spectre of Ivo.

'I can see why so many authors advertise their torture in convoluted sentences,' he said to Mary. He knew he should stop complaining, especially to someone who was part of Ivo's world, but it was this very thing that he could least ignore. The opprobrium which had briefly poured down on him had, of course, moved on months ago, but to Adam in his isolation it remained ever-present.

Candida had persuaded him to attend the *Chronicle* literary banquet, on the pretext that he had been entered for its Young Writer of the Year award. Adam had been aghast. 'Come on, Candida, what's the point? I've got as much chance of that as a celluloid duck in hell.'

'Well, I think you should be in with a chance,' she said, with the robust hypocrisy he had come to realize was characteristic of publishers. 'After all, you did have a lot of publicity, even if much of it was, um, unfavourable, and you've sold well. You need to make yourself known to the movers and shakers.'

'What, so the charm of my personality will overlay the substance of my work?'

The boredom and nastiness had, if anything, been worse than anticipated. There was something about large hotels, their veal-coloured carpets and overstuffed furniture, which made everyone look like a whore, he thought. The only suit he had was the linen one he had bought for his launch party. It hung off his thin body in swathes, ridiculous for midwinter.

'Goodness, have you been on a diet?' said Candida.

'No. Just flu.'

She looked at him speculatively. 'I hope it's not going to delay the new novel.'

'No,' said Adam.

'We've already put *Loaves and Fishes* in the summer catalogue.'

'It's coming,' he said wearily.

Candida introduced him to a couple of other authors. One of them said, 'Should I have read you?' and the other, 'Oh, yes,' in tones that indicated the opposite. He saw a boy he had known slightly at Cambridge, whom he had once slept with in the days when bisexuality had been chic; but his relief was short-lived.

'Why did you get such terrible reviews?'

'Perhaps I wrote a bad book.'

'But surely,' his interrogator persisted, 'there must have been *some* reason. I mean, it's not as if you're famous.'

Adam shrugged. He had gathered from Candida that there were various stock responses: pretending you didn't read critics, laughing it off, vowing eternal vengeance, punch-ups, etc. He said, politely, 'Perhaps it was only half bad, then.'

He had trained himself to remember what others said, the precise words and inflexions, and this training was now a torture, a gridiron of fury and self-loathing on which he turned and burned. He thought of the meeting he had had in her office to discuss the new novel, Candida nodding her glossy chestnut head.

'Will there be any sex in it? Explicit sex, I mean.'

'No,' said Adam, astonished.

Her offer to his agent had dropped by £3000.

He talked longest to Mary, knowing she was probably almost as miserable because of Mark's presence. The worst moment was when Ivo Sponge came over to talk to her, saw Adam and said, 'Ah, hallo there, old boy. No hard feelings, I hope?' and Adam, before turning his back had said, 'No.'

'Don't be a fool, Adam,' Mary said, when Ivo walked away. 'Can't you see an olive branch when it's offered?'

'I still need a long spoon.'

'Ivo's not that bad, really,' said Mary.

'So. Have you been born again?'

Mary flushed with anger. 'I haven't been to bed with him, if that's what you mean. But at least he's honest.'

'I didn't know you're a friend of Mary Quinn's,' said Candida, reappearing with magical speed. 'You must come and meet Ben. Perhaps you could write for *Grunt*.'

He was struck by Mary's air of confidence, of consequence. She would reappear by his side for a few minutes then say, 'I hope you don't mind, I must flutter off for a bit,' after no more than a minute of hectic conversation.

She had lost her Renoir roundness, the vulnerability that had made her peculiarly feminine; she was pretty, still, but with a depthless gloss, and for this, too, he blamed Ivo. Adam said, loudly, 'It strikes me as incredible that people who have nothing better than a degree in history should be considered qualified to affect the careers of living writers.'

'Oh, Adam, don't keep brooding,' said Mary, embarrassed. She noticed he had a black spot on his cheek: typical of a man not to look after his skin properly, she thought. 'It's one of those things you have to live with, a necessary evil. You've got to get over this, you know.'

'Have I? Have you got over Mark?'

Mary said angrily, softly, 'That's different.'

'Is it?'

'You can't compare a love affair and a book.'

'Can't you? I don't have a lover. I'll never have a child. All I've got is what I do.'

'And all I've got is what I do, too,' said Mary. 'Given the choice of being victim or victor, I know which to choose.'

'Can you? I don't believe in necessary evils.'

Mary looked at him, then, properly, for the first time. 'Adam, Adam, you mustn't let yourself sink. London is a terrible city for sucking you under. Terrible. I know that. If you really feel so bad, can't you go? Abroad, I mean?'

'No. I can't afford it. Look at the holes in my shoes: one genuine starving artist in a garret.'

'I wouldn't call your flat a garret.'

'Has it ever occurred to you that the only words that rhyme with "novel" are "grovel" and "hovel"?'

This really was scraping the barrel of self-pity.

'It isn't personal.'

'Of course it's bloody personal! When you read, you live inside the quick of someone's being, not what has happened to them in any plodding autobiographical sense, but the – the – growing point of their imagination. To pour such scorn on someone there, in that place, you must want to *kill* them. Don't you understand what it is that you do, even?'

'I don't know about that,' she said. 'It may be as you think, a confederacy of dunces. Myself, I see far more hype of the worthless.'

'You would,' said Adam.

He wrote, racked by sickness and self-doubt, unable to distinguish between the two. His flat was so cold he had chilblains despite wearing two pairs of socks. They burnt his toes, fiery kernels of heat surrounded by flesh so chilled it felt dead to the touch. The bathroom was warmest, because of the gas-fired water-heater, and he often worked in there, not least because he still had the gastric flu that seemed as hard to shake off as a Doberman. Everyone seemed to have flu all year round now, nobody knew why. In the months since his launch party he had lost another two stone: poor old Mabel, shuffling myopically out of her flat below had taken some persuading that he was entitled to live there. He had attacks of dizziness, especially when climbing the stairs, and could only move slowly.

He could afford neither the train fare nor the energy to go to his mother's. Every waking hour would be filled by her discussion of his wretched book. 'Now, what do you think he means, exactly, about you "sitting up and begging for attention like a dog"? I can't quite make that out, can you?' He would have thought it sadistic, but he knew her too well; she rehashed his father's defection in the same vein. Nothing very much happened in her own life, so she picked over other people's, speculating, reminiscing, endlessly recasting and reviving old grudges. Adam loathed the pettiness of her nature, yet in a way, his own interest in character came from this.

'Would you call yourself sensitive?' he asked Tom Viner, who had dropped in for a cup of tea.

'I'd hope I'm not insensitive. But you can't afford to be too tender-hearted in my job, otherwise you'd go m-m-m-, crack up. On the other hand, half of what makes people trust you, and even get better, is the relationship you make with them. You can't be a doctor if you're not interested in people.'

'Do you think it's something which has become outdated? It seems to disequip you for modern existence.'

'Superficially, perhaps. But callousness must eventually cut you off from everything worth having.'

Adam was silent for a moment. 'Do you know the most damning adjective that can now be applied to a writer? "Sensitive". It's a joke, meaning that writers are only sensitive about themselves but I wonder whether it doesn't go deeper than that. People used to read to find out things about themselves and the world. Now they read as a way of stupefying themselves more deeply.'

'Stupefaction has its points,' said his friend. 'After all, where would I be without it?'

Tom had killed a patient that afternoon. It was not his fault, but it was he who had taken a living woman and turned her into a corpse. There would be an inquest, and that might mean the end of his career. It was a relief to hear Adam's plaints, because, although he undoubtedly suffered, the cause was so trivial. At times Tom wondered whether his whole family, apart from Grub, were not junkies for other people's problems as a distraction from their own. You could not have many existential agonies when you saw those of real bereavement, real pain, real death every day of your working life. Ruth had told him long ago that people who became doctors had the highest personal fear of death, a fear that could only be countered by continuing success in combating it in others. 'It's a hopeless battle in which you have to give hope,' she said.

Tom was still shaking. There was no support system for doctors who killed patients. You had to absorb the shock, somehow, and carry on. He had been working since Friday lunchtime, and it was now Monday afternoon. In that time, he had had eight hours' sleep and two sandwiches.

He had been so disillusioned by his six months on Casualty that he was seriously considering chucking it. There were plenty of nine-to-five jobs paying twice his present salary open to ex-doctors. To be taking examinations still, working a ninety-hour week for £26,000, and lodging in other people's houses at thirty-four was more than anyone could stand. Sarah would have no more of it. 'Why should it be any worse for people who can afford it to pay for medicine than it is for them to pay school fees? What's so wrong with a two-tier system? We accept inequality in other essentials, what's so terrible about my charging thirty pounds to someone as a fee? A plumber costs twice as much.'

'A plumber hasn't been trained for five years at public expense.'

'The public have had their pound of flesh from me during all my years as a house officer,' Sarah said, her teeth flashing. 'I want the things I'm entitled to, as a middle-class professional.'

Well, Tom thought, stirring his mug of tea at Adam's flat, it may happen anyway.

The patient had been pregnant, and sectioned under the Mental Health Act. The baby had got stuck. But, whether because she had stopped taking her antipsychotic medication during pregnancy or for some other reason, she had absolutely refused to have a Caesarean. She had even refused to let anyone take her blood pressure. By dawn on Sunday, the monitor showed foetal distress, the waves of her contractions not just agonizing for her but suffocating for the child.

Everyone present was a registrar or lower; Tom was the most senior doctor there.

'Hold her down,' he said.

It had taken six people. The baby was saved, but afterwards, the monitors let out a long electronic wail in mimicry of the weak human one. The mother had bled to death under the drapes, without ever regaining consciousness.

There is no such thing as a good death, thought Tom, peeling off his gloves. Every nightmare comes true in the end: we drown in our own lungs, suffocate in our own blood, are driven out by unimaginable shock or exhaustion. Yet some deaths are worse than others, especially if you have had a hand in them.

Everyone was pale with shock. The metallic stench of iodine and blood was breathed in and out by the ventilators in the wall. They were all drenched with red, smeared and spattered as if in an abattoir.

'Jesus Christ, guv,' said his assistant.

What had made it worse was that, by unhappy coincidence

Sarah had been there, as part of her GP training. She was the psychiatric senior house officer, and had been the only one to protest at their decision to do a Caesarean, and at the time they had all shouted at her. Including Tom.

'I find it unforgivable that you didn't support me,' she said after, white beneath her tan.

'There was no other way,' he said.

'You could have let the baby die.'

'They could both have died.'

'Why did you choose to save the baby rather than its mother?'

'Oh, for Christ's sake! I was trying to save them both! The woman was insane, you know that.'

'It's probably the best thing for the baby, you know,' said the obstetric registrar, and even the pragmatism Tom had learnt was insufficient to prevent him recoiling. He lit another cigarette with trembling fingers.

'What's wrong?' said Adam. 'Did you fail your exam?'

'No. Passed.'

'We ought to be celebrating, then,' said Adam. 'Doesn't that mean you can become a consultant?'

'In theory. If I get the right references from the right people. But, in my case, I'll probably have to apply for jobs as a locum.'

He told Adam about the inquest that would have to come. Both men were silent.

'It's bloody, isn't it? All this dependency. You expect, when you're grown-up, you'll be free of the power others have over you, the cliques and bullying and school reports, but it just comes back, more and worse, in a different form.'

Page by page Adam's new book built up, and then, one day, was finished. It was different from the first, but, he thought, better.

The response from agent and publisher was curiously muted. 'You'll understand, we can't have a party or make a fuss this time,' said the publicist. 'Everything at Belgravia's being cut to the bone.'

'That's fine,' said Adam, relieved.

'Can you give me a list of people we should send advance copies to? Your friend Mary, for instance, she's a useful contact.'

'I really don't think that would be a good idea.'

'She's a reviewer.'

'But it puts her in an invidious position. If she likes it, it looks as though she's compromising herself, and if she doesn't, it's even worse.'

The proofs arrived, full of the usual misprints. He corrected it, knowing that the finished copy would still contain a printer's error per page. The typeface was shrunken, making this book seem shorter than his first though it was, in fact, longer. The dust-jacket was drab. It was being rushed out for the autumn, a good time to appear his new editor had told him, because of the run-up to Christmas when most books were sold.

'But won't mine get lost, then?'

'Oh, no,' she assured him.

Three months after he had given in his manuscript, *Loaves and Fishes* was published. He knew this because, apart from the twelve copies delivered to his door, one or two bookshops in the Charing Cross Road had copies. For a week, hope and madness made Adam patrol all the bookshops within a radius of a mile, taking his novel off the shelf and surreptitiously moving it on top of a blockbuster. *Loaves and Fishes* was always back under the display table by the next day, but as far as he could tell this method sold at least ten copies.

Then, three weeks after publication, he opened the *Chronicle* and saw a review by Mary.

'Ivo, I really do want to do this one.'

'No.'

'You crucified him.'

'He crucified himself.'

'But this is much better. Really, truly.'

Ivo shrugged.

'Adam didn't know any better then. I'm sure he regrets writing you that letter. I know he does.'

'Mary, you're his friend,' said Ivo, righteously.

'Just this once? I know I can be dispassionate.'

'The very fact you're pleading for the bugger's book, my darling, means you're not. What can he give you in return? Nothing. What can Candida Twink give you? Nothing. If you work the favours market for nothing, you devalue my currency.'

'Ivo, you know that what you wrote about Adam's first novel wasn't fair, or even accurate.'

'Really?' said Ivo, unpleasantly.

Mary saw she had handled this badly. 'What I mean, Ivo, is that it was a brilliant piece of journalism. Even I laughed. But it will look rather vindictive, won't it, killing off the second too? Not very good for the favours market?'

'Hmm,' said Ivo, stroking his bow-tie.

'I really could be quite dispassionate, you know.'

'Could you?' Ivo appeared to come to a decision. 'All right. You can have it –'

'Oh, thank you, thank you –'

'But on one condition. You must pick it to pieces, just as you do the others. Fetch! I'll need the copy by tomorrow.'

Mary struggled, with her wish to help Adam, with her need for work, with her fear of offending Ivo, with her desire to show him that she had been truly blooded.

'All right,' she said.

She did like the book, too; people who like each other very often like their work. The plot was absurd, vigorous, fantastical, squirming about like puppies in a bag – but she did not intend to do more than knock one or two of them on the head.

Yet the thing she had been trained to do took over. She had learnt how to criticize, and her mind leapt out of its scabbard like an enchanted sword, slicing and skewering and running the book through almost before she realized what she had done.

A year ago, it had taken Mary a week to write her first review; now she could produce pieces three times as long in two hours, composing as fast as she could type. There was a thrill in being up against everything – time, competition, her own inertia and lack of confidence, and, most of all, Mark – that she thought might be like the blood-lust that overtakes warriors in battle. To survive, to be revenged, this was what every child in Ireland took in with their mother's milk; Mary had only to consider that Adam was English for the sarcasm to flow.

When it was done, she tempered her review, honing it this way and that, forgetting everything but the necessity to compose a piece of journalism that Ivo would print; and then, because she was immediately onto another deadline, she faxed it.

The Heat-wave

All through her second summer as a journalist, Mary went swimming in the Ladies' Pond on Hampstead Heath. It was a long journey from Chelsea. In summer the Tube was suffocating, people packed in so densely that the stench of sour flesh and tired clothes quelled the most regular *frotteur*. The further east she travelled the shabbier the passengers became: by Leicester Square, all the chic foreign students and matrons in navy and gilt had been replaced by balding New Agers, bespectacled Trotskyites and the inevitable drunk. The advertisements promoting shops and films melted away in favour of booze and holidays. Those with pretensions to style got out at Camden; at the next stop, you could not even be sure of finding functioning escalators. Up Highgate Road, the traffic shimmered and boomed, creeping past run-down warehouses, Georgian terraces, rows of shops.

Hampstead Heath was the closest thing in London to the countryside, a countryside with tarred paths, dustbins, mown grass, but still somewhere where you could look and see nothing but trees, beech and chestnut and oak, soaring to their full size. At the bottom of Parliament Hill a chain of pools seeped into each other, fed by the Fleet, one of the lost rivers of London. The Ladies' Pond, where it rose, was clean despite its murk of mud and mallard, but the river became progressively dirtier as it sank south until, by the time it reached Fleet Street, it had become the storm pipe for a sewer.

Whenever Mary walked through its gate the wire wound round

her heart began to relax and soften until she felt that she could breathe again. The tall trees and sloping green lawn, the tranquil swimmers gliding between ducks and waterlilies were like visions of a purer world. Nobody worried about their shape or the labels on their clothes; there were no children, nothing to remind her of what she had lost.

Mary swam one slow lap, moving towards the far end of the pond and its tangle of willow and water. Sometimes women would stay a while by the rope that cut off this apex of green shadow, as if before an altar, swaying and gazing; sometimes they would turn back long before, to sunbathe on the smooth green sward, listening to the splashy quack of duck and radio. It was like a benign form of ECT, or the holiday she could not afford.

Adam had told her that all writing is made possible by a kind of surplus, not of feeling or intellect but of energy. The truth of this was every week borne in on her. Each piece became harder to write, especially as her byline became known. Yet she was only as good as the piece she had just written. In the beginning this had been exciting, but now it terrified her.

Mary would huddle fully dressed under the duvet, drinking and painting her toenails in a frantic attempt to calm down, while editors rang up copy-chasing. Sometimes she would pick up the phone and lie, like K. P. Gritts, that she had faxed it to the office already when she hadn't even sorted out the first paragraph. Sometimes she would pretend to be ill. Yet the dreadful, inescapable fact was that she had to produce it, or there would be no money and no more commissions. As soon as any cheques came in, she would spend them on frivolous things, clothes mostly, because she felt she deserved a treat; and the things she craved to fill her emptiness became more and more expensive.

'Don't you think you're spreading yourself too thinly?' Ivo asked her.

Mary shrugged. He wants to keep control of me, she thought. 'A woman can live on her looks, her wits or her back. I can't choose the first or the last.'

'Oh, I wouldn't say that,' said Ivo.

So she wrote with her big booming voice, and now the telephone calls, invitations and padded envelopes containing proofs of novels were all for her, little Mary Quinn. Sometimes she was amazed by what urgency could pull out of her, but more often she was appalled. Only the book reviews were easy: as Ivo had said, it was the lowest form of journalism and paid commensurately. Yet she could not abandon them; and indeed they became the form for which she was best known. The challenge to make her mark in five hundred words rather than the seven or one thousand allowed to the opposite sex was like a gauntlet. I can be as good as you, she said to Amelia in her mind, I can be better, and the voice would swell and swell. When she stopped to think of what she actually did, Mary became quite frightened – but she could not stop. She had not heard from Adam, since she had demolished *Loaves and Fishes*, nor from Tom. She did not want to think of the reason why this might be so.

There was never a day in which she could relax, because two or three deadlines were always looming. She left her answer-phone on continually, picking up the phone only if she heard a friend speak. Gradually, though, she realized that she had no real friends, only acquaintances – that was all she had time for. Whenever she finished one piece, she had to think of two more, because in the time it took to obtain and execute a commission she might find herself with no money for the month, and she could not let her overdraft get any higher. Even so, it did. She watched her debts rise as though they were water, and herself a prisoner in a sealed room, quite helpless to do anything to stop it.

'But don't you enjoy it at all?' Tom had asked her.

'Does your father?'

'I don't know. I suppose so. I mean, Dad was awful in the morning, trying to think up five jokes before lunch, but once he'd done them he'd be on a high. I suppose that's what got him drinking.' He looked at Mary's glass and away again.

'It's not just the deadlines,' said Mary. 'There's no creativity, no originality of thought or expression. It's dross, all of it.'

'Not all, surely?' he said.

'All,' said Mary, fiercely. 'We think we're brighter than almost anyone else, a belief reinforced by the fact that at any social event, we only talk to each other.'

'Some of my best friends are journalists.'

'Oh,' said Mary, dismissively. 'You're the token doctor. You're there to give us a touch of reality in cyberspace.'

It was not without its satisfactions, of course. There was a pleasure in turning a phrase, in cracking a joke that might just squeeze past. There was a pleasure in going to the Slouch Club once a week and being served by people with whom she had once worked, in encountering the manager who had sacked her, and seeing him go green with anxiety. She churned out book reviews, interviews, profiles, think pieces, features; all of them, she knew, tawdry, spiteful rubbish. She received hatemail by the bagful.

And for this, she was counted a rising star. Her fees jumped from £200 to £300, from £500 to £600 per thousand words. In journalism, venom is the elixir of success. It is the magic ingredient that overcomes ignorance, inaccuracy, ineptitude and even the inability to form coherent sentences. Mary displayed none of these blemishes. She worked at developing her hate. She lifted the thought of Mark and Amelia, up-down, up-down, as she might weights on a bar-bell, until malice poured out of her like sweat. Only a handful of women journalists were prepared to be nasty in print, and these either came from nowhere, like herself or, like Fiona Bamber, were so well connected that nobody dared ostracize them. In between were nice, intelligent women saying nice, intelligent things that vanished without trace. Were they too thick or too cowardly to realize what nastiness could do? Mary wondered. She met them sometimes. They always had children and husbands, and a tired sort of look like paper that had been folded too many times. If they had columns, they appeared on Mondays, when news was thin and the bile that made for good copy had not begun its weekly accretion. Real hacks wrote for the Sundays. They were immediately recognizable as belonging to a different species. The males had short bristling hair of indeterminate colour and steel-rimmed spectacles mounted on the face of a depilated pug; the females wore sticky lipstick like drying blood. They were all single, unless they married each other, but they earned anything from £40,000 a year.

Phoebe Viner had said to her, 'Really, it's a terrific stroke of luck not to marry your first great love. What you've had is a kind of inoculation against romance, which is one of the best things life can hand a young woman. The point is that when you fall in love again, you'll know what you want, instead of taking a lot of nonsense.'

'I don't think I'll ever fall in love again.'

'Nonsense, of course you will. You're the type. But you must fall in love sensibly.'

'Isn't that an oxymoron, like hurrying slowly?'

It was hard to believe she would ever marry, now. Where did they go too, all the decent men? There hadn't been a war, they couldn't all be gay, and yet there were so many more women than men.

I hope I have a daughter of my own, one day, Mary thought, stopping to watch a mother and child playing together on the grass. All those years with Mark, waiting and hoping for him to want a baby as much as she did, stupidly honourable, stupidly patient. If she had forced her fertility on him she would at least have got something out of their time together.

When she recognized that the baby's mother was Amelia, Mary felt a kind of terror, as though someone were playing a practical joke so bad it was almost funny. Then fury overtook her. This is the person who ruined my life, she thought; and then, colliding into it, That baby should have been mine. Everything about it that had charmed her seconds before was now like a splinter of glass. Her own solitude, her independence, were no more than barren desolation. She glared at them, terrified she was about to start crying.

'Hallo,' said Amelia, hesitantly.

Mary inclined her head. 'What's she called?'

'Rose.'

She was all cream and gold, new-minted, with eyes the same colour as Mary's own. The irony of this hurt her almost more than she could bear.

'She's pretty.'

'Thank you.' There was a long pause. Amelia was over-whelmed with many feelings – pity, embarrassment, envy. Look, she wanted to say, it's not all it's cracked up to be, this baby business. Enjoy your freedom while it lasts. Enjoy being young and free and slim.

'How are you finding it?'

'Oh, fine. You look well,' Amelia said, after a pause. 'I didn't recognize you, at first.'

'Yes,' said Mary. 'I've changed.'

'It suits you.'

'I had to, remember?' She felt almost sick. Was Amelia deliberately cruel, or just monumentally stupid?

'I've enjoyed your pieces,' said Amelia, politely. She was distracted by Rose, a little frightened by Mary's glittering stare.

'Have you, indeed. How gratifying,' said Mary. 'Are you writing another book?'

'Oh, eventually, I dare say.'

'Good,' said Mary, baring her teeth. 'I might review it, then.'

'I don't think Ivo would allow that, do you?'

'He couldn't stop me. In any case, I don't think he'd try. What goes around, comes around. You fucked him on my bed, do you think he's changed?' She had a sudden moment of absolute conviction. 'What do you think he's doing on it now?'

Her satisfaction at this exchange lasted until she saw Tom in Slouch's.

'What are you doing here? I didn't know you were a member.'

'I'm not. Dad is.'

'Oh, of course.'

'He's just done something rather splendid,' said Tom. 'De Monde has been on at him to do cartoons about his enemies, and Dad kept refusing. This morning, he was called up to Max's office, and Max said, "I employ you, so why won't you do what I say?" So Dad just looked at him and said, "No, Mr de Monde, you've got it the wrong way round. I employ you."'

'What a wonderful story,' said Mary. 'It's true, too, really. People do buy the *Chronicle* just to see the Felix cartoons, or some of them. Did Max fire him?'

'No,' said Tom, and he seemed to shimmer in the heat, tall and stern. 'Dad left. That's what you do, you see, if you're not a whore.'

Mary got very drunk that night. It would not have mattered – she got drunk more or less most nights – except that she was with Ivo. The mirrors threw her reflection backwards and forwards like a cat playing with a mouse. She saw her mouth open too wide, the wild laughter squeezing from her eyes, all smudged mascara and eye-liner, and Ivo watching as he filled her glass again and again. She thought of Tom's face, reproaching her, and wanted to die. It was a Thursday night, when the dregs of literary London gathered, lolling on the overstuffed armchairs and banquettes, drinking spritzers, Dos Equis or juice, their eyes darting towards the door in case each person who came in was more worthy of cultivation than those already present.

How I loathe them all, Mary thought, and her hatred was more intoxicating than drink. The fat, balding toffs, the tall lank-locked Londoners, the crop-haired guerrillas, the lipstick lesbians, the boisterous babes, the Trustafarians. Acrid smoke poured from each mouth and nostril, as if so much vanity, malice, ambition, gyrating inside each body like so many cogs in a machine must produce a physical manifestation. On every face was the same combination of weariness and avidity, occasionally lit by flashes of enthusiasm so intense it might easily have been mistaken for fanaticism. Through the open window the sounds of Soho came in stripes, the roar from other clubs and pubs spilling out onto the hot pavements, the thump of disco and salsa from slowly crawling cars, the gunning of engines, the smash of glass.

'Oh, this heat, this heat,' said Mary, fanning herself with a copy of *Private Eye*. 'I think I'll melt into a pool of grease.'

'Have you heard, Fiona Bamber's having it off with Tom Viner?'

'No! Since when?'

'I don't know. Ages, I expect.'

'I thought he had a girlfriend.'

'No, that ended some time ago. But I should think the chance of a revenge fuck must be almost irresistible.'

'I feel terrible,' said Mary, suddenly.

'I'll take you home,' Ivo offered.

He hailed a taxi in Old Compton Street and helped Mary in. She was so drunk she could hardly sit upright, and kept lolling onto his shoulder. Ivo put his arm around her.

'It's too hot.'

Nevertheless, she did not move away, and he went on determinedly.

Sweat darkened the corrugations in his hair. When he turned his thick wet mouth into hers it was almost a relief, like taking a tepid shower.

'Christ, you're a sexy little bitch,' he said, and Mary experienced a jolt of irritation that almost sobered her. She felt a kind of bored pity for him, combined with sentimental affection that she knew was mostly drink.

'Do you want to do it, then?' she asked, as the taxi turned into her street.

'Of course I do.'

'All right.'

She felt very calm and cold, although when she stood up the drink made her head muzzy again. They went down the steps to her basement, and she wanted to tell Ivo not to drool in such an absurd fashion. He was all over her as she fumbled with the keys, like a dog, thrusting his sloppy tongue into her ears so that she quickly became rather deaf.

It might as well be him as anyone, she thought, turning to face him. It was a little like losing her virginity, now she had decided to do it. She unzipped her dress and stepped out of it.

'Christ!' said Ivo, and began to tear off his clothes. He looked almost green. 'Oh, Jesus. Can't you draw the curtains?'

'No.'

Mary lay down on her bed. This was going to be easy, she thought, surprised. Ivo was not a pretty sight, it was true; all those free lunches had taken their toll, and he was splotched with large flat pink moles that made him resemble one of those terrible

English puddings made with suet and sultanas – Spotted Dick, she thought, giggling. But at least he was heavy, and it was such a relief to be pinned down by another body, after so long on her own.

'Let me in, let me in,' said Ivo, snorting and snuffling like the big bad wolf outside the door of the third little pig; and at that moment, Mary understood that she simply could not do this. What she had already done was bad enough, but if she allowed Ivo to continue it would somehow be the end. It was more than the physical act, more than a chance to obliterate Mark. If she loved anyone, it was Adam, whom she had betrayed. All this she perceived in an instant, as one who has been sinking needs only to touch the bottom of a pool in order to reverse, horrified and frightened, yet also strengthened even at the last moment; and she said, 'Ivo, I can't.'

26

Adultery and Betrayal

Mark had always taken an austere pleasure in the horror of human existence. The inevitability of the grave cast a backwards shadow on every endeavour towards perfectibility, and anyone attempting to challenge this deserved derision. Ambition, duplicity, hypocrisy, vanity – all should be crushed without exception.

There was no getting round the fact that he had kissed a princess and found a toad in Amelia. He felt angry, cheated, frustrated; he thought to himself how he had been captured and dragged to the altar just at the point when he should have been capitalizing on his growing reputation. Nothing was under his control any longer. He almost felt nostalgic for his days with Mary. At least she had been devoted to him, had seen to it that his shirts were ironed and the fridge filled – unlike Amelia who spent all hours of the day crooning to the disgusting little grub she had squeezed out of his genes.

It was awful, this friction of another human being. He could feel the disturbance of their presence even when his wife and child were sleeping, the displacement of atoms, the consumption of oxygen in his own space, and when they were awake it was utter hell, scream, scream, scream, stench, stench, stench. He would open his front door every evening with nostrils stretched wide and quivering for the least taint of nappy.

'I will not, I will *not* have the pram in the hall,' he told her, white with fury.

'It's only a folding buggy,' she said, uncomprehending. 'It hardly takes up any more room than a brolly.'

'It's the *pram*, in a hall' said Mark, who took this to be the most deadly of all enemies of promise.

When he found that Rose had lost the bird off the spout of his Alessi kettle he had been so unpleasant that Amelia had been obliged to go and buy another the next day from Heals.

It was bad enough living in a city where every house that cost less than half a million pounds shared both walls with its neighbours; where you could hear the messages left on telephone-answering machines, the rows, the cries, the roar of aeroplanes overhead and the rumble of trains beneath. He was crowded at work and crowded at home. No wonder people preferred to drive to their offices rather than face more claustrophobia commuting. But they could not afford two cars, and the Volvo was for Amelia and Rose.

Every morning there would be the descent into the murky pandemonium of the platform, people shoving and fighting to get off a train, others fighting and jostling to get on. As soon as he found a space to squeeze between, more and more people crammed in behind him, like a terrible adult version of Sardines. Then the doors would slice shut and the torpid air of the platform immediately seemed like pure cool oxygen in comparison to this steamy, stagnant broth, that had already been in and out of the mouths and lungs of every person present. Banker and builder, typist and tourist, all were packed tight in the dreadful democracy of commuting, the train hurtling through a darkness that writhed with dangling black cables, noses in each other's armpits, eyeballs on each other's blackheads, utterly silent except for the thump and hiss of an invisible Walkman. Everyone clung onto the side-bars and roofstraps, almost vertical until, in absolute pitch dark, they came to a stop with a long, dying, screeching groan.

As the *Chronicle* grew poorer, even legitimate expenses such as taxis after eight o'clock were cut. It was all very well on the toy-town train that took them to and from the Docklands, but the Underground was another matter. At night, when the carriages were half empty, gangs of tattooed skinheads or blacks in ragged jeans would charge up and down extorting money, while a wino's vomit rolled this way and that along the corrugated floor until it sank into the cracks and dried there.

In the small hours of the night, sighing as Amelia tried and failed to get Rose to sleep, he would mechanically console himself with his achievements, like a pianist playing scales. Had he not been the most brilliant historian of his year? Had he not got a starred first? Was he not political columnist of a national news-paper, beating Ivo yet again? Was he not the son-in-law of one of the richest men in Britain? Did he not possess five suits from Hackett's, two from Armani, one from Turnbull & Asser and one from Ralph Lauren? He now owned things which, seven years ago, he could see only in magazines – Lobbs' shoes, solid gold cufflinks, Mulberry luggage. People even thought he must have been to Winchester.

None of these reflections currently gave him as much satisfac-tion as his affair with Fiona Bamber. It was not just her beauty, or that she was the wife of a man he envied. She was the most manipulative person he had met, at once venal and feral, genuinely malicious in a manner only he could savour; and she loathed children.

'It never occurred to me that Andrew would seriously expect me to drop my career and become a brood mare,' she said.

'You discussed it before you got engaged?'

'No. I assumed he wanted me for myself,' said Fiona, with a self-assurance he could only admire. She was the one woman he had ever encountered who wore, as a matter of course, the kind of underwear universally expected to excite lust but disparaged by most women, including Amelia, as too uncomfort-able.

'I hang from the suspenders of disbelief,' he told her.

The only trouble was finding a place to meet. The Evenlodes had a flat in Bayswater, but it was for all the family, and there were a great number of them; Fiona herself commuted back to Oxford in the evening. His flat had, irritatingly, just been let at a sum which so nearly covered his mortgage that it would be foolish to take it back. There were freebies, of course – nights and weekends away in tolerably smart hotels, thanks to the political dinners and conferences to which he was now invited. However, the most convenient place turned out to be home.

Every week, Mark, in common with many political staff, had a day off. This was supposed to be used for writing his weekly column, a magisterial survey of the political scene or, depending on your loyalties, a compendium of spiteful gossip concerning everything from politicians' finances to whips' hotel bills. All the broadsheets had such columns, as though the heavy dough of politics needed a leaven of malice to make it palatable, but Mark's was undoubtedly of a superior nature. The scholarly irony that had inflated his career from the start still served him well. He could polish off his column in a couple of hours, but he insisted that Amelia and Rose leave the house for the day. This cleared the afternoon for Fiona.

She was not, of course, a friend, or even an ally. He suspected their pleasure sprang from more or less identical sources, that of deceiving the spouses on which they were dependent for patronage. Mark had never forgiven Andrew Evenlode for a time when, invited to dinner as a poor young graduate, he had brought a bottle of Lambrusco, seized from an off-licence in a hurry.

'Good heavens,' Evenlode said to the other guests. 'He's brought a bottle of Tizer!'

It was sordid to make love to Evenlode's wife on his own bed, surrounded by reminders not only of Amelia but of babyhood – the plastic Early Learning Centre activity boxes, dashboards, beakers and push-button telephones that currently preoccupied Rose – but also erotic.

'You're like a burglar shitting on the carpet,' said Fiona. She had been in court that day, watching the concluding speeches made in the libel case brought by Gore Tore against the *Mail*.

Mark winced at her coarseness – and, he had to admit, perspicacity. He waved at the smoke she exhaled. It was the one thing he truly detested about her, though she did it, as she did everything else, rather well. Her best asset, he thought, was her complete absence of any need for affection.

'Do you think you'll stay on if the paper loses the case?'

'I'll have to see. It was passed by the lawyers, they can't very well blame me.'

'You'd have got away with it if you'd just kept to the under-age sex – everyone expects rock-stars to do that. It's doing things to little furry animals the British can't stomach.'

'I know, I know. Such frightful sentimentality. It's going to cost the paper over a million, with the legal fees.'

There was the sound of a key in the lock, and a childish voice wailing.

'Hell. She's back.'

'Sure it's not the nanny?'

'No. The last one turned out to be a Pole with bulimia. Got through six yoghurts a day. Amelia's in charge again, though she's got our cleaner helping out some days. Something must have happened.'

Mark scrambled into his clothes. Fiona calmly slipped on her dress and picked up an old newspaper.

'Mark, I've just had a rather peculiar encounter on the – oh, hallo, Fiona. What are you doing here?'

'Just – borrowing,' said Fiona, going up the stairs to Tom's flat.

Amelia stared after her. Mary's words resounded in her mind. 'How long has *that* been going on?'

'How should I know?' said Mark. 'She just appeared.'

Out of the corner of his eye he could see a scrap of satin underwear he was quite sure was not Amelia's. 'I really do have to work.'

Amelia went on staring. Downstairs, Rose's wails were increasing in pitch and volume. She heard Tom's voice, and Fiona's laughter.

'I thought you understood that I had to have the house to myself today.'

'Mark, there's a heatwave outside. You can't really expect me to trudge round London all day while you wait for inspiration for your poxy little column that nobody reads.'

'I simply cannot work with that child screaming in the background. Just *do* something with it.'

'Do something with *her*,' said Amelia, furious. 'She's not an it, she's a little girl, she's *your* little girl, however much you try to ignore her existence. My God, I think I should have told Mary Quinn she had a lucky escape, just now.'

'Mary?'

'We bumped into each other on the Heath. It was unbelievably embarrassing. You can't imagine.'

Amelia's voice trembled; but all her misery was concentrated on the idea of Tom rolling about upstairs with Fiona on the double bed she herself had bought for him. She was mortified. If he had to sleep with a married woman, she found herself thinking, why couldn't it be me?

Tom was astonished when, roused from stuporous sleep, he found Fiona lying across the foot of his bed.

'You look like one of those dogs on a medieval tomb,' he said, yawning. He put his arms behind his head, and looked at her.

Fiona smiled. 'I'm hiding.'

'Who from?'

'Amelia.'

'Why? Oh.'

'You disapprove?'

'Yes. Is it a policy of yours to wreck the marriages of all my friends?'

'I didn't know you and she were close.'

'She's been through the mill a bit. Oh, not close in that way, in case you're thinking . . . Don't be ridiculous, she's married.'

Fiona burst out laughing.

'Do you expect me to go along with your lies?'

'I've told Ivo we're having an affair, just as an insurance policy. It's to protect Amelia, you know. Andrew and I have an open marriage.'

'I don't believe you.'

'Oh, shades of Bloomsbury, don't you know? It's in the

genes. He's in love with someone who'll suit him much better than me.'

'I don't believe you.'

'You don't know him as well as you think you do.'

'Obviously, or he wouldn't have married you.'

'Tom, my marriage has been a disaster from start to finish, but it was a joint decision.'

'You think that exonerates you from screwing around with Crawley? And implicating me? What about *my* life?'

'You're not still seeing that Sarah person? The one who looks like a horse?'

'No, as it happens I'm not.'

'Well, then.' Fiona peeped out at him from under her long blonde fringe. 'I don't suppose you'd like a quick one?'

Mary's review of *Loaves and Fishes* was not long. Adam wrote nicely, she said, about the scenery round a small Norfolk village, but the idea of a mermaid being found there was just too whimsical, his style over-lyrical and the plot frankly absurd. He should try writing travel books.

There were no others. Adam's novel had been rushed out too quickly. It was a relief, and yet it was as if this thing he had laboured and wept and suffered over during the last year did not exist. It would not go into paperback, would not be bought by libraries; would, apart from a copy at the British Museum and one or two possibly sold to friends, simply disappear as though it had never existed.

Adam's long struggle for composure now served him well. He was not wounded by Mary's piece, suspecting that Ivo was to blame for it, but he was surprised that she had not at least forewarned him. That did hurt, a little. It wasn't so bad, being demolished by someone you knew, because you understood their tastes and foibles, he thought. Much of what she disliked was perfectly reasonable, and at least accurate as far as it went. He did nothing; and heard nothing. It was summer, everyone was away. London emptied, the heat pressed down like a hot, wet, grey towel.

His agent rang before going on holiday to say that Candida had been made redundant. 'A pity you only got one review. Happens all the time with second novels, nothing personal.'

'Do you know there's a man who has the world record for being struck by lightning? Every time he sees storm-clouds, he starts running and running, but no matter how fast he runs the lightning catches up and воом!' Adam said.

'I think you'll have to do the next uncommissioned. Or perhaps try a different tack. Have you thought of writing a travel book?'

Adam remembered the anguish of the past year, and was suddenly, miraculously, free of it. What did it matter, after all? His book existed, that was victory enough; and by his own standards it failed, which was failure enough.

'No, never,' he said, and put the phone down.

So he began again, on his third and last novel. He was neither happy nor sad. Day after day, he sat in a waking dream, writing. For a month, two months, he was able to ignore the blood in the lavatory bowl, as he ignored letters and bills. Any envelope brought up by the old woman downstairs he threw into a shoe-box, and forgot about. He told Malcolm he was too unwell to come in. He took multi-vitamin tablets, gargled with diluted Dettol and ordered takeaways. He saw no one.

He sat on a foam cushion because the flesh on his buttocks and legs had wasted so that it was painful to sit up. When that became too uncomfortable, he propped himself up in bed. Had it not been for the gnawing ache in his armpit and the need to keep running to the loo he would have been completely content. The new novel glowed in his mind like a ball of witchfire, drawing him on and on, so that he did not know or care what happened as long as it could come into being.

There came a day when, hour after hour, his sickness thudded down to a new level, paused and sank again. It was like going down in a lift whose cable had snapped, but which still stopped at each floor.

He knew that the time had come to ask for help, but was too ashamed of the mess and stench to crawl for the telephone.

The diarrhoea was so bad that he was trapped on the lavatory seat like a prisoner, pulling the chain between bouts. Soon there was no paper left. He began to use newspaper, terrified this would block the exit pipe. Finally, grimly, he tore up books. His arms and hands trembled with the effort. Adam bent over his thin knees and sobbed dryly, while torrents of evil-smelling yellow water rushed out of his raw anus, splashing the backs of his thighs.

After a while, he gave up using paper, and grabbed an old sponge, rinsing and wringing it out under the bath tap that by a miracle of plumbing was beside him. Even when there was nothing left, his body kept straining and tearing as though trying to turn itself inside out. There was blood on the sponge. He was dizzy and thirsty, his mouth slimed with sores. When he scooped up a little water to drink, shuddering as he saw his hands, it went right through in minutes.

The reek of shit was frightful. He felt as if he was suffocating, and struggled on his knees to open the window. It was like lifting a mountain. Adam gripped the frame, his fingers sliding on the yellow paint and heaved. He managed to get a little air coming through, and put his cracked mouth to it. But he could not breathe. His lungs were seared, splayed, squashed flat as duck in a Chinese restaurant.

How long he stayed that way, kneeling and gasping, he could not tell. Hours, perhaps, gripping onto the side of the bath which melted and buckled in his grasp. What jerked him out of the descent was the sound of the front door being buzzed. Adam dropped onto his hands. His elbows collapsed, but lying flat made it slightly easier to breathe. He writhed on his side, trying to push with his toes. If only the person would keep ringing. The coir on the floor rippled away, sand in a desert, ridge after ridge, perfectly raked by the dry wind. There was nothing but dust, the shrilling of far-off birds waiting to pick his bones.

Then, in a dream, Mary was there, and men. He whispered to them that he could not breathe, and they put a tube into his nose. His lungs became a very little less painful. He was lifted onto a stretcher, strapped in. Everything spun and pressed. There were flashes in which he was being tilted feet first, slipping and jolting so that all his terror of falling came back, then he was out in the busy street, staring up at the sky, the beautiful blue air, reaching everywhere, endlessly.

Part Three

27

Dying Young

Adam lay in the same intensive care unit in which Mary had been placed, or one very like it. He was half raised, with a drip going into his arm and an oxygen mask on. To Mary's eye, he looked half dead already, drained and emaciated to an incarnation of pain. A host of bacteria with long, barbarous names – Aspergillus, Strongyloides, Cryptosporidium, Nocardia – was looting the city of his flesh. He had a kind of pneumonia which, though it could be kept in check by antibiotics, would return and macerate his lungs to the point at which he could suffocate.

'You have the chance of a good few years of life,' the specialist had told Adam, when he regained consciousness. 'But there will, of course, be some deterioration.'

'What?'

'Incontinence. Continuing weakness. Recurring infections. Possible blindness and dementia.'

'Unfashionable even in death,' said Adam, gasping. He had been put on steroids, which muffled pain and depression to dull thuds of understanding. The result in some strange way concentrated his essence by enlarging his sense of irony. There was a gruesome satisfaction in knowing the worst: 'Here comes a chopper to chop off your head, Here comes a candle to light you to bed'. It had always amazed him that people did not think more about their own death, when it was the only thing of which you could be absolutely, irreversibly sure. At the same time, he was stunned, his ears ringing as if he had literally been hit over the head. He heard a whimpering sound from a long way off, and wondered vaguely whether a puppy had got onto the ward. Then he realized that it was coming from himself.

'Bad luck,' said the consultant, with the distant compassion of his profession.

'Did you know?' Mary asked, when the consultant had left.

'No.'

It was hard to speak, even without the oxygen mask, for his throat was raw. There were tumours in his throat, now, great pustules that made him imagine his neck must look like a turkey's. He saved his strength, and the monitor measuring his heartbeat climbed a jagged red mountain of strain before any words came out.

'You came.'

'I had your spare keys,' she said. 'I never gave them back.'

She looked down at her hands. 'I want to say I'm sorry, Adam. What I wrote was cruel, unjust. Of course there were faults in your book, but it wasn't all fault. I didn't say that it was all bad, either. He cut out the quote for the paperback. I'm saying this so badly.'

'Ivo?'

'Yes. He hates you, you know. I don't know why. But I should have stood up to him. It's partly that he knows how fond I am of you. I think he wanted to turn me against myself – but that's all over now – oh, Adam, I'm so sorry, I had no idea.'

Adam shrugged. 'You're right. My books are. Crap.'

'No, it wasn't, it isn't. You just haven't got there, quite, yet. But you didn't deserve another roasting.'

'Not important.'

'Not important?' Mary was affronted. 'Of course it is. I've ruined your career.'

'No. Books live – or don't.'

He was too exhausted to say any more. Did he really believe that? It was a comforting thought: that someone, somewhere, would understand and value just what he had done, would pass it along to others, like some irrepressible gene.

Every day Mary went to see Adam, and every day he seemed to dwindle further, as if the will that had kept him alive was a flame consuming his waxy flesh. Adam knew he was dying. He gazed at it, calmly, despite his terrible fear. Dying young was a professional situation which he recognized. At last, he thought to himself, I'm joining a great tradition. He could finish his book. He understood everything he had done wrong before, even if there had been no other way. He had chosen words, not had them struck out of his deepest self, the only self that counted. He had been afraid of offending people, his mother especially, of not entertaining them, of assuming his own authority as an author. He had thought that writing was an escape from living, a separate yet parallel state of wish-fulfilment, but now he understood that for him it was life, terrible and chaotic and yet the only kind of life to which he was at all suited.

'Could you. Do something?' he asked Mary.

'Anything.' She expected some impossible, death-bed instruction.

'Buy me some. Pyjamas.' He felt that he must stock up for his death, as though he were a woman going into hospital to have a baby.

Mary went to Marks & Spencer and bought him five pairs of the best cotton ones she could find. She felt a grief beyond tears, beyond anything she had known. Why had she not seen that he was the one person who gave her the right advice, who truly loved her, without the will to possess? Partly it was a kind of resentment, consisting of many layers – resentment that despite everything he had had access to the same glittering world Mark inhabited, resentment of his formal education, resentment of his aloofness, even of his being a published author. Yet it was also the knowledge that a heterosexual woman is always going to feel more deeply for a homosexual man simply because she responded to him at some level as a man, whereas for Adam she was wholly *other*. They were both outsiders, but his alienation went further, for it included himself.

She could not reject him now, even if she wanted to. In a sense, she realized, her passion for Mark had been due to certain intellectual similarities between him and Adam. She had projected onto Mark all the goodness and gentleness of her friend.

He, though, had saved her; saved her not just from a physical but a second, moral, death. In the nasty, embarrassing tussle with Ivo, what Adam had said, of there being no such thing as a necessary evil, had suddenly become something on which her whole existence hung. She had thought it naïve, for what else could there be? Yet now she understood that to take such a thing as Ivo into herself would have been disaster.

'I've failed at venality,' she told Adam. 'As I've failed at everything else. But it's a failure that feels good, for once.'

'What will you do?'

'Look after you.'

'But you have to earn a living.'

'I've lost my appetite for journalism.'

'You won't know what to do.'

'I know some of it. The basics. My mother was a nurse before she had children.'

'I never knew that.'

'You never asked.'

It worried her that his illness was kept secret. 'Have you told your mother?'

'No.'

'She must suspect something. You can't – you can't just cut her out. You're her only child.'

'You know her.'

Mary did.

'Years ago, I tried to tell her about being gay,' said Adam. 'She became completely hysterical – literally wouldn't listen, started humming loudly to block out my words.'

'What shall I tell people who ask?'

'Pneumonia.'

'And Tom?'

'Visits.'

'Oh.'

So I might see him again, Mary thought.

Adam saw her blush, and closed his eyes. He looked like a sculpture she had seen of St John the Baptist, skin racked over a skeleton. The stubble on his face cast deeper shadows, but nobody wanted to shave him, even wearing gloves. An odd, sulphurous smell came off him, even in this antiseptic place, a smell like rotting flower-stems. Lilies that fester, she thought. No, no, that was wrong, it was not Adam who was corrupted but herself. The soft mechanical bleeps measured the ebb and flow of his life. Sometimes, when Mary visited, he lay in a kind of dream, at once conscious and staring down into the abyss, his body all gasping mouths and weeping eyes. His pain seemed to him like a fiery landscape, where geysers of fury and self-pity would erupt, suddenly, scaldingly. Again and again he would feel himself sink into this place, and that was more terrible than anything, the knowledge that he was going to go down there, and that nothing would stop it.

The antibiotics slowly began to win. He imagined his antibodies marshalling themselves, like the Spartans at Thermopylae, hopeless but determined to fight on until the last one was dead. It was his favourite story, his Ur-story, he thought, knowing you were going to be killed and bloody well going on anyway. He refused to take AZT, and was triumphant when, shortly after, its efficacy was questioned.

'Admit it,' he said to Tom. 'Half the time we're just guinea pigs. You haven't a clue what really happens.'

'I love it when middle-class people exercise their right to challenge twelve years of medical training and a decade of research,' Tom answered.

'I just hate authority figures.'

'Of course. Professionally, you challenge every other authority, especially God's.'

'I'm agnostic. Well, C of E, same thing.'

'You protest too much.'

'Yes, I probably do. I'd like to die a Catholic. It's the only serious religion. But the trouble is, I can see the opposite of everything too clearly to believe in one creed, including atheism. And you?'

'Oh, mutually contradictory as well. Darwinism and some sort of divinity.'

'Shall I tell you something strange? I never believed in God until I began to write. Then there was such a powerful sense of simply copying out what had already been written that I found I did – I felt as if my life was being manipulated, that in some strange way I was being made to do it. I didn't choose to be a novelist, you know. Or even the books I've written. They chose me.'

'My mother would say that was your anima at work.'

'I met Ruth, once. She's wonderful.'

'Yes,' said Tom.

'She's turned you and your brothers into the sort of man she should have married, hasn't she?'

Adam still cut too close to the bone.

'Will you promise me something?'

'That depends.'

'Don't marry unless you can be sure of loving her more than Ruth.'

'I didn't know my love-life was of such intense interest,' said Tom, embarrassed.

'Didn't you? All fiction is concerned with love, really, fundamentally, and so I must be too.'

'Perhaps that's why I prefer music.'

'It's the same thing. Not romantic love. It's the Eros that's set against Thanatos, the life-force against the death-wish. That boy Mary was so in love with is a terrible Thanatosser.'

'Yes,' said Tom. He did not understand what Adam was wittering on about, but looked at him fondly.

'You shouldn't blame Mary, you know. What was wrong was that she did it at all,' said Adam, his mind wandering.

'Friends should help each other,' said Tom.

'She did the only thing a conscientious person could do in her position, which was to say about it exactly what she'd write about a book by someone she didn't know. Ivo is the one to blame. He should have got someone else, or left it alone.'

Adam was moved to another wing of the hospital. It was the only part of the building where patients were allowed to smoke, and had its own special food. On the walls were posters saying, HAVE YOU GOT H.I.V.? HAVE YOU GOT A PROBLEM?, which always made Mary want to get out a felt tip and scribble something rude.

Then came a time when he was well enough to go home.

'You still look like death.'

'But I'm not, apparently, dying just yet.'

'Adam, you can't live alone in that flat. You *must* tell your mother. You should be with her.'

'I'd sooner die.'

'What if you have another collapse? It's hopeless. Adam, there are organizations, the Lighthouse . . .'

'No. No. I don't want some bloody buddy talking about how I should see the tofu sculptures in Derek Jarman's garden,' said Adam savagely. 'I'm brother to dragons and companion to owls. I need to be alone. I hate this place. I hate sleeping in the same room as other people – other sick people especially. I want to go home.'

So he went back to his flat. Mary helped him up the stairs; they took an hour to climb, and when they went in she found the telephone and gas had been cut off.

'Think this is cold?' said Adam, with the self-mortifying pride of Englishmen that she could never understand. 'You should have tried my prep school. If you dropped your sponge on the floor in the morning, it shattered.'

She paid the bills, and did her best to restore order. One way or another, her fate seemed bound up with this place, she thought. At least her own flat was rent-free. It was astonishing, she thought, how both of them, virtual paupers, were living in two of the smartest areas of London. How long could she go on maintaining both establishments? There were a couple of cheques for £700 each due in, and after that, nothing. She dared not think of her overdraft any more. It was going to be impossible to write journalism as well as look after Adam – assuming that Ivo's chagrin did not have repercussions on her ability to earn a living.

It was not just that she wanted to make redress. There was a happiness to domestic drudgery which took the worst off the knowledge that she was going to lose him. She liked cooking for herself and another, liked the rhythm of housework, the bustle of shopping once again in Berwick Street market for fish and fruit and pasta. He needed help to and from the lavatory, in and out of the bath. There were incontinence pads – just sanitary towels, really, which somehow they managed to laugh over. It was astonishing, thought Mary, what you could bear to do for another person. She wondered if this was what Tom felt for his patients, a more diffuse sort of passion for humanity, or if it was all just disinterested professional curiosity. She wondered if what she was doing now was to please him, just as she had been a critic to please Ivo and a common-law wife for Mark.

If that's so, she said to herself, at least it's of benefit to somebody I care for. The sheets and his pyjamas needed to be washed every day, and that hour in the launderette, reading under the whirling Cyclopean eye of the machines, was one of complete peace. Only her former training enabled her to write the few commissions that now came her way. She bathed him, overcoming his protests and her own pity at the wasted, blackened flesh beneath her strong small hands, massaging him with cream. She refused to wear gloves for this, though for other things she had to. Sometimes it occurred to her, remotely, that the last human being she had touched with any degree of intimacy had been Mark.

'You're so thin,' she said.

When he was well enough he would sit up in bed and make corrections to the manuscript he had been working on before collapsing. It dawned on her that he was extraordinarily happy.

'This is the best bit, the bit that makes it worth while,' he said. 'It's like pruning, or weaving, or hammering down.'

He made no move to try to find a publisher, though, and she did not want to offer to help.

'Sell my computer,' he said.

'Are you sure? You might be able – still – to –' She faltered, and flushed.

'It was never really me, if you know what I mean,' he said.

Mary sold it to another freelance through the notice-board at Slouch's, diving into the club as if holding her breath. With the money, she bought more sheets, bags of coal from a department store, because they delivered, interlined curtains, and two electric bar heaters. The flat warmed up considerably. She cleaned it every day, terrified of infection, and, in a burst of energy, painted all the walls and windows. Adam complained about the smell, but was grudgingly happier when it was done. Pots of flowers and herbs now adorned his window-ledge, high above the traffic rumbling between Berkeley Square and Bond Street.

'There is a kind of greatness to your domesticity,' he said.

'Don't you think there is always? The powers of order subduing the powers of chaos,' said Mary, panting a little as she wrenched the bin-liner, jammed with rubbish, out of the bin.

'I don't know that I care overmuch for order. It sounds so . . . anal. Have you ever looked at my painting?'

'Yes. I still don't like it, I'm afraid.'

'It's the burning boy,' said Adam. 'Emma told me she saw someone burn alive. But it's my burning boy, too.'

'What?'

'Elizabeth Bishop.'

He gestured. It took her an hour to find the poem, for he did not have shelves, just stacked books on top of each other.

Mary read:

> '"Love's the boy stood on the burning deck
> trying to recite 'The boy stood on
> the burning deck.' Love's the son
>   stood stammering elocution
>   while the poor ship in flames went down.
>
> '"Love's the obstinate boy, the ship,
> even the swimming sailors, who
> would like a schoolboy platform, too,
>   or an excuse to stay
>   on deck. And love's the burning boy."'

She cooked every variation of soup and stew she could think of, and hardly noticed that she had stopped drinking, only that she felt better, stronger, more alive. When Tom telephoned or visited, she took care to be as brief as possible, rushing past him on the stairs with a bundle of laundry, smiling brightly. He did not meet her eyes, either.

Adam was not easy to look after, of course. Mary discovered that he liked two-hour baths, and became sulky when these were not exactly the right temperature. He told her that she had the knack of coming in at just the wrong moment; she rented a television and he became childishly addicted to three or four serials, especially *Quantum Leap*.

'Ivo said to me, when I began reviewing, that what novelists really want is to be loved.'

Adam considered this. 'That notion seems to me to understand so little about anything as to be almost pitiable.'

'But, surely, you wanted your books to be liked at least?'

'Of course, it's more agreeable to have them liked than disliked,' said Adam, with his old irritability. 'But the idea of being loved or even liked by people I don't know is a perfectly ghastly one. I'm not soft in the head. Yet.'

'You must be feeling a bit better.'

'I'm not ready for death, if that's what you mean.' He gave his tombstone smile. 'Not ready to make an adventure out of it. I know the plot, of course.'

Georgina had moved to Notting Hill with her partner, as she insisted on terming him. He looked like the usual sort of man in publishing, Tom thought, as he pushed a piece of Wonderloaf around the cream sauce that had accompanied his two slices of duck: balding, cocky and miserable. Everyone was grabbing handfuls of bread. It was the usual Nineties thing of inviting people for supper rather than dinner, and then keeping them waiting until nine thirty, by which time two bottles of plonk and some crisps tasted like ambrosia. The first course had been a single new potato, the size of a nut, wrapped in bacon, on a few strands of salad like green barbed wire, and the second was this blasted duck. It looked elegant, he supposed. Georgina had, as she put it, 'fallen out of love with food' as well as her husband, and seemed now to live entirely on grilled vegetables. He cursed himself for forgetting to have a couple of cheese sandwiches first. The trouble is, I've got used to Mary's dinner parties, he thought to himself, smiling absently at yet another pretty girl whom Georgie had wheeled out for him to meet. At least she had served proper food in that funny little basement of hers.

'Candida used to work with Bruce, but now she's an agent,' Georgina said. 'Tom is an old friend of Adam Sands's.'

'Oh, yes, poor Adam, I published his first novel. It wasn't a happy experience for either of us. My goodness, I'm glad to be out of Belgravia.'

'Ruined when Max de Monde took it over,' said Bruce.

'For all I know, it may end up ruining him. I wonder how he's doing?' said Candida. 'Adam, I mean.'

'Poorly, I'm afraid,' said Tom.

'Flu? Everyone seems to have flu all the year round, now.'

'No. Pneumonia.'

'Good heavens, that's really rather serious, isn't it?' said Candida, opening wide brown eyes.

'Yes.'

'Oh dear. But he will get better, won't he?' she asked, with the childlike trust in modern medicine everyone seemed to have; and Tom, suddenly angry, said, 'No. As a matter of fact, he's dying.'

'Oh dear. The usual?'

'Yes.'

'Did you see that programme on Derek Jarman?' Bruce asked.

'No,' said Tom. 'Whenever I switch on a television it's about work, but with better conditions and more sex.'

Candida was still wringing her face into expressions of concern. 'You mean he –? Oh dear, why didn't he tell me? Is he gay, then?'

'Not officially. But yes,' said Georgina.

'If only I'd known,' said Candida. 'We could have marketed him so differently, made sure he captured the pink pound and . . . I did wonder, you know.'

'Heartless bitch,' muttered Georgina to Tom. 'And she flirts with Bruce a bit too much. Right, that's one off my Christmas card list. This is our first proper dinner together since I left Dick,' she confided, as they trooped upstairs to the drawing room for peppermint tea. The lavatory, as expected, had a pine seat, piles of Felix books by his father, and a Mark Boxer cartoon of Georgina's mother. The muted wail of the Eurhythmics came through the gold-starred wall. Georgina poured more smokeless coal onto the glowing grate from an antique copper bucket. In Kennington, Tom remembered, she had cheerfully and illegally burnt logs.

'Oh, bugger,' she said, seeing a black coal mark on the pale silk rug.

'You've got awfully posh, Georgie.'

'I'm still rather feeling my way. All this *haute* bohemianism can be a trifle oppressive.'

'Ah. How are the children taking it?'

'Not well,' said Georgina, her earrings trembling. 'Children are such little beasts. Do you know what Cosmo did the other day? He said, "Look, Mummy, look!" and I turned round and there he was with his willy in Flora's mouth. What the hell do you do?'

'Tell him she'll bite it off,' said Tom, cheerfully.

Georgina burst out laughing. 'Oh, Tom, you should have been a woman!'

'I'll take that as a compliment.'

'It's meant as one. I've always thought that's why women adore you, you're really one of us. I'm just riven with guilt. But, really, what could I do? He's too mad. D'you know what really held me back? I couldn't bear the thought of moving all my books. There are acres and acres of them, and one wall in our old house actually had to be strengthened to support them. But at a certain point he simply became redundant. And I discovered an awfully good firm of –'

'Lawyers?'

'No, packers,' said Georgina.

'Every woman I know seems unhappily married for the same reasons, just now,' said Tom. If only Bruce does make her happy, he thought. If only.

'Including Fiona?'

'I suppose so.'

'Tom, perhaps I shouldn't say this, but I had heard a rumour that you and she were *à deux*.'

'Untrue.'

'Is it? She's always had a crush on you, you know.'

'You don't have a crush on someone you've already been to bed with, Georgie,' said Tom. 'I've never heard such nonsense.'

'But you did give her the boot. That's generally a powerful aphrodisiac.'

'Of course. I'd been used for research purposes, as I recall.'

'Hmmm.'

'Look, Georgie, I am not, repeat *not* having an affair with Fiona. If you want to know I find her absolutely repulsive.'

'I'd have thought the temptation to pay back Andrew must have been pretty irresistible.'

'I'm not interested in her. I couldn't care less about her. I don't mess about with married women, let alone ones married to old friends. In fact, I'm –'

'Yes?' said Georgina, encouragingly, but Tom stopped.

'Tell me,' said Candida, coming up to him. 'Is Adam really ill?'

'Yes, really.'

'Dear, dear. I must see what I can do. Has he been able to write at all?'

'I don't know. There does seem to be something he's still working on.'

'It's just – I am such a fan of his,' said Candida. 'You don't buy someone unless you have a passionate belief in their work,' she said, radiating, she hoped, conviction. 'If he's written something else I'd like to have first bite at representing it. I'll drop him a line.'

Tom seemed to see her for the first time. 'Look, I shouldn't have told you, about his being so ill.'

'Never mind,' said Candida. 'I meant to get back in touch anyway, now I've become an agent. By the way, you live in Camden, don't you?'

'Yes,' said Tom; and Candida asked, 'You couldn't possibly give me a lift home?'

28

Bonfire Night

All week the air had been rent by sudden screams and bangs from firecrackers and rockets. Eldritch shrieks trailed across the sky as bristle-headed boys all over the Queen's Estate let their demons out of milk-bottles. The more enterprising made an effigy which would have pleased their teachers with its ingenious use of materials. It was a broken mop, whose long, grey-white strings looked almost too hair-like, with a ball of newspaper for a face. The stick, or body, they swaddled in rags. This they wheeled along all over Camden, as far as Baker Street, in Billy's old buggy, which they had found on the dump and mended with wire, calling, 'Penny for the gu-uy! Penny for the gu-uy!'

Of course, they expected a hundred times more than a penny, and expressed their discontent with any offering less than ten pence. The doll had no face, but seemed in its cracks and seams to suggest a kind of sad innocence. Grace shuddered when she saw it, for it reminded her of Joy. The boys never failed to get money out of people, unlike the beggars. It was strange, she thought, that people would always give money to a dummy rather than a real, live person, because the beggar might spend it on drink. What did they think the boys spent their money on? Milk?

The crack dealers had moved out from the Estate, and the smack dealers were back. It meant more syringes, but, on the whole, less violence. Sometimes Grace thought that if everyone unemployed could be addicted it would solve all the Government's problems – a bit like drugs in prisons, keeping everyone quiet while they were banged up in their cells. The gangs preyed on the addicts, most of all, and they occasionally beat up each other, in search of money for a fix, but they left mothers alone.

'Don't ever take any medicine or drugs except the ones Mum gives, Billy, understand? Even if they look like sweeties.'

'Why?'

'They're bad. They give you bad dreams, and they kill you, dead.'

'Why do they?'

'It's like the apple in *Snow White*.'

'The poisonous one.'

'Yes. The one the wicked witch gives.'

'But that's just a story,' said Billy, confidently.

'Stories are sometimes true. There are people who may not look like wicked witches, but they are. Don't eat anything except what Mum gives. And Mrs Crawley.'

Billy was quiet, then asked, 'Is Mad Maggie a witch?'

'No. She's just mad.'

'She wants to give me a kitten. I'd like it, yes, please.'

Grace sighed. Billy looked at her pleadingly, with his huge tawny eyes. He did so love animals.

'Sorry, petal. We can't afford a cat.'

'Just a little one?'

'Kittens grow up.'

Billy, too, was growing, up and away from her. Grace began to think that he needed a father, or someone other than herself. If only we could get away, she thought, looking at the nets with their repeated picture of a little cottage with trees and cows woven in.

Through the wall they heard Maggie singing,

> 'London's burning, London's burning
> Fetch the engine, fetch the engine . . .'

Outside, some boys had overturned a wheelie-bin and set fire to it with petrol. The flames were jagged and hot, and excited them. They sat, swigging lager out of cans, bouncing balls, scuffling or just staring at what they had made. The gaunt tree in the patch of green seemed to lean towards them, behind its railings, its leaves and shrivelled conkers already fallen.

What will I do if Billy joins them? Grace thought. He needed some kind of idea of what being a man meant, pretty soon, and those boys had one, if only because they had made themselves into a gang. They were scarcely even teenagers, but they were turning themselves into men; Grace heard their mums screaming their heads off at them, but it didn't do any good, just rolled off. They skipped school and stole, when they weren't fighting. There was a gang for the white kids and a gang for the blacks and a gang for the Pakis. How the hell would Billy escape being sucked into one or the other?

This was their season, this dull fag-end of the year, when the cold air sharpened their wits and stirred their blood. All over London you could see them, coming out of the estates and rampaging up and down the high streets, looking for trouble, throwing fire-crackers, getting pissed. Bonfire Night was the time when all the joy and sullen cruelty of the city was let loose, when the dying of the year and the dying of the culture came together to cause conflagration.

By tea-time excitement had spread all over the Queen's Estate. Those on the top floors, with views towards Primrose Hill and Hampstead Heath, looked out of their windows; the smack dealers even had a party. There was said to be a big tank up there with piranha fish, and guns, so people left them alone even when their sound system was turned up high enough to shatter glass.

Grace and Billy left to see the firework display before the sun went down, but by the time they got to Primrose Hill it was night.

'Look, Mum, look, a horse!' said Billy, pointing to a large lighted bay window. Inside was an antique rocking-horse.

'Isn't it lovely?'

'I'd like it. Yes, please.'

'Sorry, petal. Horses are for rich people. Don't cry, sweetie. We can see the real ones at the farm, remember?'

Grace wondered whether she could save up for one of the small corduroy ones she had seen in the toyshop on Parkway. Billy was growing so fast now, she could hardly keep up with all the new clothes he needed.

Primrose Hill rose, taller and darker than it ever seemed by daylight, lit by a bonfire that leapt twenty feet into the air, scattering sparks whenever the wind gusted, and seething with people, innumerable thousands, streaming through the gates and along the paths. Some waved sparklers that flowered with brief, fierce petals of hissing white, so intense that they left long trailing ribbons of light upon the acrid air.

'Look,' said Billy, fascinated, 'They're doing *writing*!'

He had just started to learn his alphabet, joining the dots to form ABC with intense concentration.

'Read it,' said Grace, but the letters always faded before a word or name could be spelt, and then the sparkler itself would be nothing but a thin, glowing pistil, good only to light another with its embers.

How eerie it was, this celebration, yet full of a pagan good humour. Traffic was forced to a standstill as groups charged up and down the reclaimed streets, full of vitality brought by the dying year. Some carried coloured paper lanterns with candles inside, others wore luminous rings round their necks and heads, apparently floating on the dark like wingless cherubim. The hill shivered with unearthly points of white and green, darting and wavering through the packed blackness.

Every child who had a father was riding on his shoulders, bobbing with excitement, and everyone who knew a neighbour was exchanging greetings. Grace and Billy picked their way between the leafless trees, holding hands, alert as deer to the possibility of danger in this privileged, alien world. Every now and again a group, always teenage boys, would let off their own independent fireworks, which could shoot into the crowd further up; but they were different from the boys on the Queen's Estate.

'Not frightened are you, petal?'

Billy clutched the toy horse he kept in his pocket. 'Mummy, Mummy, I'm going to take my horse and ride him up high into the sky, so he can be all colours.'

'What colours?'

'All different colours. Red an' blue an' yellow an' green. I just love colours, I just love them, I love fireworks, I love fire.'

'I love them, too,' said Grace, though the memory of how Joy had taken her to see them as a child stung her eyes. She lifted him onto her shoulders. His long legs hung down to her waist.

Above, the sky pressed heavy and dull, the colour of putty. The crowd murmured and rustled to itself, gathering into a body of expectation and then, as the first rockets rose on spangled stalks, cried with one voice, 'OOOOOOOOOOOAAAAAAAAAAA.'

Four, five, six immense blooms, seared blue and red and violet, then gold, green, blue as their petals momentarily grew, spread, fused, and dehisced into burning seeds. Electric white spiralled, shrieking, out of sight, changed into the trunks and leaves of trees, taller than the tallest building, terrible as lightning, bending this way and that; burning orbs of unearthly blue and red tumbled, ripened or rose unexpectedly to burst against the sky with a rending crack; boiling fountains of silver and gold erupted from the ground. It was as though, for this one night, all the lost fields and springs and trees of London were allowed to revisit the earth like beautiful but impotent giants before sinking back into the hard ground that had stifled them.

BOOM - RACKA - DACKA - RACKA - BOOM - BOOM - BOOM!

Every animal for miles must be scared stiff, thought Grace. The noise, thrown back and amplified by the buildings all around, boomed in her own head, and her shoulders ached from carrying Billy. She put him down, and began to usher him back towards a gate, past families and groups of friends. It was at times like these that she felt lonely, seeing people so happy together, the men so gentle and good with their kids. Where did you find such men? Of course, they looked pretty useless otherwise, flabby with kindness like that doctor-bloke at Mrs Crawley's.

Things were ever so much easier since she had got the job in Kentish Town; Mrs Crawley paid £4.50 an hour, a pound more than usual, for looking after Rose and the house. She couldn't complain, not when she had suddenly added £80 a week to her income, and Mrs Crawley was so grateful for everything she did. She put £10 a week into Billy's building society account, and he now had £200, which made her feel really good.

Just a little bit longer, thought Grace, and I could stop signing on. She had never had so much dosh. New duvet and socks, trainers for Billy, more books, a rocking-horse, even. It cost, to be honest, but her nerves were less bad, she had to admit. Buying food with her own money instead of grazing felt good, even if the idea of paying for a TV licence would always be a joke.

Joy had left very little of use. Some clothes, always useful even if they were the wrong shape, some old pans and mugs, some books and a shoe-box of papers, birth certificates and things. Grace was too tired and upset to look through these, thinking about the old days together, before Joy got really sick. She hadn't been any older when she had me than I was when I fell for my Billy, Grace thought, just twenty or thereabouts. She was so innocent, really, bet she didn't even know where babies came from, where she herself came from. She told me she'd been adopted, but then she told so many stories about herself, sitting round the blue Formica table, out in the East End. Was that what Joy had remembered when she went all the way to London Fields? At least she and Billy were clear of TB.

Gently, she began to usher him back. It was a long walk home, and she didn't want to risk him getting tired. The asthma was much better now that he had his Ventolin, but it was a fair walk back to the Queen's.

'Come on, petal,' she said, thinking to herself that she must stop calling him this. After all, he was a proper boy. He had started to notice that she had bad breath in the morning; that intimacy they had shared was changing because he was at school every day. He had fallen for one of his teachers in a big way, and now it was, 'Miss Thing this', or 'Miss Thing that'. It broke her heart because, of course, she wanted him to be independent, and yet she yearned for the way he used to nestle in to her. Maybe I should get myself another baby, she thought, though little Rose was a nice one. She and Billy played together on the nights she came to babysit, he was ever so gentle with her.

They walked back, past the beautiful houses, through the concrete passages, along the broken paving, to their tower. Some boys erupted out of the swing doors, laughing and shouting, jostling them. Billy held her hand tightly, but did not turn his body into hers as he would once have done. The fireworks popped and whistled, distracting her. She pushed the timer on the light, walking up steadily, holding Billy's hand, thinking that the smell of burning must be from outside until she was on her own landing.

There was fire between herself and her flat.

'Oh, sweet Jesus. Run down the stairs, Billy, RUN!'

But he was still a baby, after all, and clung to her.

'Billy, it's dangerous. Go down the stairs.'

She could hear Mad Maggie's cats, yowling. 'MAGG-IE! MAGGIE! GET OUT!' she yelled.

Billy was crying, terrified. The heat on their faces seemed to suck the air from their lungs. Smoke rolled towards them. Grace picked up her son and ran down the stairs, outside, to the little patch of fenced-in green. 'Stay here. Don't move. It's dangerous, you understand? Hide behind the railings.'

'MUMMY! MUMMY!'

'*Stay!*' she said, and her son clung to the rails, unable to climb over them, sobbing.

Freed of him, she ran to the nearest telephone booth. The phone was broken. And the next. She ran on and on until she found one that worked and dialled 999, hardly able to speak for the pain in her heart and lungs. Yes, said the calm voice, the fire brigade would come.

Grace thought of the traffic, and of poor Maggie, trapped, with all her cats. She ran back to where Billy was. 'Billy, sweetheart, don't cry. The fire engines are coming, but Mum has to see if she can help Maggie. She's too sick to get out. Stay here.'

He was beyond comforting, hysterical with fear.

Grace tore herself free of his fingers and ran back up the stairs in the dark. She could see quite well, because of the flames lighting up her floor.

I can't get too close, she thought. Billy comes first, he needs me. Yet at the same time, she could not leave the poor old bag to die. Maggie's flat was closer to the stairs than hers, and she had no doubt that it was her own flat that was burning. She had always known that one day they'd try something like this. Thank God they'd both been out.

The smoke rolled towards her, oily and thick. She began to cough, her eyes streaming. It was poisonous, this stuff. She got down and crawled, as far as Maggie's door.

'Maggie, Maggie, get out. There's a fire!'

She couldn't shout, and in any case, she probably couldn't be heard above the cats. Grace thumped weakly on the door, coughing until she thought she'd throw up.

It was no use. She had to get back to her son. Poor bloody Maggie was doomed, just like Joy had been. Perhaps it was even she who had started the fire, though Grace remembered the boys and doubted it.

She staggered down the steps, and out, almost collapsing in the fresher air. Billy had stopped crying, and was sucking his thumb and playing with his toy horse, oblivious, as though he had forgotten her already. People had started to gather, watching like idiots as the glass smashed from the heat. How many floors would the fire take?

'Here I am, sweetie,' she said, and took Billy in her arms. He nestled into her, wide-eyed. She looked up, and saw Maggie's window open at last. Her neighbour was all lit up from behind, like someone in heaven, or in hell, and she held something in her arms.

A cat, Grace realized, for even as Maggie jumped, it squirmed out of her arms, and landed just inside the patch of green. She tried to shield her son's eyes, but Billy broke away. 'Stop, Billy, stop!' she cried, but he turned to her with shining eyes.

'Look, Mum,' he said. 'It's my kitten.'

Tom, watching the same fireworks from the hospital cafeteria, saw the dazzling, centripetal explosions rise over the rooftops, and ate a curling cheese sandwich. The walls were hung with reproductions of paintings, a Renoir that reminded him of Mary Quinn. For me, thought Tom, friends are harder to come by. I haven't the time to invest I had at university.

He still shuddered at the thought of Candida Twink, a nice girl but just too desperate. Well, that had been a bit of a disaster. He had drunk too much at Georgina's. He thought of how shocked Klaus had been to find the opioid cupboards locked.

'It's to stop us shooting up fentanyl. In the States nobody drinks, but they all do drugs. Here, it's the other way about, but they don't trust us.'

The Bach on his Walkman calmed him. It reminded him of the drawings by Escher, in which a river became a waterfall that somehow, inexplicably, went back to its own beginning as a river. He had always been fascinated by such paradoxes. There had been a picture on the back of the packets of cornflakes he had eaten as a child, of a family eating cornflakes whose package showed the same family eating the same cornflakes, infinitely regressing. He had never forgotten it.

'A chicken is just an egg's idea of making another egg,' he said to himself. 'Is that all it is? Is what is really wrong with me that I need to get married and have children? Am I unhappy because I miss Sarah more than I thought I would?'

He considered this carefully, peeling the withered orange that was his dessert. A kind of moral inertia was clearly taking him nowhere. Sarah wanted to get married now that she was in her thirties, she had always made that quite clear from the start, even though he had always told her he was not the right man. They had split up in the summer, but he was very fond of her, and she of him. Why should he not marry her? They were both doctors, and although that would mean neither of them would ever be particularly well off, unless she did indeed go into private practice, at least they would not run out of things to talk about, like so many married couples. Tom knew he was not good at talking. The stammer still came back, under stress. Though he now had an easy manner that enabled him to get on with anyone, it did not extend to his inner being, the core that had to be shielded. That, he had shown to only two people: Andrew Evenlode and Fiona Bamber. Neither experience had encouraged him to try again.

'You really are a Jew, aren't you, underneath the gentleman?' was how Fiona had put it, and although he was proud of his mother's race, proud of its intelligence, its genius, its love of beauty and justice, its unEnglish passion and capacity to endure, he understood that for her this inner self was repulsive, alien beyond all comprehension. At that moment, he felt something in him wither, whether it was the dream of assimilation or of simply being accepted for himself.

Yet neither could he fit into the Jewish half of his inheritance. When he encountered, as so often in North London, other Jews, there was always a reaction. They seemed too flamboyant, too foreign. To them, he was a Gentile, uncompetitive, at ease.

'So, make your own tribe,' said Josh. His wife was pregnant at last, and they were going to move into the top floor of the Belsize Park house, buying it from Ruth so that the other two could buy flats of their own. Everyone was happy about this, especially Ruth.

The Bach looped back again, F to G, round and round, passion regulated by the exquisite geometry of sound. You cannot step into the same river twice, it said to him.

Should I go to Celine, then? he thought. She was still pursuing him, to his dismay, ringing up every six weeks or so to invite him to the theatre, or to a dinner-party. All he had done was sleep with her once, two years ago. What had she said to her father? It would be a disaster if he antagonized his most powerful patron and referee, particularly after the inquest. Even though the coroner had exonerated him, it could affect his chances of getting a consultancy.

Celine would be the perfect wife for a consultant. She was lovely, witty and sexy, with the warmth so many English girls lacked. And she was Stern's daughter. If he couldn't join the Masons, surely he should be working the Jewish mafia? I could have gone to that party she's having if I wasn't on call, he thought. Everyone else was out, his mother with Josh and his wife on Primrose Hill, Grub and Alice off at some other musician's.

The stench of hospital curry filled his nostrils. I am lonely, he thought. I have no personality, no anchor; everything has been sunk in work, and now work is going nowhere. He had had lunch with the old man at the French Pub that week; his father had been so glum Tom asked, 'Do you wish sometimes you hadn't left Mum?'

'Not sometimes,' Sam said morosely. 'Just every bloody day of my life.'

'Why don't you ask her if she'll take you back?'

'She's a proud woman, your mother. She wouldn't.'

'Ask.'

'No. When you decide to marry, that should be it, Tom. Don't screw up. Otherwise you'll find you've thrown away your only chance of happiness on this earth.'

Could I be faithful to Celine? Tom wondered, and immediately knew the answer.

His bleep whined.

'Dr Viner.'

'Sorry, Doctor.'

The fireworks were still going, as he walked up the stairs, trying to keep some semblance of fitness.

CRRRRACKARACKARACKA   BOOM!   BOOM-BOOM-BOOM BOOM.

He went through A and E. It was in worse chaos than usual, the combination of Guy Fawkes and a Saturday night filling the waiting area with disaster. One ward was closed down because the hospital trust was millions over budget, and management had decided to cut the number of medical beds. Casualties waited for hours, under the flat white lights, without even a trolley to lie on. There were the usual gomers wheezing and trembling, a teenager with his finger blown off, babies bawling, drunks shouting, and about four black nurses and white-faced juniors trying to cope with it all. Tom, hardened, walked past. Some of these people he would see, but the meningitis case could not wait.

The patient was already in intensive care. 'Has anyone given her antibiotics?'

'The GP gave some penicillin. The season's starting early. This is the second case we've had.'

It was a child, a girl unconscious and visibly dying. Meningococcal septicaemia: almost always fatal. They got her onto a drip, but the blood poisoning was spreading like ink-stains beneath her skin, even as they watched. Her parents watched the girl's face as if they, too, were dying with every breath, although they could hardly see it for the tubes and mask over her face. The coloured waves of her life rose and fell, each time weaker, and the accompanying beep took longer and longer to come.

For four hours, Tom, a paediatric consultant and the one nurse who could be found to work on the intensive care unit, tried everything. His bleep kept going off as other patients arrived and he was due back in theatre. Outside, the fireworks still ripped across the sky; inside the bright colours rose and fell on another kind of darkness. More ionotropes, antibiotics, steroids, saline, oxygen. Nothing did any good.

'How much longer?' asked the mother.

'She's got about six hours. We'll start dialysis if she gets renal failure, but it doesn't look like she's going to pull through. I'm sorry,' said the consultant. 'I've got to go and look at another patient. I'll be back as soon as I can.'

'Oh, God, oh, God,' said the mother, half to Tom and half to some deity which, however inadequately, she believed him to represent. 'Please, please, think of something. There must be something you haven't tried.'

It was awful, a dying child, you never got used to it. This was someone who should be out in the world, spinning with life and joy. The Escher waterfall went round and round in his head, endlessly circulating in defiance of gravity and logic.

If only I could throw a magic switch in the body, he thought, the switch in the drawing, the kink, to reverse this cruel process. And then, quite suddenly, the Escher was superimposed onto his mental image of the circulation of the blood, and he felt a click in his mind.

He turned to the nurse. 'Have we – have we got a d-d-d- oh, fuck, a filtration unit here?'

'Yes.'

'Get her onto it. Now. Don't wait for renal failure.'

Tom turned his calm, professional face to the child's parents. No point in showing the excitement he felt, in case it failed.

'I'm going to try something. There's a chance we could wash the disease out of her blood, filter it. It's very simple, and it might not work, I haven't heard of it being done before. You understand, she's probably going to have to have her leg amputated?'

It probably wouldn't work. Time to go into theatre again. He rubbed his eyes, and went down to the neonatal unit, filled with the sweet sickly smell of pure oxygen. Three newborn babies like wizened turnips lay in perspex boxes, their ECG pads and monitors at odds with the bright murals of Bambi and Pooh, the swinging mobiles and wooden rocking chair. All were boys with hernias that needed operating on as soon as possible. Tom saw with relief that one, transferred from another hospital whose list was overflowing, had a line in already. It was always a nightmare trying to find a vein in babies, their hands were so covered with fat.

'No, sweetie,' said a nurse, in a syrupy voice, 'this is good for you.'

They were all big, sweet girls whose bovine good nature sometimes made them maddening to deal with.

'Who wants a beautiful little baby?'

'Me! Oh, aren't you a cutie?'

Tom filled in the forms for each of the babies and talked to their parents over this inane babble. The mothers always insisted on coming into the antechamber and watching as their child was put under, though it made everyone more tense. Once you were scrubbed up you had to forget about everything except performing as a team, and having some poor woman pass out as he pierced her child's body was the last thing he needed.

The baby was wheeled in, crying miserably. He had had no milk for twelve hours, and became even more frantic in the heat.

'It's all right, it's all right,' said the mother, patting her son, white with terror. The baby squirmed and fought, slippery as a fish.

'Stop that, he's picking up your tension,' he said, sharply, trying to get a tiny cannula into the infant's hand.

The mother controlled herself, with a great effort.

'Don't worry, he's going to go a bit floppy and boss-eyed,' he said. 'There! Sweet dreams.'

The baby's squeaks faded into bird-like whistles. Tom placed the laryngeal tube down the child's windpipe. The oxygen in his blood dipped alarmingly, then went up as the hiatus was bridged and the ventilator took over. Everyone relaxed.

'You'll see him in twenty minutes,' said Tom, nodding to his assistant to take the mother out. She would probably collapse, then, they all did.

They wheeled the trolley through, into theatre, where the baby's abdomen was painted with orange iodine, and sliced open. Ten minutes later, the surgeon was stitching delicately, and the first patient was wheeled off to the recovery room. Another baby came in. It was like a factory belt, thought Tom, gulping coffee, and yet he knew that desperate woman would be transformed by relief. Perhaps he should marry Sarah, she would understand the high he got from this.

He glimpsed a last firework against the dull sky, a comet miraculously rising; and then he was bleeped and told that the meningitis case was responding to treatment.

BOOM! went the fireworks, all over London. BOOM! BOOM-RACKA-RACKA-RACKA-BOOM!

Sarah Meager and Klaus Dreisler ignored the stars exploding over the rooftops of Clapham.

'Will he mind, you think?' Klaus asked, and Sarah, smiling, said, 'No.'

29

Fraud

When Max de Monde had told Mark that his daughter had a trust fund of a million pounds, he spoke the truth. The trust fund did exist, had been created for her when she was a teenager, as soon as his fortunes had begun their most dizzying ascent. Amelia's grasp of business matters had always been rather hazy, but she knew that, however uncomfortable life had become since her marriage, her comparative poverty would not last long. Mark knew this too, and it softened the edge of his tongue whenever he remembered.

Having been so nearly discovered with Fiona had given him a fright. Yet he could not stop craving her. It was a little like what he had gone through with Amelia, when living with Mary, but far more intense. He could not stop thinking about Fiona, her astonishing perversity and feral innocence, her skin. Perhaps, he thought, there was something intrinsically erotic about duplicity and adultery, or perhaps it was just work. Perhaps not. She carried a sexual charge that was almost legendary, though people also said she was mad.

'Felix' Viner had never got over her. He was drinking himself to death, and if he saw Fiona would stop, theatrically, and turn his face away. Mark thought this was stupid, yet when he saw her in the corridors of the House he wanted to have her up against the wall, grinding between her white thighs. He tried it, once – he would try anything, once, except drugs – and received a sharp slap.

'Keep your paws off me, or I'll sue you for sexual harassment,' Fiona said, and there was no mistaking the bite in her voice.

'But there's nobody here.'

'What I do in private is one thing. This is work.'

Mark waited all day the following Monday. She didn't come to his house. He wondered whether to ring her in Oxford, and by evening had succumbed, despite his detestation of the telephone. She had left the answerphone on. It was a novel, and deeply unpleasant experience.

'Where were you?' he asked, on the phone the next day.

'With my husband,' she said, innocently.

'But –'

Fortunately for Mark, his words were drowned by the sound of Max de Monde's helicopter taking off. Of late, its drone had become more frequent, and the sense of oppression it created was redoubled by everyone's fear that the paper was going to fold. Already, a whole flotilla of special interest magazines had been sold off by the MDM Group, for Max was still hoping for a knighthood and owning *What Begonia?* was not going to add to his chances. Month by month, star writers who had clung on against all offers and blandishments now left for other publications. All the broadsheets were cutting their prices to levels at which, with the fall in advertising, it would be impossible to survive, and the *Chronicle* was the weakest of the broadsheets.

'Angus just doesn't seem to realize that if you go down-market you make people ashamed of either writing for or reading the paper,' Ivo said.

Media columnists began to write the *Chronicle*'s obituary. It was reported, incorrectly, that even the canteen had closed and, correctly, that freelances had to wait at least four months before being paid the miserable sums for which they were commissioned. As Christmas approached, a rumour went round that the annual pay rises would not be automatically made, and that this year nobody would receive a bonus.

'God dammit, I was counting on that five hundred for my Christmas presents,' Lulu said. 'This really is outrageous.'

Groups of disgruntled journalists gathered by the spluttering coffee machines, trying to get enough feeling together for a union meeting.

'After all, every time Max uses his bloody chopper he spends five thousand pounds. Why should we be the ones to suffer?'

Only Angus looked reasonably cheerful. If he were sacked, he knew he would get a pay-off of at least £300,000: it was in his contract. Yet he dreaded the bawlings-out he got every week from de Monde, after faxing the *Chronicle*'s front page to him.

'Why has the *Times* got this story about the Princess and not us?'

'Pure luck.'

'There's no such thing. You have to make your own luck,' growled de Monde; and Angus, who had handed out this bromide several hundred times to others in the course of his career, swallowed hard. Only this week he had taken his lead investigative reporter, pinned him against the wall and nutted him – a little violence being, in his experience, a useful way of getting the goods. To his amazement, the little wimp promptly resigned and sicced his lawyer onto them. Lawyers! They were the bane of every paper, whether for you or against.

It went without saying that the annual literary banquet had to be cancelled. A mere thirty people, including two investors, were invited to a Christmas lunch at the Slouch Club.

'Look on my works, ye mighty, and despair,' muttered Ivo.

'You're very low, these days,' said Lulu, who had squeaked onto the guest-list only because some editor had flu.

'Who isn't?'

'Cheer up. Things are bound to get better. The recession can't last for ever. What goes down must come up.'

'Some things are like one's waistline, my darling, and some are like one's hair. At the current rate of loss, I don't think any of us will be here in a year's time,' said Ivo.

'It doesn't matter so much to you, does it? After all, you don't have a wife and family.'

'No,' said Ivo. 'I don't.'

'How's the baby?' an editor asked Mark, in a friendly tone. Ivo and Lulu held their breath, for it was understood that Rose was taboo. 'Girl, isn't it?'

'Quite well. As a matter of fact,' said Mark, 'she really looks astonishingly like me.'

Christmas for Mark was an annual nightmare of bad taste, even worse than spring with all its vulgar pink blossom and yellow forsythia. Amelia insisted on having a tree, saying that Rose was old enough now to appreciate it. She was certainly old enough to be fascinated by the baubles and fairy lights, which, now that she could walk, she was determined to pull down on herself; and after the struggle to wedge their Nordstrom pine safely in the hand-painted Deruta planter, Mark and Amelia glared at each other in naked hate.

'I said to wedge it between some bricks, you fool.'

'If the water rises any higher, I'll electrocute myself. Is that what you want?'

'Now that you mention it, yes.'

'Right, *you* finish this bloody tree on your own, then. Rose, if you yank at it one more time, I'll smack you. There! What did I say?'

'WAAAAAAH!'

'How dare you? How *dare* you! She doesn't understand.'

'Then why the fuck are we putting on this charade?'

'WANT! WANT! WANT BALL!'

'Because I want it,' said Amelia. 'I want us to pretend to be a real family, just for a few days.'

Mark glanced at his daughter. She really was quite fascinatingly like himself, and slightly less boring now that she could talk. On the other hand, his wife was so loathsome it made him shudder. Oh, Fiona, he thought.

'Why pretend?' he said.

'Why indeed?' said Amelia. 'You've always been more concerned with how many angels dance on a pin than real life.'

'The real life is the life we do not lead,' said Mark, at his most robotic.

'Is that a quotation? I'm sure it is. Am I supposed to feel inferior?'

'It's Oscar Wilde.'

'Oh,' said Amelia. 'Well, he was a writer, wasn't he? That's what a writer can say, though I shouldn't think they'd be much cop if they really believed it. You're just a hack. Get a life.'

Amelia was feeling less tired. Rose was sleeping through the night, at least until six a.m., and Grace could come every day. She was completely brilliant, and the house was now immaculate. She had only been late once, and that, Amelia discovered, was because her flat had been burnt down.

'That's terrible. Where will you live?'

'We're in a bed-and-breakfast.'

'What's that like?'

'Bloody awful. All my stuff's gone, too, and Billy's things.'

Amelia was horrified. 'You mean, you've no clothes? For either of you?'

'No. He minds most about his books, and his toy horses.'

'I'll get him some more. Yes, don't be silly.' She looked at Grace's thin figure. 'What size are you?'

She gave Grace a bundle of old clothes that she could no longer fit into, throwing in a couple of cashmere jumpers that had holes in the sleeves, a pair of Calvin Klein jeans, a dowdy old skirt.

'This is good stuff, I can't take it, they'll never believe I'm broke,' said poor Grace, envisaging being burgled at the bed-and-breakfast.

'No, I insist,' said Amelia, glowing with philanthropy. 'And you must do all your laundry here, too, and have baths, if that's a problem. At least until the council rehouses you.'

'Well – thanks,' said Grace, touched. 'You're really good to me.'

'No,' said Amelia, 'it's you who're good to me.'

She now had enough energy to drag herself up the road and into a gym where, thank God, she was unlikely to meet anyone she knew socially. It was full of vast, knobbly men like winter parsnips, but there was a line of exercise bikes and step machines, and a circuit trainer.

Grimly, Amelia started working out. She could not afford the smart places she had gone to before, or a personal trainer, and tennis was out of the question. Every day she pushed and pedalled and sweated, and as she did so her weight fell and her rage grew.

Why do I keep putting up with all this nonsense from Mark? she kept asking herself, watching the red dot flash round the computerized circuit. The leaves fell from the trees, and the cold, dull air of winter sharpened her thoughts. Why am I afraid of him? – for she now recognized the sensation he aroused in her so powerfully as being fear, not desire. Is it true, as Mary had implied, that he's sleeping with Fiona? She pounded for a few minutes, turning in her mind the exchanges she had had with both women that summer. Did she care very much if it were true? No, she had to admit, she did not. It was unpleasant when she thought that her child's father was unfaithful, but for herself, well, in her own mind she was no less so.

The understanding that she was in love with Tom had put everything around her in a harsh, exact light. Just as there had been a Rose-shaped hole in her life, that she had never known about until her child was born, now she found there was a Tom-shaped one – rather like the plastic objects her daughter was now busily pushing through individual slots, she thought. But it was a hole that so far had not been filled.

She was consumed by a jealous desire, as if by slow fire. Could it possibly be true about Fiona having an affair with him? It seemed much more likely than the notion of one with her own husband. If only, she thought now, she could be rid of Mark; and this was the perfect excuse. She could kick him out while Rose was still little, keep the house, even get him to contribute half his salary if she divorced him. He'd just been the stud, as Grace had said.

Amelia remembered Mark's prediction that if Tom moved in she would fall in love with him. Why had she not seen before how attractive he was? It wasn't just his beauty, it was the way he looked at you with a kind of absent-minded twinkle in his eye. She thought about what he would feel like against her skin in great detail; she had dreams that would wake her, they were so powerful.

How did one go about letting a man know you were, well, available? She was sure he liked her, but the old certainty that every man, heterosexual or not, fancied her belonged to another life. Besides, she didn't want Tom Viner just to fancy her. She wanted to make him feel for her what she felt for him. Much as she adored

Rose, her baby could not be the only thing in her life. Her sap was rising again, thought Amelia, pedalling furiously at the bicycle that went nowhere, pushing herself up invisible hills and round non-existent race-tracks. She lay on the carpet with Rose on her knees and did stomach crunches, ten, twenty, thirty, fifty a day. She assumed positions hitherto known to her only during sexual intercourse, flexing, contracting. Alas, though the jelly belly diminished somewhat, she still saw the depressed middle-aged woman in the mirror.

I must get my hair done again, she thought, and as soon as she could squeeze herself back into her largest smart suit, albeit with the zipper half-way down, she went to Mayfair to be regilded.

'My hair's got a bit thinner since I had the baby,' she told the stylist, apologetically.

'The only thing that will make it grow properly is if we cut it quite short,' he said, and Amelia, sighing, agreed. Snip, snip, snip, her straggly shampooed locks fell to the ground like wet fur, this was going to cost at least £80, and she had no idea whether her credit card would bounce or not. Glumly she flicked through *Harpers* and *Vogue*, noting that models this year were thinner than ever. A woman could not be too rich or too thin, it had been said. Had she ever been a size eight to ten? She certainly wasn't rich any more. All her income from her trust fund, every penny of it, seemed to go to paying Grace and the butcher. Even if she could still afford the clothes she saw, she doubted she would fit into them. Why didn't designers make things for women who were size sixteen? Wasn't over half the female population supposed to be this? Oh, if only she could get hold of that million pounds now, instead of waiting another six months for it! At the end, shorn and streaked, she handed over her Visa card and listened to the grudging chatter of the machine as it checked her credit. It squeaked and spat and droned loudly to itself while she waited, turning redder and redder, convinced that a message was going to flash up on the screen that she should be arrested for exceeding her limit.

'Sorry, Mrs Crawley, it shouldn't take so long. I'll try again,' said the receptionist, and only her pride prevented Amelia from falling to her knees and confessing that she had no money now, none at all, that despite her jewellery she was an utter sham.

'Excuse me, I –'

The machine uttered a piercing screech, and spat out a ticket for her to write on.

Amelia came home in a temper.

'I can't bear it, I can't bear being this poor. It's just killing me. We don't buy new clothes, we don't go on holiday, we only drive one car and live in one house, but even when I go to have my hair done for the first time in months I can't afford it.'

'Why don't you ask Max to release some more of your trust fund?'

'I have. I've left message after message, with his secretary, with his Filipina, even with Mummy. He's not replying.'

'Well, then, we're broke.'

'How can we be, on what my father pays you?' she said. 'It's impossible. You must be spending money on something you aren't telling me. You've got your mortgage covered on that horrid little flat of yours – there has to be a reason for it.'

'It's just what middle-class life costs. Even if we were to move out to somewhere really grim and family, like Muswell Hill.'

'Muswell Hill! All that red brick! I'd die.'

'You could take out an overdraft,' Mark said. 'The bank knows a million's coming – there must be some point to having a Coutts cheque book.'

'Yes, I suppose I could.'

But Coutts were awful. They insisted on sending round someone to value their house, and it was obvious he had never even heard of Kentish Town, and couldn't wait to shake its dust from his velvet-collared overcoat.

'Of course, we'll move as soon as my trust fund matures later this year,' said Amelia, in her best social manner.

'Of course,' the valuer agreed. 'But, meanwhile, it looks as if you'll need some underpinning to make up the value of the house when you bought it.'

'Oh, we had it all done when we moved in two years ago,' said Amelia, confidently.

'Umm. Unfortunately, it looks like they didn't do a good enough job. See those cracks?'

Another month passed. They were living off the rent Tom paid them, there was no avoiding the fact.

She rang her lawyer. 'Look, Jim,' she said, 'I'm going to get all this money from my trust fund in six months' time. Isn't there something you could do to get us some of it now? I don't mind losing a few thousand in interest, we're absolutely desperate. Daddy's the trustee, but he just won't talk to me.'

'I'll see what I can do.'

Another month passed, and she had begun to think he had forgotten when he rang again. Ivo was there, soaking up her whisky, and amusing her. She picked up the call just as the answerphone clicked on.

'Amelia?'

'Yes?'

Her message was murmuring in the background.

'Is this a good time to talk?'

'Not very,' she said, mindful of Ivo's presence. 'Let me take this on another phone.'

She raced upstairs and picked up the telephone in the study. 'Hallo?'

The answerphone gave a piercing beep.

'Hallo, Jim. That's better now.'

'Amelia. I need to ask you a question.'

'Ask away.'

'Nobody else had access to your trust fund, did they? There were no other trustees?'

'No, just Daddy.' Amelia's heart began to beat with such rapidity it felt like a small bird in a smaller cage. 'You must know that. McKenna and Carter drew it up.'

The lawyer sighed. 'I'm afraid I have some bad news for you. The trust has been drained.'

'*Drained?*'

'Yes. There's nothing in it, apart from a couple of thousand pounds. I couldn't believe it myself, at first.'

'You mean, my father –?'

There was a long, echoing pause. Amelia sat down.

'He reinvested it in another of his companies. It's sort of legal, I'm afraid, because he was the sole trustee.'

'Well, get it out again.'

'I can't. I've started to trace it, but each company seems to feed off the other. They're all called similar things, Max de Monde General, Max de Monde Publishing, MDM Holdings, it's a rat's nest. God knows how he keeps track of them.'

'Daddy said he was the only one I could trust,' Amelia said, blankly.

'I've drafted a letter to send to him, but from what I hear, there's not much chance of getting it back.'

'How could he do this to me?'

'He's pretty desperate.'

'So are we. Look, don't tell anyone just yet. Write to him saying I must see him about the trust fund. Oh, and, Jim?'

'Yes?'

'Could you get us the remaining two thousand now?'

Amelia heard the front door close. Rose began to wail.

'Grace, *Grace*!'

'Coming!'

'Sorry, Jim.'

'I'll try,' he said, ringing off.

She went downstairs, but Ivo had gone. She was too upset to be anything but relieved by this. Only days later did she realize that the incoming message tape inside her answerphone, which had presumably recorded the entire conversation, had gone too.

30

Happiness

'Just try another spoonful, my dear, just one.'

'No.'

'Please.'

'Can't.'

As Adam grew weaker, he regressed to a kind of babyhood. Thrush weakened his teeth and inflamed his gums and throat; cancerous tumours made it hard to swallow. His breath was terrible, sulphurous, for when she tried to brush his teeth the flesh around them bled until they were raw. It became impossible to get him to eat anything but ice-cream and mashed banana. Haägen-Dazs was the best, they agreed, though when Mary saw the advertisements, with their beautiful entwined couples feeding each other, she felt the wire cut round her heart again.

Every day there were new lesions on Adam's body, not just the large, hard purplish lumps and red blotches, but rashes that formed multiple blisters which burst and crusted over.

'I feel like that man in *The Fly*,' he said.

He was scarcely recognizable, so gaunt, bearded, haggard. His appetite dwindled. From periodic, excruciating visits to the hospital, they learnt that tumours were multiplying internally too, along his intestines, making it harder to digest food. A Macmillan nurse now visited once a week, and Mary learnt that his blisters were shingles, and could be treated with a drug called acyclovir. There was nothing to be done for the other except repeated chemotherapy, and as this often made no difference except to induce more nausea, Adam refused it.

His earlier mood of acceptance had changed into bouts of anger, often taken out on Mary.

'I'm only trying to help.'

'I didn't ask you to,' he snapped.

'Oh, Adam. There's nobody else.'

'You've just been waiting to step into this role, haven't you? Do you know the real trouble with you and Mark? He invented himself out of novels, and you tried to read him as if he were a book.'

'Yes,' she said, struck. It was the excessive literariness about their affair which she had yearned for, the endless, obsessive discussions of what they had read. 'You're right. That was precisely his attraction for me.'

'The only trouble is,' he said, with infantile cruelty, 'you're such a crappy reader.'

She was terrified of getting ill, because it would mean he would have nobody to help with the daily business of dying. She could kill him even with a simple cold. Again and again she pleaded with him to let his mother know, but after listening to one of Mrs Sands's rants on the telephone, she understood why he simply wished to shut her out. After all, she had not wanted her own mother to know about her suicide attempt, and Adam had respected that.

He stopped writing, whether because he had finished or because he had exhausted his last reserves of energy she didn't know. Slowly, painfully, his detachment was replaced by bitterness.

'Do you know what the medical name for thrush is? Candida. That's a good one, isn't it?'

'She wasn't so bad, Adam. At least she liked your work enough to publish it.'

'Unlike you. You'd have killed it stone dead, wouldn't you?'

Mary sighed. That life now seemed impossibly remote. She still found invitations to parties piling up on her mat when she went back to Chelsea, and instantly threw them away, along with the catalogues and the books that were pushed through her door-flap.

'Just bugger off, bogtrotter. I don't want to be moved. There must be some less clumsy way of changing the sheets.'

'It's what the nurse showed me to do. At least the council will pay for the laundry to be done. You're pampered.'

'Pampered!' he said in a suppressed shriek. 'Is that what you call it?'

They could not share jokes any longer. His irony was melting, as if before a blowtorch, as his agony and tiredness increased. Every cell of his body seemed to be withering, screaming. The effort not to scream almost consumed him, when the bouts of stomach cramps came again. I'm shitting myself to death, he thought horrified. It was agony even to swallow the painkillers and penicillin prescribed in a syrup. He could no longer bear to have more than the lightest of sponge-baths. The look in his eyes was terrible. She could not begin to imagine what it was like for him, and almost preferred it when he was difficult, more like his acidulous old self. It was when he apologized that she felt her composure crack. 'I'm sorry, I've got cabin fever,' he said, after one particularly foul outburst.

'Yes.'

'I keep thinking of all the places and countries I should have gone to when I was able, wishing I'd travelled more. Even if I didn't have the money, I should have managed, somehow. I'm glad I went to Sicily. Taormina was beautiful. I feed off so few memories now, they're all used up.'

'Wouldn't you like to go out now? We could go to Green Park.'

'The visits to the hospital nearly kill me as it is.'

'I could call Tom to help you downstairs.'

'No. No.' He turned his face into the pillows. 'I don't want him to see me like this.'

'It wouldn't matter to him. He's probably seen it all before.'

'But it would matter to *me*,' said Adam, with great passion.

She thought of him now no longer as the lover she could never have had, but as a kind of child, pitifully ruined but still needing everything she could give. The GP prescribed him painkillers and vitamins, but there was so much that she had to buy. He had to sleep on a lambskin to avoid bedsores, he needed nappies, and food was so expensive. Mark had liked to observe that crippled men never wanted for wives, as though this was proof of some sinister

314

female desire for dominance over his sex, but she knew now that all they wanted was someone to love, that the female hunger to give was even stronger than the desperation to get. She could not imagine ever having a baby, now, or a husband and the family she had hoped for. That Christmas, she wandered round the streets between Chelsea and Mayfair, looking at twilight into the warm, brightly lit living rooms, each with its glittering tree and cargo of happiness, for ever out of reach. Her own family seemed even more distant when she telephoned them, apologizing that for the second year running she could not afford the ferry over, or expensive presents. She bought Adam a silk scarf from Liberty, though, and he gave her his black leather jacket.

'You need a new coat,' he said. 'And I won't be wearing this again.'

Mary wished he had not rejected his sexuality so completely, that he could have found other gay friends instead of battling it out in such dreadful solitude; that he had not been so filled with self-hatred and shame. To him, his disease seemed like the natural culmination of a lifetime of concealment and suffering. She reflected that, in another era, he would probably have got married and had children, led a double life and been quite happy with it. Being homosexual now seemed so much worse, with its enforced outings.

He had said, once, 'I hate the word "gay". It suggests happiness, frivolity, about a condition which is anything but.'

'Do you know what the Edwardians called it? Earnest.'

'As in, *The Importance of Being*?' Adam laughed. 'Good for Wilde, slipping one past his audience. Yes, "earnest" would do fine; and people like me could be called, "deadly".'

Spring came, and the crocus bulbs she had planted flowered, both in Adam's flat and in her own. She wished, now, that she had saved the money. All her ingenuity could not stop her debts from continuing to rise. She sold everything she had which could generate money, from designer dresses to costume jewellery, preserving only her own computer, printer and answering machine, for she still hoped to rescue something after the worst had happened. One or two newspapers still gave her the occasional book to review, especially after she explained why she had disappeared, but not the *Chronicle*. Ivo had clearly not forgiven her for his mortification. In any case, there were too many rumours about de Monde being on the verge of bankruptcy for her to want commissions from such a source; and she had lost her appetite for the chase.

Her voice dwindled and fell into silence. The magic beanstalk of rage was being cut down, strand by strand. Her fingers were roughened by too much housework, she could not imagine them rattling a keyboard, so she sold her computer and printer. All the same, when she accepted a cheque for them both, from someone who answered her advertisement in *Loot*, it was a death-knell to all her hopes.

She solved her problems, at least temporarily, by taking out a bank loan for £5,000. How she was to pay this off she did not know, for she was too busy even to start the labyrinthine procedure of signing on for the dole. There were supposedly all sorts of things she could claim for, from Meals on Wheels to something called Invalid Care Allowance, but because Malcolm had never paid Adam's National Insurance it seemed exceedingly difficult to prove that they were entitled to it. Adam simply could not be left alone for the hours and hours it took to explain all this, either on the telephone or in person; she filled in forms from the DSS and sent them off with his GP's covering letter, and just hoped for the best.

Malcolm was one of the few visitors Adam allowed in, and it was obvious, when Mary saw him, that he was doing it out of pure charity.

'I dread these scenes so much,' he confided to Mary, in an undertone over a cup of tea. 'I go to a funeral a month at the moment. Everyone I know is dead, or dying. You become obsessed by the disease, even if you haven't tested positive yourself, touch wood. I'm terrified Carlos is going to get it, he's such a naughty boy, so beautiful. People just can't resist him. But if Carlos were to go, I think I'd die too. He's the love of my life, you know. It's a terrible thing when you find that, it makes you so frightened.'

'Yes,' said Mary, 'I can see that.'

Georgina visited, too, in a cloud of scent and gossip. She

brought an enormous bunch of hyacinths and narcissus, wrapped in cellophane and tied with luxuriant ribbon that, Mary reflected sourly, probably would have paid for a month's heating bills.

'Haven't we met before?' she said to Mary, puzzled; and Mary, who had once been so curious about this handsome, formidable woman, said, 'Adam's launch, perhaps.'

'My dear, how frightful, whatever's happened to your face?' Georgina said, on entering the bedroom. Mary wanted to hit her, but Adam, oddly, seemed quite cheered up by the question. What he needed, Mary realized, was for this to seem normal, a passing thing.

'Has Tom told you, the Evenlodes are divorcing? Fiona has been having it off with that ghastly creep at the *Chronicle*, you know, the one who shotgunned poor Amelia, and Andrew has decided to leave Fiona anyway, and the big question is, what will Amelia do? She's been in purdah practically since her wedding, you know, though someone told me she'd put on a lot of weight. At least there are no children involved on Andrew's side.'

Mary hovered, making tea, while Adam murmured inaudibly. So, Ivo and I were right first time, she thought.

'By the way, has Candida Twink got in touch? No? She's an agent now, heard you'd written another novel. She's dead keen to read it.'

'Over my dead body,' said Adam.

'Well, she probably will, won't she?' said Georgina, 'One way or another. But the fact is, you didn't write it without intending it to be published, did you? Nobody does, that's the rub, even if, unlike me, you don't write drivel for money. What have you done about your manuscripts? They could be worth something.'

'Unlikely, very.'

'They might, you never know. Americans get all excited about that sort of thing. Have you made a will?'

Mary could not bear it. She said, feeling like a servant, 'If you'll excuse me, Adam, I think I'll go out.'

She went back to Chelsea, thinking she would use the time to give Phoebe her six hours' cleaning. Recently, she had been splitting it up into patches of an hour here or there, because of the need to get to Adam and see if he had survived the night. This was not as satisfactory for either of them, and as Mary started to go down the stairs to her basement, Phoebe opened the door and said, 'Oh, hallo, come upstairs for a cup of cha.' It was not a request.

'Look, my dear,' said Phoebe, sucking at her cheroot. 'I hate to say this, but our arrangement isn't really working out, is it?'

'I'm sorry,' said Mary. 'I've been looking after a sick friend these past months.'

'Ah,' said Phoebe. 'Well, perhaps you could move in with him. That would solve everything. You see, I'm getting a bit too shaky on my pins not to need help myself these days. I was thinking of some sort of housekeeper type, you know? And that basement, well, it's not quite as uninhabitable as I thought.'

'Indeed,' said Mary, drily, thinking of all the hours she had spent making it very much habitable.

'I could probably get some little Croatian or something, I hear they're quite diligent,' said Phoebe, her purple turban sliding sideways. Her skull was filmed with soft, thin hair. She really was rather ancient, underneath the thick black eyeliner and red lipstick.

'Look,' said Mary, determined not to be pushed around, 'I'll have to ask my friend if I can move in. It's a one-bedroom flat, and he really is very ill. It would be more convenient for me not to have to travel so far every day, and I quite see your point about the housekeeping. Could you give me six weeks? You've been so kind about everything, and I promise I'll get the cleaning back up to scratch.'

'Yes, of course,' said Phoebe, disarmed. 'What's your boyfriend got?'

'He's not my boyfriend, nor ever could be,' said Mary, looking steadily at her. 'He's gay.'

'Ah. Oh,' said Phoebe. 'How sad. More cha?'

One morning, when she turned the key in the lock, she heard Adam say, 'Mary? Is that you?'

'Yes.'

'Come in and turn the light on, would you?'

She did as he asked, though the room was already brimming with the lemony sun of spring. 'Better?'

'No.'

'What's wrong?'

'I can't see. I can't see, except blurrily, out of one eye. Oh, Mary – I won't even be able to read, now.'

They were both silent. Then Mary sat down beside him, and held his hand, stroking it.

'You understand, don't you? It's the end.'

'Yes,' she said, and she did, for it was, after all, the thing that had bound them from the beginning, the imaginative state produced by moving the eyes across marks on the page. It was this that had led her into his shop on Charing Cross Road, all those years ago when she was fresh from across the water, with her first wages from the club in her pocket, and the hunger to read and have books of her own. They had talked, and talked, and talked, all about books and reading and writing, until they had become friends.

'Let me call the doctor. Maybe there's something, some way of reversing it –'

'There's none.'

'There are books on tape –'

'I can't go on.'

Tears began to flood down Mary's face. 'Adam, you never know. There might be new drugs just round the corner, something. You might get better again, try the chemotherapy, something might work. I'll get you water from Lourdes, oh, God, don't give up, don't give up, my dear, please don't –'

'I'm dying Mary. I don't want to die blind.'

'We're all dying,' said Mary, on the edge of hysteria. 'It's all hopeless.'

'Get a grip on yourself.'

'Well, get a grip on *your*self.'

'I have,' said Adam. He paused. Every word was such an effort, a knife of pain going into his heart. 'Look. I'm buggered if I'm going to let this foul thing kill me. I'm going to do it. Myself. Help me.' He was so weak now that it took him a convulsion of will just to move his hand. 'You've done it.'

Mary thought back to when she had tried to take her own life, for a reason that now seemed so petty and self-indulgent she understood Tom's scorn. 'I'll have to get Tom.'

'Yes.'

He closed his eyes, exhausted.

'I can't do it,' said Tom.

They sat in a reconditioned pub in Covent Garden, glaring at each other. It had taken all her courage to ring him, and he had suggested this hideous venue as reasonably close to the hospital where he was working as a locum. Back on the wheel of fortune, sending out letters of application, ringing round anyone who might help him get into doctor heaven. Outside, the pub's pillars had been painted to resemble malachite and onyx; inside, its seats were turquoise button-backed velvet, its tables mahogany veneer, its bar formerly a church screen complete with large wax candles. False coals burned soundlessly; overhead, imported brass fans hung motionless. A pale plane of light turned red by the leaded glass in the pub's windows stained both their faces.

'Why not?'

'I'm a doctor. If it was discovered, I'd be struck off.'

'Oh, for God's sake! You can't be so straight,' Mary hissed at him. 'Who's to discover?'

'A coroner.'

'You must have access to drugs that wouldn't be easily detected.'

'Do you think they aren't all checked? Mary, I can't.'

'What do you mean, you can't? Have you never done abortions? Have you?'

She looked at him, sulking over the table with his pint of bitter, and the light flashed red on her teeth.

'Abortions are legal,' said Tom. 'Euthanasia isn't. You know that.'

'The law, the law. What is the law? This is your friend, Tom. He wants to die now, not blind, with every shred of what he is stripped from him. How can you kill an innocent baby in its mother's womb and not someone who's dying anyway – who wants to die?'

'Do you think I like doing what I do? Do you think these

questions don't come into my mind too? Every day? I – it's the law, Mary. I can't break it.'

'And you called me a whore for doing what Ivo wanted! You utter, craven coward.'

They stared at each other, locking wills.

'I'm sorry. I shouldn't have said that about you and Ivo,' said Tom. 'But I'm not a coward. I've saved thousands more people than I've ever killed, in conditions you can't even begin to imagine. Things aren't going well for me professionally, but I just can't throw away twelve years of my life, my training.'

'Not even for a friend?'

'No. But I could tell you, theoretically, how many painkillers would be fatal.'

'Tom,' said Mary, after a pause. 'I never went with Ivo, you know.'

'I never said you did.'

'No, but you – I wrote what I did to help Adam, you know. It was the only review he got. I didn't mean to harm him. I'm not going to review any more.'

'That's a pity. You're good at it.'

'I didn't know you read them.'

'Criticism isn't bad. It's a necessary thing.'

'It's corrupt and corrupting.'

'So is any profession, done badly. But done well, it's a fine thing, a great thing, even. Writers can't exist without readers, without a matching intelligence and sympathy.'

'But critics aren't readers. That's what's so destructive.'

'I don't know enough about your world, but I'd be surprised if everyone in it hated books,' said Tom, gently.

She stared down at the table. Its surface was covered with ghostly circles, left by wet glasses, overlapping and blurring but distinct, preserved in fine layer upon fine layer of polish. So many lives, she thought. He lives with Mark, of course he must have discussed this with him.

'He should ask his GP for morphine', said Tom. 'It must be taken with care, though. Too much is fatal.'

'Yes,' said Mary.

'A sympathetic GP is very important,' Tom said, slowly. 'You might also ask – him?'

'Her.'

'Adam might also ask her how she would feel about signing a death certificate for someone who dies at home, peacefully, after a long illness.'

His face swam in the red gloom. Guiltily, miserably, she looked up at him. They would always be tied by death, now.

'Thanks.'

31

A Picnic

Spring came, and it was the loveliest Mary could remember. Never had the parks seemed so full of blossom; even the withered trees in concrete tubs along Oxford Street, trees which seemed so broken, cramped and meagre they were little more than supports for fairy lights at Christmas, burst into flower. The ugliest buildings were screened by a haze of green while the handsome stood like brides beneath spirals of floating white petals.

Even Adam seemed to be improving. He could get up, and sat by the front window, turning his skull to the gentle sun, and complaining that there was far too much chat and not enough music on Radio Three.

'What can you see?'

'A sort of wavery impressionistic blur. It's quite interesting, really. Your hair has grown back a lot, hasn't it?'

'Yes. I haven't the time to get it cut. It's an awful mess, though.'

'It's better long. When you've got such a nice colour, you should make the most of it.'

'You should come out into the parks. Kensington Gardens is full of tulips, all pink and yellow and maroon and white. It's lovely going past on the bus.'

'Sounds vulgar.'

'Yes, but it isn't. Anyway, what's wrong with a bit of vulgarity?'

'I've always preferred Queen Mary's Rose Garden, myself. There are too many Arabs in Hyde Park.'

'Oh, *Adam*!'

'Well, you know what I mean. Hot dogs and ghetto-blasters.'

'And rollerblading, now. Why don't we go to the Rose Garden? It's not too far. We could take a picnic.'

Slowly, Adam became persuaded, even enthusiastic. 'We could ask Andrew, and Tom and Georgina.'

'I've never met Andrew.'

'He's nice. You'll like him, you really will. He looks stuffy, the archetypal English toff but he's not, not inside, he makes you notice all sorts of things about buildings and paintings. I never noticed the little cast-iron flames on top of old traffic lights before I knew him. He fell out with Tom when he got engaged to Fiona –'

'It's terrible, the way you've all had affairs with each other. Like *La Ronde*,' said Mary, without thinking. 'Oh – not you of course –'

'Well, Andrew was a bit at school, you know. I was his fag.'

She burst out laughing, appalled. 'You mean –?'

'Claws to the ceiling, darling, claws to the ceiling. Anyway, you're part of it, too. Through Mark.'

'Ugh.'

'Mary, listen, you *must* give up hating him. Not because he hasn't been a shit, but because it's such a pointless waste of mental energy.'

'It taught me to write.'

'I think you always could.'

'Perhaps. But only a real emergency got it out of me. It isn't as bad as it was, you know – I mean, I don't feel like throwing up every time I see or hear his name any more. I suppose after a couple of years that counts as progress. The trouble is, I've got used to it. You can become addicted to hating someone, just as you can to loving them.'

'You're frightened of what would be left if you stopped.'

'Yes. That's it, exactly. At present I'm in check, between you and him. It's shameful to need a focus for my life, but I do. I wish I were strong enough to do without men, to be completely absorbed in work without ever seeing how trivial it is. I didn't mind waitressing, you know, when I had Mark. Of course, I sort of knew I was bright enough to do something else, but it was fun, the buzz and the people at the club.'

'You wouldn't want to go back to it?'

'No.' She sighed. 'No, that's all behind me, another life.'

'Good. Sometimes, when I listen to you, I think feminism has never happened.'

'You forget, I'm not really middle class.'

'All the same, hatred is so destructive of the hater. It devours itself, and yourself, and feeds off that devouring. It's the original vicious circle.'

'What's done can't be undone.'

'I know. I know. But it can be overcome, subsumed if you yourself become larger than the thing that caused you so much pain. That's what I want for you, Mary, for you to be free. You must become bigger than he is, not as a critic but in yourself.'

The tenderness with which he spoke brought hot tears to her eyes. For the first time she understood how fond he was of her, that he might love her, even, in the same way she loved him.

'Oh, Adam,' said Mary, 'you make me so ashamed.'

'Do I?' His ugly face flickered with a smile. 'Perhaps that's my revenge.'

'Well, it's finely drawn, then.'

'He was never worthy of you, Mary. He's such a small, mean sort of man. Those snake's eyes should have warned you.'

'Better than Ivo.'

'Was that your only choice? Besides, Ivo, toad though he is, strikes me as having been rather better than you give him credit for.'

'You surprise me.'

'I surprise myself. That's the great advantage of illness, you know. It gives you such a lot of time to think about what people are really like. Ivo may be a toad and a scumbag, but he's actually quite a kind man, in his way. He was only doing his job, trashing me, because it was a rotten book. Yes, it was, Mary, I know that. It's just a pity he did it in a way which was personal.'

'But he's corrupt.'

'Oh, I'm not saying he isn't. On the other hand, he didn't put you in a cage and try to rip your heart out. He tried, in a fumbling sort of way, to help you become a different person.'

'It certainly was fumbling,' said Mary, drily.

'You should marry, you know. Whatever else you do. It's your natural state, as solitude is mine. You've been good to me, Mary, I want to see you happy.'

'Oh, hush, don't talk so. I haven't been good, I've been awful. I betrayed the only real friend I ever had. Can anything be worse? What can you think of me?'

'Whatever you did was trivial. Looking after me, nursing me, isn't.'

'Adam, if I could die,' said Mary, bursting into sobs, 'if I could die and save you instead, I'd do it. My life is worthless, anyway. I'll never do any of the things you could do.'

'You're just young.'

'That's not how I feel. Inside, I'm an old crone.'

'You won't stay one. You'll grow young again. That's how I see you, happy and surrounded with love.'

'I can't believe it.'

'That's what's so foolish about being grown-up,' Adam said. 'You train yourself to believe only in the terrible things. Yet there is so much that's wonderful and good. Happiness is a little like learning to swim, you know. You have to stop fighting and panicking, just let it come.'

The fine weather continued, and she rang round Adam's handful of close friends to ask them to the picnic. All agreed, offering to bring food and even champagne in a tone of guilty enthusiasm. She knew they all felt they should have visited more often, but she also knew that, unlike her, they had lives of their own to get on with, and were frightened of someone they knew dying so young.

What will I do when he dies? she thought. Her six weeks of grace in Chelsea were almost up, and she had barely begun the arduous search for another flat or room. She could not move in with Adam – that would drive them both crazy. For a couple of mornings she had bought copies of *The Times* and the *Evening Standard* to look for flatshares, but just getting through on the telephone was a nightmare. And how was she to pay any rent, living on a massive overdraft?

The day of the picnic came. The buzzer sounded, and Tom

came up to help Adam down the narrow stairs. As they passed Mabel's flat, Tom said, 'Look, it's all nailed up.'

'They've got her out, then.'

'Either that, or she's died.'

'There's a notice from the pension fund.'

'I never heard a thing. What if she's inside?'

'She had relatives in the country. Perhaps she's gone to them. She really was pretty old, you know.'

'So, you're the last one left, Adam. Well, they can't evict you.'

'No, I know.' He gave a curious smile.

Tom had brought a collapsible wheelchair from the hospital. It was a relief when Adam consented to sit in it. Georgina and Andrew were waiting for them, carrying plastic bags that clinked invitingly.

'You can drink, Adam, can't you?' asked Georgina, struck.

'Oh, yes. I intend to. This is beautiful. I'm in a sort of – scented, coloured mist. Would you mind – wheeling me round – for a while?'

'No, no, not at all,' they all said.

So they pushed him round, a little self-conscious at times because of the stares that his thinness and poor, ravaged face elicited, and from which his near-blindness shielded him.

'We should have done this before,' said Georgina.

'No,' said Adam. 'Today is perfect. That's what I wanted, a perfect day.'

He listened to the waterfall.

'I've always liked the idea of this place so much. The Inner Circle of London being full of beauty, and such terribly bad statues. It is almost at the exact centre, you know, not of the actual city but of our own mental map of it.'

'Have you ever been to the Open Air Theatre?'

'No.'

'We should –' And then Georgina remembered, and fell silent.

'It's odd, the way ducks always remind you of people you know,' said Andrew Evenlode, easily.

'Animals nearly always do. There's a camel in the Zoo who's a dead ringer for Tennyson.'

'That was how my father taught himself to draw cartoons,' said Tom. 'There was one I still remember, of a man trying to use a rhinoceros to pick his teeth.'

Mary, who had been silent, intimidated again, laughed.

'Where do you want us to stop, Adam?'

'Not in the Rose Garden. Closer to that appalling fountain of the triton. There's lots of grass there.'

They found a place, and spread out blankets and cushions. Adam was helped out of the wheelchair and lowered slowly onto the ground. The scent of drying mown grass was everywhere. There was no sound from the city, only birds and falling water.

'What food!' exclaimed Mary, salivating as she unwrapped the greaseproof paper. There were fillets of salmon in pastry, wild rice sprinkled with tiny nuts and segments of red and yellow pepper, potatoes in mayonnaise, puddings in which meringue, fruit, cream and chocolate were so intermixed as to constitute a kind of layering of the senses. Tom opened the champagne carefully, but at the last moment of easing the cork out, it shot forward and hit Andrew on the forehead.

There was a moment's dreadful silence, and then both men began to laugh. They laughed and laughed, rolling round on the rugs like dogs.

'Boys, boys,' said Georgina.

'Oh, shut up,' said Mary, irritated.

How trivial it was, all this concern about who loved whom . . . She thought of the poem Adam had made her read, its delicate wit and sadness. You couldn't go around like that, burning with love, you needed a more ordinary, bread-like kind of passion. Yet who among us has not been scalded? she thought. There were Andrew and Georgina both in the throes of divorce, there were Adam and herself. Only Tom seemed largely unmoved.

'Won't you eat? You seem to live on air.'

Adam roused himself to say he would. Slowly his thin hand conveyed a few crumbs of each food to his mouth. Mary watched, anxiously, maternally, fearing he would choke. She knew any kind of food brought him to the edge of nausea. He ate, then said, calmly, as if it were the most natural thing, 'I've collected these.

But I need someone to crush them up.' From his pocket he withdrew a bottle of pills. He addressed Tom. 'I think there's enough.'

'Adam, you can't be serious!'

'Look at him,' said Mary, rounding on Georgina, her latent antipathy suddenly turning to fury. 'How can you doubt it? It's his right.'

'I thought you were getting better,' Georgina said, her mouth turning down like a child's.

'I can never get better, Georgie. Only worse.'

'But you've enjoyed today, haven't you? There could be other good days.'

There was a long silence. Adam sat patiently.

'He wants to go on a good day, don't you see?' said Andrew Evenlode.

'I'm so tired,' said Adam. 'I just want to die, now, while I'm still myself.'

They sat, thinking, in the warm haze. A blackbird burst out of a bush, chattering.

'Tom?'

'Living is dying,' said Tom. 'It's a paradox I'm not allowed to solve.'

'But Adam is dying anyway,' said Mary.

'Mary is right,' said Andrew, and, somehow, it was decided.

'I'll need a spoon,' said Tom. 'You should have something stronger than champagne, though. Brandy, gin, spirits of some kind.'

From her bag, Mary took out her flask of Jameson's. She had not touched drink for months, but had kept it, just in case.

'Is that enough?'

'Yes,' said Tom.

How beautiful it was, that day, the trees in new leaf and the birds all singing. The air, warm and sweet, rose off the streets and parks in a barely perceptible shimmer, the buzz of a helicopter scarcely louder than a bee. Max de Monde, looking down like God in his heaven, considered the city that had taken him in and turned him out. It was not gorgeous, like Paris or Rome, not a product of energy and inspiration like New York, nor an aesthetic creation like

Florence. Its river wound under many bridges, both functional and fantastic, a broad, glittering stretch of brackish brown water that rose and fell with the tides. It could look drab and squalid, or serenely elegant. It had grown great on the principle of lending you money only when you could prove you didn't need it, but that particular piece of circular thinking was one he had circumvented for as long as possible with his own form of banking.

I have had my time, he thought; and the whirling blades that kept him miraculously suspended, as his own will and lies had done, suddenly lost their power, falling down, down, down, unstoppably, the irresistible force meeting the immovable object, until he was consumed by the shadow he had cast for so long.

The instinct of one such as Ivo is always to spread bad news. What to do, though, when the information concerned his own paper? Clearly, he could not tell just anyone that Max de Monde had gone as far as embezzling his own daughter's trust fund before finding himself a new job. The others could sink or swim; it had been perfectly clear for some time that the fortunes of the *Chronicle* were beyond reasonable hope of recovery. Of course, one was always on the look-out for a better offer, but now Ivo sloughed off his idleness and produced a series of dazzlingly funny pieces. He wrote about the body in fiction, about the mania for centenaries, about the popularity of the detective story and the perennial attempts to make politics fashionable. Ivo was casting his bread upon the waters. Fortunately the editors whose eye he wished to catch had such short memories that they did not stop to enquire why he had not written more. They suddenly remembered that Ivo Sponge was a talented journalist, wasted on the *Chronicle*, which was what he wanted them to think.

Ivo circulated the Slouch Club. He had his piece of stupendous gossip to give in exchange to the right buyer, news that would bring down not only de Monde, but, more importantly, Mark. What he had overheard on the Crawleys' answerphone had all the hallmarks of a real plum – and he had the tape with him to prove it. It would mean the end of his friendship with Amelia, but she had, in any case, served her purpose.

The only person who failed to notice his sudden efflorescence was, to his mixed relief and chagrin, Mark.

Against his will, and very much to his surprise, Mark was wholly absorbed by his daughter. It was a biological thing, he thought, they were designed by nature to be appealing at their most vulnerable and irritating time of life. Yet Rose so resembled himself, and this consoled him for the absence of Fiona in his life and bed more than he would have thought possible. To see his own eyes gazing out of her flawless face was extraordinarily affecting; but what really excited his interest was her passion for books.

Patiently, he sat now with her on his lap, reading *The Tale of Jemima Puddleduck* for the fiftieth time, consciously attempting to modulate his atonal voice while pondering the semiotics of Beatrix Potter. For the first time since he graduated he began to buy books, marvelling at the world that unfolded, at the delicate yet robust imaginations that had produced such work for the very young. Together, Mark and Rose raced through Hairy Maclary, Mog the Cat, the Large family and the Ahlbergs. Fairytales illustrated by Patrick Lynch and Errol le Cain unfurled before their astonished gaze; and Mark, whose cramped mind, crammed with a thousand books and books on books, had never been forced to consider just what constituted a dragon, or a hero, or a family, felt within himself a strange stirring.

'*Spot the Dog* is now banned,' he informed Amelia.

'Would you prefer her to be reading Proust? "Where's the madeleine, Albertine? Is it on the bed? Is it in the cupboard? Is it – under the cork tile?"' Amelia said this with angry jocularity, but to her amazement, Mark gave his machine-gun laugh.

'That really is rather a good joke. I didn't know you'd read Proust.'

'Only the first two,' said Amelia, who had given up her habitual lying about which authors she had or had not read. (Many years later, when she actually came to some of them, and was ravished by one in particular, one that seemed to her to tell her whole story, she exclaimed to herself, 'Oh, I would never have married him if I'd known this!' But, then, had she not married Mark she would

never have turned to such authors.) She gave him a look of contempt. 'The ones about love. That's all most people get through.'

'I don't really care for most people, do you?'

'Well, yes, actually,' said Amelia, rising to answer the doorbell.
'I do.'

32

Too Late

Nothing in life flattered Max de Monde as greatly as his leaving it. For a week after the crashing of his helicopter, every national newspaper carried obituaries in which he was described as a modern Colossus, a lovable tyrant, a dashing entrepreneur. The reason for this was less the antique fear of speaking ill of the dead than the more modern one of proprietors not wishing to display that they, too, were mortal and had feet of clay. Other, lesser beings in finance and the media had been bought off or silenced, and were too ashamed of the memory of this to counter de Monde's hagiographies.

So praises rolled out for him as the man who had saved the *Chronicle*, and the memory of his splendid parties was still uppermost in the minds of many who mourned him. The Thames was dragged for the black box of his helicopter, and arrangements made for a grand funeral.

Then, as Amelia knew it must, the news of her father's crimes began to seep out.

'BANKRUPT TYCOON STOLE FROM DAUGHTER', said one headline, and the floodgates opened. In one day, shares in MDM Group fell almost as sharply as de Monde himself. As much as £300 million was found to be missing. Old stories and nicknames resurfaced, and soon it was proved: the Levanter had absconded from life leaving his employees, wife and heirs without a penny. Freed of libel restrictions, the stories became wilder and wilder. There were tales that he had been used to launder money from both guns and drugs, tales of orgies and disgusting personal habits, tales of enormous sums owed to everyone from the bank to the butcher. Mrs de Monde was generally pitied, for her husband's infidelities and tyrannies were well known, and she had remained modest in her tastes. All the pent-up hatred people felt for Max was visited on his daughter.

How utterly, now, Amelia regretted ever having published her travel book. Every interview she had given, every column she had written, her choice of clothes, partner, words were now laid bare to ridicule. Her vanity, her vulgarity, her shrewishness, her insincerity, her social ambition – all were excoriated. It was useless to protest that the Amelia of which these things were written was long gone, that she herself had lived in a delusion fostered by her father. The professional and social resentment from which he had protected her throughout his life gathered and poured itself down on her head like black rain.

For Mark, this was the final blow to married life. All his wife's pretensions and affectations, which another nature might have modified or condoned, were poison to him; and all the scorn that had been held back by the thought of her trust fund poured out.

'You smack your lips when you eat, like a peasant,' he would say at meal-times; or, 'Your nose really is large, isn't it? Do you know, a nose is the only thing that goes on growing throughout your life? You're going to look like a rhinoceros by the time you're forty.'

Amelia, spinning off into the outer darkness of bereavement, hardly understood what he was saying, only that it was intended to destroy her. She did not listen to it, except as a kind of irritating background buzz. Her love for her father, and her hatred of him, were so much larger than the sickly thing that was Mark, his opinions scarcely mattered to her. She remembered a thousand things about Max – how as a child she had adored him so much that she would fantasize about giving him all the blood in her body for a transfusion, dreaming of how she would lie there getting paler and paler while he flushed redder and redder, until he would start up his great roaring laugh, and catch her lifeless body in his arms; how he had taught her to ride a bicycle, and, later to drive; how he had told her she was beautiful, and how she had always been able to get any present, no matter how expensive, out of him.

Yet she also remembered his capriciousness, his cruelty, his coarsely reductive attitude to every other human being. He had whipped her when she disobeyed him, and taught her his own disrespect for anyone with pretensions to higher moral values.

'Everyone shits, 'Melie,' he said. 'Never forget that,' and he would leave the face flannels he used instead of lavatory paper on the floor for the maids to wash, and the contents of his bowels for them to flush.

He treated me just as he treated his employees, she thought, one day. While I tried to break free, he gave me everything; but once I left, I was nothing, I was shown only the dark, cold, lightless side of him, sent into the outer circle of London.

It took her a long time to work this out, and while she was doing so she could not stop reading the papers or watching the news. She was the least of her father's victims, it transpired – and few saw her as such.

What saved her in all this time was Rose, whose love and need for love was like a miniature sun, and Grace.

'I don't care what the papers say, I know you're a good person,' said Grace, 'and so do your neighbours, and so does my Billy. Kids are like animals, they know when someone isn't good-hearted.'

Amelia smiled at this – for had she not herself been deceived since childhood? – but appreciated it. Billy came to play with Rose every afternoon, and this was another lifeline.

'Looks good for your street-cred, doesn't it, having a nig-nog coming in the front door?' said Mark, sarcastically.

'Rose needs all the friends she can get, especially as she isn't likely to have a brother or sister,' said Amelia, choking back her rage at hearing Billy so described. 'He's a lovely boy, bright and gentle, and Rose adores him.'

Grace's bed-and-breakfast was quite close by. It sounded terrible: up to two families crammed in each room, a stench of frying-oil and pee everywhere, unwashed clothes and bodies and people in constant terror of being robbed. Grace and Billy were lucky:

they had a room the size of a cupboard to sleep, wash and cook in, but they were always on edge, and Grace visibly tired.

'The council keeps saying they'll rehouse us, but it's been nine months now,' said Grace. 'I don't know what to do. What really makes me mad is that it costs them three hundred a week to keep us there. Still, it's such a mess nobody minds about the cat.'

She told Amelia of the fights and yells, and the Asian family next door who locked their daughter in a cupboard because she was refusing an arranged marriage. Billy had already had hysterics because one of his new toy horses had been snatched by an older girl; he kept the other deep in his pocket, and only brought it out when he came to play with Rose.

How Grace could stand it, Amelia didn't know, but she helped in every way she could think of. 'I don't know how you keep going,' she said.

'Well, there's no choice, is there?' said Grace. Increasingly, she became less an employee than a friend, embarrassed about taking money at the end of every week.

What upset Grace most of all about what she had lost in the fire was the little photograph album she had had of Billy from babyhood on; and her mother's papers.

'I don't care about the rest, it was all crappy, but those pictures and things, they was my history,' she said.

Amelia closed and barred the shutters across the front window. A dozen reporters and photographers were gathered in the street and her front garden, trampling on her wallflowers and standing on her dustbins. She had taken the telephone off the hook the day before, but even so it was impossible to get any peace.

'Piss off or I'll call the police!' she had yelled down at them, when they had actually taken to banging on her door at six a.m.; but it was the police, come to interrogate her. She knew nothing, of course, and her lawyers could prove it, but it only added to the strain, and the hue and cry to get a photograph of Max's daughter.

Only Mark and Grace could enter or leave, and the latter started to come in at the back, over the garden wall. The Crawleys' neighbours, politely agog, all felt sorry for Amelia: after all, she was a mother like themselves, overweight, harassed, unglamorous. They had only known her after she became pregnant; and several had children the same age as Rose. Whatever the papers said, they agreed, Amelia had never been stuck-up: she had taken their hesitant offerings of second-hand clothes and cots with gratitude, and given them flowers, books, meals in return. They helped her, now, in a hundred small ways, having Rose to lunch or tea, doing the shopping, and enjoying the scandal hugely.

Mark wanted none of it. 'I can't do my column if I don't get my sleep,' he said. 'And I don't want those nosy people dabbling in our lives.'

'Your column is probably going to disappear, along with the newspaper,' said Amelia. 'Your family isn't. Can't you, for once in our marriage, give me some support?'

Rose said in her clear little voice, 'Why do you always come in at the window and go *bzzz, bzzz, bzzz?*'

A photographer had climbed a ladder and was peering over the top of the wooden shutters into the gloom. Amelia sprang forward and drew the curtains just as his flash went off.

There was more knocking at the door.

'GO AWAY!' she shrieked.

This time, however, it was her mother. 'Come on, darling, give them what they want and then they'll go away. Let's brush your hair, now, and put on a bit of make-up. There!'

Amelia, too weary to protest, allowed herself to be shepherded out to the front door and photographed with her mother and daughter. As predicted, the worst of them, satisfied, went away.

'Shall I make us all a cup of tea? We should make some for the people outside, too, you know.'

'You seem to be taking it very calmly, Mummy.'

'I've had them camping on my doorstep, too. Besides, I always knew Max was dishonest,' said Mrs de Monde.

'You forgave it?'

'Not exactly. But at least he was honest about his dishonesty. Few people are.' She sipped her tea.

'Yes,' said Amelia, thinking with some bitterness about her relations with Mark. 'That is a kind of virtue.'

'How is Mark taking this?'

'Badly. He's very puritanical, you know, very Cambridge. There's something about all that flat land that makes people censorious, I think. Oxford people are more, well . . .'

'Hilly?'

They both smiled.

'As a matter of fact, I think we're probably going to call it a day.'

'I'm sorry to hear that.'

'Well, it's never been much of a marriage. We aren't really suited, you know. If it hadn't been for Rose, it'd probably have burnt itself out in a couple of months. Oh, I wish Grace would get here!'

Rose, bored, was whining, 'Mummy, Mummy, wead-a-book!'

The doorbell rang again.

'It's electric, isn't it? Let's disconnect it,' said Mrs de Monde, briskly. Amelia had never seen her mother so decisive before. 'I've done the same in Holland Park. Where's your supply?'

She went down into the cellar, armed with pliers. 'I've always hated electric bells. Nasty things.'

'This is so weird,' Amelia said. 'The last time I had so many photographers trying to take pictures of me was on my wedding day, do you remember? He wouldn't talk to me then, he must have known what was coming.'

'Possibly. But Max always believed in something turning up at the last moment, you know, like any gambler.'

'Why *did* you marry him, Mummy?'

'You never knew my people,' said Anne de Monde, washing her hands. 'They were pretty typical for their class and time – stiff, undemonstrative, rigid with convention and family pride. Max, well, he wasn't English, for a start.'

'What made you go to Beirut?'

'Oh, it used to be a terribly glamorous place, like the South of France but more exotic. You can't imagine how drab England was after the war, especially in the country: no colour, everything rationed, crippling taxes, not even Land Girls to talk to, just a huge, icy, echoing house we couldn't afford, all covered with dustsheets. I wanted to travel. My parents wouldn't hear about it, until – until I discovered I was pregnant.'

'You? *Pregnant?*'

'Yes.'

'Unmarried?'

'Yes.'

'So that's what you meant when you said about it being in the family. Who was the father?'

Mrs de Monde said, wearily, warily, 'Someone I couldn't possibly marry.'

'Why? Was he married already? Was he poor?'

'No.'

'He raped you?'

'No. No! I adored him. I was desperate for affection, attention, love. It wasn't his fault. But I had to be sent away, to have the baby.'

'You mean, you *had* it?'

'Yes. I was sent to Beirut. Daddy pulled strings to get me a job at the embassy afterwards. There was a convent there, and the nuns helped people in my situation get their babies adopted. It was a dreadful birth, and they took her away from me immediately. It hardly felt real, it didn't become real, until I had you, almost a decade later. Then I began to feel what I'd done was a terrible thing.'

'Do you mean that I've got a half-sister? Oh, be quiet, darling! Where? How old?'

Mrs de Monde said, 'She would be forty-four now.'

'Have you never tried to trace her?'

'I thought it best not. Because of Max, you know. She was adopted by excellent people – English people – I left a letter to be given her when she was grown-up. But that was before the war there. The convent is long gone.'

'What was she called? Oh, there's Grace, thank goodness.'

'I called her Joy,' said Mrs de Monde, as the key turned in the front door.

After Adam's funeral, Mary moved into his flat. She had to leave Phoebe's, and it seemed the logical thing to do, when she had been paying his rent for the last nine months anyway. She packed up all the things she could fit into a taxi, just as she had long ago outside Mark's flat in Brixton. I've come full circle, she thought, except now it's lonelier, because there's no Adam.

She kept expecting to see him, whenever she went from the living room into the bedroom. She slept on his bed, the bed she had made so many hundreds of times, and which she had never shared with him. He had died with her, not lived with her, and that was a far greater intimacy, she thought.

Mary talked to him all the time, both aloud and in her head. Strange to think that she had once talked to Mark this way, after he had left her. Those conversations, as far as she could recall, had never been so interesting. She formulated explanations for this: Adam had lived in the quick of his imagination, Mark in the dead, Adam was a writer, Mark a hack. But the real reason was that she had loved him, more than she had ever loved Mark.

She had such a strange feeling, even now, even after all the grinding business of the death certificate and the funeral, and telling Adam's mother that he had died of cancer, and enduring her terrible tears, that Adam was not dead but mysteriously alive. The air seemed to ring with expectation, as if he had just asked her a question which she had not heard and was waiting for an answer. It prevented her from sinking absolutely into grief, even as she told herself that it was a trick of the mind, a self-deception.

One day she began to sort through his papers. Mrs Sands was supposed to do this, but remained in Norfolk, apparently prostrated. Mary made up a bundle of clothes to give her, but did not think she would appreciate them, or his books.

The papers should be easier. Adam had been more than usually bad at keeping these in some sort of order, and she kept coming across final demands for the payment of this or that utility, printed in red, and dated years back.

Eventually, however, she came across a shoe-box full of unopened letters. The private ones she did not want to touch. Most were bills, or statements from his publishers about how much was still unearned of his advances, but one was from the pension company that owned the building. She opened it.

Dear Mr Sands,

Following our recent conversation, I can confirm that we are prepared to pay you the sum of £20,000 to vacate the top flat of the above address. This is our final offer. Please confirm your acceptance in writing.

Mary gaped. Twenty thousand pounds! If only Adam had known. Then she looked again. He *had* known. It was four months old, and there was mention of a telephone conversation. What had happened? Was the offer still valid?

She rang the pension company. Yes, the offer was still valid. Everybody had been down with flu, which was why it had not been pursued more quickly.

'You do realize that Mr Sands died last month?' said Mary.

Discreet commotion. They had not realized.

'I have been paying his rent for the last year – two years, intermittently,' said Mary, taking a deep breath and remembering the cheque she had written just before Adam had gone on holiday. 'I was living with him, as his common-law wife. I am equally a protected tenant. However, I am perfectly willing to vacate the flat for the sum which you offered.'

When she put down the telephone, she felt faint. If only she'd known, she could have been spared so much worry. She could have moved them into a comfortable rented flat, bought him more ice-cream, employed a cleaner. Then it occurred to her that Adam simply hadn't grasped the extent and depth of her burden. He had never been domestic, had always expected either to live like a pig or be served by women. Nor had he known how long his illness would last. He had wanted to stay here, in the same little flat, like Montaigne in his tower. But he had also, she discovered, wanted to leave her something.

He had made a will, after all. It had been witnessed by Georgina, and the man in the art gallery downstairs. He had left her the rights to his novels, published and unpublished. The manuscript of his third was in a file under the bed, with a note. The handwriting was wavering, but clear.

Dear Mary,

If you think it worthwhile, send this to Candida. Otherwise, burn it. I wish I could have given you more.   Adam.

'Oh, *Adam*!' said Mary, exasperated, touched, appalled.

She looked at the wodge of paper in her hands, but did not attempt to read it. To make such a decision was beyond her. He had written it while ill, and she was still too close to that. She did not want to pry into what his last thoughts had been, or take the decision whether they should survive or not. Yet neither did she want to destroy the little that remained of her friend.

In the end, she took the file to the post office, bought a padded envelope and sent it to Candida with a covering letter. When she returned, she found that a booklet of backdated Giro cheques had at last been sent by the DSS. They amounted to £700.

The cheque from the pension company would be given to her as soon as she handed over her keys, so she set about packing and finding herself a new place to live. She was feverish with impatience to be out of debt at last, though her bank, now that they knew she would be paying off her loan, were showering her with offers of extended credit.

I need not even rent, she thought. With twenty thousand pounds, I could actually put down a deposit on a flat, get some security at last.

These thoughts kept those of Adam at bay. When she left his flat, she knew that the haunting would stop, and the real process of grieving would begin.

On the day before she was due to move out, when she was coming down the stairs with a bin-liner full of rubbish, she found an envelope on the doormat by the front door. Inside was an invitation engraved on stiff white card. She thought at first it must be from a publisher, but it was from Andrew Evenlode.

'At Home', it said, puzzlingly, giving his address in the Cotswolds.

Mary rang Tom, the one person she could think of to whom she did not mind exposing her ignorance.

'What exactly does it mean?'

'He's giving a party. A d-, a ball. On Midsummer Eve.'

'Oh. That sounds –' she thought it sounded terrifying '– fun.'

'It'll probably be quite sad. The family are selling up, because of

Lloyd's. They've been there for centuries, you know, and now they've lost all their money.'

'Well, lucky them to have had it in the first place,' said Mary. 'Is it worth seeing?'

'Yes, very. I could give you a lift, if you like.'

She said, after a pause, 'I've never been to a ball. I won't know anyone there.'

'You'll know Andrew, and Georgina.'

'And you.'

'Yes,' said Tom. 'You'll know me.'

'How are you?'

'Fine. You?'

'I'm fine, too. I've got a new job.'

'A consultancy?'

'Yes.'

'Oh! I am pleased for you. What did the trick? Or wasn't there one?'

'Well,' said Tom, 'it was just Buggins' turn, you know.'

She heard the pride, and the diffidence, in his voice. 'Is it a good hospital?'

'Yes. I'm running the intensive care unit. Unfortunately, like so many London hospitals, it's under threat of closure.'

Mary laughed. 'It's one step forward and two steps back, isn't it?'

'Well, others get different moves. Have you heard about Amelia's father?'

'Yes. How is she?' Mary felt genuinely sympathetic. It was strange, she thought. She had met this person only twice, and yet their lives had been intimately connected. I don't hate her any more, she thought. In fact, when I consider what her life must be like with him, and what she must feel like about her father, I actually pity her.

'All right,' said Tom, in his usual, guarded way.

'Are you still living there?'

'I've moved out, actually. I can get a place of my own. Now that I've got a bit more job security – if it can be called that.'

'Will they really close your hospital down?'

'I don't know. Nobody does. There's lots of protest. But it still

343

has to keep on working. People don't stop having cardiac arrests just because a bunch of arseholes in government want to save money.'

'Tom,' said Mary, then stopped.

'Yes?'

'Tom, I think –' She could not bring herself to say it, so instead she said, formally, 'I'd like it very much if you would give me a lift.'

33
The Ball

Mary had now lived in England for twelve years, but she had never seen any of its countryside except that on the journey to and from Belfast. Sitting beside Tom Viner as he drove them to the Cotswolds, she was ashamed of her incuriosity.

'How beautiful this is, how beautiful. I never imagined England could be.'

'We're lucky it's such perfect weather.'

It had taken a long time to get out of London, the Marylebone fly-over petering out into interminable crowds of ugly semi-detached houses, many boarded-up, uninhabitable even by immigrants because of the traffic and fumes. The sun was still quite high in the sky, and shone directly into their eyes. Tom put on dark glasses.

'You look absurdly filmic, Ray Bans and black tie,' said Mary. 'It's a change from your usual old clothes.'

Tom felt the stammer rise up in his throat. He said, drily, 'I need them to see where I'm driving. There should be another pair in the glove c- in front of you, if you want.'

'Your girlfriend's?'

'Don't have one.'

Mary clenched her fists, then consciously relaxed them. 'What happened to that doctor?'

'She's engaged to be married to a friend of mine. A German. Also a medic. Very nice bloke.'

'Do all your ex-girlfriends marry your friends?' Mary blurted out, before she could stop herself, but Tom laughed.

'Only one or two.'

'Of course, you've had thousands.'

'Hundreds of thousands,' he agreed.

'Oh!' said Mary, for the motorway, slicing between a chalky hill, suddenly came out on a rise, and the whole of Oxfordshire lay below them, rippling away. 'We've really left London, now.'

'Yes, that's what I always feel here when I drive along this road. I haven't been to Lode for years.'

'Are the Evenlodes really divorcing?'

'Yes. Fiona's moved out.'

'It's odd, isn't it, how all the rich ones do.'

'They don't have to wait. To marry, I mean.'

'Like Mark and Amelia.'

'Yes. But then, the converse can be true, too. People can wait too long, until all the excitement has drained out of everything.'

'Like Mark and me,' said Mary. Her hands stopped sweating. She smoothed her dress. It was exquisitely embroidered with silver thread, and she had bought it with all the backdated Giro cheques from the Gallery of Antique Costumes and Textiles. Adam would have approved, she thought. He had told her often that luxuries were the only real necessities, because they fed the spirit.

'Will Mark and Amelia be there?'

'I expect so, though I don't know. Andrew and Amelia are friendly, and I don't expect Mark will want to pass up the chance to sniff around such a place.'

'No, indeed, I don't expect so, either,' said Mary, amused by the dislike in his voice. She felt a sudden nervousness. 'Where have you moved to?'

'Your old flat at Phoebe's, as it happens.'

'So, she hasn't found herself a nice little Croatian?'

They both laughed. The verges shimmered with ox-eye daisies, and beyond them impossibly verdant trees and fields stretched away into a bowl of gold.

'No. Not yet. She's lonely, poor old bat. I think she just wanted someone to talk to about her days as a Muse. But I am going to buy a place of my own. It's time I joined the grown-ups.'

'Oh, you've worked that out?'

346

'Yes. Yes, I have. Where are you living now?'

Mary had come to his mother's house in a taxi. He had been relieved to see her, not even having her new number. Since she had left Adam's, it was as if she had disappeared into the churning whirl of London, and he had been anxious in case something had gone wrong.

'I expect I'll be buying, too.'

'Lode is the most *perfect* country house anyone can imagine.'

'The garden is even better. Have you seen the marble lake?'

'Heavenly herbaceous borders.'

'Oh, the pleached limes!'

'That topiary.'

'Have you seen the folly?'

'It would break my heart to have to leave such a place.'

'It breaks mine I've never had it.'

'*So* unjust. How were they to know they should have reinsured? Everyone who was anyone had money in Lloyd's. A whole swathe of society has been cut low.'

'I wonder if de Monde invested in them?'

'Shh, there's Amelia.'

'I'd heard she'd blown up like a balloon. Looks just the same, though.'

'God, those *curtains*! Have you seen them? Acres of red silk. Just too divine, pure Bunuel.'

'Hallo, Ivo.'

'Amelia, my darling. What can I say?'

Amelia was wearing the crushed gold dress she had bought for her launch party. When she had decided, at the last moment, that she would go to the dance at Lode, it had been one of her few moments of real happiness to discover that she could fit into it again. It was still fashionable (£9000 did ensure that much) and perfectly suitable for midsummer.

Of course, the body underneath it had changed. She had to wear a brassière, now, because her breasts had lost their elasticity, and a girdle, because her stomach was never going to be flat again.

347

The tan on her skin really did come out of a bottle, as she had once claimed: she could not afford a holiday, and she was still afraid of going out, even in her own back garden. The photographers had gone away, but she found the cringing fear that at any moment her privacy might be invaded by someone with a long lens harder to get rid of.

The thought of Tom being at Lode, however, was too powerful a lure. As long as he had stayed on her top floor, she had felt quite strong, as though he was her secret lifeline – as his telephone line, unknown to reporters, had been during the days when she had to keep her own permanently off the hook. When he announced that he was moving out, across London to Chelsea, she felt her heart begin to break.

I'm more upset about his leaving than I am about Daddy's death, she thought to herself sometimes. What she felt changed from day to day. Mostly, it was anger, now, a continuing resentment that he had not confided in her, had dumped her and her mother in the scandal which he dared not face. Yet she was also consumed with sadness that he had never even met Rose, his own granddaughter.

Was I only ever a puppet for him, a toy? she wondered. Did he lose interest as soon as he could no longer manipulate me? Was that what made me, accidentally on purpose, conceive? Was I trying to cut free myself, with all those long trips abroad? Or was he trying to cut me free from him, knowing what was to come?

Mark was utterly useless. He had done everything to antagonize reporters and make the stories worse. He even drove like a robot, efficiently, but without any instinctive sense of how a gear-shift worked; and he would not leave her side now, when she wanted him to.

'Well, Ivo,' she said, 'you could start by saying sorry. It was you, wasn't it?'

'I couldn't help overhearing your conversation with the lawyer.'

'But you could help taking the tape from my answerphone.'

'I needed proof. The trouble with Max was, nobody dared print what they suspected because he kept everything locked up in his head. That lawyer would never had spoken out. Also, I needed a new job on another paper. The two were – interdependent.'

'You really are scum,' said Mark.

'No more than you, old boy,' said Ivo.

'You're *both* scum,' said Amelia.

A small crowd began to gather, attracted to their acrimony like fish to blood.

'You're both the most scheming, lying, cowardly pair of men I've ever encountered,' she said. All the rage that had been smouldering inside her towards Ivo for the past two months, and towards Mark for the past three years, burst out. 'I don't know how you have the nerve to go anywhere among decent people.'

'There's no such thing as decent people, my darling,' said Ivo. 'There's just people who get away with behaving badly, and people like your father, who don't. Mark, for instance, did that hatchet-job on you in the *New Statesman*.'

'Do you think I care about that now?'

'Well, you were pretty furious about it at the time.'

Amelia remembered she had been. 'You wrote that, when you were sleeping with me?'

Mark said nothing. He should have been proud of his incorruptibility, yet the humiliation of being exposed in public was almost more than he could stand.

Amelia regarded both men with a kind of amazement. 'Well, Tweedledum and Tweedledee,' she said.

Mark just shrugged, but Ivo laughed. That about summed the two of them up, she thought: the one indifferent, the other unrepentant.

'Oh, *go away*, both of you, all of you,' she said, exasperated.

Tom was not dancing, though he had been for several hours. 'You're looking remarkably pretty,' he said to Celine. 'More so than usual, I mean.'

'I'm surprised you remember what I usually look like,' she said.

'Look, Celine, I'm sorry – I don't want you to be hurt but –'

'Is that why you haven't been returning my calls? Oh, Tom!' She laughed. 'That was just a nice time for both of us, wasn't it? You didn't think it meant any more? It was ages ago, anyway.'

'No – no,' said Tom, profoundly relieved, and slightly cross at the same time.

Celine looked at him mischievously. 'No, what I wanted to tell you – look, it's still a bit of a secret, but we can trust you – is that Andrew and I are getting married as soon as his divorce comes through.'

What a complete idiot I am, Tom thought, blushing and blurting out his congratulations. Of course she wasn't in love with me – and of course her father wasn't blocking my chances of promotion. He put back his head, and laughed to himself. 'I couldn't be more delighted,' he told them both, and meant it. Yet why was he still restive and discontented?

He was sitting, now, on his favourite bench at Lode. It was inside a weeping ash tree, and completely concealed the sitter in a round green room of whispering leaves. Candles in coloured glass vases hung from shrubs and trees, casting a flickering light. There was the great yew, with its long swing on which generations of Andrew's ancestors had swung, the monkey-puzzle tree, the walled garden, the wild one. There was its topiary, like gigantic chess pieces, its maze, its vegetable garden, its orchard, its croquet lawn.

It was a little dream of England, this place, the idyll which people with money had dreamt of escaping to from London. How much longer would it remain? he wondered. The village had crept, bungalow by bungalow, almost to its front gates, and the house was burgled at least once a year. Beyond a row of Italian cypress trees and across a muddy field stood a factory, and beyond that, a motorway, whose faint hum could be heard whenever the band stopped playing. Above him, if he stepped out of his green womb, he would see stars, as people had seen them for centuries, but on the horizon there was the dull red glow that was creeping across England, street by street, blotting out the heavens and people's apprehension of their own littleness.

He could hear the jazz band playing behind him. The gravel crunched nearby.

'I didn't expect to see you here,' said Mark Crawley.

'Why not?' said Mary's voice. 'I know Andrew.'

'I didn't know that.'

There was a long pause. Tom, unseen, shifted uncomfortably. He did not want to eavesdrop. It occurred to him that the one girl he had really wanted to dance with was Mary. Why didn't I ask her? he thought.

'You've changed, no?' said Mark.

'I cut my hair off.'

'It's grown back.'

'I'll never be able to sit on it again.'

'I didn't mean changed like that.'

'No?'

'Where did you get your dress?'

'That's none of your business.'

'Oh. Hired.'

'My own.'

'You must be doing well. Are those real diamonds?'

Tom heard the insolence as clearly as Mary.

'No.'

'Funny, I thought they were.' Mark paused. 'I've often tried to find the distinction between a woman who's beautiful as opposed to one who's pretty. A beautiful woman makes costume jewellery look real.'

'Your wife has real jewels,' said Mary, coldly.

'Yes. And isn't it odd? They always look fake.'

'Are you trying to make some sort of apology?'

'That would be a waste of time, wouldn't it? You were right, though, when you said Amelia was a tourist.'

Mary said nothing.

'Just think what we could be,' said Mark. 'Like two lions hunting together.'

'No.'

'There hasn't been anyone else, has there?'

'No.'

She sighed, drearily. Tom thought of the way she had looked in hospital, and was suddenly overwhelmed with a rage so complete it

351

was like lightning. 'It's no good, Mark. I don't feel anything for you, except –'

'You just haven't been fucked –'

'Contempt,' said Mary.

There was a long pause.

'There's someone else, isn't there?'

'No.'

'Yes there is. Ivo?'

'Don't insult me. Why can't you believe that I can live by myself?'

'Because you're not that sort of woman. I know you, Mary, remember? I lived with you for five years.'

'Yes,' she said. 'That's why you don't know me. If you'd ever had a grain of love in you, you'd understand that what you did to me is precisely what made me change.'

There was a long silence.

'Oh, no,' said Mark, suddenly. 'It isn't the doctor, is it? Tom Viner.'

Mary said nothing. Tom felt his ears burning.

'Well,' said Mark, with an exasperated laugh. 'Join the club. He got Amelia in such a lather she practically had an orgasm when he put his key in the lock. Tom was our lodger, in case you don't know.'

'I do know.'

'So,' said Mark, mocking. 'Tom Viner, the man who can't keep his plonker in? You'd be better of with Sponger-boy.'

'I'll keep it in mind,' said Mary, evenly.

'Well,' said Mark, 'my regards, then.'

There was a sound of footsteps moving off.

Thank God, thought Tom, sick with embarrassment. What an ugly, ugly scene. I didn't know anyone talked like that, with such malice. What the hell did women see in him? He patted his pockets mechanically, looking for cigarettes.

A saxophone raised its voice in a musical bray, ending a number. He came out of the ash tree, and saw, appalled, that Mary was still there, staring at the water. A look of horror crossed her face.

'I'm sorry, you shouldn't have heard that,' she said, putting her hands to her cheeks.

'What a shit.'

'I think he must be mad,' she said. 'As well as bad.'

'He's been having an affair with Fiona,' said Tom, drily. 'She does have a certain effect.'

'Yes. Yes. She's very beautiful,' Mary said, in a distracted voice.

'No. What he said was true –'

'I know, I know, you have affairs –'

'About the difference between beauty and prettiness. I'd never seen it that way before.'

She said, after a slight pause, 'That's one of the things that makes him such a good writer. He puts his finger on things. Only, they wither at the touch.'

'You aren't withered.'

'Aren't I? Aren't I?'

She burst into tears, and ran away from him, up the slope – like Cinderella, he thought, starting after her. Except that Mary left no slipper, and though he searched all over the house and grounds, he could not find her.

34

The Rose Garden

Everything looked drear, in the hour before dawn. The colour had been leached from Mary's hair and dress, and the shining fields she had passed only a few hours before were as cold as porridge. Ivo drove his BMW along the motorway back to London, the kedgeree from his breakfast fermenting in two bottles of champagne.

'I don't need your help,' Mary said.

'Yes, you do.'

'No, I don't.'

'You've always needed help, and I'm the only person who's ever given it to you.'

'I am grateful to you.'

Ivo almost howled, 'I don't want gratitude!'

Mary said, 'I've got twenty thousand pounds for Adam's flat. Well, fifteen, now I've paid off my debts.'

'Oh, yes? Do you think you'll be able to live on that?'

'No. But it's enough. I can put down a deposit on a flat. Or I could go on renting. I've got a bit of freedom, a piece of pure luck, and I'm going to make the most of it.'

'What will become of you?'

'Why does anything have to become of me? Why can't I just *be*?'

'I'll tell you what will happen,' said Ivo, angrily. 'You'll go on being a hack, for a while, because you're on the circuit now and you're still pretty, even if you never went to university and come from nowhere. You'll get a flat, and a cat, and you can earn a few hundred pounds here and there pontificating about crappy little novels, and crappy little ideas, and then one day you'll wake up and find nobody wants you. You'll be one of the hundreds of raddled has-beens who litter the fringes of journalism.'

Mary listened in horror.

'Then you'll start to drink again. Just a little bit, now and then, and then more and more until you become a drunken, middle-aged whore, shuffling along in rags and sleeping on park benches. You can only rise or fall in London. There's no middle way. Look at me. Twelve years ago I was nobody, just like you, and now I've got a company BMW with an airbag. I'm offering you the chance to rise with me, and if you don't take it you'll sink back to the very bottom. Nothing will get you back then, nothing.'

'I don't doubt that some of the things you say are true,' said Mary. 'I know my looks will go, as all looks must, and I know that I didn't go to university. But I don't come from nowhere. I come from Belfast. Even if I'll never go back there to live, I'm as Irish as the day I was born.'

'Oh, for Christ's sake!' said Ivo.

'And my parents aren't nothing. You don't know anything about them. It's true they're not society people, but so what? They're honest, unlike Amelia's marvellous father, and they're brave, too. My father's a baker. He had a heart attack at forty-five after the IRA threatened him for not paying them extortion money. My mother brought up seven children, in a house just two up, two down, and now she's a social worker in South Armagh.'

'But you must have hated it, to leave. You don't belong there any more.'

'I hated some things,' said Mary. 'I got tired of the social life, just going down to the pub, seeing people stagnate. I wanted more than pettiness and hatred and narrow-minded restrictions. I was fed up with guys always trying to check out whether I was Protest-ant or Catholic, and fed up with having my bag searched every time I went into a shop, the soldiers pointing guns. And I hated, hate, the IRA. Not just for what they did to my father. They blew up the library, they blew up all sorts of things people need, trying to wreck the economy, they kill innocent people, my best friend from school. I always knew I'd go away. But that doesn't mean I'm ashamed of where I've come from.'

'You were a waitress until I picked you up out of that hospital bed,' said Ivo. 'Remember?'

'I didn't want to be one, you know,' said Mary, frankly. 'It was the only job I could find. As a matter of fact, I wanted to be a journalist.'

'Ha!'

'Oh, not your sort of journalist, not like you and Mark. That never crossed my mind. I told you, I believe – believed – believe in reading for pleasure. I wanted to work on a women's magazine, get all the latest clothes and things. I didn't aspire to anything more intellectual when I was eighteen. All the nuns said I should go to university but I was wild to go abroad. I thought that somebody would be dying to give me a job, but people didn't even want to see me. They kept saying, "You haven't any experience, come back in three years' time," but how was I to get experience? I had nothing to bargain with, nothing to make me stand out. My cousin had a flat in Shepherd's Bush, and I could sleep on her sofa, that's what saved me. That, and walking into the club one day, off the street, and asking if they needed a waitress.'

'But you'd have gone on as a waitress if you hadn't been forced out.'

'Perhaps. I liked the glamour, the people, the awfulness, in a way. And then there was Mark. I wanted him to succeed for me. I've never been that ambitious, or I wasn't until you took me to that party of Amelia's. That's what changed me.'

'No,' said Ivo, gripping the wheel. 'I changed you, me, I, Ivo. I'm your Pygmalion.'

'My Mephistopheles, more like,' said Mary. 'You're too close to the kerb, incidentally.'

'What made you so upset? Was it seeing Mark again?'

'No. Just something he said.'

'What?'

'I'm tired, Ivo.'

They were re-entering the city now. The sky was turning a clear, cold pink. She had loved seeing the sky so much in London, after the weather at home, being able to see the trees and the buildings. It made up for the loneliness.

'Mary, be sensible for once in your life. You can't go on floating about in some eternal Irish psychodrama, lurching from one crisis to the next. You need someone like me to look after you, but I can't do that if you don't play the game.'

'What game is that?'

'You know perfectly well what game.'

'Oh,' said Mary, 'you mean, fucking.'

'Yes, if you choose to put it that way.'

'Well, that's what it is, isn't it? The Sponge Lunge, only it goes all the way.'

Ivo swore.

'I'll never do it with you, Ivo. Not just because you're a snob and a racist, and always trying to make yourself out to be smarter than everyone else. Not just because no woman in her right mind can fancy you when you wear those stupid bow-ties and try to behave like something out of Evelyn Waugh.'

They were passing the outskirts of Little Venice, now, creamy Georgian houses dreaming at their own reflection in the canal, oblivious to the ugliness beyond.

'I can't do fucking, Ivo, I can only make love, and I couldn't do that with you, not in a million years. That part of me is just gone. It did me too much damage. I had to cut it out.'

'You're talking absolute rubbish, Mary, as usual,' said Ivo. 'Unless, of course, you're trying to tell me your fanny has been surgically removed.'

'No,' said Mary, half laughing, exasperated.

'Well, then,' said Ivo, slamming his foot on the brake, and grabbing, more or less simultaneously.

Nothing had ever been more important to Tom Viner than that he should find Mary now. Had he been thinking rationally, he could have found a way to trace her once she disappeared into the metropolis, but all he could think was that he had neither her telephone number nor her new address.

He ran all over Lode and its grounds. The moon had set, and it was dark, the thick dark of the countryside. Some people were still dancing, half asleep, in the marquee, others were slumped at the breakfast table, dinner jackets and gloves mashed with smoked haddock and rice. He saw people he hadn't seen since university, perfectly recognizable fifteen years on despite the bloating or shrivelling of time.

'Why, Tom!' they cried, 'Tom Viner!' but he just waved, and ran on. He saw Candida Twink, whose face contorted with some emotion, and swerved, ashamed. Into the famous library, up the wide oak staircase and past the suits of armour that would all soon belong to another man, in and out of chintzy bedrooms where he had once slept, where people were too tired or too randy to notice his brief incursion.

'Have you seen a girl with dark hair in a silver dress?' he asked anyone who looked conscious. 'It's urgent.'

No, they all said, no, they had not.

He ran along the herbaceous borders, blanched blue delphiniums lit by guttering flares, and through the topiary that stood dreaming in the pre-dawn mist; ran past marble statues and trellised arbours, dived through hedges so thick that the tunnels in them were like small rooms. There was a folly, ahead, made entirely of shells, and a woman wearing a shining dress sat in it.

'Mary?' he asked, then saw it was Amelia. 'Oh, hallo.'

'Hallo,' said Amelia.

'I've been looking everywhere f-f-f –'

'Oh, Tom,' said Amelia. 'I'm so glad, dearest Tom, I knew that you must want –'

'Mary', said Tom, his desperation leaping over his stutter and her babbling.

'*Who?*'

'Mary Quinn. Have you seen her? She's wearing a silver thing.'

Everything suddenly became appallingly clear. It was Mary he wanted, Mary, whose lover, long ago, she had taken away.

At this moment, Amelia discovered that she could not forget the things that she had learnt, things that were now engraved on her deepest being. She was simply not as selfish as she had been, nor as confident; and she had Rose.

'Mary left with Ivo,' she said.

'With Ivo? Are you sure?'

'Yes.'

'When?'

'Not more than an hour ago. He's got a navy BMW.'

She had noted this, thinking, rightly, that it was the price of her betrayal.

'Oh, Jesus,' said Tom, and ran back through the gardens, to his car. He never even said thank you, thought Amelia, staring after him.

Tom had never understood the attraction of having a good car before. He wanted one that was reasonably safe and reliable, having seen too many people scraped off the roads, but otherwise it was just something to get you from one place to another. Apart from that, it was a waste of money, a necessary boredom.

Yet now he wished he had the fastest sports car in the world. If I can only overtake Ivo on the motorway, he thought. That's my only chance.

He pushed the car, eighty, eighty-five, ninety, until it was shuddering with strain. The sky turned lemon, then apricot, and then the sun rose up, a radiant ball, and the chill air seeping through his windows warmed a little. The sky slowly changed, like litmus paper, into pale, pure blue. His speedometer touched ninety-five. He was filled with a wild exhilaration, singing along with Fats Waller, the rich, laughing pagan voice contradicting the self-mocking words. You proposed to someone because your postman told you to, or to break the ice, or because you were pretending there was a moon – anything rather than say what you felt. But there came a point when you just had to say, believe it, beloved: and Tom knew that somehow, he had to say the most terrifying three words in any language, I love you.

He passed one car, but it was not Ivo's, then a lorry and a van. Where were they? Where did Ivo live? What was he doing to her? The Marylebone flyover approached, its roads carrying the occasional car, people stopping for a second at traffic lights, none of them a BMW. His exhilaration faded. The air was so clean and warm, the faint, bitter tang of a million car exhausts not yet tainting it – but they would. How was he to find her? He thought of Adam, making him promise not to marry any woman he loved less than his mother. Poor Adam. They had waited all afternoon for him to die, he thought; and suddenly, he was quite certain, as certain as if he had been given a magic mirror in which to see his heart's desire, that he knew where Mary must be.

The ornate black and gold gates of the Rose Garden were open. Ahead, a plume of water from the fountain floated in the fresh, warm air, and on either side, beds of roses released a faint, soapy scent. Blackbirds hopped across the grass, pulling on elastic worms, indifferent and energetic, chattering.

There was no other sign of life.

This is stupid, he thought, of course I'm wrong, of course she's gone home, or off with Ivo, and I've blown it like I've blown everything else. He was so convinced that when he turned the corner he thought he must be dreaming.

Mary was sitting in the place where they had had the picnic. The silver on her dress was like tears, endlessly falling. She looked up.

'I thought you'd be here.'

'I miss him so much.'

Tom went down, awkwardly, on the grass beside her.

'How can you bear it, thinking that all the people you love are going to die?' she asked, looking away.

'By thinking of all the people I'll love who are not yet born.'

'Is that it? That's what really makes you able to carry on?'

'That, and knowing I'll have children.'

'Lucky you.' She bent her head, and said, 'Ivo prophesies that I'll end up as a wino with a cat.'

'Unlikely. What's happened to Ivo? I thought you got a lift with him?'

'He's been knocked out.'

'What? By you?'

'No. He braked too suddenly – trying, you know? And the airbag whooshed out and biffed him. So I just left.'

Tom began to laugh, and, after a moment, Mary did too.

'A windbag and an airbag.'

'Poor Ivo. He was terribly pleased with that car. He told me he's on some staggering new salary.'

'I don't expect I'll ever have such a thing. Or such a car,' said Tom, picking up a daisy, and shredding its petals, clumsily.

'No. You're too honest.'

'Too dull.' He picked another daisy.

'No, no, you're not.'

'I wish I could talk like you,' said Tom. Mary looked at him in astonishment. 'I love the way you talk. I wish I could be so f-f-f –'

'You have a stammer?'

'Luent. Yes. It only comes out when I don't r-make the effort to switch. You know, words.'

Oh, poor Adam, thought Mary, understanding at last. 'Mark hated the way I talk,' she said. 'He told me so, when he – when we had our last conversation. Apart from the one you overheard,' she said, and colour flooded her.

'Well, I don't. I don't. I'm trying to say, very badly, that I love you, Mary. I don't want you to, to d-d-disappear.'

The expression of relief on his face at having said this almost made her smile. She shook her head. 'You don't know me. Not really.'

'I do know you. I want to marry you. I've known about you for years. Adam told me.'

'He told you about *me*?'

'Yes,' said Tom.

'He told me about you, too. A lot –' She looked down, wondering if Tom had ever known how much Adam had talked. 'He said you were incapable of fidelity. That's why I can't be in love with you. I can't be in love with anyone, though if I – I can't have it, all over again, understand?'

'Don't you think people are capable of change?' asked Tom.

'Mark said they weren't.'

'Don't you think it's time you forgot about what Mark said?' he asked.

'Besides, you're doing it the wrong way round. You don't just tell someone you love them and want to marry them, like that, not in the twentieth century.'

'Why not?'

'I can't sleep with you because then I would love you, even if you didn't me, and that would be so dreadful, so dreadful, you can't begin to imagine. Ten times worse than before.'

She rose, and he seized her. She said, 'I can't – I can't – I can't – Go away –'

'Is that what you want?'

He released her at once, and she almost sank down.

'I don't know – I need to make my own mind up, not have it made for me. I've been so unhappy for so long, I don't know if I can recognize its opposite –'

'I don't know, either,' said Tom. 'Feel. I'm shaking, too. It's not just you. But I do know, Mary, that I love you, and choose you, and that you, also, can choose.'

35

One Year Later

While the present century was in its last decade, and on one Thursday evening in midsummer, a boxy black taxi made its way from Camden to Soho at a rate of three miles per hour with two passengers sitting uncomfortably on its back seat. All around them, traffic rumbled and jammed, spilling out invisible poisons, but on the pavements people walked, and talked, and pushed their children in pushchairs shaded by lacy umbrellas that bobbed and danced irrepressibly. It was a warm day, a luminous afternoon, and for miles around the sky overhead was piled with feathery, ornate billows that might or might not indicate a change in the weather.

Both passengers were tense. They were going to a party, a big party, a party that would be written up and cried down as one of the parties of that year; and both were invited.

'I don't know why I got an invitation, too,' said Amelia de Monde, who had gone back, not without defiance, to using her maiden name since her divorce. 'After all, I hardly knew him.'

'No, I don't know either,' said Ivo Sponge. 'I expect it was Mary's idea. You two have been like buckets in a well. I expect she wants you to see her at the top.'

'She has risen very high, hasn't she?'

'Yes. Higher than I ever got to in that world. Luckily, it isn't my world any longer, or I should be rather jealous. Becoming the keeper of Adam's flame is the best career move she could have made. The media are all over her. All the same, I don't think she's ever going to make what I do. Christ, this traffic is a drag. I actually miss the recession, sometimes.'

Ivo was a different man. Gone were the striped shirts, the bow-ties and the rolls of flab. He had found his natural apotheosis as a television critic. His wardrobe now consisted of American shirts, Italian suits, and, most importantly, a pair of Ray-Bans for which he had become rather famous. There were those who claimed he had lost his eyesight as a result of so much television – but this was envy. He was now acknowledged as the most attractive bachelor in journalism.

'Oh, do stop grumbling. Look what good weather we're having.'

'Pathetically fallacious,' muttered Ivo. 'I don't know how you can bear to go on living in this area.'

'Kentish Town?' said Amelia, in surprise. 'I love it. I know the high street is ugly, but it's got the Heath, and two swimming pools, and a fish shop, and a brilliant florist, and a cobbler, and a butcher who delivers – all the things that have been priced out of places like Chelsea. I like the fact it isn't a middle-class ghetto.'

'But what about the people?'

'Oh, I love my neighbours,' said Amelia. 'I've got to know them, you see.'

'You do seem to have become fashionably left-wing. Is it something they put in the water round here?'

Amelia shrugged. She looked at a couple of other mothers she knew in the high street, and smiled. 'I am rather surprised, given your past history, Ivo, that you were invited too.'

'Of course. Everyone who's anyone comes to Mary's parties.'

'But I'm not anyone,' said Amelia. 'I used to be, but now I'm nobody, except the daughter of someone everyone condemns, trying to scrabble a living on the fringes of journalism.'

'Oh, never mind,' said Ivo. 'There'll be such a crowd, nobody will notice.'

'I wouldn't have come, except – I'm curious. I've only met her a couple of times. What's she like?'

'Mary? Mary is . . . ' Ivo's cherubic face flattened. 'Well. You shouldn't ask.'

'I always thought you were in love with *me*,' said Amelia, piqued by sudden realization.

'Oh, I adore *you*, my darling.'

'Yes,' said Amelia. 'Only – one does get rather tired of being adored, you know.'

'That's the penalty for being a fashionable beauty.'

'Oh, well,' said Amelia, touched that he still bothered to flatter her. 'Too late to change now.'

'We've all changed,' said Ivo, looking at her over the tops of his dark glasses. 'Mary most.'

'And all because of Mark?'

'Well, partly. A single hack can't make a book successful, you know, any more than he or she can turn it into a failure.'

The success of Adam Sands's novel *The Burning Boy* had taken everyone by surprise. There was nothing the public liked as much as a dead author, especially a dead homosexual author, particularly if he had died in Chattertonesque poverty and obscurity, Ivo thought. Adam's photograph, the one that looked so strikingly unlike him, now brooded over every bookshop counter in the land; the marketing department of Slather and Rudge, astonished to find they had the makings of a commercial and critical success on their hands, had descended magnificently to the occasion, even including a box of matches in the publicity material.

Ivo was right: a single critic could not make or unmake an book. Yet he was unpleasantly aware, as perhaps he was intended to be, that without the unstinting enthusiasm of Amelia's former husband, and his own former friend, *The Burning Boy* might not have achieved such prominence. Mark Crawley had not only written an enormously long piece in the *Times* about why it was brilliant, he had gone on *Snap, Crackle, Pop!* to argue its merits. Ivo often wondered whether his motives for doing so were entirely pure. It crossed his mind that perhaps Mark had at last discovered that the favours market afforded greater and more subtle possibilities for revenge than the fear one; and the fact that both Mary and he himself had roasted Adam's first two books could have played a powerful part in Mark's advocacy. Whatever the reason, a single, influential journalist, which Mark, despite being replaced by Lulu at the *Chronicle*, still undoubtedly was, could do much to propel a novel into the public eye.

'Do you really think it's marvellous?' Amelia asked him. 'I haven't read it, yet, but I've been listening to the serialization on *Woman's Hour*.'

'Oh, it's all right,' said Ivo. 'Yes, I suppose it is rather good in its way. Certainly better than anything he did before.'

'But not a work of genius?'

'Oh, for heaven's sake, what is? Perhaps five books a century. It's fashionable to admire it, that's all. It's the *Zeitgeist*. It might be a minor classic. It certainly seems to have struck a chord with a lot of people.'

'It's so desperately sad, unrequited love. Who was it about, really?'

'I don't know. Some other poof, I expect. I only met him once, you know. As a matter of fact, I asked him if he'd like to review for the *Chronicle*, before his first novel came out, and the silly ass said no. The funny thing is, everyone knew who he was at Cambridge, but nobody apart from Mary really knew him that well.'

'Do you think he was in love with Mary?'

'No. That wasn't the sort of thing they had. Mind you, I think he was the love of *her* life.'

'I'd have thought she has other things to think about now.'

'Yes,' said Ivo, and they both sighed.

I'm so lucky, thought Amelia. I've come out of the whole business with a roof over my head, even if I now have to slave for every penny. 'I wonder how Mark finds it, back in Brixton? Pretty depressing, I should think. I'd rather have a nanny than a husband, any day,' said Amelia. 'Grace has absolutely saved me. I didn't begin to realize how miserable he was making me until she came along.'

'Rather risky, isn't it, having a single mother in your house? Her little boy's black, isn't he? You know what they're like when they grow up.'

'That's disgusting,' said Amelia. 'But I shouldn't think they'll stay for too long. Grace is doing night-classes, she wants to be a teacher. But I hope they will. It's more like having a sister around than a nanny. It's all worked out so well for both of us. She and Billy live at the top – you know, Tom Viner's old flat.'

'I've never seen the point of Tom Viner,' said Ivo.

'There's a lot of things, one way and another, that you haven't seen, aren't there?' Amelia answered, not without malice; and Ivo, looking up at the clouds, slowly shifting, and piling and sculpting themselves into blazing forms – into angels and demons, chariots and ships – had to agree that, really, all things considered, there were.